DORCHESTER TERRACE

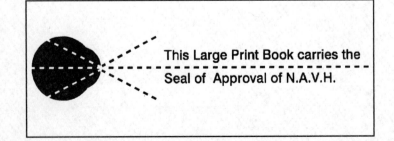

This Large Print Book carries the
Seal of Approval of N.A.V.H.

A CHARLOTTE AND THOMAS PITT
NOVEL

DORCHESTER TERRACE

ANNE PERRY

THORNDIKE PRESS

A part of Gale, Cengage Learning

Detroit • New York • San Francisco • New Haven, Conn • Waterville, Maine • London

GALE
CENGAGE Learning

Thorndike Press® Large Print Basic.
The text of this Large Print edition is unabridged.
Other aspects of the book may vary from the original edition.
Set in 16 pt. Plantin.

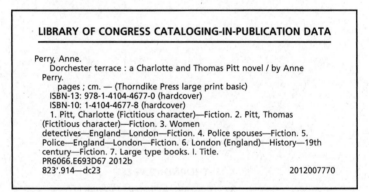

LIBRARY OF CONGRESS CATALOGING-IN-PUBLICATION DATA

Perry, Anne.
   Dorchester terrace : a Charlotte and Thomas Pitt novel / by Anne Perry.
      pages ; cm. — (Thorndike Press large print basic)
      ISBN-13: 978-1-4104-4677-0 (hardcover)
      ISBN-10: 1-4104-4677-8 (hardcover)
      1. Pitt, Charlotte (Fictitious character)—Fiction. 2. Pitt, Thomas (Fictitious character)—Fiction. 3. Women detectives—England—London—Fiction. 4. Police spouses—Fiction. 5. Police—England—London—Fiction. 6. London (England)—History—19th century—Fiction. 7. Large type books. I. Title.
PR6066.E693D67 2012b
823'.914—dc23   2012007770

Published in 2012 by arrangement with The Ballantine Publishing Group, a division of Random House, Inc.

Printed in the United States of America
1 2 3 4 5 6 7 16 15 14 13 12

To Donald Maass
and Lisa Rector-Maass
for their friendship and
help over the years

CHAPTER 1

It was mid-February and growing dark outside. Pitt stood up from his desk and walked over to turn the gas up on the wall lamps one by one. He was becoming used to this office, even if he was not yet comfortable in it. In his mind it still belonged to Victor Narraway.

When he turned back to his desk he half expected to see the pencil drawings of bare trees that Narraway used to keep on the walls, instead of the watercolors of skies and seascapes that Charlotte had given him. His books were not so different from Narraway's. There was less poetry, fewer classics perhaps, but similar titles on history, politics, and law.

Narraway had of course taken with him the large, silver-framed picture of his mother. Today, Pitt had finally put in its place his favorite photograph of his family. In it, Charlotte is smiling; beside her stands thirteen-year-old Jemima, looking very grown-up, and ten-year-old Daniel, still with the soft face of a child.

After the fiasco in Ireland at the end of last year, 1895, Narraway had not been reinstated as head of Special Branch, though he had been exonerated of all charges, of course. Instead, Pitt's temporary status as head had been made official. Even though it had happened several months earlier, he still found it hard to get used to. And he knew very well that the men who had once been his superiors, then his equals, and now his juniors, also found the new situation trying at best. Rank, in and of itself, meant little. His title commanded obedience, but not loyalty.

So far they had obeyed him without question. But he had had several months of very predictable events to deal with. There had been only the usual rumblings of discontent among the various immigrant populations, particularly here in London, but no crises. None of the difficult situations that endangered lives and tested his judgment. If such a crisis were to occur, it was then, he suspected, that he might find his men's trust in him strained and tenuous.

Pitt stopped by the window, staring out at the pattern of the opposite rooftops and the elegant wall of the nearby building, just able to discern their familiar outlines in the fading light. The bright gleam of streetlamps was increasing in all directions.

He pictured Narraway's grave face as it had been when they last spoke: tired and deeply lined, the effect of his difficult escape from total disgrace and from the emotional toll of his experiences in Ireland. Pitt knew that Narraway had accepted, at last, the existence of his feelings for Charlotte; but as always, Victor's coal-black eyes had given little away as they talked.

"You will make mistakes," he had said to Pitt in the quietness of this room, with its view of sky and rooftops. "You will hesitate to act when you know it could hurt people or destroy a life. Do not hesitate too long. You will misjudge people; you've always thought better of your social superiors than you should have. For God's sake, Pitt, rely on your instincts. Sometimes the results of your decisions will be serious. Live with it. The measure of your worth is what you learn from the errors you make. You cannot opt out; that would be the worst mistake of all." His face had been grim, shadowed by memories. "It is not only the decision you make that counts, but that you make it at the right moment. Anything that threatens

9

the peace and safety of Britain can come under your jurisdiction."

Narraway had not added "God help you," though he might as well have. Then a dry humor had softened his eyes for a moment. Pitt had seen a flicker of compassion there for the burden that lay ahead, and also a hint of envy, regret for the excitement lost, the pounding of the blood and the fire of the mind that Narraway was being forced to give up.

Of course, Pitt had seen him since then, but only briefly. There had been social events here and there, conversations that were polite, but devoid of meaning beyond the courtesies. The questions as to how each of them was learning to bend, to adapt and alter his stride to a new role, remained unspoken.

Pitt sat down again at his desk and turned his attention to the papers in front of him.

There was a brief knock on the door.

"Come in," he said.

The door opened at once, and Stoker entered. Thanks to the events in Ireland, he was the one man in the Branch that Pitt knew for certain he could trust.

"Yes?" he said as Stoker came to stand in front of Pitt's desk. He looked worried and uncomfortable, his lean face more expressive than usual.

"Got a report in from Hutchins in Dover, sir. Seen one or two unusual people coming over on the ferry. Troublemakers. Not the usual sort of political talkers — more like the ones who really do things. He's pretty sure at least one of them was involved in the murder of the French prime minister the year before last."

Pitt felt a knot tighten in his stomach. No wonder Stoker looked so worried. "Tell him to do all he can to be absolutely sure of their identities," he replied. "Send Barker down as well. Watch the trains. We need to know if any of them come up to London, and who they contact if they do."

"It may be nothing," Stoker said without conviction. "Hutchins is a bit jumpy."

Pitt drew in his breath to say that it was Hutchins's job to be overcautious, then changed his mind. Stoker knew that as well as he did. "Still, we should keep our eyes open. We've enough men in Dover to do that, with Barker."

"Yes, sir."

"Thank you."

Stoker turned and left. Pitt sat without moving for a moment or two. If it really was one of the French prime minister's assassins, would the French police or secret service get in touch with him? Would they want his help, or prefer to deal with the man themselves? They might hope to get information about other anarchists from him. Or, on the other hand, they might simply contrive for him to meet with an accident, so the whole matter would never reach the public eye. If the latter were the case, it would be better if the British Special Branch pretended not to be aware of the situation. Pitt would have to make the decision about whether to involve the Special Branch, and to what extent, later, when he had more information. It was the type of decision Narraway had referred to: a gray area, fraught with moral difficulties.

Pitt bent back to the papers he had been reading.

There was a reception that evening. A hundred or so people of social and political importance would be gathered, ostensibly to hear the latest violin prodigy playing a selection of chamber pieces. In truth it would be a roomful of people attempting to observe and manipulate any shifts in political power, and to subtly exchange information that could not be passed in the more rigid settings of an office.

Pitt walked through the front door of his house in Keppel Street just after seven o'clock, with plenty of time to get ready for the reception. He found himself smiling at the immediate warmth, a relief after the bitter wind outside. The familiar smells of baked bread and clean cotton drifted from the kitchen at the far end of the passage. Charlotte would be upstairs dressing. She was not yet used to being back in the glamour and rivalry of the high society into which she had been born. She had found it shallow when she was younger, and then, after marrying Pitt, it had been out of her reach. Now he knew, although she had never once said so, that at times she had missed the color and wit of it all, however superficial it was.

Minnie Maude was in the kitchen preparing Welsh rarebit for him, in case the refreshments at the event were meager. Her hair was flying out of its pins as usual, her face flushed with exertion, and perhaps a certain excitement. She swung around from the big stove as soon as she heard his footsteps.

"Oh, Mr. Pitt, sir, 'ave yer seen Mrs. Pitt? She looks a proper treat, she does. I never seen anyone look so . . ." She was lost for words, so instead held out the plate of hot savory cheese on toast. Then, realizing the need for haste, she put it on the kitchen table, and fetched him a knife and fork. "I'll get yer a nice cup o' tea," she added. "Kettle's boiled."

"Thank you," he said, hiding at least part of his amusement. Minnie Maude Mudway had replaced Gracie Phipps, the maid who had been with the Pitts almost since they were married. He was still not entirely used to the change. But Gracie had her own home now, and he was happy for her. Minnie Maude had been hired on Gracie's recommendation, and it was working out very satisfactorily, even if he missed Gracie's forthright comments about his cases, and her loyal and highly independent support.

He ate in silence, with considerable appreciation. Minnie Maude was rapidly becoming a good cook. With a more generous budget at her disposal than Gracie had ever had, she had taken to experimenting — on the whole, with great success.

He noticed that she had made enough for herself, although her portion was much smaller. However, she seemed unwilling to eat it in front of him.

"Please don't wait," he said, gesturing toward the saucepan on the stove. "Have it while it's hot."

She gave an uncertain smile and seemed about to argue, then changed her mind and served it. Almost at once she was distracted by a stack of clean dishes waiting to be put away in the Welsh dresser, and her meal went untouched. Pitt decided he should speak to Charlotte about it; perhaps she could say something to make Minnie Maude feel more comfortable. It was absurd for her to feel that she could not eat at the kitchen table just because he was there. Now that she had taken Gracie's place, this was her home.

When he had finished his tea he thanked her and went upstairs to wash, shave, and change.

In the bedroom he found Jemima as well as Charlotte. The girl was regarding her mother with careful appreciation. Pitt was startled to see that Jemima had her long hair up in pins, as if she were grown-up. He felt proud, and at the same time, felt a pang of loss.

"It's wonderful, Mama, but you are still a little pale," Jemima said candidly, reaching forward to straighten the burgundy-colored silk of Charlotte's gown. Then she flashed Pitt a smile. "Hello, Papa. You're just in time to be fashionably late. You must do it. It's the thing, you know."

"Yes, I do know," he agreed, then turned to look at Charlotte. Minnie Maude was right, of course, but it still caught him by surprise sometimes, how lovely Charlotte was. It was more than the excitement in her face, or the warmth in her eyes. Maturity became her. She had an assurance now, at almost forty, that she had not had when she was younger. It gave her a grace that was deeper than the mere charm that good coloring or straight features offered.

"Your clothes are laid out for you," Charlotte said, in answer to his glance. "Fashionably late is one thing; looking as if you mistook the arrangements, or got lost, is another."

He smiled, and did not bother to answer. He understood her nervousness. He was trying to counter his own anxiety over suddenly being in a social position that he had not been born into. His new situation was quite different in nature from being a senior policeman. Now he was the head of Special Branch and, except in the most major of cases, entirely his own master. There was no one with whom to share the power, knowledge, or responsibility.

Pitt was even more aware of the change in his circumstances as he alighted from the hansom and held out his arm for Charlotte, steadying her for an instant as she stepped down. The night air was bitterly cold, stinging their faces. Ice gleamed on the road, and he was careful not to slip as he guided Charlotte over to the pavement.

A coach with four horses pulled up a little ahead of them, a coat of arms painted on the door. The horses' breath was visible, and the brass on their harnesses winked in the light as they shifted their weight. A liveried footman stepped down off the box to open the door.

Another coach passed by, the sound of iron-shod hoofs sharp on the stones.

Charlotte gripped his arm tightly, though it was not in fear that she might slip. She wanted only a bit of reassurance, a moment to gather her strength before they ventured in. He smiled in the dark and reached over with his other hand to touch hers for an instant.

The large front doors opened before them. A servant took Pitt's card and conducted them to the main hall, where the reception had already begun.

The room was magnificent. Scattered columns and pilasters stretching up to the painted ceiling gave it an illusion of even greater height. It was lit by four massive, dazzling chandeliers hanging on chains that seemed to be solid gold, though of course they weren't.

"Are you sure we're in the right place?" Pitt whispered to Charlotte.

She turned to him with a wide-eyed look of alarm, then saw that he was deliberately teasing her. He was nervous. But he was also proud that this time she was here because *he* was invited, rather than because her sister, Emily, or her aunt, Lady Vespasia Cumming-Gould, had been. It was a small thing to give her, after all the years of humble living, but it pleased him.

Charlotte smiled and held her head a little higher before sailing down the small flight of steps to join the crowd. Within moments they were surrounded by a swirl of color and voices, muted laughter, and the clink of glasses.

The conversation was polite and most of it meaningless, simply a way for everyone to take stock of one another while not seeming to do so. Charlotte appeared perfectly at ease as they spoke to one group, then another. Pitt watched her with admiration as she smiled at everyone, affected interest, passed subtle compliments. There was an art to it that he was not yet ready to emulate. He was afraid he would end up looking as if he were trying too hard to copy those born into this social station, and they would never forget such a slip.

Some junior minister of the government spoke to him casually. He could not remember the man's name, but he listened as if he were interested. Someone else joined in and the discussion became more serious. He made the odd remark, but mostly he just observed.

Pitt noticed an acute difference in the way people behaved toward him now, as compared to a few months ago, although not everyone knew who he was yet. He was pleased to be drawn into another conversation, and saw Charlotte smile to herself before turning to a rather large lady in green and listening to her with charming attention.

". . . Complete ass, if you ask me," an elderly man said heartily. He looked at Pitt, raising an eyebrow in question. "No idea why they promoted the fellow to the Home Office. Must be related to someone." He laughed. "Or know a few secrets, what?"

Pitt smiled back. He had no idea who they were referring to.

"I say, you're not in Parliament, are you?" the man went on. "Didn't mean to insult you, you know."

"No, I'm not," Pitt answered him with a smile.

"Good job." The man was clearly relieved. "My name's Willoughby. Got a little land in Herefordshire. Couple of thousand acres." He nodded.

Pitt introduced himself in turn, hesitated a moment, then decided against stating his occupation.

Another man joined them, slim and elegant with slightly protruding teeth and a white mustache. "Evening," he said companionably. "Rotten business in Copenhagen, isn't it? Still, I dare say it'll blow over. Usually does." He looked at Pitt more carefully. "Suppose you know all about it?"

"I've heard a thing or two," Pitt admitted.

"Connections?" Willoughby asked.

"He's head of Special Branch!" the other man said tartly. "Probably knows more about either of us than we know about ourselves!"

Willoughby paled. "Oh, really?" He smiled but his voice rasped as if his throat were suddenly tight. "Don't think there's much of any interest to know, ol' boy."

Pitt's mind raced to think of the best way to reply. He could not afford to make enemies, but neither would it be wise to belittle his importance, or allow people to assume that he was not the same master of information that Narraway had been.

He made himself smile back at Willoughby. "I would not say you are uninteresting, sir, but you are not of concern to us, which is an entirely different thing."

Willoughby's eyes widened. "Really?" He looked mollified, almost pleased. "Really?"

The other man looked amused. "Is that what you say to everyone?" he asked with the ghost of a smile.

"I like to be courteous." Pitt looked him directly in the eye. "But I can't deny that some people are less interesting than others."

This time Willoughby was very definitely pleased and made no attempt to hide it. Satisfaction radiated from him as he took a glass of champagne from a passing footman.

Pitt moved on. He was more careful now of his manner, watching but speaking little, learning to copy the polite words that meant nothing. It was not an art that came to him easily. Charlotte would have understood the nuances within what was said, or unsaid. Pitt would have found direct openness much more comfortable. However, this form of socializing was part of his world from now on, even if he felt like an intruder, even if he knew that beneath the smiles, the

21

smooth, self-assured men around him were perfectly aware of how he felt.

A few moments later he saw Charlotte again. He made his way toward her with a lift of spirits, even a pride he thought was perhaps a little silly after all these years, but nevertheless was quite real. There were other women in the room with more classic beauty, and certainly more sumptuous gowns, but for him they lacked warmth. They had less passion, less of that certain indefinable grace that comes from within.

Charlotte was talking to her sister, Emily Radley, who was wearing a pale blue-green silk gown with gold embroidery. Emily's first marriage had been a match to make any mother proud. Lord George Ashworth had been the opposite of Pitt in every way: handsome, charming, of excellent family, and in possession of a great deal of money. After his death, it was held in trust for his and Emily's son, Edward. A suitable time later, Emily had married Jack Radley. He was another handsome man, even more charming, but with no money at all. His father had been a younger son, and something of an adventurer.

It was Emily who had persuaded Jack to enter politics and aspire to make something of himself. Perhaps some of Emily's hunger to affect other people's lives had come from her observation of Charlotte and her involvement in several of Pitt's earlier cases. To be fair, at times Emily had also helped Charlotte, with both flair and courage. The sisters had exasperated and embarrassed Pitt, driving him frantic with fear for their safety, but they had also very thoroughly earned his respect and gratitude.

Looking at Emily now, the light from the chandeliers gleaming on her fair hair and on the diamonds around her neck, he thought back with a little nostalgia to the adventure and emotion of those times. He could no longer share information about his cases, even with Charlotte. It was a loss he felt with surprising sadness. Now his assignments were not merely confidential, but completely secret.

Emily saw him looking at her and smiled brightly.

"Good evening, Thomas. How are you?" she said cheerfully.

"Well, thank you. And I can see that you are," he responded. Emily was naturally pretty, with her golden hair and wide, dark blue eyes. More important, she knew exactly how to dress to complement the best in herself, whatever the occasion. But, perhaps because it was his job to watch people and read the emotions behind their words, he could see at once that Emily was uncharacteristically tense. Could it be that she was wary of him, too? The thought chilled him so much that he could barely gather himself enough to acknowledge Jack Radley.

"My lord, may I introduce my brother-in-law, Thomas Pitt?" Jack said very formally, as Pitt turned automatically toward the man with whom Jack had been speaking. "Thomas, Lord Tregarron."

Jack did not mention Tregarron's position. Presumably he considered the man important enough that Pitt should have been familiar with his title.

It was then that Pitt remembered Charlotte telling him of Jack's promotion to a position of responsibility within the government, a position that finally gave him some real power. Emily was very proud of it. So perhaps it was defensiveness, then, that he could see in her quick eyes and in the slight stiffness of her shoulders. She was not going to let Pitt's promotion overshadow Jack's.

It came to Pitt suddenly: Tregarron was a minister in the Foreign Office, close to the Foreign Secretary himself.

"How do you do, my lord?" Pitt replied, smiling. He glanced at Charlotte, and saw that she too understood Emily's tension.

"Lord Tregarron was telling us about some of the beautiful places he has visited," Emily said brightly. "Especially in the Balkans. His descriptions of the Adriatic Coast are breathtaking."

Tregarron gave a slight shrug. He was a dark, stocky man with thick, curling hair and a highly expressive face. No one could have thought him comely, and yet the strength and vitality in him commanded attention. Pitt noticed that several women in the room kept glancing at him, then looking away.

"That a Cornishman admires anyone else's coast has impressed Mrs. Radley greatly," Tregarron said with a smile. "As so it should. We have had our share of troubles in the past, between shipwreck and smuggling, but I have no time for separatists. Life should be about inclusion, not everyone running off to his own small corner and pulling up the drawbridge. Half the wars in Europe have started out of that type of fear. The other half, out of greed. Don't you agree?" He looked directly at Pitt.

"Liberally helped with misunderstanding," Pitt replied. "Intentional or not."

"Well put, sir!" Tregarron commended him instantly. He turned to Jack. "Right,

Radley? A nice distinction, don't you think?"

Jack signaled his approval, smiling with the easy charm he had always possessed. He was a handsome man, and wore it with grace.

Emily shot Pitt a swift glance and there was a distinct chill in it. Pitt hoped Jack had not seen it, lest it upset him. Pitt knew he himself would dislike it if Charlotte were so defensive of him. In his experience, you do not guard anyone so closely, unless you fear they are in some way vulnerable. Did Emily doubt that Jack had the steel in his nature — or perhaps the intelligence — to fill his new post well?

And had Tregarron chosen Jack, or had Emily used some connection of her own, from her days as Lady Ashworth, in order to obtain the position for him? Pitt could not think of anyone Emily knew who was powerful enough to do that, but then, the whole world of political debt and preferment was one he was unfamiliar with. Narraway had been excellent at figuring out the truth in this type of situation. It was a skill Pitt needed to arm himself with, and quickly.

He felt a sudden, powerful empathy with Jack; they were both swimming with sharks in unfamiliar seas. But Jack was used to using his charm and instinctive ability to read people. Perhaps he would manage to survive, and survive well.

The conversation had moved from the Adriatic Coast to a discussion about the Austro-Hungarian Empire in general, and from there went on to Berlin, and finally to Paris, that city of elegance and gaiety. Pitt said little, content to listen.

The musical interlude for the evening began. Much of its exquisite beauty was wasted on the audience, who were not so much listening as waiting in polite silence until it was over and they could resume their own conversations.

But Charlotte heard the haunting beauty of the pieces and wished the musician could play all evening. However, she understood the rhythm of such gatherings; this break was to allow a regrouping of forces. It was a time in which to weigh what one had observed and heard, and to consider what to say next, whom to approach, and what gambit to play next.

She was sitting beside Pitt, a hand resting lightly on one arm. She could see Emily, seated in a gold-painted chair several rows in front of her, between Lord Tregarron and Jack.

Charlotte had known Jack's promotion was important, but she had not realized until now how steep a climb it had truly been. And tonight she had recognized that, under Emily's usual charming manner, lurked fear for Jack in his new position.

Was it because Emily knew Jack too well, was aware of a fundamental weakness in him that others did not see? Or could it be that she did not know him well enough and so was unable to see the strength of will beneath his easy manner, his charisma that seemed so effortless?

Charlotte suspected that the real truth was that, after a decade of marriage, Emily was finally realizing that she was not only in love with Jack, but that she also cared about his ability to succeed not just for what it might bring her, but also for what it could give Jack.

Emily had been the youngest and prettiest of the three Ellison sisters, and the most single-mindedly ambitious. Sarah, the eldest, had been dead for fifteen years. Her death now seemed a lifetime ago. The fear and pain of that time had receded into a distant nightmare, one Charlotte seldom revisited. Their father had also died, about four years ago, and some time later their mother had remarried. This was another subject fraught with mixed emotions, though Charlotte had completely accepted her mother's choice, and Emily largely so. Only their grandmother remained horrified. But then, Mariah Ellison had made a profession out of disapproving. Caroline's second husband, Joshua Fielding, belonged to an acting troupe, was Caroline's junior by many years, and was Jewish to boot. Caroline's marriage to him gave Grandmama more than ample opportunity to express all her pent-up prejudices. That Caroline was thoroughly happy with Joshua only added insult to the injury.

It made Charlotte happy to think that Emily seemed to be learning how to love in a different, more unselfish way, a way that was more protective, more mature. It meant she herself was becoming more mature. Not that the ambition was gone! It was very much present, woven into the fiber of Emily's character.

Charlotte also understood the defensive posture Emily had adopted earlier. Charlotte felt the same tigress-like instinct to protect Pitt; but she also knew that in his new position, there was little with which she could help. He was on far more unfamiliar ground than even Jack was; though Jack's family had had no money, it did have aristocratic connections in half the counties in England. Pitt was the mere son of a gamekeeper.

But if Charlotte *were* to attempt to protect him, she would not signal it as clearly as Emily had done earlier. Charlotte knew Pitt would hate that! She wasn't sure whether Jack would too.

When the performance was over and the applause died down, the conversations resumed, and Charlotte soon found herself talking to a most unusual woman.

She was probably in her late thirties, like Charlotte herself, but in all other ways she was quite different. She was dressed in a huge-skirted gown the color of candlelight through brandy, and she was so slender as to look fragile. The bones of her neck and shoulders appeared as if they might break if she were bumped too roughly. There were blue veins just visible beneath her milk-white skin, and her hair was so dark as to be nearly black. Her eyes were dark-lashed and heavy-lidded above her high cheekbones, her mouth soft and generous. To Charlotte it was a face that was instantly likeable. She felt the moment their eyes met that the mysterious woman had a great strength.

She introduced herself as Adriana Blantyre. Her voice was very low, just a trifle husky, and she spoke with an accent so slight that Charlotte had to strain her ears to make certain she had really heard it.

Adriana's husband was tall and dark, and he too had a remarkable face. At a glance he was handsome, yet there was far more to him than a mere balance or regularity of feature. Once Charlotte had met his eyes, she kept looking back at him because of their intelligence, and the fierceness of his emotion. There was a grace in the way he stood, but no ease. She felt Pitt watching her curiously as she looked at the man, and yet she did not stop herself.

Evan Blantyre was an ex-diplomat, particularly interested in the eastern Mediterranean.

"A marvelous place, the Mediterranean," he said, facing Charlotte, and yet speaking almost to himself. "Part of Europe, and yet at the gateway to a world far older, and civilizations that prefigure ours and from which we are sprung."

"Such as Greece?" Charlotte asked, not having to feign interest. "And maybe Egypt?"

"Byzantium, Macedonia, and before that Troy," he elaborated. "The world of Homer, imagination and memory at the root of our thoughts, and the concepts from which they rise."

Charlotte could not let him go unchallenged, not because she disbelieved him but because there was an arrogance in him that she was compelled to probe.

"Really? I would have thought Judea was the place at the root of our thoughts," she argued.

He smiled widely, seizing on her interest. "Judea certainly, for the roots of faith, but not of thought, or, if you prefer, philosophy, the love of wisdom rather than commanded belief. I chose my words with care, Mrs. Pitt."

Now she knew exactly what he meant, and that he had been deliberately baiting her, but she also saw that there was intense conviction behind what he said. There was no pretense in the passion of his voice.

She smiled at him. "I see. And which of our modern civilizations carry the torch of that philosophy now?" It was a challenge, and she meant him to answer.

"Ah." Now he was ignoring the others in their group. "What an interesting question. Not Germany, all brightly polished and looking for something brave and brash to do. Not really France, although it has a uniquely piquant sophistication. Italy has sown the seeds of much glory, yet it is forever quarrelling within itself." He made a rueful and elegant gesture.

"And us?" Charlotte asked him, her tone a little sharper than she had meant it to be.

"Adventurers," he replied without hesitation. "And shopkeepers to the world."

"So no present-day heirs?" she said, with sudden disappointment.

"Austro-Hungary," he replied too quickly to conceal his own feelings. "It has inherited the mantle of the old Holy Roman Empire that bound Europe into one Christian unity after the fall of Rome itself."

Charlotte was startled. "Austria? But it is ramshackle, all but falling apart, isn't it? Unless all we are told of it is nonsense?"

Now he was amused, and he allowed her to see it. There was warmth in his smile, but also a bright and hard irony.

"I thought I was baiting you, Mrs. Pitt, and I find instead that you are baiting me." He turned to Pitt. "I underestimated your wife, sir. Someone mentioned that you are head of Special Branch. If that is indeed true, then I should have known better than to imagine that you would choose a wife purely for her looks, however charming."

Pitt was smiling now too. "I was not head of Special Branch at the time," he replied.

"But I was ambitious, and hungry enough to reach for the best with no idea of my own limitations."

"Excellent!" Blantyre applauded him. "Never allow your dreams to be limited. You should aim for the stars. Live and die with your arms outstretched and your eyes seeking the next goal."

"Evan, you are talking nonsense," Adriana said quietly, looking first at Charlotte, then at Pitt, judging their reactions. "Aren't you ever afraid people will believe you?"

"Do you believe me, Mrs. Pitt?" Blantyre inquired, his eyes wide, still challenging.

Charlotte looked at him directly. She was quite sure of her answer.

"I'm sorry, Mr. Blantyre, because I don't think you mean me to, but yes, I do believe you."

"Bravo!" he said quietly. "I have found a sparring partner worth my efforts." He turned to Pitt. "Does your position involve dealing with the Balkans, Mr. Pitt?"

Pitt glanced at Jack and Emily — who had now moved farther away and were engaged in conversation elsewhere — then back at Blantyre.

"With anyone whose activities might threaten the peace or safety of Britain," he replied, the levity wiped from his face.

34

Blantyre's eyebrows rose. "Even if in northern Italy, or Croatia? In Vienna itself?"

"No," Pitt told him, keeping his expression agreeable, as if they were playing a parlor game of no consequence. "Only on British soil. Farther afield would be Mr. Radley's concern. As I'm sure you know."

"Of course." Blantyre nodded. "That must be challenging for you, to know when you can act, and when you must leave the action to someone else. Or am I being unsophisticated? Is it actually more a matter of *how* you do a thing rather than *what* you do?"

Pitt smiled without answering.

"Does your search for information ever take you abroad?" Blantyre continued, completely unperturbed. "You would love Vienna. The quickness of wit, and the music. There is so much music there that is new, innovative in concept, challenging to the mind. I daresay they are musicians you have never heard of, but you will. Above all, there is a breadth of thought in a score of subjects: philosophy, science, social mores, psychology, the very fundamentals of how the human mind works. There is an intellectual imagination there that will very soon lead the world in some areas."

He gave a slight mocking shrug, as if to

deny the heat of his feelings. "And of course there is the traditional as well." He turned to look at Adriana. "Do you remember dancing all night to Mr. Strauss's music? Our feet ached, the dawn was paling the sky, and yet if the orchestra had played into the daylight hours, we could not have kept still."

The memory was there in Adriana's eyes, but Charlotte was certain she also saw a shadow cross her face.

"Of course I do," Adriana answered. "No one who has waltzed in Vienna ever completely forgets it."

Charlotte looked at her, fascinated by the romance of dancing to the music of the Waltz King. "You actually danced when Mr. Strauss conducted the orchestra?" she asked with awe.

"Indeed," Blantyre responded. "No one else can give music quite the same magic. It makes one feel as if one must dance forever. We watched the moon rise over the Danube, and talked all night with the most amazing people: princes, philosophers, artists, and scientists."

"Have you met the emperor Franz Josef?" Charlotte pursued. "They say he is very conservative. Is that true?" She told herself it was to keep the conversation innocuous,

but she was caught up in this dream portait of Vienna, the new inventions and new ideas of society. It was a world she herself would never see, but — at least as Blantyre had told it — Vienna was the heart of Europe. It was the place of the genesis of new ideas that would spread throughout the whole continent one day, and beyond.

"Yes, I have, and it is true." Blantyre was smiling but the emotion in his face was intense. There was a passion in him that was urgent, electric.

"A grim man, with a devil on his shoulder," he went on, watching her face as closely as she was watching his. "A contradiction of a man. More disciplined than anyone else I know. He sleeps on an army bed and rises at some ungodly hour long before dawn. And yet he fell madly in love with Elisabeth, seven years younger than himself, sister of the woman his father wished him to marry."

"The empress Elisabeth?" Charlotte said with even sharper interest. There was a vitality in Blantyre that intrigued her. She was unsure whether he spoke with such intensity merely to entertain, or possibly to impress, or whether his passion for his subject was really so fierce that he had no control over it.

"The very same," Blantyre agreed. "He overrode all opposition. He would not be denied." Now the admiration in his face was undisguised. "They married, and by the time she was twenty-one she had given birth to her third child, her only son."

"A strange mixture of rigidity and romance," she said thoughtfully. "Are they happy?"

She felt Pitt's hand touching her arm, but it was too late to withdraw the remark. She glanced at Adriana and saw in her eyes an emotion she could not read at all: a brilliance, a pain, and something she was trying very hard to conceal. Becoming aware of Charlotte's gaze on her, she looked away.

"No," Blantyre said frankly. "She is somewhat bohemian in her tastes, and highly eccentric. She travels all over Europe wherever she can."

Charlotte wanted to make some light remark that would ease the tension and turn the conversation away from her misjudged question, but she thought now that such a thing would be obvious, and only make matters worse.

"Perhaps it was a case of falling in love with a dream that one did not really understand," she said quietly.

"How very perceptive of you. You are

rather alarming, Mrs. Pitt." Blantyre said this with pleasure, and a distinct respect. "And very honest!"

"I think you mean 'indiscreet,' " she said ruefully. "Perhaps we had better return to Mr. Strauss and his music. I believe his father was a noted composer as well?"

"Ah, yes." He drew a deep breath and his smile was a little wry. "He composed the 'Radetzky March.' "

At the farther side of the room was Victor Narraway, newly elevated and a somewhat reluctant member of the House of Lords. He suddenly smiled as he saw Lady Vespasia Cumming-Gould. She was now of an age that it would be indelicate to mention, but she still had the beauty that had made her famous. She walked with the grace of an empress, but without the arrogance. Her silver hair was her crown. As always, she was dressed in the height of fashion. She was tall enough to carry off the huge, puffed upper sleeves that were in style, and she clearly found her great sweeping skirt no encumbrance.

He was still watching her, with the pleasure of friendship, when she turned slightly and saw him. She did not move, but waited for him to come to her.

"Good evening, Lady Vespasia," he said warmly. "You have just made all the trivialities of attending such an event worthwhile."

"Good evening, my lord," she replied with laughter in her eyes.

"That is unnecessary!" Now he felt self-conscious, which was a very rare thing for him. He had held extraordinary power, discreetly, for most of his adult life, first as a member of Special Branch, then for the last decade and a half as its head. But it was a new experience for him to be given such social deference.

"You will have to get used to it, Victor," she said gently. "Elevation to the peerage gains a different kind of influence."

"Their lordships' deliberations are mostly a lot of pontificating," he replied a trifle sourly. "Very often for the sound of their own voices. No one else is listening."

She raised her eyebrows. "Have you just discovered that?"

"No, of course not. But now that no one is obliged to listen to me, I miss the pretense of respect, but far more, I miss the knowledge of my own purpose."

She caught the pain in his voice, even though he had tried to mask it with lightness. He knew she had heard it and he was not sure if he wished he had been cleverer at concealing it, or that she knew him less well. But perhaps the comfort of friendship was of greater value than the privacy that came from not being understood.

"You will find a cause worth risking something for," she assured him. "Or if none presents itself, you will create one. There is enough stupidity and injustice in the world to last us both the rest of our lives."

"Is that supposed to comfort me?" he said with a smile.

She raised her silver eyebrows. "Certainly! To be without purpose is the same as being dead, only less peaceful." She laughed very delicately. It was a mere whisper of amusement, but he knew she meant it passionately. He remembered her speaking once, only briefly, of her participation in the revolutions against oppression that had fired Europe almost half a century ago. They had rocked the entire continent. For a few short months, hope of a new democracy, freedom to speak and write as one chose, had flared wild and bright. People met together and talked all night, planning new laws, an equality that had never existed before, only to see their hope snuffed out. In France, Germany, Austria, and Italy, all the old tyrannies were restored with barely any change. The barricades were swept away and the emperors and kings sat back on their thrones.

"I have grown used to being given my causes without the effort of looking for them," he admitted. "I accept the rebuke."

"It was not meant as a rebuke, my dear," she answered. "I would welcome your assistance in finding something worthy of doing myself."

"Nonsense," he said very softly, looking across the room to where Pitt and Charlotte were speaking with Evan Blantyre. Looking at Charlotte caused a sudden catch in his breath, a twist of his heart. The memories of their time in Ireland were still far from healing. He had always known that it was his dream alone; she had been there only to help him, and in so doing, to help Pitt. It was Pitt whom she loved. It always would be. "Right now I am sure you are very much occupied in worrying about whether Pitt is going to be eaten by the lions," he said, looking back at her.

"Oh, dear! Am I so transparent?" Vespasia looked momentarily crestfallen.

"Only because I am worrying about the same thing," he told her, pleased that she had not denied it. It said something for their friendship that she had owned the concern.

Now she met his eyes, her anxiety undisguised.

"Are you afraid he will retain his respect for the upper classes, and defer to them even if he suspects them of treason?" he asked her.

"Certainly not!" she responded without hesitation. "He has been a policeman far too long to do anything so idiotic! He is painfully aware of our weaknesses. Have you already forgotten that miserable affair at the palace? I assure you, the Prince of Wales has not! Were it not for the queen's own personal gratitude to Pitt, he would not have the position he does now, nor, very likely, any position at all!"

Narraway pulled his mouth into a bitter line at the memory. He knew His Royal Highness was still carrying a deep grudge about the whole fiasco. It was not forgiveness that stayed his hand, it was his mother's iron will and strong personal loyalty to those who had served her with grace, and at the risk of their own lives.

But Victoria was old, and the shadows around her were growing ever longer.

"Does the prince's anger concern you?" he asked Vespasia.

She gave a shrug so slight it hardly moved the deep lavender silk of her gown. "Not immediately. By the time the throne is his, he might have more pressing issues to occupy him."

He did not interrupt her brief silence. They stood side by side, watching the swirl and shift of the glittering party in front of them.

"I am afraid that mercy will override the necessity for action," Vespasia said at last. "Thomas has never balked from looking at the truth, however harsh, or tragic, or compromised by blame in many places. But he has not previously had to do more than present the evidence. Now he may have to be judge, jury, and even executioner himself. Decisions are not always black-and-white, and yet they must still be made. To whom does he turn for advice, for someone who will reconsider, balance what might be a mistake, find a fact he had not seen, which may well change everything?"

"No one," Narraway said simply. "Do you think I don't know that? Do you imagine that I have not lain awake all night staring at the ceiling and wondering if I had done the right thing myself, or perhaps sent a man wholly or partially innocent to his death because I could not afford to hesitate?"

Vespasia studied him carefully: his eyes,

his mouth, the deep-etched lines of his face, the gray in his thick shock of black hair.

"I'm sorry," she said sincerely. "You wear your worries with sufficient grace that I had not seen the burden they've created clearly enough."

He found himself blushing. It was a compliment he had not expected from Vespasia. He was a little alarmed at how much it pleased him. It also made him vulnerable — something he was not used to, except with Charlotte Pitt — and he knew that he must force it to the back of his mind again.

"You must have thought me inhuman," he replied, then wished he had not been so open.

"Not inhuman," Vespasia said ruefully. "Just far more certain of yourself than I have ever been. I admired that in you, even if it left me in awe, and kept me at some distance."

Now he was really surprised. He had not imagined Vespasia in awe of anyone. She had been flattered by emperors, admired by the tsar of all the Russias, and courted by half of Europe.

"Don't be so silly!" she said sharply, as if reading his thoughts. "Privilege of birth is a duty, not an achievement! I admire those who have mastered themselves in order to be where they are, rather than having been handed it by circumstance."

"Like Pitt?" he asked.

"I was thinking of you," she said drily. "But yes, like Thomas."

"And did you fear for me, when judgment lay in my hands?"

"No, my dear, because you have the steel in your soul. You will survive your mistakes."

"And Pitt?"

"I hope so. But I fear it will be far harder for him. He is more of an idealist than you ever were, and perhaps more than I. He still has a certain innocence, courage to believe in the best."

"Was I wrong to recommend him?" Narraway asked.

She would have liked to answer him easily, reassure him, but if she lied now she would leave them isolated from each other when perhaps they might most need to be allied. And she had long ago given up telling lies beyond the trivial ones of courtesy, when the truth served no purpose.

"I don't know," she said quietly. "We shall see."

CHAPTER 2

Two days after the reception, Vespasia received the news that a woman she had known and admired some time in the past, Serafina Montserrat, was ill and confined to her bed.

It is seldom easy to visit those who are not well, but it is far harder when both you and they know that recovery is not possible. What does one say that has any kind of honesty, and yet does not carry with it the breath of despair?

Vespasia had contemplated this while taking a bath perfumed with her favorite mixture of essences: lavender, rosemary, and eucalyptus in bicarbonate of soda crystals, which always invigorated and lifted the spirits. Now she sat in her dressing room before the looking glass while her maid arranged her hair before assisting with the tiny buttons of her dress. Today Vespasia had chosen a gown of indigo-shaded wool, which was both flattering and warm. She firmly believed that one should dress for the sick with as much care as for a party.

Still, she had not made up her mind about what to say; whether to speak of the present, which was so different for Vespasia than for Serafina. Perhaps remembering the past — rich, turbulent, filled with both triumph and disaster — would be a happier choice.

It was also difficult to know what to take as a small gift. In February there were few flowers; those that were available had been forced to grow in artificial circumstances, and seldom lasted long. There was hardly any fruit at all. Vespasia had then remembered that Serafina liked good chocolate, so a box of carefully selected and beautifully wrapped Belgian chocolates with cream centers seemed a good choice.

She had considered a book of memoirs, or foreign travels, but she did not know if Serafina was well enough to read. She still lived in her house in Dorchester Terrace, with her great-niece as a companion, but was there anyone who would read to her with spirit and charm, if she was not well enough to read for herself?

"Thank you, Gwen," Vespasia said as her maid finished dressing her hair. Kindness required that she make this visit generously and with good spirits. It would be best that she do it quickly, before her anxiety got the better of her mood.

The morning was brisk and cold, but fortunately she did not have far to go. Her carriage was waiting at the door. She gave the footman the Dorchester Terrace address, and accepted his hand to step up. Seating herself as comfortably as possible in the chill, she arranged her skirts around her so as not to crush them more than necessary.

She watched the tall houses pass by, the few people out walking in the windy streets, heads bent against the first spattering of rain, and thought back nearly fifty years to her first meeting with Serafina Montserrat. The world had been in a turmoil of excitement then. The revolutions of '48 had filled them with hope and the willingness to sacrifice everything, even their lives, for the chance to overthrow the old tyrannies. It was illusory — perhaps it always had been — but for a brief space their ideas were passionately alive, before the barricades were destroyed, the rebels were dispersed, imprisoned, or killed, and everything was put back as before.

Vespasia had come home again, settled into an acceptable marriage, and had children, but never again had she felt so profoundly passionate about anything as she had then. Serafina had also married, more than once, but remained a fighter, both physically and politically.

Their paths had crossed since, many times. Vespasia had traveled all over Europe. She used her beauty and intelligence to effect good where she was able to, but with a degree of discretion. Serafina had never been discreet.

They had chanced across each other in London, Paris, Rome, Berlin, occasionally Madrid, Naples in the spring, Provence in the autumn. When they met they had spoken with laughter and grief, and exchanged new hopes and old memories. This might be their last meeting. Vespasia found herself stiff. Her hands were clenched as if she was cold, yet she was well supplied with rugs, and the carriage was not uncomfortable.

They pulled up outside the entrance in Dorchester Terrace and Vespasia's coachman opened the door for her to alight. She accepted his hand and took from him the ribboned box of chocolates. "Thank you. Please wait for me," she instructed him, then walked across the pavement and up the steps. It was early for a call, and she was very aware of that, but she wished to see

Serafina alone, before any others might come at a more usual hour.

The door opened and she handed her card to the footman.

"Good morning, Lady Vespasia," he said with only mild surprise. "Please do come in."

"Good morning," she replied. "Is Mrs. Montserrat well enough to receive visitors? If the hour is too early, I can return."

"Not at all, my lady. She will be delighted to see you." He smiled, closing the door behind her. She thought she detected something more than good manners in his voice, perhaps even a thread of gratitude.

She walked into the wide hall with its beautifully parqueted floor and sweeping staircase. She noticed that there was a very handsome lamp built into the newel post at the bottom.

"I'm certain Mrs. Montserrat will wish to see you, but of course I will take the precaution of going up to ask her maid," he explained. "If you would be good enough to wait in the withdrawing room, where the fire is lit, I shall return in a few moments. Would you care for a cup of tea?"

"Thank you, that would be most welcome. It is inclement weather." She accepted because it would make him feel less uncomfortable about leaving her, if it should require several moments of assistance before Serafina was ready to receive anyone.

The withdrawing room was warm and elegant in a most unusual manner. The floor carpeting was pale blue, and the walls were papered in the darkest possible green. The somberness of it was brilliantly relieved by furnishings in Indian red and warm amber brocade, with cushions also in amber and green. Thrown carelessly across them were silk blankets with tasseled edges, woven in the same beautiful colors.

The fire was low, but had clearly been lit since early morning, filling the air with the scent of applewood. There were paintings of northern Italian landscapes on the walls: one of Monte Bianco gleaming white in a clear evening sky; another of early morning light on Isola San Giulio, catching the roofs of the monastery, and making shadows in the clear water of Lago d'Orta, where half a dozen small boats lay motionless.

The decor was chaotically eclectic, and full of life, and Vespasia smiled at a score of memories that crowded her mind. She and Serafina had sat at a pavement café in Vienna and drunk hot chocolate while they made notes for a political pamphlet. All around them had been excited chatter, laughter at bawdy jokes, voices sharp-edged, a little too loud with the awareness of danger and loss.

They had stood on the shore at Trieste, side by side, the magnificent Austrian buildings behind them and the sweeping Adriatic skies above, high-arched with clouds like mares' tails fanned out in the evening light. Serafina had cursed the whole Austrian Empire with a violence that twisted her face and made her voice rasp in her throat.

Vespasia returned to the present with a jolt when the tea was brought. She had nearly finished it by the time a young woman came in, closing the door softly behind her. She was in her mid-thirties, dark-haired, but with such unremarkable brows and lashes that the power of her coloring was lost. She was slender and soft-voiced.

"Lady Vespasia. How gracious of you to call," she said quietly. "My name is Nerissa Freemarsh. My aunt Serafina is so pleased that you have come. As soon as you have finished your tea I shall take you up to see her. I'm afraid you will find her much weaker than you may remember her, and somewhat more absentminded." She smiled apologetically. "It has been quite some time since you last met. Please be patient with her. She seems rather confused at times. I'm so sorry."

"Please think nothing of it." Vespasia rose to her feet, guilty that it had been so long since she had come to see her friend. "I daresay I forget things myself at times."

"But this is . . ." Nerissa started. Then she stopped, smiling at her own mistake. "Of course. I know you understand." She turned and led the way out across the parqueted hall again and up the handsome staircase. She walked a little stiffly, picking up the dark, plain fabric of her skirt in one hand so she did not trip.

Vespasia followed her up and across the landing, and — after a brief knock on the door — into the main bedroom. Inside it was warm and bright, even in the middle of this dark winter day. The fire was excellent; the logs must be applewood here also, from the sweet smell. The walls were painted light terra-cotta, and the curtains were patterned with flowers, as if Serafina wanted to carry the summer with her, regardless of the iron rule of time and season.

Vespasia looked across at the bed and could not keep the shock from her face.

Serafina was propped almost upright by the pillows at her back. Her hair was white and dressed a little carelessly. Her face was devoid of any artificial color, although with her dark eyes and well-marked brows she did not look as ashen as a fairer woman might have. She had never been beautiful — not as Vespasia had been, and still was — but her features were good, and her courage and intelligence had made her extraordinary. Beside her, other women had seemed leached of life, and predictable. Now all that burning energy was gone, leaving a shell behind, recognizable only with effort.

Serafina turned slowly and stared at the intruders in her room.

Vespasia felt her throat tighten until she could barely swallow.

"Lady Vespasia has come to see you, Aunt Serafina," Nerissa said with forced cheerfulness. "And brought you some Belgian chocolates." She held up the box with its beautiful ribbons.

Slowly Serafina smiled, but it was only out of courtesy. Her eyes were blank.

"How kind," she said without expression.

Vespasia moved forward, smiling back with an effort that she knew marred any attempt at sincerity. This was a woman whose mind had been as sharp as her own, whose wit nearly as quick, and she was no more than ten years older than Vespasia. But she looked empty, as if her fire and soul had already left.

"I hope you'll enjoy them," Vespasia said, the words hollow as they left her lips. For a moment she wished she had not come. Serafina appeared to have no idea who she was, as if the past had been wiped out and they had not shared the kind of friendship that is never forgotten.

Serafina looked at her with only a slow dawning of light in her eyes, as if shreds of understanding gradually returned to her.

"I am sure you would like to talk for a little while," Nerissa said gently. "Don't tire yourself, Aunt Serafina." The instruction was aimed obliquely at Vespasia. "I'll put another log on the fire before I leave. If you need anything, the bell is easy to reach and I'll come straightaway."

Serafina nodded very slightly, her eyes still fixed on Vespasia.

"Thank you," Vespasia replied. There was no escape. It would be inexcusable to leave now, however much she wished to.

Nerissa went over to the fire, poked it a little, which sent up a shower of sparks, then carefully placed another log on top. She straightened her back and smiled at Vespasia.

"It is so kind of you to come," she said. "I'll return in a little while." She walked over to the door, opened it, and went out.

Vespasia sat down in the chair next to the bed. What on earth could she say that would make sense? To ask after her friend's health seemed almost a mockery.

It was Serafina who spoke first.

"Thank you for coming," she said quietly. "I was afraid that no one would tell you. I have bad days sometimes, and I don't remember things. I talk too much."

Vespasia looked at her. Her eyes were not empty anymore, but filled with a deep anxiety. She was desperately searching Vespasia's face for understanding. It was as if the woman Vespasia knew had returned for a moment.

"The purpose of visiting is to talk," Vespasia said gently. "The whole pleasure of seeing people is to be able to share ideas, to laugh a little, to recall all the things we have loved in the past. I shall be very disappointed if you don't talk to me."

Serafina looked as if she was struggling to find words that eluded her.

Vespasia thought immediately that, without meaning to, she had placed further pressure on Serafina, acting as if she was hoping to be entertained. That was not what she had meant at all. But how could she retrace her steps now without sounding ridiculous?

"Is there something you would particularly care to talk about?" she invited.

"I forget things," Serafina said very softly. "Sometimes lots of things."

"So do I," Vespasia assured her gently. "Most of them don't matter."

"Sometimes I muddle the past and the present," Serafina went on. Now she was watching Vespasia as if from the edge of an abyss in which some horror waited to consume her.

Vespasia tried to think of a reply, but nothing seemed appropriate for what was clearly, at least to Serafina, a matter of intense importance. This was no mere apology for being a little incoherent. She seemed frightened. Perhaps the terror of losing one's grip on one's mind was deeper and far more real than most people took time or care to appreciate.

Vespasia put her hand on Serafina's and felt the thin bones, the flesh far softer than it ever used to be. This was a woman who had ridden horses at a gallop few men dared equal; who had held a sword and fought with it, light flashing on steel as she moved quickly, lethally, and with beautiful grace. It was a hand that so swiftly coordinated with her eye that she was a superb shot with both pistol and rifle.

Now it was slack in Vespasia's grip.

"We all forget," Vespasia said softly. "The young, less so, perhaps. They have so much less to remember, some of them barely anything at all." She smiled fleetingly. "You and I have seen incredible things: butchers, bakers, and housewives manning the barricades; sunset flaming across the Alps till the snow looked like blood. We've danced with emperors and been kissed by princes. I, at least, have been sworn at by a cardinal . . ."

She saw Serafina smile and move her head in a slight nod of agreement.

"We have fought for what we believed in," Vespasia went on. "We have both won and lost more than the young today have dreamed of. But I daresay their turn will come."

Serafina's eyes were clear for a moment. "We have, haven't we? That's what I'm afraid of."

"What frightens you, my dear?"

"I forget who is real and who is just memory," Serafina replied. "Sometimes the past seems so vivid that I mistake the trivia of today for the great issues that used to be — and the people we knew."

"Does that matter?" Vespasia asked her. "Perhaps the past is more interesting?"

The smile touched Serafina's eyes again. "Infinitely — at least to me." Then the fear returned, huge and engulfing. Her voice shook. "But I'm so afraid I might mistake some person now for someone else I knew and trusted, and let slip what I shouldn't! I know terrible things, dangerous things about murder and betrayal. Do you understand?"

Frankly, Vespasia did not. She was aware that Serafina had been an adventurer all her life. She had never let her causes die from her mind. She had married twice, but neither time had been particularly happy, and she had no children. But then she could outride and outshoot so many men, she was not an easy woman to be comfortable with. She had never learned to keep her own counsel about her political opinions, nor to temper the exercise of her more dangerous skills.

But this was the first time Vespasia had seen fear in her, and that was a shock. It touched her with a pity she could not have imagined feeling for such a proud and fierce woman.

"Are any of those secrets still dangerous now?" she asked doubtfully. It was hard to sound reassuring without also sounding as though she was patronizing Serafina, implying that her knowledge was outdated and no one would still be interested. It was a judgment so easy to mishandle. Vespasia herself would hate to be relegated to the past, as if currently not worth bothering about, even though one day that would assuredly be true. She refused to think of it.

"Of course they are!" Serafina told her, her voice husky with urgency. "Why on earth do you ask? Have you lost all interest in politics? What's happened to you?" It was almost an accusation. Serafina's dark eyes were alive now with anger.

Vespasia felt a flash of her own temper, and crushed it immediately. This was not about her vanity.

"Not at all," she replied. "But I cannot think of anything current that might be affected by most of my knowledge of the past."

"You never used to be a liar," Serafina said softly, her mouth a little twisted with unhappiness. "Or at least if you were, you were good enough at it that I did not know."

Vespasia felt the heat burn up her face. The accusation was just. Of course some of the events she knew, the acutely personal ones, would still be dangerous, if she were to speak of them in the wrong places. She would never do so. But then she always knew exactly where she was, and to whom she was speaking.

"Those sorts of secrets you would keep," she told Serafina. "You would not mention them, even to the people involved. It would be such awfully bad taste."

Suddenly Serafina laughed, a rich, throaty sound, taking Vespasia back forty years in the time of a single heartbeat. Vespasia found herself smiling too. She saw them both on the terrace of a villa in Capri. The summer night was heavy with the scent of jasmine. Across the water Vesuvius lifted its double peaks against the skyline. The wine was sweet. Someone had made a joke and laughter was swift and easy.

Then a log burned through and fell in the fireplace with a shower of sparks. Vespasia returned to the present: the warm bright room with its flowered curtains, and the old, frightened woman in the bed so close to her.

"You had better ask Miss Freemarsh to be sure that certain people do not call on you," Vespasia said with absolute seriousness. "There cannot be so many of them left now. Give her a list, tell her you do not wish to see them. You must have a lady's maid who would help you?"

"Oh, yes. I still have Tucker," Serafina said with warmth. "God bless her. She's almost as old as I am! But what reason shall I give?" She searched Vespasia's eyes for help.

"No reason at all," Vespasia told her. "It is not her concern who you will see, or not see. Tell her so if she presses you. Invent something."

"I shall forget what I said!"

"Then ask her. Say, 'What did I tell you?' If she replies by repeating it, then you have your answer. If she says she can't recall, then you may start again too."

Serafina lay back on her pillows, smiling, the look in her eyes far away. "That is more like the Vespasia I remember. They were great days, weren't they?"

"Yes," Vespasia answered her, firmly and honestly. "They were marvelous. More of life than most people ever see."

"But dangerous," Serafina added.

"Oh, yes. And we survived them. You're here. I'm here." She smiled at the old woman lying so still in the bed. "We lived, and we can share the memories with each other."

Serafina's hand slowly clenched the sheets, and her face became bleak with anxiety again. "That's what I'm afraid of," she whispered. "What if I think it's you, but it's really someone else? What if my mind takes me back to the days in Vienna, Budapest, or

Italy, and I say something dangerous, something from which secrets could be unraveled and understood at last?"

Her frown deepened, her face now intensely troubled. "I know terrible things, Vespasia, things that would have brought down some of the greatest families. I dare not name them, even here in my own bedroom. You see . . ." She bit her lip. "I know who you are now, but in thirty minutes I might forget. I might think it is the past, and you are someone else entirely, who doesn't understand as you do. I might . . ." She swallowed. "I might think I am back in one of the old plots, an old fight with everything to win or lose . . . and tell you something dangerous . . . a secret. Do you see?"

Vespasia put her hand on Serafina's very gently, and felt the bones and the thin, knotted tendons under her fingers. "But, my dear, right now you are here in London, in late February of 1896, and you know exactly who I am. Those old secrets are past. Italy is united, except for the small part in the east still under Austrian rule. Hungary is still lesser in the empire, and getting more so with each year, and the whole Balkan peninsula is still ruled from Vienna. Most of the people we knew are dead. The battle has passed on from us. We don't even know who is involved anymore."

"*You* don't," Serafina whispered. "I still know secrets that matter — loves and hates from the past that count even now. It wasn't really so long ago. In politics, perhaps, but not in the memories of those who were betrayed."

Vespasia struggled for something to say that would comfort this frightened woman.

"Perhaps Miss Freemarsh will see that you are not left alone with anyone, if you ask her?" she suggested. "That would not be unnatural, in the circumstances."

Serafina smiled bleakly. "Nerissa? She thinks I am fantasizing. She has no idea of the past. To her I am an old woman who enlarges her memories and paints them in brighter colors than they were, in order to draw attention to herself, and to make up for the grayness of today. She is far too polite to say so, but I see it in her eyes." Serafina looked down at the coverlet. "And she has other things on her mind. I believe she might be in love. I remember what that was like: the excitement, the wondering if he was coming that day or the next, the torment if I thought he favored someone else." She looked up at Vespasia again, laughter and sadness in her eyes, and questioning.

"Of course," Vespasia agreed. "One does not forget. Perhaps one only pretends to now and then, because the sweetness of it comes so seldom as one gets older. We remember the pleasure and tend to forget the pain." She drew her mind back to the present issue. "Does Nerissa have any idea who you are, and what you have accomplished?"

Serafina shook her head. "No. How could she? The world was different then. I knew everybody who mattered in one empire, and you did in the other. We knew too many secrets, and I wonder if perhaps you still do?"

Vespasia was momentarily discomfited. She did know far more of the present world and its political and personal secrets than she would tell anyone, even Thomas Pitt. How had Serafina seen through her so easily, and in a mere quarter of an hour?

The answer was simple: because at heart they were alike, believers who cared too much, women who used their courage and charm to influence men who held power and could change nations.

"A few," Vespasia admitted. "But old ones, embarrassing possibly, but not dangerous."

Serafina laughed. "Liar!" she said cheerfully. "If that were true there would be sadness in your voice, and there isn't. I hear no regret."

"I apologize," Vespasia said sincerely. "I underestimated you, and that was rude of me."

"I forgive you. I expected it. One has to lie to survive. My fear is that as I get worse, I shall lose the judgment, and possibly even the ability to lie anymore."

Vespasia felt another, even more painful, wave of pity for her. Serafina had been magnificent, a tigress of a woman, and now she lay wounded and alone, afraid of shadows from the past.

"I shall speak to Miss Freemarsh," she said firmly. "What about your Tucker? Is she still able to hold her authority with the other servants?"

"Oh, yes, God bless her. I wouldn't have anyone else. But she is seventy if she is a day, and I cannot expect her to be here all the time. Sometimes I see how tired she is." She stopped; no more explanation was necessary.

"Perhaps it would be possible to get you a nurse who would be by your side all the time, at least all day, when people might call," Vespasia suggested. "Someone who understands sufficiently to interrupt any conversation that might veer toward the confidential."

"Do such people exist?" Serafina asked dubiously.

"They must," Vespasia said, although she had only just thought of it. "What happens to people who have been in high positions in the government or the diplomatic service, or even the judiciary, and know things that would be disastrous if spoken of to the wrong person? They too can become old and ill — or, for that matter, drink too much!"

Again Serafina laughed. It was a light, happy sound, an echo of who she used to be.

"You make me feel so much better," she said sincerely. "I am growing old disgracefully, shabbily in a way, and becoming a liability to those I loved and who trusted me. But at least I am not alone. If you are not too busy doing great things, please come and see me again."

"I shall come with pleasure," Vespasia replied. "Even if I should be fortunate enough to have some great thing to do — which I doubt." She rose to her feet. "Now I must see Miss Freemarsh, and Tucker, if I can. Then I will look for a nurse with intelligence and discretion."

"Thank you," Serafina replied, her voice

for an instant husky with gratitude, and perhaps relief.

Vespasia left the room and went farther along the corridor, hoping to find Tucker. She could remember her as a young woman, just starting out in Serafina's service when they were all in Italy, when Vespasia herself was not yet twenty. She had seen her again briefly, maybe a dozen times over the years, but would she recognize her now? She must be greatly changed.

There was a young laundry maid with a pile of freshly ironed sheets coming toward her.

"Excuse me, will you tell me where I might find Miss Tucker?" Vespasia asked.

The maid dropped a half-curtsy. "Yes, m'lady. She'll be downstairs. Can I fetch 'er for yer?"

"Yes, please. Tell her that Lady Vespasia Cumming-Gould would like to speak to her."

Tucker appeared within a few moments, walking stiffly but with head held high along the passageway from some stairs at the farther end. Vespasia knew her without hesitation. Her face was wrinkled and pale, her hair quite white, but she still had the same high cheekbones, and wide blue eyes, which were a little hollow around the sockets.

"Good morning, Tucker," Vespasia said quietly. "I am grateful that you came so quickly. How are you?"

"I am quite well, thank you, m'lady," Tucker replied. It was the only answer she had ever given to such a question, even when she had been ill or injured. "I hope you are well yourself, ma'am?"

"Yes, thank you."

The ritual civilities observed, Vespasia moved on to the subject that concerned them both. "I see that Mrs. Montserrat is not well, and am very anxious that she should not cause any ill feeling by her possible lapses of memory." She saw instantly in Tucker's face that she understood precisely what Vespasia meant. They were two old women, an earl's daughter and a maid, standing in a silent corridor with more shared memories and common understanding than either of them had with most other people in the world. And yet it was unthinkable, especially to Tucker, that the convention of rank should ever be broken between them.

"It might be advisable if you were to remain in the room as often as you may, whether Mrs. Montserrat thinks to ask you or not. Even if you do no more than assure her that she said nothing indiscreet, it would comfort her a great deal."

Tucker inclined her head very slightly. "Yes, m'lady. I'll do my best. Miss Freemarsh . . ." She changed her mind and did not say whatever it was she had been about to.

"Thank you." Vespasia knew she had no need to add more. "It is nice to see you again, Tucker. Good day."

"Good day, m'lady."

Vespasia turned and went to the main staircase.

"It was kind of you to call," Nerissa said when she met Vespasia at the foot of the stairs by the lamp on the newel post.

"Nonsense," Vespasia replied rather more briskly than she had intended to. The comfort of speaking to Tucker the moment before slipped away from her. She was deeply disturbed, and it had taken her by surprise. Physical decline she was prepared for — to a degree it was inevitable — but the slipping away of mental grasp, even of identity, she had not considered. Perhaps because she did not want to. Could she one day be as isolated and afraid as Serafina was, dependent on people of a generation who neither knew nor understood anything

71

of who she was? People like this cool young woman who imagined that compassion was no more than a duty, an empty act performed for its own sake.

"I came because Serafina and I have been friends for more years than you are aware of," Vespasia said, still tartly. "I am gravely remiss in not having come before. I should have taken the care to know how ill she is."

"She is not in pain," Nerissa said gently. Something in the patience of her tone irritated Vespasia almost unbearably. It was as if, in her perception, Vespasia was also unable to grasp reality.

Vespasia bit back her response with a considerable effort, because she needed this young woman's cooperation. She could not afford to antagonize her.

"So she assured me," she said. "However, she is in distress. Maybe she has not told you so, but she is convinced that in her memory lapses she may be indiscreet, and the thought of it troubles her profoundly."

Nerissa smiled. "Oh, yes, I'm afraid she is not always quite sure where she is, or what year it is. She rambles quite a bit, but it is harmless, I assure you. She speaks of people she knew years ago as if they were still alive, and frankly I think she romanticizes the past rather a lot." Her expression became even

72

more patient. "But that is quite understandable. When the past is so much more exciting than the present, who would not want to dwell in it a little? And we all remember things with perhaps more light and color than they really possessed."

Vespasia wanted to tell this young woman, with her indifferent face and healthy young body, that Serafina Montserrat had a past with more vivid color than any other woman Nerissa was likely to meet in her lifetime. But her purpose was to safeguard Serafina, to remove the fear, whether founded or not, rather than put Nerissa Freemarsh in her place.

"The reality doesn't matter," she said, ashamed of the evasion but knowing that it was necessary. She could not afford to tell Nerissa more than a suggestion of the truth, since the young woman clearly did not consider it important enough to guard with discretion.

"Serafina is anxious that she may unintentionally speak of someone else's private affairs," she continued. "Would it not be possible to see that her visitors are limited, and that someone is with her who would interrupt if she seems to be wandering in her mind? Such assurance might relieve her anxiety. Tucker is excellent, but she cannot be there all the time. I can look for someone suitable and suggest a few possible names."

Nerissa smiled, her lips oddly tight. "You are very kind, but Aunt Serafina would dismiss such a person within a short while. She hates to be fussed over. Her fantasy that she knows all kinds of state secrets and terrible things about the private lives of archdukes and so on is complete imagination, you know. The few people who call on her are quite aware of that. It pleases her to daydream in that way, and it does no harm. No one believes her, I promise you."

Vespasia wondered if that was true. In the past, thirty or forty years ago, Serafina had certainly known all manner of things about the planned rebellions within the vast Austro-Hungarian Empire. She had been part of some of them. She had dined, danced, and very possibly slept with minor royalty — even major, for all Vespasia knew. But that was all long ago. Most of them were dead now, and their scandals were gone with them, along with their dreams.

Nerissa smiled. "It is kind of you to care, but I cannot limit Aunt Serafina's visitors. It would leave her terribly alone. To talk to people, to remember, and perhaps romance a little is about the only real pleasure she has. And it is generous of you to consider another servant, but that is not the answer. I don't wish to tell Aunt Serafina, but it is not economically wise at present."

Vespasia could not argue with her. It would be both impertinent and pointless. She had no idea as to Serafina's financial situation. "I see."

"I hope you will come again, Lady Vespasia. You were always one of her favorites. She speaks of you often."

Vespasia doubted it, but it would be ungracious to say so.

"We were always fond of each other," she replied. "Of course I shall come again. Thank you for being so patient."

Nerissa walked with her across the parquet floor toward the front door, and the carriage waiting at the curbside, the horses fretting in the wind.

Victor Narraway was already extremely bored with his elevation to the House of Lords. After his adventure in Ireland and his dismissal from Special Branch — which had stretched him emotionally far more than he had foreseen — he wanted something to occupy his time and his mind, a position that had use for at least some of his talents.

But for Narraway to interfere in Special

Branch now that Thomas Pitt was head would imply that he did not have confidence in Pitt's ability; it would undermine any action Pitt took, not only in Pitt's mind, but also in the minds of those he commanded and those to whom he reported. It would be the greatest disservice Narraway could do him, a betrayal of the loyalty Pitt had always shown. Pitt had trusted in Narraway's innocence in the O'Neil case when no one else believed him and his guilt seemed clear — indeed, it was morally true that he was partly at fault. Still, Pitt had refrained from blaming him for anything.

So Narraway was left bored, and felt more acutely alone than he had expected to; able to watch but unable to participate.

Not that there was much to participate in; in the months since Pitt had been in charge, nothing out of the ordinary had occurred, nothing to challenge the imagination or the nerve.

Narraway had considered foreign travel as an option, and indeed had taken a late autumn trip to France. He had always enjoyed its rich countryside. He had walked around some of its older cities, reviving his half-forgotten knowledge about them, and adding to it. However, after a while it became stale, because he had no one with whom to share it. There was no Charlotte this time, no one else's pleasure to mirror his own. That was a pain he still preferred not to think of.

He had had the time to attend more theater. He had always enjoyed drama. Comedy was, for him, profoundly bereft without the presence of Oscar Wilde, who had been stigmatized for his private life, and whose work was no longer performed on the stage. It was an absence Narraway felt with peculiar sharpness.

There was always opera, and recitals of music, such as that of Beethoven or Liszt — two of his favorites. But all these pursuits only stirred in him the hunger for something to do, a cause into which to pour his own energy.

He sat in his book-lined study with its few small watercolor seascapes, the fire burning and the gaslamps throwing pools of light on the table and floor. He had eaten a light supper and was reading a report of some politician's visit to Berlin; he was looking desperately, and without success, for a spark of intrigue or novelty in it. So he was delighted to be interrupted by his manservant, announcing that Lady Vespasia Cumming-Gould had called.

He sat upright in his chair, suddenly wide awake.

"Ask her in," he said immediately. "Bring the best red wine."

"White, sir, surely?" the manservant suggested.

"No, she prefers red," Narraway replied with assurance. "And also bring something decent to eat. Thin brown toast, and a little pâté. Please."

"Yes, my lord." The man smiled, rolling the title around on his tongue. He was inordinately proud of his master. He did not say so, but he thought Narraway was a great man, underappreciated by his government, a trespass for which he did not forgive it.

Vespasia came in a moment later. She was wearing a deep shade that, in the gaslight, was neither blue nor purple but something in between — muted, like the night sky. He had never seen her in anything jarring; though she was always dressed subtly, when she was in the room, one looked at no other woman.

He considered greeting her with the usual formalities, but they knew each other too well for that now, especially after the recent fiasco in Ireland, and then with the queen at Osborne.

78

"Good evening, Victor," she said with a slight smile. She had taken to using his Christian name recently, and he found it more pleasing than he would have admitted willingly. There was no one else who called him by his first name.

"Lady Vespasia." He looked at her closely. There was anxiety in her eyes, though she maintained her usual composure. "What has happened? It's not Thomas, is it?" he asked with sudden fear.

She smiled. "No. So far as I am aware, all is well with him. It is possible that what I have to tell you is nothing of importance, but I need to be certain."

Narraway indicated the chair opposite his own. She sat with a single, graceful movement, her skirts arranging themselves perfectly without assistance.

"You would not come unless it mattered to you," he replied. "I have not made my boredom so obvious that you would come simply to rescue me. At least, I hope not."

She smiled with real humor this time, and it lit her face, bringing back all the grace of her beauty and the sharp realization of how radiant she could be.

"Oh, dear, I had no idea," she murmured. "Is it that dreadful?"

"Tedious beyond belief," he answered,

crossing his legs and leaning back in his chair comfortably. "Nobody tells me anything of interest. Either they assume I already know it — and very possibly I do — or else they are afraid they will be seen talking to me and people will assume they are passing me dark secrets."

The manservant reappeared with the wine and food. He served it with only the barest questions as to its acceptability, and then retreated.

Narraway waited as Vespasia sipped her wine.

"Do you know Serafina Montserrat?" she finally asked, in a quiet voice.

He searched his memory. "Is she about our age?" he asked. That was something of a euphemism. Vespasia was technically several years older than he, but it was of no importance.

She smiled. "The manners of their lordships are rubbing off on you, Victor. It is not like you to be so . . . oblique . . . toward the truth. She is somewhat older than I, and considerably older than you."

"Ah. Yes, I have heard of her, but only in passing. Mostly in reference to certain European matters, those brief sputters of revolution in the Austro-Hungarian Empire and Italy," he replied.

"She would not like our efforts to be referred to as sputters," Vespasia observed drily. There was amusement in her eyes, but also pain.

"Indeed. I apologize. But why do you ask? Has something happened to her?" he asked.

"Time," she replied ruefully. "And it has affected her rather more severely than it affects most of us."

"She's ill? Vespasia, it is not like you to be so evasive." He leaned forward uneasily. "What is it that concerns you? We know each other well enough not to skirt around the truth like this."

She relaxed slightly, as if she was no longer bearing her great tension alone.

"She is becoming very severely forgetful," she said at last. "To the point of slipping back into the past and imagining she is young again, and in the midst of all manner of intrigues with people who are no longer alive — or, if they are, are long since sunk into decent retirement."

He was still not sure why this would trouble her so much. So he waited, watching the firelight on her face.

She took a slice of toast and spread pâté on it, but did not eat.

"She is afraid that she will accidentally betray some secrets that still matter," she told him. "Do you think that is possible? Her niece, Nerissa Freemarsh, feels that Serafina's talk is largely fancy. She did not say so in so many words, but she implied that Serafina is creating a daydream to make her essentially tedious life more exciting than it is. And it is true that she would not be the first person to embroider the truth in order to gain attention."

She lowered her gaze, as if she was ashamed of what she was about to say. "In her circumstances it would be easy enough to understand. If I were bound to my bedroom, alone and dependent upon others for virtually everything, and those others were far more concerned with their own lives, I might well retreat into memories of the days when I had youth and strength, and could do what I wished and go where I pleased. No one likes to be constantly obliged, and to have to plead where they used to command."

Narraway nodded. He also dreaded such a fate; he was still in excellent physical health and his mind was as sharp as it had ever been, but here he was becalmed in a professional backwater. Perhaps a slow decline into complete obscurity was what awaited him, and eventually even the help-lessness Vespasia spoke of with such pity.

"What would you like me to do?" he asked.

She considered for only a moment. "I know something about Serafina, but what I know has mostly to do with the revolutions of '48, and of course the Italian unification and freedom from Austrian rule. But we have met seldom since then, and when we have spoken, it has been without details. I know she fought hard, and was physically extraordinarily brave, far more so than I. But does she really know secrets about anything that could matter now? Those revolutions were so long ago. Does anyone care anymore who said or did what at that time?"

Narraway thought about it for several minutes before answering her. The coals settled in the fire and he took a pair of delicate brass tongs to replace them.

"Politically, I doubt it," he said finally. "But if she knew of some personal betrayal . . . people's memories can be long. Although, as you say, most of the people from that time are gone. But I can ask a few discreet questions, even if it is just to set your mind at rest, and to confirm that there is no one left whose life she might jeopardize. I'm afraid that is the best I can think of to do, at present. I wish I knew how we might persuade her that it is 1896, rather than whatever year she believes it to be."

Vespasia smiled at him, gratitude warming her face. "Thank you. It will be a beginning, and perhaps all we can do."

"Is she afraid for her own safety?" he asked.

The question startled Vespasia. "Why, no. I don't think so. No. She's concerned that she might unintentionally betray someone else, not being fully aware of who she is talking to or where she is."

He looked at her steadily across the low table with its tray of food. The firelight winked on the dusty glass of the wine bottle.

"Are you sure?"

Her eyes widened. "No," she said very softly. "I thought it was the confusion of not knowing that frightened her most, the dread that she might betray all that she has been in the past by speaking too much now. But maybe you are right. Perhaps she is afraid of someone trying to ensure her silence for some reason, even at the cost of her life. But why would she worry about such a thing?"

"I don't know," he admitted, picking up a slice of toast. "But finding out will give me something worthwhile to do. I shall be in touch with you as soon as I learn anything beyond what you already know."

"Thank you, Victor. I am grateful to you."

He smiled. "I can do nothing tonight. Have some more wine and let us finish the pâté."

The following morning Narraway began to search for any reference he could find to Serafina Montserrat. In the past he would have had access to Special Branch files. Or — even more simply — he could have gone to his predecessor and asked him for whatever information he could recall. But now he had no authority, no position from which to ask anything, and — perhaps more important — no ability to demand that whatever he said be kept private.

He could have gone to Pitt, but Pitt had enough to be concerned with in his new command. Moreover, he certainly would know nothing himself; he was far too young. He had been a child at the time of Serafina's activities.

Narraway began at his club on the Strand, approaching one of the oldest members quite casually. He learned nothing at all. A second inquiry gained him exactly the same result.

By midafternoon he had exhausted the obvious avenues, which were certainly few enough. He did not want to raise interest or suspicion, so he had kept his questions very general. He simply asked about the times and places that concerned Serafina, but mentioned no individual people. The answers had been interesting: memories of a year that had contained a brief hope for freedom, a hope that remained elusive, even now. Vespasia's name had come up briefly, but not Serafina's. If indeed she had known anything of danger or embarrassment to anyone, she had kept her own counsel quite remarkably.

By late afternoon it was growing colder, and he was beginning to believe that Serafina's imagination was a great deal more colorful than the reality had been. Walking briskly across Russell Square under the bare, dripping trees, he accepted that he would have to go to a more direct source and ask his questions openly.

He smiled at his own inadequacy. He should have more sympathy with Serafina Montserrat, especially if she had been as dynamic as Vespasia had said. To lose power, he thought, is like watching yourself fade away, pieces of you slipping out of your control and vanishing so that you grow ever smaller and more helpless, until there is nothing left of you except a tiny heart that knows its own existence, but can do little to affect anything else.

He should have more pity for the old, treat them with the same dignity he would have given someone more powerful than he. He made the resolution then and there to do so, hoping he would always be able to keep it.

He came out in Woburn Place and hailed a passing hansom. Giving the driver his home address, he climbed in with some relief.

The next day he telephoned Lord Tregarron at the Foreign Office, an acquaintance from his days at Special Branch. He arranged to call upon him that evening. Tregarron's father had been dead some years now, but he had been an expert on the Austro-Hungarian Empire. He had spoken both German and Hungarian, the predominant two of the twelve different languages spoken among the mass of peoples and nationalities that had been loosely joined in the empire.

Narraway spent most of the day reading in the library of the British Museum, reminding himself of the history of the Austro-Hungarian Empire in the last fifty to sixty years, the empire that claimed to be the descendant of the Holy Roman Empire of medieval Europe, heir of the might and influence of Rome itself. He read about the various rebellions of each of its constituent parts, their passion to gain more autonomy.

Serafina was Italian. Venice and Trieste were swallowed up by Austria, losing their ancient culture and their ties to their own people. Venice had regained its freedom, but Trieste and its surrounds had not yet done so.

But he found little mention of Serafina's name, and even when he did it was oblique. Was she in fact making up her knowledge of dangerous secrets, as Vespasia half feared, to color in retrospect a life that was rapidly slipping away from her?

It was after dinner when Narraway reached Tregarron's house in Gloucester Place. He stepped out of his hansom into the first scattering of freezing rain. The footman showed him immediately into the oak-paneled study, where rows of bookcases were filled with leather-bound volumes, and pictures of Cornish seascapes hung in the panels free for such decoration. Tregarron himself came in a moment later.

"Evening, Narraway," he said cheerfully. "Can I offer you something? Brandy? A decent cigar? It's a miserable night. It must be a matter of some importance, to bring you away from your own fireside at this hour." He waved toward a large leather chair, indicating that Narraway should be seated.

"No, thank you." Narraway declined the offer, but sat down comfortably. "I don't want to keep you longer than I need to. It is gracious of you to spare me the time."

"Old habits," Tregarron said drily, sitting in the companion chair opposite him and leaning back, crossing his legs. "How can I help you now? You said something about the Austro-Hungarian Empire. Pretty good shambles, especially after that awful business in Mayerling." He pulled his face into an expression of regret and a certain unmistakable degree of disgust. "Emperor's only son, heir to the throne, commits suicide with his mistress in a hunting lodge. If that's what it was, of course." He let his words hang in the air. "Maybe it was just the best interpretation they could put on it, under the circumstances."

"I think it's rubbish," Narraway said briefly. "Unless he was insane. No royal prince takes his own life because he can't marry his mistress. His wife might have been any kind of a bore, or a harridan —

even then, you just live separately. It's been done by more kings than I've had good dinners. The old emperor himself has a mistress, in spite of having married for love."

Tregarron smiled widely, showing strong teeth. "My father spent years in Vienna. He said Franz Josef was supposed to marry the empress's elder sister, but he fell madly in love with Sisi on sight and wouldn't have anyone else."

"Yes. And your father probably would've been the man to know," Narraway agreed. "But that makes it even more unlikely that Rudolf would have taken his own life. Simply because he couldn't possibly make her empress, when the time comes? I don't believe it."

"Was it the Mayerling business you wanted to speak to me about?" Tregarron asked curiously. "How does that concern our government, or Special Branch, for that matter?"

"No, it has nothing to do with Mayerling, or Rudolf," Narraway said quickly. "It goes back much further than that, possibly thirty years or more, forty, even fifty."

"Good heavens!" Tregarron looked startled, and amused. "How old do you think I am?"

Narraway smiled. "I was actually thinking

of your father. You said he spent years in Vienna . . ."

There was a brief tap on the door and, without waiting for a reply, Lady Tregarron came in. She was in her mid-forties but still extremely attractive in a quiet, comfortable way. Her features were unremarkable, her coloring quite ordinary, but she carried with her a kind of serenity. It was impossible to imagine her troubled by any sort of ill temper.

"Good evening, Lord Narraway," she said with a smile. "How pleasant to see you. May we offer you something? Perhaps a fresh cup of tea? I assume you have dined already, but if not, I'm sure Cook could find you a good sandwich, at the very least."

"A cup of tea would be excellent," Narraway accepted. "It's a miserable night."

"Are you sure that's all?" she asked with concern.

"I don't want to disturb you for long. In fact, I can come to the point rather more quickly than I have been doing." He turned to Tregarron. "Have you heard of a woman named Serafina Montserrat? Perhaps in some connection with Austrian affairs?"

There was a slight flicker across Tregarron's face, but it was impossible to read. "Montserrat?" he repeated. "No, I don't think so. It's the kind of name one would remember. Italian? Or Spanish, perhaps?"

"Italian," Narraway answered. "From the north, Austrian-occupied territory."

Tregarron shook his head. "I'm sorry, I have no idea."

Lady Tregarron looked from one to the other of them, then excused herself to ask the maid to bring tea.

Narraway knew Tregarron was lying. The expression in his eyes, the repetition of the name to give himself a moment to consider before denying, gave him away. But there was no point in asking again, because he had already chosen his position. He could not go back on it now without admitting he had lied. And what explanation could there be for that? If Narraway had asked him with Lady Tregarron not present, would the answer have been different?

Was Tregarron's denial due to a desire to remain uninvolved in something? Surely anything Serafina knew was too old to affect anyone now, and certainly couldn't affect any current government concern. But could it affect someone's reputation? Or a friend?

Or was it simply that since Narraway was no longer in Special Branch at all, let alone head of it, Tregarron did not trust him, but did not want to say so? That thought was peculiarly painful, which was ridiculous. It had been months now since his dismissal. He should be over it. He should have found some new passion to consume his energy. There were years of spare time stretching ahead of him.

He forced his voice to sound light, free from emotional strain.

"I don't suppose it matters," he said lightly. "It was an inquiry for a friend. Something to do with informing those who might wish to contact her before it's too late. Apparently Mrs. Montserrat is getting very frail."

Tregarron did not move at all. "Do I take it from your remark that Mrs. Montserrat is dying?" he asked.

Narraway shrugged. "That was what I gathered. I think she is of very advanced years."

Tregarron blinked. "Really? I suppose it was all a very long time ago. One forgets how the years pass." He smiled ruefully, but the expression stopped far short of his eyes.

Narraway hesitated. Should he let Tregarron see that he had observed the slip, or might he learn more if he let it pass? He decided on the latter.

"Yes," he agreed with a sigh. "We were all

a lot younger, with dreams and energy that I, at least, no longer possess."

Tregarron appeared to relax, easing further into his chair. "Indeed. Matters are always more complicated than the young suppose them to be. Perhaps that's just as well. If they grasped all the reasons why things won't happen, or can't be made to work, nothing would ever be tried. It's certainly a hell of a mess now. We don't need firebrands of any sort, especially in Austria. They have got little enough grip on their crumbling empire as it is, without harebrained idealists running amok."

He shifted a little and recrossed his legs before continuing. "The emperor's son died in one of the ugliest scandals of the century, and God knows, there have been other bad ones. We've had the odd few ourselves. Now his nephew, the only heir left, is wanting to marry a woman the old emperor considers beneath the position that will be thrust upon her. The Hungarian situation is bad, and growing worse. Most of Europe recognizes that the poor devils are second-class citizens in their own land. Italy and the Balkans are increasingly restless. And I'm afraid all of that is to say nothing of the chaos in Russia, and the very considerable rising power of Germany, which, united, is now tasting its own strength."

He bit his lip and stared gravely at Narraway. "We have more than enough to worry about. Let the past lie in whatever peace it can."

"It wasn't important," Narraway lied. "A passing kindness I might have been able to do." He smiled apologetically. "I'm a trifle bored with listening to their lordships in the House. Perhaps I should find myself a country pursuit, except I am not a countryman, apart from the odd weekend."

"Perhaps you should remain in London and listen more closely to their lordships. I'm sure you could find something to argue about, concentrate their minds now and then on a useful issue." Tregarron frowned slightly. "I . . . I hate to ask this, but are you confident in this fellow Pitt that they've put in your place in Special Branch? I know he was a good policeman, but this is not quite the same thing, is it? He'll need judgment, a keenness of perception that police experience won't have taught him. He might be brilliant at solving mysteries and be able to unravel criminal activity and tell you exactly who's involved, but can he see the larger picture, the political ramifications? Has he actually mastered anything beyond the art of solving crime? Does he understand anything deeper than that?"

Narraway knew exactly what Tregarron meant, but he affected a slight confusion to give himself time to think.

Tregarron leaned forward, filling the silence in an abrupt way, as if worried that he had offended Narraway. "I know he's a good chap, and probably as honest as the day is long, and after that disaster with Gower, we'll destroy ourselves without honesty. But for God's sake, Narraway, we need a little sophistication as well! We require a man who can see ten jumps ahead, who can outwit the best against us, not just put a hand on the shoulder of the actual perpetrator of a crime, the fanatic with a stick of dynamite in his pocket."

"I think one of Pitt's greatest assets will be that men who think they are clever will always underestimate him," Narraway replied.

Tregarron's eyebrows shot up and a faint humor lit his face. "Should I consider myself suitably rebuked?" he inquired.

Narraway smiled, this time with genuine amusement. "Not unless you wish to," he said smoothly. "I have every confidence in Pitt, and you may also."

But as he went outside into the rain half an hour later, he was less certain than he had led Tregarron to suppose. Was Pitt's own innate honesty going to blind him to the degree of deviousness in others?

Pitt had been born a servant, and had spent his boyhood with respect for the master of the estate, Sir Arthur Desmond, a man of unyielding honor and considerable kindness. Might Pitt, at some level below his awareness, expect others of wealth and position to be similar?

How would he cope with the disillusion when he discovered that it was very often not the case?

Then Narraway remembered the affair at Buckingham Palace, and thought that very possibly his anxieties were unnecessary. He lengthened his stride toward Baker Street, where he would assuredly find a hansom to take him home.

CHAPTER 3

Pitt's office was warm and comfortable. The fire burned well, and every time it sank down, he put more coal on it. Outside the rain beat against the windows, sharp with the occasional hail. Gray clouds chased across the sky, gathering and then shredding apart as the wind tore through them. Down in the street passing vehicles sent sprays of water up from the gutters, drenching careless pedestrians walking too close to the curb.

Pitt looked at the pile of papers on his desk. They were the same routine reports that greeted him every day, but if he did not read them, he might miss one thread that was different, an omission or cross-reference that indicates a change, a connection not made before. There were patterns that anything less than the minutest care would not disclose, and those patterns might be the only warning of a betrayal or an attack to come.

He was disturbed in the rhythm of his reading by a sharp rap on the door. He turned the page down reluctantly.

"Come," he answered.

The door opened and Stoker came in, closing it silently behind him. His face was difficult to read, as usual. Pitt had learned to interpret his agitation or excitement by studying the way he moved, the ease or stiffness in his body, and the angle of his shoulders. Now he judged Stoker to be alert and a trifle apprehensive.

"What is it?" he asked, gesturing toward the chair opposite his desk.

Stoker sat obediently. "Maybe nothing," he replied.

"If it was nothing, you wouldn't be here," Pitt pointed out. He trusted Stoker's instincts. He was the only one who had believed in Narraway when Narraway had been accused of treason in the O'Neil case. Everyone else had believed only what the evidence seemed to show them. Stoker had had the courage to risk not only his career but also his life to work secretly with Pitt against those who had corrupted and usurped the power. It was Stoker who had saved Pitt's life in the desperate struggle at the end.

Stoker's mastery of small observations was acute. He heard the evasions that skirted around a lie, saw the smile that indicated nervousness, the tiny signs of vanity in a conspicuous watch chain, a folded silk handkerchief a shade too bright, the overly casual manner that concealed a far better acquaintance than that admitted to.

"What is it?" Pitt insisted.

Stoker frowned. "Down Dover way. There have been a few questions about railway signals and points."

"Railway points?" Pitt was puzzled. "You mean where the tracks join, or branch? What specifically is being asked? Are you sure it's not just routine maintenance?"

Stoker's face was grim. "Yes. It's a stranger, asking about how the signals work, where they're controlled from, can it be done by hand, that sort of thing. Thought it might just be some fellow wanting to explain it to his son, at first. But there have been questions about timetables, the freight trains and passenger trains from Dover to London, and branch lines as well, as if someone wanted to figure out where they cross."

Pitt thought for a moment or two. Some of the possibilities were ugly. "And you're sure it's the same man asking?"

"That's a bit hard to tell. Extremely

ordinary-looking, except he had very pale, clear eyes. The man who asked about the freight trains had on spectacles. Couldn't see his eyes."

"And the man who asked about the signals and points?" Pitt asked, a tiny knot of anxiety beginning to tighten in his stomach.

"Different hair, as much as you could see under his hat. Doesn't mean anything. Anybody can put a wig on."

"What's being moved in and out of Dover on the lines he asked about?" Pitt pressed.

"I looked into that. Heavy industrial stuff, mostly. Some coal. Fish. Nothing worth stealing, not with a rail crash anyway."

Pitt thought for a moment. "And you said he asked about passenger trains, as well?"

"From Dover to London. Think it's some passenger they could be after?" Stoker asked.

"It's a lot of trouble to go through for one passenger," Pitt replied. "It sounds more like some kind of anarchist thinking to create a major disaster, just to show us that he can."

"What for?" Stoker was frowning, puzzled. "Couldn't even pretend there's any idealism or political motive in that."

"That's what worries me," Pitt admitted. "It doesn't make sense. We haven't understood it yet. But you're right, there's something planned, even if this is just a distraction, something to keep us occupied so we miss the real thing. But we can't ignore it. And if, as you say, someone is prepared to cause a train crash just to kill one person, then it has to be someone of overwhelming importance."

Stoker moved his thin, strong hands in a very slight gesture of helplessness. "Whatever they are planning, it would have to be soon. They wouldn't want to risk a change in the timetables wrecking their plan."

Pitt took a deep breath, and suddenly the room felt colder, even though the fire was still burning and the windows were still closed.

"So who could it be?" he asked. "Who's coming from Dover to London in the next couple of months? Who would anarchists want to kill?"

"Nobody that matters, far as I can tell." Stoker shook his head. "Some Russian count is coming to stay for a private visit. Might be visiting some of our royal family at the same time, I suppose. One or two politicians, but no one important: a Frenchman and an American. Can't see why any of them would be worth killing, especially here. Probably far easier to do it at home, if you wanted to. Oh, one minor Austrian duke, Duke Alois, but he doesn't hold any office, and he'd be easy enough to kill in Vienna. And whoever did it could escape there. Whole of Europe to go to. We're an island: A foreigner would stick out like a sore thumb, unless he hid in one of the immigrant communities in London. But why bother? It makes no sense."

"Then this is to divert us from something else," Pitt answered. "Something more important."

Stoker nodded, his jaw tight. "More important than a foreign count or duke being assassinated right here in London, under our noses?"

"Well, if it's a diversion, that's the point," Pitt said grimly. "They can't hold our attention unless they do something drastic. Keep looking. And tell me what you find."

Stoker rose to his feet. "Yes, sir. Maybe it's a dry run to see if we pick it up?"

"I thought of that," Pitt agreed. "Learn everything you can. But discreetly."

When Stoker was gone, Pitt sat back in his chair and considered. Many cases in the past had begun as a whisper, a rumor that seemed trivial at first, a fact that didn't quite fit, an alliance that was outside the usual pattern. Narraway had years of experience in seeing the anomaly that was the first indication of a new plot, or an attack on a new target.

Until his arrival at Special Branch, Pitt had been used to being called in only after a crime had been committed. He then worked backward to unravel it, the history, the motives, and the proof of guilt that would stand up at trial. It was a new discipline for him to be faced with an event before it occurred, and to be responsible for preventing it.

Did those who had appointed him in Narraway's place really have any understanding of exactly the skills involved in this process? Had they misjudged Pitt's abilities because they had seen Narraway's successes, and had known that Pitt had contributed to most of the later ones? Could they be so naive?

He had a gnawing fear in the pit of his stomach that they could be.

His own judgment had sometimes been desperately flawed. He had been taken in completely during the whole O'Neil affair; he had been just as duped as the rest of them, until close to the end. And he had believed Narraway innocent out of personal loyalty, which had nothing to do with reason, logic, or ability.

He thought of Narraway's Irish past, the tragedies and compromises, the things Narraway had done that Pitt would not have. Narraway was subtler, more experienced, and infinitely more devious than Pitt, a loose cannon, whereas Pitt was predictable. And yet even Narraway had come within an inch of being ruined, despite all his skill and experience.

Was Special Branch itself on trial now? Was that the crux of it? Was this all part of a larger plan to ultimately proclaim it a failure and get rid of Special Branch altogether? Pitt knew that even within the government, not everyone wanted them to succeed.

Pitt made it his first priority to learn whatever he could regarding possible assassination targets. If the intended victim was indeed someone visiting a member of the royal family, then the minister in the Foreign Office responsible for Central and Eastern Europe would be a good person to begin his inquiries with. Accordingly, he was at Lord Tregarron's office a little after half-past two. If there was anything in the rumor, then foiling the plot was a matter of urgency. An assassination on British soil would be one of the most acute embarrassments imaginable, whoever the victim was.

He was still a trifle self-conscious announcing himself as Commander Pitt of Special Branch, but he managed to hide it. He was received with courtesy by a smart young man, who was presumably a secretary of some sort, and who invited him to wait in a very comfortable room.

The armchairs were of brown leather, and there were newspapers and quarterly magazines on the table before a briskly burning fire. He was even offered whisky, which he declined. The secretary made no move toward the tantalus on the sideboard when he offered, as if he had expected Pitt to refuse.

"Right, sir," he said smoothly. "We'll not keep you longer than we have to."

Ten minutes later it was not the secretary who returned, nor Lord Tregarron himself, but Jack Radley. He came in and closed the door behind him. He was dressed in a black coat and striped trousers. He looked extraordinarily elegant, and slightly uncomfortable.

"Good afternoon, Thomas," he said with a half-smile. "I assume this must be important for you to have come here in person. May I tell Lord Tregarron what it concerns?"

Pitt was a trifle taken aback. He had not

expected to have to explain his errand to anyone else, but he had not called on Tregarron before. Perhaps he should have foreseen it.

"I urgently need some information on visitors any of the royal family may be expecting from overseas within the next month or so," he replied a little stiffly.

Jack's eyes widened, curious but unconcerned. "Anyone in particular?"

"I don't know. That is what I have come to ask. It might be either official or private."

"Is there some concern for Her Majesty?" Now Jack looked more anxious. "Special Branch doesn't usually bother Lord Tregarron with this sort of thing."

"Not so far as I know," Pitt replied a little coolly. He had heard Jack's implied criticism that he was wasting their time. "My information suggests that the danger may be to the visitor, but it could be extremely unpleasant either way. I need to speak to Lord Tregarron as soon as possible."

Jack nodded. "I'll inform him." He turned and left, closing the door behind him with a click.

Pitt waited, pacing back and forth across the deep red Turkish carpet, until Jack returned several minutes later, alone. Pitt started toward the door, but instead of opening it for them both to leave, Jack closed it again.

"This seems rather general," Jack said unhappily. His finger was still on the handle, his body blocking the way out. "What is it that makes you believe there is some threat? You made it sound as if it could come from almost any quarter. Who do you suspect, and of what, precisely? If I could take that information to Lord Tregarron, he might be able to help you."

Pitt was not easily ruffled. Years in the police had taught him the virtue of patience, and also that when people are shocked or frightened, they often react aggressively. However, this faintly patronizing tone from Jack, of all people, was as abrasive as vinegar on a cut.

"You make it sound as if I'm looking for some kind of personal favor to help me out of a predicament," Pitt said tartly. "It is Special Branch's duty to prevent any assassination attempts on British soil, and doing so is as much in the interest of the Foreign Office as it is in Special Branch's."

Jack paled and the skin across his cheekbones tightened. "An assassination attempt? Is that likely?"

"I don't know! Because I don't know who's visiting, apart from the official government list."

Jack stiffened. "Exactly what *do* you know, Thomas? I'll see how it squares with the information we have. After all the recent problems with Special Branch, you must understand why Lord Tregarron is cautious." There were spots of color on Jack's cheeks, but his gaze did not waver.

"That is why I came in person," Pitt said between his teeth. He was on the verge of adding that if Tregarron didn't trust him, then he had better ask the prime minister to have Pitt replaced, because nothing would ever get done. Then he realized how childish that would have sounded, and how appallingly vulnerable. Had he heard someone else say such a thing, he would have immediately seen their weakness.

He took a breath and spoke more levelly. "I am aware of the delicacy of the situation, and Special Branch's one recent near failure," he said, faintly emphasizing the word "near." "I would remind Lord Tregarron that in the end we succeeded — rather spectacularly."

Jack stood motionless. "I will remind him. He will still want to know the details behind your concern. What shall I tell him?"

Pitt was prepared. He had expected to answer to Tregarron personally, but he could see that it was going to have to be through Jack. He outlined what Stoker had told him.

"It doesn't seem like much," Jack said gravely.

"By the time it does seem like much, it will be too late to deal with it quickly and discreetly," Pitt pointed out. "You might mention that also. Special Branch's job is not to stage dramatic rescues. It is, if possible, to avoid the danger and embarrassment in the first place."

Jack bit his lip. "I'll go and tell him. Please wait."

Again Pitt was too restless to sit in any of the chairs, comfortable as they were. He stood by the window, then paced, then stared out the window again at the busy street below. The blustering wind whipped at coattails, caught umbrellas, and endangered hats. He could imagine the hiss and splash as the wheels of passing carriages sent arcs of muddy water up into the air behind them.

It was a quarter of an hour later when Jack finally reappeared. This time he looked distinctly embarrassed.

"I'm sorry, but we can offer no practical help. Lord Tregarron says that he has considered the information you passed to us, and he does not feel that it refers to any of the private visits of which we are aware, nor does it seem connected to any of the anarchist groups in Europe of which we know. In his opinion, it is no more than careless gossip, and there is no need for you to be anxious."

He gave a bleak smile. "He asked me to convey to you his thanks for passing on your concern, and for taking the trouble to come personally, especially in view of recent past events." He seemed about to add something further, then changed his mind. Perhaps a glance at Pitt's face told him that he was already beyond the point of condescension.

Pitt felt acutely like the policeman he had once been, whom well-trained butlers would send to the servants' entrance when he had been bold enough to knock on the front door. As if they felt that the gamekeeper's son was putting on the airs of a gentleman and needed to be put in his place.

What would Narraway have done in this situation? The answer was obvious: He would not have *been* in this situation. Tregarron would have seen him, regardless of what he thought of the evidence.

Or would Narraway have been confident enough to judge the entire situation more accurately, and thus not needed Tregarron's opinion? Was that where Pitt had failed?

"Thank you for attempting to help," Pitt said coolly. "I shall have to acquire the information from some other source. This has been a waste of time, but it seems that neither you nor I have the power to avoid that. Good day."

Jack started to say something, then changed his mind. He was pale, but his cheeks were flushed. He opened the door for Pitt, who went out and into the long corridor without looking back.

Jack watched Pitt until he was out of sight, then returned to Tregarron's office, knocking lightly. He was answered immediately.

Tregarron looked up from his desk, the question on his face.

Jack closed the door behind him. He found this embarrassing. Pitt was his brother-in-law, and he both liked and respected him. But he knew something of the circumstances of Pitt's promotion to Narraway's position, and how close the whole affair had come to disaster. He knew that Pitt must be nervous now, perhaps leaning too far toward caution, afraid of missing a clue, and consequently overreaching himself, and his authority. If he became officious, he would make enemies.

"I think he was just being careful, sir," he said to Tregarron.

Tregarron smiled, but it was tight-lipped. "Don't let him be a nuisance over this, Radley. If people realize he's jumpy, they may start to imagine that there's something real behind it. We can't have Europe thinking we don't know what we're doing. Keep a tight rein on him, will you?"

Jack stood very straight. "Yes, sir." He considered adding something more, then thought better of it. He was new to his position too. Tregarron was one of the most dynamic figures in the Foreign Office. He had clearly taken a liking to Jack, much to Emily's delight.

He sincerely hoped Emily had had no hand in his promotion. It was extremely important to him to succeed on his own merit.

Early in their marriage, he had been content to live very comfortably on the wealth Emily had inherited from George Ashworth, but as time had gone by he had become less happy with it. Possibly that was due in part to the sense of purpose he saw in Pitt, and Charlotte's confidence in him because of it. He wanted Emily to look at him with the same regard: a regard born of belief, not duty.

Tregarron cleared his throat impatiently.

Jack smiled. "Yes, sir, I'll see that he doesn't embarrass himself, or us."

"Thank you," Tregarron said. "You'd better look over those papers from the German ambassador."

After dinner that evening, Pitt sat in the parlor in the big chair opposite Charlotte. The gaslight was bright, and the heavy velvet curtains were closed. The fire burned well, and the sound of the wind in the trees outside, mixed with the faint spatter of rain on the glass, was oddly comfortable. They were discussing moving house, but seemed to be deciding against it, at least for the time being.

"Are you sure you don't want to?" he asked, looking at her. She was mending one of Jemima's dresses. The faint click of the needle against her thimble was the only sound from inside the room, except for the whisper of the flames. "We could afford it," he added.

"I know." She smiled. "The job is enough change for the moment."

"You mean, it might not last?" he interpreted, recalling Jack's stiff figure standing by the door, relaying Tregarron's dismissal. Should he tell Charlotte about it? Not being able to discuss his concerns was the highest price of his promotion. It left him alone, in a way he had not been used to in fourteen years of marriage. He tried to put the warmth back into his eyes, to take the sting — and perhaps the fear — out of his words. She was just as sharply aware as he was that if he failed he would not be able to go back into the ranks again, that there was nowhere else for him. He had no private means, unlike Narraway or Radley.

"No," Charlotte said firmly, looking up and meeting his eyes. "I mean that I like this house and I'm not ready to leave it yet — if I ever will be. We've had a lot of good times here, and bad — or they've looked bad for a while. Victor Narraway, Aunt Vespasia, Gracie, and you and I have sat up all night in the kitchen, and fought some desperate battles." She shook her head a little, ignoring her sewing. "A new house would be empty in comparison. And I'm not ready to let the old one go. Are you?"

"No, perhaps I'm not." He smiled, feeling the warmth blossom inside him. "Every time I go down the corridor to the kitchen I see Gracie standing on tiptoe, still a couple of inches too short to reach the plates on the top of the dresser. I'm not used to seeing Minnie Maude, five inches taller. But she's a good girl. You're happy with her, aren't you?"

"I'll always miss Gracie, but yes, I am," she said with certainty. "And Daniel and Jemima like her, which is almost as important." Then she frowned, aware that something was wrong. She was uncertain whether he was not telling her because it was confidential, or because he did not want to spoil the evening. She could read the tension in him as easily as if he had spoken. For more than fourteen years they had been friends, as well as husband and wife. He kept all manner of secrets from the government, the police, and the general population, but he kept only the most specific, confidential details from her.

She saw in his eyes that he had made a sudden decision.

"I saw Jack today," he said, after a moment.

Charlotte waited, watching his face, reading the conflicting emotions.

"I had to see Tregarron about something, or at least try to," he went on. "But he sent Jack for me to report to, and relay his replies back."

"Jack's new promotion," she said with a little tightening of her lips. "I think Emily's prouder of it than he is."

"Did she push him into it?" he asked.

"Possibly." A shadow crossed her face. "Was he arrogant?"

Pitt relaxed at last, allowing his shoulders to ease and his body to sink into the familiar shape of the chair. "Not really. I was annoyed because I was damn sure Tregarron wouldn't have dismissed Narraway like that, but I think I went to them with too little information. Tregarron didn't believe there was any cause for concern, and it may well be that he is right. I need to know a lot more. I should have waited. Narraway would have."

"And you expect to walk in and be as good in your first year as he was after twenty?" she asked, her eyebrows raised.

"I need to be," he said quietly. "Or at least as near as makes no visible difference."

"He failed sometimes as well, Thomas. He wasn't always right."

"I know." He did know, but that did not ease his anxiety, or change the fact that he knew what failure would cost not just him, but the entire Branch.

Charlotte left home at nine o'clock the following morning, stepping out onto the pavement feeling a trifle self-conscious in her new riding habit. She looked extremely smart in it, which she was happily aware of, but it had been a long time since she had worn such a flattering and rather rakish outfit. It had not been possible until lately. Money had been reserved for essentials, which this most certainly was not, especially when one had children who seemed to grow out of every piece of clothing within months.

A week ago she had agreed to meet Emily in Rotten Row in Hyde Park, to spend an hour or two on horseback. Accordingly she now walked briskly toward Russell Square, where she was certain she could find a hansom cab. The wind had dropped, and there was a very slight frost in the air. It was a perfect winter morning for a ride.

However, when she alighted in Hyde Park she felt far less enthusiastic than she had expected to when the arrangement had been made. She could not put from her mind Pitt's conversation about his meeting with Jack in Lord Tregarron's office.

The trees of the park were bare, a fretwork of black lace against the sky. The earth of the long bridle path was already churned up by hooves, and the grass beyond was the strange, almost turquoise color that the frost crystals lent it. In the distance there were at least twenty riders already out: women sidesaddle, graceful in perfectly cut habits;

men riding astride, some of them in military uniform.

The sound of laughter drifted on the slight breeze; she also heard the jingle of harnesses and the thud of hooves as a horse broke into a canter.

Charlotte walked across the hard, frosty earth toward the group of horses still held by their grooms, and she wondered how much of the previous day's encounter Jack had relayed to Emily. Did he consider his work also to be bound by secrecy? More probably he had imagined that she would hear of it from Charlotte today, and would have prepared her for that, regardless of protocol.

She saw Emily standing by her horse. She was easily distinguishable from the other women there by her slenderness, and the gleam of winter light on her knot of fair hair, visible beneath the brim of her exquisite riding hat, which was like a shallower version of a gentleman's top hat, its brim slightly curled. Charlotte estimated the cost of it, and felt a flicker of envy.

She walked onto the gravel, which crunched under her boots.

Emily turned. She saw Charlotte and immediately started toward her.

"Good morning," she said with a tentative

smile, her eyes searching Charlotte's. "Are you ready to ride?"

"Very much," Charlotte replied. "I've been looking forward to it." It was a strangely stilted conversation, nothing like the ease and good humor they usually shared.

Side by side, without meeting glances, they walked back to the grooms standing with the animals. They mounted and moved out at a walk. They nodded to other riders they passed, but did not speak to anyone, as there was no one with whom they were acquainted.

The longer the silence lasted, the more difficult it would be to break it. Charlotte knew she must say something, even if it was completely trivial. Words often meant little; it was the act of speaking that mattered.

"We've been thinking about moving," she began. "Thomas asked me if I would like to, but I'm fond of the house on Keppel Street. A lot of important things have happened while we've been there, memories I like to live with, or at least I don't want to let go of yet."

Emily looked sideways at her. "But wouldn't you like to live somewhere slightly larger? Perhaps on one of the squares? Or do you think it's just a little early to move?" She meant, was Charlotte certain that Pitt would measure up to the job?

For a moment Charlotte did not answer. She was the elder, but she would always be socially the junior because of Pitt's humble beginnings, and because Emily had a wealth Charlotte could never even dream of.

Emily colored uncomfortably and looked away, fussing with her reins as though she needed to guide her horse along this safe, flat, fine gravel and earthen path.

"It is always a good idea not to take success for granted," Charlotte replied levelly. "Then, if one does fail, one has so much less distance to fall." She saw Emily's expression tighten. "But actually, I simply meant that I am not yet ready to leave a house so full of happy memories. I have no intention of entertaining, so we don't require the extra rooms."

"Surely you'll have to entertain?" Emily asked. "And anyway, it's such fun!" A smile flickered across her face.

"Yes, we will have to entertain. But only friends," Charlotte said quickly, keeping her horse even with Emily's. "And our friends are perfectly content with Keppel Street."

"But in Thomas's new position he will be expected to entertain people who are not necessarily your friends." Emily raised her fair eyebrows. "There are certain social obligations with promotions, you know? Head of Special Branch is a great deal more than just a policeman, even a gifted one. You will have to get used to speaking easily to government ministers, ambassadors, and all kinds of other ambitious and useful people."

"I doubt we would ever be able to afford a house fit to entertain people like that," Charlotte said drily. "It's a promotion, not an inheritance."

Emily winced. "I didn't realize you felt so badly about it. I'm sorry."

Charlotte reined in her horse. "It?" she questioned.

Emily stopped too. "Money. Isn't that what we're talking about?"

"It's what *you're* talking about," Charlotte corrected her. "I was talking about living in a house where I'm comfortable, rather than buying a bigger one that I don't need and that is a strange place to me, without familiarity or memories. I'm not you, Emily, and I don't want the same things."

"Don't be so pompous!" Emily snapped back. "This is really about Jack having to tell Thomas he couldn't see Lord Tregarron, isn't it?" Her tone was challenging, almost daring Charlotte to deny it.

"Well, if we're speaking of pompous . . ."

Charlotte began.

"It was not —"

"Really?" Charlotte cut across her. "Well, it seems you know far more about it than I do. But then Thomas's work is secret. He can't tell anyone, even me." She urged her horse on, moving ahead of Emily. She hated quarreling, especially with someone she cared for so deeply. It left her feeling unhappy and oddly alone. But she would not let Jack's sudden promotion go to Emily's head, or Jack's for that matter, and allow them to thoughtlessly make worse Pitt's sense of being out of his depth. Perhaps she was being unnecessarily protective, but then, so was Emily.

She reined in her horse again and waited until Emily caught up with her. Without meeting Emily's eyes she started again.

"I don't want to move yet. It's taking things for granted that haven't happened for certain. I would have thought you, of all people, would understand that. Your social position is assured, and your financial one, but you've a long way to go before you can say the same politically."

"Is that Thomas's opinion?" Emily was not yet mollified.

Charlotte forced herself to laugh. "I have no idea. He didn't mention it. Why? Do you think Jack has very little further to go? That would be a shame."

Emily muttered under her breath, and Charlotte knew very well that what she said was distinctly impolite.

While Charlotte was riding in Hyde Park, Pitt was already in his office at Lisson Grove asking for all the recent information Special Branch had gathered about any dissident groups in Central or Eastern Europe, particularly within the vast Austro-Hungarian Empire. The empire stretched from Austria itself eastward to include Hungary; south into northern Italy and down the Balkan Peninsula, encompassing Serbia, Croatia, Slovenia, and Romania; and north to Bohemia, Moravia, Slovakia, and parts of Poland and Ukraine. Within its borders, twelve different languages were spoken and several major religions were observed, including Roman Catholicism, Eastern Orthodoxy, and Islam. Additionally, there was a large number of Jews in prominent and highly influential positions in Vienna, a place where anti-Semitism was deep, ugly, and growing. Unrest of one sort or another was normal there.

Vienna might be the cradle of all sorts of new thoughts in politics, philosophy, medicine, music, and literature, but it was also a city of sporadic violence, with a shadow of unease, as if there was some doom just beyond the horizon, waiting for the moment when all the gaiety would end.

Pitt had requested to see Evan Blantyre, whom he had met at the recent musical evening. Evan's knowledge of the Austro-Hungarian Empire was extensive, and he might be able to offer the information and assistance Lord Tregarron had declined to provide.

He was pleasantly surprised when Blantyre agreed to see him almost immediately. Less than an hour later, Pitt stood in a pleasant anteroom, which had paintings of the Austrian Tyrol on the walls. He was there only briefly before he was ushered into Blantyre's office. This was a large, comfortable room with a fire burning in the hearth, and armchairs on either side of it. There were worn patches on the carpet, and the color was faded from age and sunlight. The desk was old, the wood gleaming like satin.

"Good morning, Commander," Blantyre said with interest, holding out his hand.

"Good morning, sir," Pitt replied, accepting the greeting. "I appreciate your taking the time to see me so quickly. It may prove to be nothing of importance, but I can't let this matter go until I know for sure."

"Quite right," Blantyre said. "Although I must say from the little you told my secretary, it all seemed rather coincidental, no real reason to suspect that any foreign visitor is the focus of an attack, if indeed an attack is even being planned." He indicated the chairs near the fire and they sat down opposite each other.

"It is probably nothing," Pitt agreed. "But a lot of issues start out as a whisper, one coincidence, and then another too soon after it, people showing an unexplained interest in something that appears to be harmless, but then isn't."

Blantyre smiled ruefully, curiosity lighting his face. "Well, how the devil do you know which coincidences matter? Is there an intellectual formula for it, or is it instinct, a particular skill?" His eyes were steady and bright. "Or something only experience can teach you, and perhaps one or two very near misses?"

Pitt shrugged. "I'm tempted sometimes to think there's a hell of a lot of luck in it, but I suppose to call it luck is just a different way of saying that it requires constant observation and the need to run down everything that strikes a jarring note." He

126

smiled. "And, as you say, one or two close shaves."

Blantyre nodded. "In other words, paying attention to detail, and a lot of damned hard work. Tell me more about exactly what alarms you in these particular inquiries. Do you really think this is about some intended violence? Against whom, for God's sake? And if Duke Alois really is the target, why here? It sounds unlikely to me, conspirators setting up an attack in a foreign country. It would require them to go into a place where they have no network of friends nor many sympathizers. Every man's hand would be against them."

"True," Pitt conceded. "But they would also be unknown to the general public. Fewer people here to recognize or betray them. And there is the other possibility."

Blantyre frowned. "What's that?"

"That they don't intend to escape. If they feel passionately enough about their cause, they may be prepared to sacrifice their own lives in the process."

Blantyre looked down at the worn pattern of the carpet. "I hadn't thought of that," he said grimly. "Of course, men do such things — and women too, I suppose. Patriots, misguided or not, come in all forms. Martyrs as well." He looked up at Pitt again. "I still don't find it very likely. That sort of great sacrifice isn't something you offer in order to kill a nonentity. In sheer practical terms, the world doesn't take enough notice." He pulled his mouth into a bitter smile, and then let it fade. "Tell me exactly what you've found, and I'll do all I can to learn if it's part of a greater plot. God knows, the last thing we need is some Austro-Hungarian duke blown to bits on our front doorstep."

Pitt told him the core of what he had gathered from Stoker's reports, and added the further information he had received since then. As he spoke he watched Blantyre's expression grow darker and more troubled.

"Yes, I see," Blantyre said as soon as Pitt had stopped speaking. He sat pensively, with his strong hands held so the fingertips touched. "If there were substance to it, it would be appalling. But how seriously have you considered that it is a wretched string of coincidences making a few unconnected inquiries look sinister, when in fact they are not at all? Or else — and this seems more likely to me — someone deliberately concocting this stuff to take your attention away from something else that *is* serious, and far more relevant?" Blantyre raised his eyebrows.

Pitt nodded and smiled bleakly. "I considered that as well. That it could all be a bluff." He thought for a moment. "Or perhaps a double bluff?"

Blantyre let out a sigh. "Of course you are right. I really don't think there is any likelihood of an assassination here at the moment, but I will look into it, ask a few discreet questions, at least about the possibility."

"Thank you." Pitt rose to his feet. "I can't afford to ignore it."

Blantyre smiled and stood also. He held out his hand and Pitt took it, returning the firm grip before he turned to go.

Pitt left the office feeling relieved, if only because Blantyre had taken him seriously. He had treated him as he would have treated Narraway.

Pitt smiled to himself as he went down the steps and out into the street and the heavy traffic.

Two days later, Pitt was sitting alone in his office. It was close to the end of February, and the daylight faded all too quickly. Within the next quarter-hour he would have to stand up and turn on the gaslight.

129

There was a knock on the door, and Stoker put his head around it.

"Mr. Evan Blantyre here to see you, sir," he said, his tone a mixture of surprise and respect. "Says it's pretty urgent."

Pitt was surprised too. He had accepted that Blantyre, for all his courtesy, had still mostly seemed to think that the whole possibility of a threat to any visiting Austrian dignitary was largely a misreading of the information.

"Show him in," he said immediately, rising to his feet.

A moment later Blantyre came in, closing the door behind him. He shook Pitt's hand briefly, and started to speak even before both of them were seated.

"I owe you an apology, Pitt," he said gravely, hitching his trousers a little at the knees to preserve their shape as he crossed his legs. "I admit, I didn't take this theory of yours very seriously. I thought you were jumping at shadows a bit. Understandable, after some of the recent tragedies."

Pitt presumed he was referring to the Gower case and Narraway's dismissal. He said nothing. It was ridiculous to have hoped that some of that wretched betrayal would have remained secret, but it still hurt him that so many people seemed to know of it. He waited for Blantyre to continue.

Blantyre's face was very solemn. "I looked into the information you gave me," he went on. "At first it seemed to be very superficial, a series of odd but basically harmless questions, unconnected to each other. But then I examined them a little more deeply, one at a time, beginning with the tracing of the most likely route from Dover to London, which of course is by train."

Pitt watched Blantyre's face, and the intensity in it alarmed him. He waited without interrupting.

"It seemed to mean very little." Blantyre gave a slight shrug. "Hundreds of people must make such a journey. Inquiries would be natural enough, even several days in advance of travel. Then I looked at the signals you mentioned, and the places where such trains would pass a junction on the track. You are perfectly right, of course. Freight trains also travel there regularly, and a series of accidents — signals green when they should be red; points changed and a freight train diverted onto the wrong track — could create a disaster with enormous proportions. You would have far more than just one man dead."

He drew his breath in slowly, then let it out again.

"But I thought I had better see if the route tied in with any known person of importance. It did, rather more than I supposed. It turns out that you are right. One of the minor Austrian dukes is coming. He is of no importance himself, but he's still a member of the imperial family, and grandnephew of our queen, or something of the sort. He is making a private visit to a grandson of the queen's. It is not a government matter at all. But his coming, and the time that the inquiries concern coincide precisely with the plans made for him to travel from Vienna to Paris, then to Calais, and across the Channel. From Dover he goes by train to London. He'll be staying at the Savoy."

"Not the palace?" Pitt asked in surprise.

"It seems he wants to do a little entertaining himself," Blantyre said with a tight little smile. "But you see my point. When I made a few inquiries of certain friends in Europe, they also investigated, and found that questions had been asked about the entire route. It seems he will be bringing only a few servants: a secretary, a valet, that sort of thing."

He hesitated only a moment. "I'm sorry, Pitt. Your instincts were correct. This is something you have to take seriously."

132

Pitt was cold, in spite of the embers burning in the grate only a few feet from him. Until now he had been allowing himself to think that he was probably imagining the danger, as Tregarron and even Blantyre had said, but Blantyre's news changed everything.

"Here." Blantyre held out a small bundle of papers. They looked to be hastily scribbled notes, perhaps half a dozen sheets in all. "You will need to follow up on it, of course, so I have given you the names of the people I spoke to, the facts and references I checked. I cannot oblige you to keep them secret, but I would ask that you tell as few people as possible, and only those you are certain you can trust absolutely, not only their honesty but also their discretion. Usually, I would not have committed anything to paper, but I fear this is far too serious to bother with the usual protocol. This is, potentially at least, a monstrous crime, which would kill not only a member of the Austrian royal family, but also God knows how many innocent Britons, if we don't prevent it." He held the notes out for Pitt to take.

Pitt met Blantyre's gaze, then took the papers and looked down at them. They were exactly as Blantyre had said: names, places, dates — all the information Pitt needed to check the routes, and, above all, the names and descriptions of known anarchists involved in assassinations in Europe and the methods they had used. Particular emphasis had been given to those who resembled the man who had inquired about railway signals and points.

He looked back up at Blantyre.

"I'm sorry," Blantyre said again, gravely. "I know you would rather have been wrong, but I'm afraid it seems that you are not. Something is planned that could, at its worst, set us at war with Austria."

Pitt's mind raced. He did not have enough military or diplomatic knowledge to understand why anyone would want to do such a thing. If a British train was wrecked, though, feelings would be high in both countries. Accusations would be made, things said that would be impossible to deny later. Grief and confusion would turn to anger. Each country could so easily blame the other.

"God knows who or what is behind it," Blantyre said softly. "It may be no more than yet another petty uprising of one of the Balkan nations wanting more independence, and resorting to their usual violence. It happens quite regularly. But it may also be a far deeper plan, intended to damage

Britain. Otherwise, why do it here?"

"You mean someone prompting them to do it?" Pitt asked quietly. "In order to accomplish . . . what?"

"I don't know," Blantyre admitted. "The possibilities are considerable. Maybe there is some treaty these people wish broken, and this is the easiest way to go about it."

"Thank you. I shall look into all these." Pitt rose to his feet and offered Blantyre his hand.

The following day Pitt sent for Stoker, who came into the office looking unusually cheerful. However, his lightness of mood disappeared as soon as he sat down obediently and waited for Pitt to speak.

"You'll remember that Evan Blantyre came here yesterday afternoon," Pitt said quietly. "I'd given him the information we had. At first he thought it was all irrelevant, but he looked into it anyway . . ."

Stoker sat up a little more stiffly.

"And there are plans for Duke Alois Habsburg to visit London from March sixteenth to nineteenth. He is to travel first from Vienna to Paris, then Calais, to take the steamer to Dover, lastly the train to London. He won't stay at the palace, but at the Savoy Hotel. There are plans to throw a party at Kensington Palace for his friends." He grimaced as he saw Stoker's face. "It is exactly the route we were concerned about, and on the day for which inquiries were made."

Stoker let out his breath with a sigh, his eyes wide. "So it's real!"

"It could be," Pitt answered. "Or it could be something we have been very subtly allowed to know about in order to draw our attention away from something else. But either way, we can't afford to ignore it. This is the information Mr. Blantyre gave me." He passed it over. "Read it. Check each of the details and each of the names."

"Yes, sir. What are you planning to do?"

"Learn all I can about Duke Alois Habsburg, and look into anyone who could have the slightest interest in assassinating him," Pitt replied.

Stoker picked up Blantyre's papers, looked at them, and made very brief notes from the top two. "I'll come back and get more tomorrow," he said, rising to his feet.

"Anything else?" Pitt asked.

"No, sir." Stoker looked slightly surprised.

"You looked unusually cheerful," Pitt answered, leaving the question in the uplift of his voice.

Stoker smiled. "Yes, sir." He hesitated, a

faint color in his cheeks. He realized Pitt was waiting for him to elaborate. "Had to follow someone yesterday evening; he was a bit suspect."

"And?" Pitt pursued. "What did you catch him doing? Don't make me pull your teeth, Stoker!" He heard his own words, and how much he sounded like Narraway. Now the heat burned up his own face.

"Nothing, sir, actually. Turned out to be a blind alley."

"And?" Pitt snapped.

"He went to a concert, sir. The music was rather good. I thought I'd hate it, but it was . . . sort of beautiful." He looked embarrassed but happy, as if the memory still lingered with him.

"What was it?" Now Pitt was curious. Even after all this time, he knew nothing of Stoker beyond his professional skills and his indisputable courage. His personal tastes, and his life apart from Special Branch, were a complete mystery.

"Beethoven, sir. All piano."

Pitt masked his surprise. "Yes, you're right," he agreed. "It must have been good."

Stoker smiled, then excused himself and went out.

Pitt bent to study the rest of Blantyre's notes. He added to them a large sheaf of papers he had borrowed from the Special Branch files, and began to study the history of the last ten years, quickly moving forward to the present, and the character and politics of Duke Alois Habsburg.

Two hours later, his eyes stung and his head ached. He had read a mass of facts, opinions, and fears. The Austrian Empire was geographically enormous and a single entity, as far as land was concerned. It was nothing like the British Empire, which was composed of countries, islands, and — in the cases of India, Australia, and Canada — parts of other continents, half the earth away from each other. Austria was one large mass loosely held together by a dual monarchy: one in Austria, one in Hungary. It included the best part of a dozen other countries and territories, each with its own history, language, and culture, and frequently, its own religions as well.

It had always been an empire of unease. Its history was marked with plots, protests, uprisings, suppressions, the occasional assassination attempt, and of course plenty of individual executions.

Franz Josef had been emperor for nearly fifty years. In some ways he ruled with a light hand, allowing a considerable degree of individuality to remain, but in other ways he was rigid, conservative, and autocratic. The very nature of the ramshackle empire meant that it was only a matter of time before it fell apart. The question was, which of all the many divisive elements was going to be the catalyst?

Socialism and its reforms had raised their voices in Vienna. Pitt was startled to learn that the dead crown prince, Rudolf, the heir to the throne who had died at Mayerling, had believed in its principles so passionately that he had expressed his intent to declare the Austrian Empire a republic and to rule as its president upon his succession to the throne.

Pitt sat motionless with the papers in his hands and tried to imagine what old Franz Josef had thought of that. And what now of the new heir, Archduke Franz Ferdinand?

Blantyre had written a long note about him. Apparently, for all his radical differences with the old emperor, Ferdinand had no sympathies of the socialist nature. He abhorred socialism and its reforms just as heartily as did his uncle.

Blantyre's conclusions were the only ones likely, given the evidence. There was a plot to assassinate Duke Alois Habsburg when he was on British soil, presumably in London, since there had been anonymous inquiries about arrangements at the Savoy Hotel and Kensington Palace.

If it happened, it would be a tragedy, and an appalling embarrassment for Britain. And it would be a disaster for Special Branch.

The next morning Pitt went again to see Lord Tregarron. He must make the Foreign Office minister aware of the threat, at the very least, and possibly see if he could have the trip altered in time, place, or even route of travel, at the last minute. And Duke Alois himself must also be made aware of the danger.

As before, he was met first by Jack, who was again very smartly dressed in a black coat and striped trousers. He looked just as uncomfortable as he had previously, when he came into the room where Pitt had been asked to wait. He closed the door behind him and took a deep breath.

"Good morning, Thomas. How are you?"

It was an obvious attempt at civility in a situation he already foresaw as being awkward.

Pitt had anticipated resistance, until Jack made Tregarron aware of the seriousness of the threat. He was determined to keep his temper, not only for Charlotte's sake — she had told him of her encounter with Emily at Hyde Park — but also because the moment he lost control of himself, he would lose control of the situation.

"Well, thank you," he replied. "But concerned." He tried to keep his expression neutral. "I took the various pieces of evidence I have to Evan Blantyre, as he is the best expert I know on the Austro-Hungarian Empire. I asked him to evaluate the likelihood of it being linked to serious trouble in Britain within the next couple of months." He saw Jack's face darken.

"Apparently Duke Alois Habsburg is visiting one of our royal family in a few weeks' time. He plans to travel from Vienna to Paris, then to Calais, by ferry to Dover, and lastly by train to London —"

"The obvious route," Jack interrupted.

"I am aware of that," Pitt replied. "The exact timetable might be less obvious, but people are making inquiries about it, even so far as the Savoy Hotel, where it is known he will stay, and Kensington Palace, where a party will be given."

A flash of anxiety crossed Jack's face. "Really? Is it Austrian officials making sure the route is well planned and safe?"

"No, the people who are checking are known agitators and anarchists," Pitt replied. "One or two of them are implicated in bombings in Paris."

"Arrest them," Jack told him.

"For what? Checking railway timetables?"

"Exactly. Aren't you being a bit alarmist? Alois is a very minor figure, you know." Jack gestured with his hands, as if appealing to reason. "Or maybe you don't? If somebody planned an assassination, Alois wouldn't be worth their time, or the risk."

"Are you certain?" Pitt asked very seriously.

"Yes," Jack responded immediately. However, his tone of irritation made Pitt wonder if he really was certain, or if he had actually not given the matter any thought until that moment. Either way, he would defend his superior's opinion instinctively, and ascertain the details later. That was what a loyal second-in-command did.

Pitt shook his head. "I think there is quite a lot about the Austrian royal family and its difficulties that we do not know. For example, did you expect the suicide at Mayerling?"

Jack was angry, caught off-guard by Pitt's question. "No, of course not. No one did," he said with considerable annoyance.

"But with hindsight, we can see that perhaps we should have," Pitt pointed out.

"It was a tragedy waiting to happen."

"How do you know that?" Jack demanded, coming farther into the room.

Pitt smiled. "It's my job to know a certain number of things. Unfortunately, I didn't piece together then what I now realize were signs, and I doubt Narraway did either. Or if he did, then no one listened to him."

Jack winced and his eyes became harder. "I'll go and ask his lordship, but honestly, I think you are scaremongering, Thomas, and I believe he will think so too. There is no earthly reason to assassinate Alois Habsburg. He's harmless, a lightweight junior member of the Austrian royal family, of which there are hordes, just as there are of ours." Without adding anything more, he turned and went out of the room, leaving Pitt to wait again.

This time it was no more than five minutes before he came back into the room looking tense, as if he now wanted to say far more than he dared.

"Lord Tregarron will see you, but he can only spare a few minutes." He held the door open for Pitt to go through. "He has a meeting with our ambassador to Poland in a very short while."

"Thank you," Pitt accepted, going out and following Jack down a wide, elegant corridor. About thirty feet along, Jack stopped and tapped quietly on a large, arched door.

Tregarron greeted them stiffly but with the necessary courtesy, then looked only at Pitt as Jack retired to the back of the room, making himself all but invisible.

"Radley informs me that Evan Blantyre seems to believe there is some assassination attempt planned against Duke Alois Habsburg when he visits London next month." He spoke quickly, giving Pitt no chance to interrupt him. "I imagine you have to take notice of these things, but in my opinion, someone is trying to distract you from your more urgent business. Duke Alois is, as Radley has told you, a charming, somewhat feckless young man of no importance whatsoever. It would be completely senseless for anyone to waste their time harming him, let alone to set up an elaborate plot to do it in a foreign country."

He shook his head with annoyance. "It is out of the question that we should admit to the Austrian government that we cannot look after him or guarantee his safety in the capital city of our own empire. I imagine they would find it impossible to believe we were so incompetent, and so would see it as a rebuff. If you think Special Branch cannot deal with it, I will ask the Home Secretary to take care of the matter. He has the ordinary police at his beck and call." He smiled bleakly. "Perhaps you should ask Narraway's advice. I'm sure he would make himself available to you."

Pitt was so angry he could think of no words he dared say. His hands were shaking. He could feel the color burn into his skin. He knew Jack was looking down at the floor, too embarrassed to meet his eyes.

"Good day, Mr. Pitt," Tregarron said bluntly.

"Good day, sir," Pitt replied, and swung on his heel to go out. He passed Jack without even glancing at him, nor was he aware of the rain in his face as he stepped into the street.

Walking into his own house that evening was like walking into a warm embrace, even before Charlotte met him at the kitchen door. She took a long, careful look at his face, and guided him away from the kitchen's savory cooking smells and into the front parlor. The fire was burning and the gaslamps were lit but turned low. This enveloping comfort was new since his promotion, and the ability to afford so much coal.

"What is it?" she asked as soon as she had

closed the door.

"What's wrong with sitting in the kitchen?" he countered, avoiding answering her.

"Thomas! Minnie Maude is not Gracie, but she's far from unobservant. You are the master of the house. She watches you to see if all is well, if the day is good or bad, what she might do to please you. This is her home now, and it matters to her very much."

Pitt breathed out slowly, letting some of the anger ease from him. He realized with self-conscious displeasure how little he had appreciated the effect his mood had on others. He had been born in the servant class; he should have known better. Without any warning, he was whisked back to his childhood and saw his mother in the kitchen of the big house and remembered the look on her face, the sudden anxiety that would descend when Sir Arthur Desmond had been in one of his rare dark moods, or when word had come down that he was not feeling well.

"I saw Lord Tregarron today," he told Charlotte. "First Jack, of course, who suggested, obliquely, that I am fussing over nothing. Then Tregarron implied that if I can't manage my job, I should ask for Narraway's help." He could not keep the bitterness out of his voice.

She considered it for a moment before replying. "That is extremely rude," she said at length. "I wonder what is bothering them, that they should descend to such ill manners."

"Are you asking in a sideways fashion if I was rude first?" he said with a tight smile. He knew every word he spoke was driving a further wedge between her and Emily, and yet he could not stop himself. He felt horribly vulnerable. "I wasn't. I told Jack my information came from Blantyre. He's as good a source as there could be."

"Perhaps that is the problem," she said thoughtfully. "Are you sure you are right, Thomas?"

"No," he admitted. "I'm just sure of the price if I am right and we do nothing."

CHAPTER 4

Vespasia returned to call again on Serafina Montserrat a week after her first visit. It was a bright, fresh day, but surprisingly cold. She was pleased to come inside the house, even though it had an air of emptiness about it. Pale flowers were arranged carefully in a vase on the hall table, but without flair, as if whoever had done it was afraid to be criticized for individuality. All the pictures were straight, the surfaces dust free, but it looked in some way as if the mistress of the establishment was not at home. There were no small articles of daily use visible: no gloves or scarves, no outdoor boots on the rack below the coat stand, no silver- or ebony-topped cane.

She was waiting in the cool, green morning room where the footman had left her when Nerissa came in. She closed the door so softly behind herself that Vespasia was startled to see her there.

"Good morning, Lady Vespasia. It is so kind of you to call again," Nerissa began. Her unremarkable face was marred at the moment by tiredness and lack of color. Her plain, dark dress did nothing to help, in spite of a pale fichu at the neck.

Vespasia felt something vaguely patronizing in the younger woman's tone, as if visiting an old lady was a thing one did out of charity rather than friendship.

"It is not kind at all, Miss Freemarsh," she said coolly. "Mrs. Montserrat and I are more than acquaintances. We have memories in common of times of marvelous hopes and dangers, and too few people with whom to share them, and others to recall of friends we will never see again."

Nerissa smiled. "I'm sure you do," she replied. "But I'm afraid you will find Aunt Serafina somewhat less lucid than even a week ago. She is failing very quickly." She gave a brief, apologetic smile. "Her memory has become even more disjointed, and she has longer lapses into complete fantasy. She cannot now appreciate the difference between what she has read or been told and what has really happened in her own experience. You will have to be patient with her. I hope you understand?"

"Of course I do," Vespasia assured her.

"And even if I do not, it hardly matters. I have come to visit a friend, not to cross-examine a witness."

"I did not mean to offend you," Nerissa said, lowering her eyes. "I only wished to prepare you for the deterioration you will see in her, even in so short a time, in case it causes you distress. It really is rather serious. And I hardly know how to put this delicately, but . . ." She stopped, as if unable to find the right words.

"But what?" Now Vespasia was ashamed of herself for having been so cool. The younger woman was clearly concerned. Perhaps other visitors had been tactless, or had allowed their own embarrassment to show too plainly. "What is it that disturbs you, Miss Freemarsh?" she asked more gently. "Age and illness? Forgetting things is something that happens to most of us who are fortunate enough to have long lives. It can be frightening to realize that we may all be affected one day, but it is not something to be ashamed of. There is no need for you to apologize."

Nerissa looked up and met her eyes. "It is more than forgetting, Lady Vespasia." She lowered her voice to a mere murmur. "Aunt Serafina creates fantasies, imaginings as to what she did in the past, and it is embarrassing because her accounts are very colorful, and some of them involve real people and events." She chewed her lower lip until it was pink. "I wish I could protect her from anyone seeing her like this, with no control over her mind, and most of the time very little discretion with her tongue." She turned away and lowered her gaze until she was staring at the floor. "She has a great admiration for you, you know."

Vespasia was startled. She and Serafina were not quite contemporaries, Serafina being a decade older, and they were completely unalike. Vespasia had used her wit, intelligence, and extraordinary beauty to learn information and persuade men of great power to act, as she believed, either wisely or generously. Serafina had been an adventurer in the most physical sense: brave, skilled, and with an iron nerve. She had ridden with the insurgents in Croatia, and manned the barricades, rifle in hand, in the streets of Vienna, before the ignominious collapse of the revolution and the emperor's return to power in '48.

Vespasia had done that only once, in Rome, far back in her youth. Their paths had crossed, perhaps half a dozen times since then. They had known of each other through allies in the common cause.

151

"Are you sure?" she asked quietly. "I think perhaps 'respect' would be more accurate, as I have for her. And of course we have a friendship now, in our later years, born possibly out of the understanding of what we fought for then, and the passion, and the losses of those days."

"You are very modest," Nerissa replied, a very faint edge of bitterness in her voice. "But admiration is what I meant." She looked at Vespasia squarely, even defiantly. "She will try to impress you. I'm sorry. It is humiliating to see. It might be better if you simply left a card. I will tell her you called when she was asleep, and you did not wish to disturb her."

"She will not believe you," Vespasia replied. "She will know perfectly well that you are keeping people from visiting her because you are ashamed of her. I will not be party to that."

The color swept up Nerissa's pallid cheeks, and her eyes were hot with anger. But she was not yet mistress of the house, and she dared not retaliate.

"I was merely trying to save your feelings," she said very quietly. "And to save Aunt Serafina from being remembered as she is now, rather than as the proud and discreet woman she used to be. I'm sorry if you do not see that."

"I see it very well," Vespasia told her, finding herself torn between pity and irritation. "And I assure you, my feelings are of no importance. I shall remember Serafina as I knew her in the past, regardless of what happens now. I am well acquainted with the idea that as we grow older we change, and it is not always either easy or comfortable."

"You have not changed," Nerissa said with candor that bordered on resentment.

"Not yet." Vespasia was now embarrassed herself, as if her health and good fortune were blessings she had not deserved. "But no one knows about the future. In another ten years I may be profoundly grateful if my friends still remember me at all, and call upon me even if I am tedious, and ramble a little, or lose myself in a time when I was more alive, more able, and still dreamed of great accomplishments."

Nerissa did not reply but turned and led Vespasia up the wide stairway to the landing and across it to Serafina's bedroom door. Before she entered, Vespasia heard the footman open the front door to another caller.

"Good morning, Mrs. Blantyre. How pleasant to see you. Please do come inside; the weather is most inclement."

Nerissa half turned and Vespasia caught sight of the amazement in her face. There was also an expression there that might have been resolve, and then a flash of emotion quite unreadable.

"I think Aunt Serafina has another visitor," she said quickly. "I must go down and welcome her." She tapped sharply on the door in front of them. Then, without waiting for an answer, she pushed it open for Vespasia, and excused herself again to go downstairs.

"Of course," Vespasia acknowledged her, and went into the room alone.

Tucker was standing near the door to the dressing room, a silver-backed hairbrush in her hand. The moment she saw Vespasia she smiled and her face filled with relief.

"Good morning, m'lady. How are you?"

"Good morning, Tucker," Vespasia replied. "I am very well. I am glad to see you with Mrs. Montserrat. How are you?" It was a purely rhetorical question, a matter of good manners. She smiled at Tucker and nodded slightly, then turned toward the bed.

Serafina was sitting up, her hair dressed. She looked wide awake, and as soon as she met Vespasia's eyes she smiled back. Only when Vespasia was closer did she see a vacancy in her look, an expectancy, as if she had very little idea who her visitor was.

Vespasia sat down in the chair beside the bed and for a moment felt exactly the embarrassment and distress she had told Nerissa were unimportant. Unexpectedly, they were overwhelming. She had no idea what to say to this person in front of her, helpless, a spirit trapped not only in an aging body but also in a mind that had betrayed her.

Serafina was waiting, staring at her hopefully.

"How are you?" Vespasia asked. She felt that it was completely inane, yet how else could she begin?

"My leg hurts," Serafina replied with a rueful little shrug. "But if you break bones, you can expect that to happen. I've broken enough; I shouldn't be surprised."

Vespasia felt a twinge of alarm. Was it possible Serafina really did have a broken bone? Could she have tripped and fallen? Old bones break easily.

"I'm sorry," she said with sincerity. "I hope the doctor has seen it? Has it been properly cared for?"

"Yes, of course it has," Serafina answered her. "It was in a cast for weeks. What an incredible nuisance. I can't ride a horse with a cast on, you know."

Vespasia's heart sank. "No, of course not," she said, as if it had been a perfectly ordinary comment. "And it still aches?"

Serafina looked blank. "I beg your pardon?"

After glancing at Tucker, who shook her head almost imperceptibly, Vespasia looked back at Serafina and struggled for something to say. Surely Adriana Blantyre had called to see Serafina and was even now on her way up? Or was it possible she'd come to see Nerissa? They were not so very different in age — six or seven years, perhaps. But socially they were worlds apart: Adriana the wife of a man of privilege, wealth, and accomplishment, Nerissa a simple woman of no standing, and past the usual age of marriage. Vespasia found herself listening for another footfall on the landing beyond the door, expecting interruption at any moment. Knowing how vague and distracted Serafina was today, surely Nerissa would thank Adriana for calling, but advise her to come again another day?

She turned to Tucker. "I saw Mrs. Blantyre arriving. Perhaps you might suggest to Miss Freemarsh that she call at a more fortunate time?"

Tucker was about to reply when there was a knock on the door. A moment later Adriana Blantyre came in. Clearly Nerissa had warned her that Vespasia was already here.

"Good morning, Lady Vespasia," she said with a smile of pleasure. Then she turned to Serafina. "How are you today? I brought you some lilies from the hothouse. I gave them to Nerissa to put in water." She perched on the edge of the bed, far from where she would disturb Serafina's feet.

"I'm well, thank you," Serafina replied, blinking and looking puzzled. "In fact, I can't think what I'm still doing in bed. What time is it? I should be up." A look of alarm filled her face. "Why are you here in my bedroom?"

"You've been unwell," Adriana said quickly. "You are recovering, but it's too soon to be out yet. And the weather is very cold."

"Is it?" Serafina turned to face the window. "Is it autumn? The tree is bare. Or winter?"

"Winter, but nearly spring," Adriana told her. "Rather raw outside. The sort of wind that bites through your clothes."

"Then it was nice of you to come," Serafina remarked. "Do you know Lady Vespasia Cumming-Gould?"

"Yes, we have met," Adriana assured her.

"Vespasia and I are old friends," Serafina

said, nodding a little. "We fought together."

Adriana looked confused.

"Oh!" Serafina gave a little laugh. "Side by side, not against each other, my dear, never against each other." She shot a glance at Vespasia, a secret, amused communication.

Adriana looked at Vespasia for confirmation, or perhaps for help.

Vespasia tried to keep the surprise from her face.

There was no possible course but to agree. "Certainly," she said with as much enthusiasm as she could. "Each in our own fashion." She must steer the conversation away from further trouble. How much did Serafina remember? Was she now recalling actual past events, or was she about to start one of the rambling journeys of the imagination that Nerissa had referred to?

"It sounds exciting," Adriana said with interest. "And dangerous."

"Oh, yes." Serafina leaned back a little against her pillows, her dark eyes gazing far away in the distance of recollection. "Very dangerous. There were deaths."

"Deaths?" Adriana's voice was a whisper, the color fading from her face.

Vespasia drew in her breath to interrupt. There had been, of course, but it was long ago, and there was no point in raking over tragedy now. But Serafina continued before she could break in.

"Brave people," she said softly. "Passions were very high. Men and women sacrificed their lives for the cause of freedom." She frowned and studied Adriana closely for several moments. "But you know that. You are Croatian. You know all these things."

Adriana nodded. "I've heard the stories." Her voice choked, and she coughed to clear her throat, and perhaps to give herself a moment to master her feelings. "I wasn't there myself."

Now Serafina seemed lost. "Weren't you? Why not? Don't you want freedom for your people? For your language, your music, your culture? Do you want to wear the Austrian yoke forever?"

"No," Adriana whispered. "Of course I don't."

This time Vespasia did interrupt, politely but firmly. "That was all ages ago, my dear. Mrs. Blantyre was hardly even born then. Those are old griefs. Much has happened since that time. Italy is united and independent, at least most of it is."

Serafina looked at her as if she had momentarily forgotten Vespasia's presence.

"Trieste?" she asked, hope flaring in her eyes.

Vespasia thought for an instant of lying, but it was such a condescension, such a denial of respect, that she could not do it.

"Not yet, but it will come," she assured her.

"What are you doing about it?" Serafina asked. She was puzzled, as if raking her memory, but there was also challenge in her question.

"Do you not think it wiser to discuss other things just now?" Vespasia suggested. "Fashion, perhaps, or the latest art exhibition, or even politics here at home?"

"Prince Albert is German, you know," Serafina said. "The Saxe-Coburgs are everywhere. Everybody who is anyone at all has at least one of them in the family."

"Prince Albert is dead," Vespasia assured her firmly.

"Is he? Oh, dear." Serafina blinked. "Who killed him? And for heaven's sake why? He was a good man. How terribly stupid. What is the world coming to?"

"Nobody killed him." Vespasia glanced at Adriana and back again to Serafina. "He died of typhoid fever. It was many years ago now. And yes, you are quite right, he was a good man. Perhaps next time I come I shall bring you the latest edition of the *London Il-lustrated News,* and you can look at the current gossip, such as there is, and some of the fashions for spring."

Serafina turned her hands outward in a gesture of resignation. "Perhaps. That would be kind of you." She closed her eyes. Her face looked pale and strained, her brows a little wispy, her eye sockets hollow.

Vespasia rose to her feet, staring at Adriana. "I think perhaps we should leave Mrs. Montserrat to have a little rest. She seems tired."

"Of course," Adriana agreed reluctantly. She looked at Serafina. "I'll come back and see you again soon."

Serafina did not answer. It appeared that she had drifted off to sleep.

Adriana led the way out, followed by Tucker. Vespasia was at the door when she turned one more time to look at Serafina. The older woman was staring wide-eyed, suddenly very much awake, her expression one of terror. The next moment the look was gone, and her face was completely blank again.

Vespasia closed the door and, leaving Adriana outside on the landing with Tucker, she went back to Serafina. Gently putting her hand over the stiff, blue-veined ones on

161

the coverlet, she asked, "What is it? What are you afraid of?"

The fear returned to Serafina's eyes. "I know too much," she whispered. "Terrible things, plans of murder, the dead piled up . . ."

"Plans about whom?" Vespasia asked, trying to keep the pain out of her voice. "My dear, most of them are gone already. These are old quarrels you are remembering. They don't matter anymore. It's 1896 now. There are new issues, and they don't involve us as they used to."

"I know it's 1896," Serafina said quickly. "But some secrets never grow old, Vespasia. Betrayal always matters. Brothers, fathers, and husbands sold to the executioner for the price of advancement. Blood money can never be repaid."

Vespasia stared at her and saw the clear, sharp light of intelligence in her eyes. There was nothing blurred now, nothing uncertain. But she was afraid, and she could not hide it. Perhaps that was what shocked Vespasia the most. In all the times they had met — in London, Paris, and Vienna, in the ballrooms or at a secret rendezvous in some hunting lodge or backstreet room — she had never seen Serafina white with terror.

"Who are you afraid of?" she whispered.

Serafina's eyes filled with tears, and one hand closed over Vespasia's, her thin fingers desperate. "I don't know. There were so many. I'm not even sure which ones matter anymore. And half the time I don't know what I'm saying!" Tears filled her eyes. "I'm not sure who is allied with whom these days, and if I make a mistake, they'll kill me. I know too much, Vespasia! I thought of writing it all down, and letting everyone know that I had, but what good would that do? Only the guilty would believe me. It's all so . . ."

Vespasia held Serafina's hand with both of hers. "Are you certain there are still secrets that matter, my dear? So much has changed. Franz Josef is a relatively benign old man now, broken by tragedy . . ."

"I know. And I know what that tragedy was, more than you do, Vespasia."

"Mayerling?" Vespasia asked with surprise. "How could you know more about that than what was public information? They burned the place to the ground, and all the evidence with it."

"Not all," Serafina said softly. "I know people. I've only lost my wits in the last year." She searched Vespasia's eyes. "But there are other secrets, older ones. I know who shot Esterhazy, and why. I know who

163

Stefan's father really was, and how to prove it. I know who betrayed Lazar Dragovic." The tears spilled down her tired cheeks. "I'm so afraid I'll forget who I'm talking to, and say something to give it away."

Vespasia realized that Serafina was frightened not only of letting the secrets slip, but also that whoever was involved would fear the revelations enough to kill her before that happened.

Today she knew what year it was, and she knew Vespasia. But when Adriana Blantyre had been there, Vespasia was uncertain whether Serafina had truly been aware and was only pretending to be confused, or whether she had actually believed it was a different time. Remembering the look in Serafina's eyes, the blank helplessness, she feared it was the latter. Anyway, what purpose could there be in trying to mislead Adriana?

"Perhaps it would be a good idea to see fewer people for a little while?" she suggested. "It might even be possible to make sure the ones you do see are those who would know little of such things anyway, so even if you mistook who they were, what you said would be incomprehensible to them. I know that could be terribly boring, but at least it would be safe."

Serafina understood that and sadness filled her face. "Perhaps it would be smarter," she agreed. "But will you come back again? I . . ." Embarrassment prevented her from finishing the request.

"Of course," Vespasia assured her. "We could talk of whatever you wish. I would enjoy it myself. There are too few of us left."

Serafina nodded with a smile, and sank back into the pillows, her eyes closed. "And Adriana," she whispered. "Take care of her for me. But . . ." She gulped and her voice choked. "But perhaps I shouldn't see her again . . . in case I say something . . ." She stopped, unable to finish her thought.

Vespasia remained a few minutes longer, but Serafina seemed to have drifted into a light sleep. Vespasia moved the sheets a little to cover her thin hands — the old get chilled very easily — then she walked softly from the room.

She went down the stairs and asked the maid in the hallway to send for Nerissa so she might express her good wishes and take her leave.

Nerissa appeared within moments, her face shadowed with anxiety.

"Thank you for coming, Lady Vespasia," she said a little stiffly. "I'm sorry you had to see Aunt Serafina so . . . so unlike the person she used to be. It is distressing for all of us. You will know now that I was not being alarmist when I said she is sinking rapidly."

"No, of course not," Vespasia agreed. "I'm afraid she is considerably worse, even in the few days since I last saw her. I think it might be wise, in view of her . . . imagination, if you were to restrict her visitors rather more. I suggested to her that it might be a good idea to see only those who are young enough to know little or nothing of the affairs with which she used to be concerned. She was pleased with the suggestion. It will ease her fears. And of course, as you say, it would be very sad if people were to remember her as she is now, rather than as she used to be. I would much prefer not to have it so, were I in her position."

She was uncertain exactly how to phrase Serafina's request regarding Adriana.

"You might gently turn aside Mrs. Blantyre, if she calls again," she began, and saw the puzzlement in Nerissa's face. "She is of Croatian birth, which seems to awaken particular memories and ideas in your aunt," she continued. "You do not need to give explanations."

Nerissa bit her lip. "I can't ask Mrs. Blantyre to call less often, or to leave earlier. She is an old friend. It would be . . . very discourteous. I couldn't explain it without causing offense and saying more than I know Aunt Serafina wishes. But of course I shall do my best to discourage anyone from staying very long. Tucker is already helping greatly with that. She very seldom leaves my aunt alone. Thank you for your understanding, and your help." It was final. She was not going to accept any advice.

"If there is anything further, please call me." Vespasia had no choice but to leave the matter.

"I will," Nerissa promised.

Vespasia walked down the steps to her carriage with her feeling of unease in no way lifted. Serafina had seemed so sure that she did not want to see Adriana again, but for whose sake? There had been a tenderness in her when she spoke the younger woman's name that was deeper than anything Vespasia had ever seen in her before. And Adriana, in turn, had seemed to care more than casually, more than a mere act of kindness would require. Was it simply because they were fellow exiles, with a love of country, or something else?

Vespasia was in her carriage and more than halfway home when she suddenly changed her mind and rapped her cane against the ceiling to draw the coachman's attention. He stopped and she asked him to take her instead to the home of Victor Narraway.

As she had expected, when she arrived Narraway was not in, but she left him a note asking him to call her at his most immediate opportunity. The matter was of some urgency, and she required his advice, and probably his assistance.

Narraway came home in the late afternoon, tired from the boredom of having sat most of the day in the House of Lords listening to tedious and exhaustively repetitive arguments. Vespasia's note gave him a rush of excitement, as if at last something of interest might happen. Never in his life had Vespasia disappointed him. He put through a telephone call to her, even before taking off his coat. Her invitation was simple, and he accepted without hesitation.

He found himself sitting forward a little in his seat in the hansom as he watched the familiar streets go by. His imagination raced as to what it might be that concerned her to this degree; there had been a haste in her handwriting, as though she were consumed by a deep anxiety, and the tone of her voice on the telephone had confirmed it. Vespasia

168

did not exaggerate, nor was she easily alarmed. His mind went back over other tragedies and dangers they had been concerned about together, most of them involving Pitt. Some had come very close to ending in defeat; all had held the possibility of disaster.

As soon as he reached her house he sprang out of the cab and hurried up the steps. The door opened before he had time to pull the bell. The maid welcomed him in, took his coat, and showed him to Vespasia's peaceful sitting room, its windows and French doors offering views of the garden.

"Thank you for coming so promptly," she said, rising to her feet. It was an unusual practice for her. He noticed that she did not quite have her customary composure. There was something almost indefinably different in her manner. She was as exquisitely dressed as always, in a blue-gray gown with deep décolletage, pearls at her ears and throat, and her hair coiled in a silver crown on her head.

"I presume you have not eaten? May I offer you supper?" she asked.

"After you have told me what it is that troubles you. Clearly it is urgent," he replied.

She gestured for him to be seated, and

resumed her own place beside the fire.

"I visited Serafina Montserrat again today," she told him. "I found her considerably worse; her mind has deteriorated a great deal — I think." She hesitated. "Victor, I really do not know at all quite how much she is losing her wits. When I first arrived she seemed lucid, but her eyes were filled with fear. Before I had the opportunity to speak with her for more than a few moments, Adriana Blantyre called."

"Evan Blantyre's wife?" He was startled. Blantyre was a man of considerable substance and reputation. "Courtesy, or friendship?" he asked quietly.

"Friendship," she answered without hesitation.

He watched the deepening anxiety in Vespasia's eyes, and noted the presence of another emotion he could not read. "Perhaps you had better tell me the heart of it," he said quietly. "What is it you fear?"

Vespasia spoke slowly. "As soon as Adriana came into the room, Serafina seemed to begin rambling, as if she had no idea what year it was. Adriana was very patient with her, very gentle, but it was disturbing."

"What year does she imagine she is in?" Narraway was beginning to feel the same intense pity he knew Vespasia was feeling, even though, as far as he was aware, he had never met Serafina Montserrat.

"I don't know," Vespasia replied. "Possibly the fifties, or early sixties, not very long after the revolutions of '48."

"And who does she believe Adriana to be?" he asked, puzzled. "She cannot be more than forty, at the very outside. I would have thought less."

"That's what makes so little sense," Vespasia answered. "Serafina took her for a Croatian patriot, which is not completely divorced from the truth. But she was rambling. Her eyes were far away, her hands clenched on the sheets. And then when Adriana left, I remained behind for a few moments, and suddenly Serafina was completely herself again, and the fear returned." She took a deep breath. "Victor, she is afraid that someone may kill her in order to prevent her from revealing the truths she knows. She spoke of betrayals, old grudges, and deaths that cannot be forgotten, but as if they were all current, and there was more violence to come. She mentioned Mayerling."

"Mayerling?" He was incredulous. "But Serafina was living here in London at the time, wasn't she?" he asked. "And she must have been well into her seventies and surely not privy to the inside circles of the Austrian court anymore. Vespasia, are you sure she isn't . . . romanticizing?"

"No, I'm not sure!" Her face was full of grief. "But her fear is real, that I have absolutely no doubt of. She is terrified. Is it possible that there is something for her to fear?" Her voice dropped. "Something apart from loneliness, old age, and madness?"

He felt the pain strike him; to his shame, not for Serafina Montserrat, but for Vespasia, and for himself. Then the instant after, it became pity.

"Probably not," he said quietly. "But I promise that tomorrow I shall begin to look into it. I had better do it discreetly; otherwise, if by any wild chance this is true, I shall have given whoever she fears more to fear from her."

"Yes, please be careful." Vespasia hesitated. "I am sorry if I am asking you to waste your time. She seemed so sure, and then the next moment completely lost, as though she were alone in a strange place, searching for anything familiar."

Narraway brushed it aside. He did not want her to feel obliged to him. He told her the truth, startled at how simple it was for him to confess to her.

"I'm glad of something to do that is a

challenge to my mind rather than my patience," he told her. "Even if it should prove that Mrs. Montserrat has nothing to fear, as I hope it will."

Vespasia smiled, and there was amusement in it as well as gratitude. "Thank you, Victor. I am grateful that you will do it so quickly. Now that that is decided, would you like some supper?"

He accepted with pleasure. It would be very much more enjoyable to share the evening with her than to eat alone. Before the O'Neil business, before going to Ireland with Charlotte on that desperate mission, he would have considered dining at home a peaceful end to the day, and the idea of company would have been something of an intrusion. Solitude, a good book, the silence of the house — all would have been comfortable. Now there was an emptiness there, a deep loneliness he was incapable of dismissing. No doubt it would pass, but for the moment, Vespasia's quiet sitting room held a peace that eased his mind.

Narraway gave Vespasia's request a great deal of thought as he sat quietly in his own chair by the hearth, after midnight, still not ready to go to bed. Was he afraid of sleep, of nightmares, of waking in the dark in

173

confusion, for an instant not knowing where he was? Or perhaps for longer than just an instant? Would that time come? Would he be alone, pitied, no one remembering who he used to be?

Physical changes were part of the tests of life, and they included loss of the senses and perception. It was not pathetic to lose some of one's awareness of the present and slip back to happier times.

He could recall his own youth with sharper detail than he had expected: his early years in Special Branch, long before he was head of it; when he was only learning, newer than Pitt ever was, because he had not had the decades of police experience. He had had authority, and traveled to some of the most exciting cities in Europe and beyond. He smiled now at the memories. They seemed happy and exciting, looking back, even though he knew he had at times been lonely then. And there had been failures, some of them quite harsh.

Now he thought of Paris only for its grace, the old quarters steeped in the history of revolution. In his youth he had been able to stand in the Cordeliers with his eyes closed and imagine that if he opened them he would see the ghosts of Robespierre, the giant Danton, and the raving Marat, hear the rattle of tumbrels over the stones, and smell the fear. The passion haunted the air.

He had been gullible then, believed people he should not have believed, one beautiful woman in particular, Mireille. That had been a mistake that had nearly cost him his life. He had felt a starry-eyed pity for her that had bordered on love. He had never been so stupid again.

Thinking of that brought back sharp recollections of what Herbert, his commander at the time, had said to him. And with his memory of Herbert, he knew who he should seek for answers to Vespasia's questions.

He was at the railway station by half past seven the following morning, and caught the train southward into the bleak, rolling countryside of Kent before eight o'clock. At Bexley he alighted into a hard, driving wind and walked along the main platform to look for a carriage.

By nine o'clock he was knocking on the door of an old cottage just off the high street. Bare, twisted limbs of wisteria covered most of the front walls, but he imagined that in the summer they would be covered with soft, pale, lilac flowers. He could smell rain in the wind, and the bitter, clean aroma of woodsmoke drifting from the chimney.

The door was opened by a middle-aged woman wearing an apron over her dark skirt. She looked startled to see him.

"Mornin', sir." She seemed uncertain what to say next.

"Good morning." Narraway saved her the trouble of finding the words. "Is this the home of Geoffrey Herbert?"

"Yes, sir, it is. Mr. Herbert is just eating his breakfast. May I tell him who is calling?" She did not add that it was an uncivil hour to visit, especially unannounced, but it was in her eyes.

"Victor Narraway," he replied. "He will remember me."

"Mr. Victor Narraway," she repeated. "Well, if you would come in out of the cold, sir, and take a seat in the sitting room, I'll tell him you're here." She grudgingly pulled the door open wider.

He stepped inside. "Actually . . . it's Lord Narraway." He was not used to the title himself, but this was an occasion when the respect it might command would be of service.

She looked startled. "Oh! Well . . . I'll tell him, I'm sure. Would you like a cup o' tea, sir, I mean, Your Lordship?"

Narraway smiled in spite of himself. "That would be most appreciated," he accepted.

The sitting room was architecturally typical of a cottage: low-ceilinged; deep window ledges; large, open fireplace with heavy chimney breast. But there the ordinariness ended. One entire wall was lined with bookshelves; the carpets were Oriental with rich jewel-colored designs; and there were Arabic brass bowls on several of the surfaces. It all brought back sharp memories of Herbert, a man of vast knowledge and eclectic tastes.

Herbert himself came into the room twenty minutes later, when Narraway had finished his tea and was beginning to get restless. He had not seen Herbert in fifteen years and he was startled by the change in him. He remembered him as upright, a little gaunt, with receding white hair. Now he was bent forward over two sticks and moved with some difficulty. His clothes hung on him, and his hands were blue-veined. His hair had receded no further, but it was thin. The pink of his scalp was visible through it.

"Lord Narraway, eh?" he said with a faint smile. His voice was cracked, but his eyes were bright, and he maneuvered himself to the chair without stumbling or reaching to feel his way. He sat down carefully, propping the two sticks against the wall. "It must be important to bring you all the way down here. Dawson told me you are not in the Branch anymore. That true?"

"Yes. Kicking up my heels in the House of Lords," Narraway replied. He heard the edge of bitterness in his tone and instantly regretted it. He hoped Herbert did not take it for self-pity. He wondered what to add to take the sting from it.

Herbert was watching him closely. "Well, if you're not in the Branch, what the devil are you doing?" he asked. "You aren't here looking up old friends; you don't have any. You were always a solitary creature. Just as well. Head of the Branch can't afford to be dependent on anyone. You were the best we had. Hate to admit it, but I'd be a liar not to."

Narraway felt a surge of pleasure, which embarrassed him. Herbert was a man whose good opinion was worth a great deal and had never been easily won.

"So what do you want?" Herbert went on, before Narraway could find any gracious way of acknowledging the compliment. "No need to explain yourself. I wouldn't believe you anyway. If you could afford to tell me, it would hardly be worth the bother."

"Austria-Hungary," Narraway replied.

Herbert's sparse eyebrows shot up. "Good God! You're not still raking over Mayerling and Rudolf's death, are you? Thought you had more sense. Poor bastard shot the girl, then shot himself. He was always a melancholy creature, other than the occasional attack of good cheer on social occasions. Give him wine, laughter, and a pretty face, and he was fine, until the music stopped. Just like his mother. He was always a disaster waiting to happen. Could have told you that years ago."

"No," Narraway said succinctly. "It's not about Rudolf at all, so far as I know."

"Then what? You said Austria-Hungary."

"Going back thirty years, or more maybe, to uprisings, planned or actual," Narraway said.

"Plenty of them." Herbert nodded. "Autocratic old sod, Franz Josef. Relaxed his hold a bit recently, I'm told, but back then he ruled with a rod of iron. He and Rudolf never saw eye to eye. Chalk and cheese. What about it?" He frowned, leaning forward a little and peering at Narraway. "Why do you care? Why now?"

"Thought you weren't going to ask me," Narraway said pointedly.

Herbert grunted. "Of course there were uprisings. You know that as well as any of us. Stop beating around the bush and tell me what it is you're really asking."

"A major revolt, drawing in other countries as well. Possibly a Hungarian uprising?"

A look of contempt flickered across Herbert's gaunt face. "You can do better than that, Narraway. You know as well as I do — or you ought to — that the Hungarians are content to be a safe, second-rate power, ruled by Vienna while having a very comfortable life, if not quite cock of the walk. If they rose up against the Austrians they'd lose a great deal, and gain nothing. They are quite clever enough to know that."

"The Croatians?" Narraway suggested.

"Different kettle of fish altogether," Herbert agreed. "Erratic, unstable. Always plots and counterplots, but nothing has ever come of them, at least not yet. That's not what all this is about, is it? Foreign Office thinks there's going to be another Croatian problem of some sort, do they?"

"Not so far as I know," Narraway said truthfully.

"Blantyre's your chap," Herbert observed. "Evan Blantyre. Knows the Croatians as well as anyone. Lived there for a while. Wife's Croatian. Beautiful woman, but unstable, so I hear. Delicate health, always

180

sick as a child. Not surprising, family caught up in rebellions and things."

Narraway leaned back in his chair. "I'll ask him, if things look like they're heading that way. What about the Italians? They still haven't got some of their northern cities back. Trieste and that region, for example."

Herbert thought about it for a few moments. "Italian nationalists," he said thoughtfully. "Could be trouble there. Disorganized, though, in spite of Cavour and Garibaldi and all the unification stuff. Still quarrel like cats in a bag. Thought they'd quieted down a bit."

"Perhaps," Narraway said dubiously. "Do you remember in the past an Italian woman by the name of Montserrat?" He watched Herbert's face for even the slightest flicker of recognition.

Herbert smiled a long, slow curl of amusement, his eyes bright. "Well, well," he said with a sigh. "Serafina Montserrat. Why on earth are you asking about her? She must be seventy-five at least, if she's still alive at all. I remember when she was thirty. Rode a horse better than any man I knew, and fought with a sword. Used to be quite good myself, but I was never in her class. Knew better than to try. Saved me from making a fool of myself."

"Italian nationalist." Narraway made it more a statement than a question.

"Oh, yes." Herbert was still smiling. "But not averse to lending a hand to anyone who was against Austria, wherever they were from."

"Openly?" Narraway asked.

Herbert looked shocked. "Good God, no! Secretive as a priest, and devious as a Jesuit too."

"You make her sound religious."

Herbert laughed. It was a purely happy sound, bringing to his face for a moment the shadow of the young man he had once been. "She was as far from a nun as a woman can get. Although I didn't know most of that at the time."

"How did you learn?" Narraway asked. "Perhaps more important to me, when did you learn and from whom?"

"From many people, and over several years," Herbert replied. "She worked very discreetly."

"That's not what you implied," Narraway pointed out.

Herbert laughed again, although this time it ended in a fit of coughing. "Sometimes, Narraway, you are not nearly as clever as you imagine," he said after several moments, still gasping for breath. "You should have taken more notice of women. A little self-indulgence would have helped you learn a great deal, not only about women in general, but about yourself as well, and therefore about most men." His eyes narrowed. "Too much brain and not enough heart, that's your trouble. I think secretly you're an idealist! It's not pleasure you want — it's love! Good God, man, you're a total anachronism!"

"Serafina Montserrat," Narraway reminded him sharply. "Was she a wild woman, riding and fighting beside the men, and sleeping with a good few of them, or was she discreet? I'm not here simply because I have nothing to do and need somebody else's business to meddle in. This could be important."

"Of course you need something to meddle in!" Herbert said without losing his smile. "We all do. I'd have died of boredom if I didn't meddle in everything I could. The locals all loathe me, or pretend they do, but they all come to see me now and then because they think I know everybody's secrets."

"And do you?" Narraway inquired.

"Yes, mostly."

"Serafina," he prompted.

"Yes, she was as tough and skilled as most

183

of the men, better than many," Herbert responded. "Not really a beauty, but she had so much vitality that you forgot that. She was . . ." He seemed to be staring back into memory. "Elemental," he finished.

Narraway could not help wondering how well Herbert had known her himself. That was a possibility he had not considered before. Was he asking for information about a past lover of Herbert's? Or was that merely imagination, and a little wishful thinking?

"You have not so far touched on anything remotely discreet about her," he pointed out.

"No," Herbert agreed. "She seemed to be so obvious in her support of Italian freedom fighters that most people assumed she was as open about everything else. She wasn't. I deduced, completely without proof, that she knew a great deal about Bulgarian and Croatian plans as well, and even had connections with early socialist movements in Austria itself. That last I am convinced of, but I couldn't produce an iota of evidence to support it."

"A clever woman," Narraway said ruefully. "Bluff and double bluff."

"Exactly," Herbert agreed. He leaned forward in his chair, wrinkling his jacket.

"Narraway, tell me why you want to know. It's all water under the bridge now. You can't and shouldn't prosecute her for anything. And if you ask me officially, I shall deny it."

Narraway smiled, meeting the other man's eyes. Herbert's thin cheeks colored very slightly.

"She is ill and vulnerable," Narraway answered, wondering, even as he said it, if he was wise to do so. "I want to make sure she is protected. To do that, I need to know from what directions attacks might come."

Herbert's face lost all its good humor. "Attacks?" he snapped.

"The threat may be more imagined than real. That is why I need to know."

Herbert sat still without answering for several moments, staring past Narraway to the rainswept garden, with its sharply pruned roses and budding leaves fattening on the trees. When at last he returned his gaze to the present, his eyes were clouded.

"I've realized how little I actually knew about her," he said quietly. "She was a creature of intense passion. Everything done with a whole heart. I assumed I knew why, and what her loyalties were, but since what you need now is far deeper than that, I have only observations and beliefs to offer you —

for what they are worth."

"It will be more than the little I know now," Narraway replied immediately. "First, is she image or substance, in your belief?"

"At first, I thought image," Herbert said with an honesty that clearly pained him. "Then I came to believe there was substance. I am still of that opinion."

"What changed your mind?"

"A betrayal," Herbert said very quietly. "There is no point in asking me the full story of it because I don't know. At the time I only knew of the execution, and that it was for plotting an assassination . . ."

Narraway felt a sudden chill. "An assassination?"

Herbert looked at him sharply. "For God's sake, man, it was thirty years ago, and it didn't happen anyway. The whole thing was abortive. The leader himself was captured, beaten, and shot. Most of the others escaped."

"But Serafina Montserrat was involved?" Narraway persisted. "How? Are you skirting around saying that she was the one who betrayed the leader?"

Herbert was horrified. He glared at Narraway as if he had blasphemed. "No! She was all kinds of things: willful, reckless, arrogant at times — certainly promiscuous, if you want to call it that — but she would have died for the cause. It was only through a mixture of extreme skill and courage, and the loyalty of others, that she survived. And a degree of luck. 'Fortune favors the bold' was never truer of anyone than it was of her."

Again Narraway wondered exactly how well Herbert had known her. Not that it mattered, as long as what he was saying was the truth, as far as he knew it.

"So she could be in danger?" he concluded. It was barely a question anymore.

"I don't know," Herbert said honestly, but there was more emotion in his eyes than Narraway could ever recall having seen there before. "It was so long ago, and from the standpoint of anyone in London, far away. Who do you know who gives a damn about Croatian independence now?"

"No one," Narraway admitted. "But betrayals always matter. The time and place of them are irrelevant."

"They do matter," Herbert agreed. "Far too much to wait thirty years for revenge."

Narraway could not argue with that. Almost certainly all the people concerned were dead, or too old to execute revenge anymore, just as Serafina herself was.

"Thank you." He acknowledged the point.

"Can you think of anyone else who might shed more light on the subject of why she is so afraid?"

"The current expert in that area of the Foreign Office is Tregarron. But you know that. And, of course, for northern Italy, with which Serafina was most concerned, it is Ennio Ruggiero, and for Croatia, Pavao Altabas."

Narraway got to his feet. "I'm much obliged." He held out his hand. "Thank you again."

Herbert smiled. "It's good to see you, Narraway. I always knew you'd do well."

"You taught me well," Narraway replied sincerely. "I hope to hell I taught my successor as much." He hesitated.

"Why do you say that?" Herbert asked.

"Did you worry about me?" Narraway asked him. "Whether I would succeed, whether I had the steel, and the judgment?"

Herbert smiled. "Of course, but I had more sense than to let you know it at the time."

"Thank you," Narraway said wryly.

"Wouldn't have done you any good," Herbert replied. "But you caused me a few sleepless nights — unnecessarily, as it turned out."

Narraway did not ask him about what.

■ ■ ■ ■

Narraway went to see Ruggiero, as Herbert had suggested, and spent over an hour without learning anything beyond what Herbert himself had already mentioned. Ruggiero was an old man and his memory was clouded by emotions. Italy was now united, and he wanted to forget the frictions and griefs of the past. He especially wanted to forget the losses, the sacrifices, and the ugliness of fighting.

Narraway thanked him also. To have probed and argued, perhaps caught the old man in lies, not of intent but of wishful thinking, facts covered over by dreams, would have benefited no one.

Next he went to visit Pavao Altabas and found only his widow. He had died recently, and Herbert had been unaware of it.

The widow was much younger than Pavao had been, and she knew nothing of the uprisings. The name of Serafina Montserrat meant nothing at all to her.

Lastly, he went to see Lord Tregarron, not at the Foreign Office but at the club where both were members. It was the end of the day and Tregarron was tired and unwilling to talk. However, Narraway gave him no civil alternative, short of getting up very conspicuously and leaving.

They sat opposite each other in armchairs on either side of a huge log fire. Narraway ordered brandy for both of them. The steward brought it with murmured words of apology for interrupting them, although they were not as yet in conversation.

"Leave us to talk, will you, Withers?" Narraway asked him. "No interruptions, if you please!"

"Certainly, my lord," Withers said calmly. "Thank you." He bowed and withdrew.

Tregarron looked grimly at Narraway, waiting for him to explain his intrusion.

"Damned long day, Narraway," he said quietly. "Is this really necessary? You're not in Special Branch anymore."

Narraway was surprised how deeply the reminder cut him, as if his position had defined his identity, and without it he had no standing with those who had so recently treated him with something akin to awe. He hid his hurt with difficulty. If he had not needed Tregarron, he would have found a way to retaliate, even though, at the same moment, he realized that any retaliation would betray his own vulnerability.

He forced himself to smile, very slightly. "Which removes the responsibility from me, but does not take away the freedom to meddle, if I can do it to the good," he replied.

Tregarron's dark face tightened a little. "Am I supposed to deduce from your last remark that you are justifying some interference in foreign affairs that I otherwise might object to?"

Narraway's smile grew bleaker. "I have no intention of interfering in foreign affairs, justifiably or not. But my concern is with information about the past that may prevent an action in the present of which I am uncertain, and I need to know more."

Tregarron's heavy eyebrows rose. "From me? You must know that I cannot tell you anything. Do not keep obliging me to remind you that you are no longer head of Special Branch. It is uncomfortable, and ill-mannered of you to put me in a position where I have no choice."

Narraway kept his temper with difficulty. He needed Tregarron's information, and he no longer had any means of forcing it from him, as Tregarron knew. It was this aspect of having lost power to which he was finding it hard to accustom himself.

"I am not seeking any current information," he said levelly. He found himself suddenly reluctant to explain his reasons to Tregarron. "It is the general climate of issues thirty or forty years ago."

"Thirty or forty years ago? Narraway, what the devil are you playing at? Thirty or forty years ago where?" Tregarron leaned forward a little in his chair. "What is this about? Is it something I should know?"

"If I should come to believe that it is, I shall certainly tell you," Narraway answered. "So far it is only rumors, most of which seem to me more like overheated imagination. I wish to prove, or disprove, them before I bother anyone else with them."

Tregarron's attention sharpened. "Regarding what, exactly?"

Now Narraway had no choice but to either tell the truth, or very deliberately lie. "Certain whispers about a woman named Serafina Montserrat," he answered.

A shadow crossed Tregarron's face. "How on earth could she matter now?"

Narraway changed his mind about what to say next.

"Memories, stories," he said fairly casually. "If I know the truth, or something close to it, I can dismiss them safely."

Tregarron tensed. "Who is talking about Mrs. Montserrat?" he asked. "This all sounds like gossip. But it could be dangerous, Narraway. Damage can be done that is hard to reverse. You did the right thing in coming to me. I have looked into her past since we last spoke. She worked mostly in the Austro-Hungarian sphere. She apparently knew a lot of people, and was regrettably free with her favors."

"But all years ago," Narraway pointed out. He was surprised how much he resented Tregarron's implication, even though he had never met Serafina himself. She was Vespasia's friend. He took a deep breath before he continued. "I imagine most of the men concerned are also dead, and their wives, who might have cared, as well."

"Would you like it said of your father?" Tregarron snapped.

Narraway could not imagine it. His father had been rather dry, highly intelligent but remote, not a man who would have been accessible to a woman such as he imagined Serafina Montserrat to have been. He smiled at the thought, and saw a flash of fury in Tregarron's face; it was gone again so rapidly that he was not certain if it had been real, or his imagination.

"The thought amuses you?" Tregarron asked. "You surprise me. Would it have amused your mother too?"

That was a sharp wound, a territory Narraway did not wish to explore. "Of course not," he said quietly, his voice tighter than he had meant it to be. "It is so far from the truth of what I was inquiring into that it had an oblique humor. No one's reputation in that area is in jeopardy, so far as I am aware."

"So what area is it to do with, then?" Tregarron asked, his face now all but expressionless.

Narraway chose his words carefully, thinking of what exactly Vespasia had said. "It is to do with political freedom, old plots and current ones regarding Croatia throwing off the Austrian yoke. And possibly northern Italy."

"Perhaps you don't understand me," Tregarron said, now allowing a faint smile onto his face. "Serafina Montserrat must be in her mid-seventies, at least. According to what I have heard, she was reckless and something of a troublemaker. She created an unfortunate reputation for herself, although some of the stories about her are probably apocryphal. If even half of them are true, she was a highly colorful character, and a passionate Italian nationalist. She would have been quite capable of planning an assassination, and she had the steel in her nature to carry it out. However, so far as I know, she never succeeded in actually doing so."

He crossed his legs, easing back in his chair a little, his eyes never leaving Narraway's face.

"The only event anything like that," he continued, "I heard as a story. I'm not sure what truth there is in it."

Narraway watched him intently.

Tregarron assumed the air of a raconteur. "A group of dissidents plotted to assassinate one of the leading Austrian dukes who was particularly vehement in his grip on the local government in northern Italy. It would be fair to say that he was oppressive, and at times unjust. The emperor Franz Josef has always been excessively military, but he used to be less dictatorial than he is now. Nevertheless, this dissident group planned the assassination of some duke — I forget his name — and very nearly succeeded. The plot was clearly thought out and very simple in essence. No clever tricks to go wrong, nothing left to chance."

"But it didn't succeed?" Narraway questioned him.

"Because they were betrayed by one of their own," Tregarron answered. "They fled. It seems Montserrat was among those who fought the hardest to save them, but she couldn't. She was wounded in the struggle that followed, and the ringleader was taken, summarily tried, and executed."

It was the kind of bitter tale that Narraway had heard often enough, especially when he had been in Ireland. He thought of Kate O'Neil, and of the actions he had thought responsible for his own loss of office. And then, in spite of himself, he thought of Charlotte Pitt, of love, loyalty, and wounds that would ache eternally.

Was this what it was about, a retreat into ancient sorrows, coming back to haunt one in old age? Was Serafina going back in her mind to that time, or another like it? Could she have been the one who betrayed the would-be assassin, and now feared some final revenge? Or justice?

Tregarron interrupted his thoughts.

"What can this have to do with anything today, Narraway? I can't help you if I don't know what on earth you're really looking for. Or why."

"From what you say, I rather think it has nothing to do with anything today," Narraway lied. "As you point out, she must be in her seventies, at least. That is, if she is still alive at all, of course." He rose to his feet, smiling very slightly. "Thank you for your time, and your candor."

But that was far from what Narraway thought as he rode home in a hansom through the wet streets, glancing every now and then at the cobblestones gleaming in the reflected lamplight.

Tregarron had lied to him, if not in words, then in intent. There was something Tregarron feared, but Narraway was not sure if it was an old danger resurfacing, some past error that would jeopardize Tregarron's present reputation or relationships, or if it was some totally new issue of which Narraway was unaware. But then, if it concerned the Austrian Empire, even had he still been in Special Branch, he might not have been informed. Regular diplomatic affairs had nothing to do with Special Branch.

If Serafina believed she had made lasting enemies, then it was certainly possible that she was right. The idea of such a once-magnificent woman lying old and broken, fearing for her life, deeply and painfully aware that she could no longer protect herself, hurt him with a disturbing depth.

Was he becoming soft, no longer able to judge an act impartially? Yes, he did love Charlotte. It was time to admit that to himself. In fact, after Ireland, it would be absurd to deny it. He had always despised self-delusion in others, and he had come very close to practicing it himself. That she would never care for him as more than a friend was something he had to accept. If he did so with grace, then he could keep her friendship at least.

Had that devastating vulnerability changed him?

Yes, perhaps it had. For one thing, it had given him a tenderness toward Vespasia he had not felt before: a greater understanding of her as a woman, not merely her formidable courage and intelligence. She too could be hurt in ways she would never have allowed him to see, had he not also newly experienced personal pain, surprise, and self-doubt.

It was a frightening change, but not entirely a loss.

He was determined to learn a great deal more than the very general picture he had of Austro-Hungarian affairs, particularly in reference to the dictatorial emperor Franz Josef, whose only son, Crown Prince Rudolf, had died so tragically at Mayerling.

The old man's heir was now his nephew, Archduke Franz Ferdinand, a man of whom Franz Josef did not approve. For one thing,

Ferdinand had chosen to love a woman inappropriate to become the wife of the heir to the empire. The poor creature was merely some countess or the other. That made Ferdinand, in the old man's opinion, of unsound judgment, and lacking in the dedication to duty necessary to succeed him. But he had no choice. The laws of heredity could not be argued with, or the legitimacy of the entire monarchy would be destroyed.

Should Narraway tell Vespasia the little he had learned? Perhaps so. It would be a courtesy to Serafina. Then she would know that at least one person believed her. Next time he saw Vespasia he would do so. It would be a good reason to see her again.

And should he speak to Pitt?

Not unless anything he learned about present-day Austrian affairs indicated that there could be an assassination attempt on some visiting royalty. Pitt had more than enough to do without chasing the current danger of that, if any existed, as well as all the usual Special Branch fears of anarchist bombings, and the constant rebellions in Ireland. There were Russian dissidents in London, fleeing from the ever-increasing oppression and grinding poverty at home. Additionally, there were British-grown socialists who believed that the only way to improve life for the poor was to commit outrages against the Establishment.

Pitt did not need to hear rumors about a betrayal that happened thirty years ago and a thousand miles away. Narraway had done the job himself long enough to know the importance of leaving alone what did not matter. Telling Vespasia would be sufficient.

CHAPTER 5

It was the last day of February, bright, gusty, and cold. Stoker came into Pitt's office looking grim.

Pitt waited for him to speak.

"More bits of information keep coming in that look like they're about this assassination attempt." He was ill at ease, his shoulders stiff. "We're fairly certain as to the identity of the man asking about train signals near Dover, and we have at least a possible identification of one of the men asking about how points are changed."

"Who are they?" Pitt asked.

"The man who asked about the signals was Bilinsk, we think. The French are pretty sure about it. They've been following him for a while, in connection with an assassination in Paris. He was seen at least once with Lansing —"

"Our Lansing?" Pitt asked sharply.

Stoker's face tightened. "Yes, sir. That's

the worrying part. We thought Lansing was in prison in France, but they let him go."

Pitt felt a sudden chill. Lansing was English, a cold, clever man with allegiance to no one, and — as far as they could tell — to no cause. Why the French had released him was irrelevant now, but Pitt would find out later. It could have been some technicality of the law. A good lawyer could often find one, and Lansing would be both willing and able to employ such a man. Or, worse, someone else might have paid for his lawyer, just to get him loose.

Pitt looked up at Stoker. "And Lansing was the one who asked about the points and the freight trains?"

"Yes, sir," Stoker answered. "Word is that he's an expert on transport, especially trains: signals, altering the switches on lines, diverting trains, blowing the couplings, that sort of thing. Exactly what Mr. Blantyre said."

"Any others?"

"Not yet, but we're still working."

"Anything else about Alois Habsburg?"

"Nothing. I can't see any reason at all anyone should want to assassinate him," Stoker admitted.

"Except to embarrass Britain, and Special Branch in particular," Pitt replied. "Which it most certainly would."

Stoker nodded. "That's what it looks like. The queen thinks well enough of us after the business at Osborne House, but there are plenty who don't. And most people don't even know about Osborne House, and never will."

"I know." Pitt pushed his hands deeper into his pockets, his shoulders tense. "There are quite a few who think our power is a threat to their freedom, and to their privacy. A few decades ago, people thought the same of the police."

"Idiots," Stoker said under his breath. "They send for the police fast enough if there's a burglary, a riot, or even a kidnapping. We're like the army: Nothing's too good for us if there's a war, and then when it's over they want us to become invisible — until the next time." The contempt in his face carried an uncharacteristic bitterness.

Pitt could not help but agree with him, even if he chose not to voice it.

"We need more information," he replied. "Who is Duke Alois Habsburg, exactly? What sort of entourage is he bringing with him? I don't care if that's a breach of his privacy or not!"

Stoker pulled a sour face. "Difficult to find out anything much about him, except the usual, superficial things: where he was born, his parents, where he is in reference to the succession — which is nowhere. He's not really a politician, more of a philosopher, and a dabbler in science. Very clever fellow, by all accounts, but a dreamer. He might invent something brilliant one day. Or maybe write a couple of books about existence, or identity, or something. At least that's what his own people say. So far, he's never done anything that makes any difference."

"And he's related to our queen?" Pitt pursued.

"By marriage, yes. Distantly — so is half of Europe." Stoker's face still reflected his exasperation. "Alois may be a favorite of hers. I'll find out, but he doesn't sound the sort. He's nice enough, but she doesn't go in for a lot of heavy thinking." He stopped abruptly, a faint pinkness in his cheeks, aware that he had expressed his opinion rather too freely.

"He could just be looking to impress her, and perhaps he also feels like a trip to London," Pitt replied with a faint smile. "But he may just be pretending to be an academic dreamer, when he's really a brave man doing an important job."

"I suppose that's true," Stoker conceded

with obvious reluctance. "I hadn't thought of that."

"Who's coming with him?" Pitt asked. "How many of the entourage are actually guards of one sort or another?"

Stoker sighed. "From what we're told, they're mainly domestic servants: valets and butlers — that sort of thing. Probably couldn't tell a stiletto from a fire iron." He blinked. "Doesn't the palace supply servants for guests?"

Pitt found himself smiling. "Butlers, of course; valets are different. Each gentleman wants to have his own, who knows his likes and dislikes, probably carries all the remedies he might need, and is fully aware of his weaknesses."

"It's another life, isn't it?" Stoker observed, smiling thinly.

"As are ours, to many of the people we meet," Pitt noted.

Stoker shook his head but he was still smiling. "We've got to protect this man, sir, whoever he is. If he's killed anywhere in our territory, it's going to get very ugly indeed. Some bastard's going to come out of the woodwork and blame us." He winced. "Not to mention however many of our own people get killed or crippled at the same time."

"I know," Pitt agreed, thinking of Blantyre's warning. "That could even be the purpose of the whole thing. Poor Duke Alois might simply be the means."

Stoker's face paled. He said something under his breath, but would not repeat it aloud when Pitt looked up at him.

Pitt returned to the Foreign Office that afternoon, knowing he had no possible alternative. As before, the first person he was directed to was Jack Radley. They stood facing each other in the luxurious but impersonal waiting room with its formal portraits of past ministers on the walls.

"I hope this is about something different," Jack said. He shifted his weight very slightly from one foot to the other.

"It is about new coincidences," Pitt replied, also unable to relax. Neither his professional responsibility nor their personal relationship allowed him any ease. He knew how deeply it would affect Charlotte if this new situation divided her from Emily. All the past experiences they had shared, the family memories and the adventures, would be shadowed by the present tearing of loyalties.

Jack's face had tightened, turning the corners of his mouth down.

"I have much more information regarding the probability of an assassination attempt against Duke Alois Habsburg," Pitt began. "The duke may be only a minor relation of the queen, but you don't have to be in the Foreign Office to imagine what it would do to Britain's reputation in Europe, and everywhere else, if the man was shot while he was here, visiting Her Majesty — do you?"

He was a little more sarcastic than he had intended, his own fear lending an edge to his voice.

"I imagine Lord Tregarron would not be indifferent to such an event, or to his own position in the matter if it should occur," he added.

Jack stared at him in silence, but his face was distinctly paler. For several seconds he weighed the new situation.

"You're sure you are not being unnecessarily alarmed?" he asked.

"The job is about thinking ahead, Jack. If you mean am I jumping at shadows — no. I think there's enough evidence now to take the threat seriously. Am I certain I'm not being distracted by a deliberately manufactured plot, in order to draw my attention away from something else, something more important? No, of course I'm not. Bluff?

Double bluff? I don't know. Is Tregarron prepared to take the chance that a member of the Austrian royal family will get killed in a train crash, along with a few score of Britons? If he is, then we should replace him with somebody who is a little less free with human life, and our reputation. Someone who can see the scandal, the outrage, the reparations likely to be demanded if such an assassination were to happen. Not to mention someone prepared to explain it to Her Majesty, with full inclusion of the fact that Special Branch told you details of the possibility, and you decided it was not worth your trouble to listen."

Jack took a deep breath, then clearly changed his mind.

Pitt smiled bleakly.

"I'll tell Lord Tregarron what you have said," Jack answered. "If you would wait here, I shall come back as quickly as I can."

It proved to be a full quarter of an hour before Jack returned. The minute Pitt saw his face, he knew Tregarron would see him, but under a degree of protest.

Pitt followed Jack out of the waiting room and along the corridor to the arched door. At the word of answer, Jack opened it.

"Commander Pitt, my lord," he announced, and stepped back for Pitt to go inside. This time he left them alone.

Tregarron was standing behind his desk, silhouetted against the late winter sunlight in the window beyond. He turned to face Pitt. His face was shadowed and therefore difficult to read.

"Radley tells me that you have continued to pursue this idea of a potential assassination attempt on Duke Alois. That you seem to be sure there may be something in it." He said it almost expressionlessly. "He advised me that we should take it seriously, at least insofar as, if there was even a shred of reality behind it, then it could be disastrous in its effect on our reputation, as well as costing a great many British lives. Is this your view?"

"Yes, sir," Pitt replied, grateful that Jack had put the core of the matter forward so succinctly. "It is a threat we cannot afford to ignore. Even if the attempt is completely abortive, we would look incompetent if we did not act. And worse, the Austrian government might assume that we were indifferent to the situation, or even complicit."

He was pleased to see the immediate concern in Tregarron's face, even though it was accompanied by considerable irritation.

"That seems to be rather more decisive than when you first mentioned it to Radley a few days ago," he observed critically. "Why on earth should any dissident faction in Austria wish to cause such a disaster in order to assassinate a relatively harmless and, may I point out, powerless young minor aristocrat, of no political interest at all? It makes no sense, Pitt. Have you consulted Narraway on this extraordinary idea of yours?"

Pitt felt as if the blood was burning in his face. He hoped Tregarron would not see it. He made a supreme effort to keep his voice calm and level.

"No, I have not. Lord Narraway is no longer privy to the information gathered by Special Branch, and it would be a breach of my oath of discretion to discuss with him such matters as he does not need to know. And as far as political knowledge and judgment of affairs in the Austro-Hungarian Empire are concerned, I am advised that you are the expert, and therefore the appropriate person for me to consult with, sir."

Tregarron's mouth tightened. The irritation in his expression was clear as he turned slightly and walked over to the fireplace. He sat down in the large, comfortable chair facing the door, still with his back to the light, and waved for Pitt to sit opposite him.

"Then I suppose you had better tell me

the precise evidence that led you to this extraordinary conclusion," he said, reaching to poke the fire. "Duke Alois is a man of negligible importance in Austrian affairs, let alone European. He is coming here solely because he has a certain charm and Her Majesty apparently likes him — or, to be more precise, likes his mother, who is no longer able to travel. Who on earth would possibly benefit from assassinating him? And I would point out that if anyone did wish to, they have had ample opportunity to do so in his own home, without taking a trainload of innocent people with him." He stared at Pitt, his heavy eyebrows raised, disbelief written in every line of his face.

Pitt swallowed. The thought came to his mind that Tregarron would not have spoken to Narraway in this tone, but he dismissed it, not as untrue, but as hampering his own ability to deal with Tregarron with confidence. He must not allow comparisons to cripple him. He had weaknesses Narraway did not, but he had strengths too.

He sat a little more comfortably in his chair and crossed his legs.

"If I had the answer to that question, sir, I would not need to ask you for anything more than confirmation of the fact, possibly merely as a courtesy. Duke Alois appears to be a pleasant young man with nothing to commend him except his royal connections. That doesn't mean he is of no importance at all. Sometimes such men are the perfect pawns for others."

A shadow crossed Tregarron's face, but he did not interrupt.

"However, I think it seems likely that he would be a target, not for who he is, but simply because he is available," Pitt continued. "If he were to be killed while here in England it would be extremely embarrassing to Her Majesty's government, and there are always those who would find that to their advantage —"

"In Austria?" Tregarron said with open disbelief.

"There is nothing to prove that the plan is specifically Austrian," Pitt pointed out, seeing the surprise in Tregarron's eyes with sharp satisfaction. Clearly that thought had not occurred to him. "It could be German, French, Italian, even Russian," he added. "Our power makes it inevitable that we have many enemies."

Tregarron leaned a little forward, the whole attitude of his body altering. "Details, Pitt. I am perfectly aware of our position in Europe, and in the world. Most of what you say has always been true. Why now? Why this particular young man? You had better tell me the precise facts and observations that have come to your notice, and leave the interpretation of them to me."

Pitt remained silent. His mind was racing. The man's arrogance was breathtaking. He was treating Pitt like some junior policeman reporting a burglary but incapable of seeing it in the context of a larger plan. Narraway would have had a response to wither Tregarron so that he never presumed to override him again in such a way.

But the words, the confidence, even the composure to do so eluded Pitt, and he felt like the gamekeeper's son he used to be, called up before the master of the house. Except that Sir Arthur Desmond had never treated him with such contempt.

If Pitt refused to offer the details now, it would imply that he did not have them. It was on the tip of his tongue to offer sarcastically that all Special Branch junior staff would report, in writing, to Tregarron, but he dared not. He could not function if he made an open enemy of this man.

With the difficulty of it almost choking him, he replied, "How much detail would you like, sir? There are regular sources up and down the country who give us information, and we have connections in France,

Germany, and Austria with relation to this particular event. We have our own people, and we also have relations with the equivalent to Special Branch that most European countries have, in one form or another." He watched Tregarron's face and saw a flash of anxiety. Perhaps it was a sudden realization that Pitt was better informed than he had supposed.

"Most of what we hear is merely observation of people we know altering their habits or movements," he continued. "People they talk to, places they frequent. Such changes can be indicative of planning . . ."

"Don't treat me like some policeman in training, Pitt!" Tregarron snapped. "I have neither the desire to become a detective, nor the time. For God's sake, man, do your job! You are supposed to be commander of the Branch, not some young constable on the beat!"

Pitt clenched his teeth. "I am giving you my opinion based on the evidence, Lord Tregarron. You asked me for the details. They are a collection of small observations made of changes in habit; of people asking unusual questions; new alliances between people who have no known past in common; people spending money for no obvious reason; unusual patterns of travel;

information about known dissidents meeting each other and dealing with new people; evidence of guns or dynamite being moved; people disappearing from their usual haunts and turning up elsewhere. Even, on occasion, people dying unexpectedly in accidents or murdered. Do you want me to continue?"

Tregarron's face was slightly pink. "I wish you to tell me why you think any of this points to the attempted murder of some wretched minor prince of the Austrian Empire while he is traveling on one of our trains on his way to visit our queen. I can't understand why it is all so plain to you. You seem to expect me to put this man off without any other reason beyond the uncertainty, perhaps the jitters, of our very new head of Special Branch."

There was a slight curl of contempt on his lip, which he did not bother to hide.

"It looks to me as if you've lost your nerve, man!" he went on. "Promoted beyond your ability. I told Narraway that, at the time. You're an excellent second-in-command — the best. I'll give you your due. But you are not born or bred to lead! I'm sorry you pushed me into the position where I am obliged to tell you so to your face." He did not sound sorry as much as simply angry.

"You may be right, sir," Pitt said stiffly, struggling to get his breath. "On the other hand, Lord Narraway may be. We had both better hope that his assessment of what abilities are required to lead Special Branch is better than yours." He rose to his feet. "If not, then we can expect some extremely unpleasant consequences, beginning with an assassination in London, a serious embarrassment for Her Majesty, and possibly an icy relationship with the Austro-Hungarian Empire, with a demand for reparations. Good day, sir."

Tregarron shot to his feet. "How dare you —" He stopped suddenly.

Pitt stood still, his eyes wide, waiting.

Tregarron took a deep breath. "How dare you imply that I do not take this threat seriously?" He slammed his fist into the bell on his desk. A minute later there was a brief tap on the door, and Jack came in, closing it behind him and stopping just inside the room.

"Yes, sir?" he said unhappily, deliberately avoiding Pitt's glance.

"Come in," Tregarron barked.

Jack walked a few steps closer and then stopped again. "Yes, sir?"

Tregarron stared at him. "Pitt seems to believe that Duke Alois Habsburg is the possible target of an assassination attempt, albeit an ignorant, messy, and pointless one. He doesn't know who the would-be assassin is, nor the purpose of the exercise, only that the outcome would be very ugly indeed."

"It would be, sir," Jack agreed, "and it would also give Austria an enormous weapon to use against us for years to come."

"For God's sake, I can see that!" Tregarron snapped. "The point is, we can't jump at every shadow. We have to exercise our critical judgment, not dance around like puppets on strings to the tune of every fear, real or not, likely or not, even possible or not. What is your assessment of this one, Radley? Do you agree with Pitt, on the basis of this host of minor alterations in behavior of informants, spies, and general hangers-on? Or do you think that they are part of the climate at large and that we should hold steady and not lose our nerve?"

Pitt was seething. "I certainly did not recommend losing our nerve, sir," he said hoarsely.

Tregarron's glance did not waver from Jack. "You recommended telling Duke Alois not to come," he retorted. "That is losing our nerve, Pitt. That is telling the emperor Franz Josef, and the rest of the world, that

we cannot manage to protect visiting prince-
lings from mass murder in a train wreck, so
they had better stay in Vienna, or Budapest,
or wherever the devil it is they come from
— where they have the ability to keep their
trains safe!"

"Where it is not Britain's responsibility if
they are killed or not," Pitt countered.

Jack's face went white. He still avoided
Pitt's eyes.

"Then what do we do?" Tregarron demanded. "Do we make him welcome, or do
we tell Her Majesty that we cannot protect
her great-nephew, or whatever he is, and
she had better tell him to stay at home?"

"We would be the laughingstock of Europe, my lord," Jack replied very quietly. "I
think we should give Commander Pitt all
the extra men he may need, regardless of
the cost and the inconvenience, in order to
protect Duke Alois."

Tregarron looked at him with surprise and
some disbelief. "You think this whole thing
could be real?"

"No, sir," Jack answered. "I think it is so
unlikely as to be all but impossible, but we
cannot afford to ignore it. Commander Pitt
has twenty years' experience with intrigue
and murder, and if we ignore his warnings
we will be entirely to blame if something

should happen. Our position then would be untenable."

"But bloody unlikely!"

"Yes, my lord, unlikely, but not impossible."

"I'm obliged for your advice." Tregarron turned to Pitt, looking at him sourly. "I suppose you have to come to me with what you judge to be some serious threats, but I can't be second-guessing you at every turn. You're supposed to make your own judgments. As soon as you get a little more used to your position, I expect you to do so. Good day."

Pitt was too furious to speak. He inclined his head very slightly, then turned on his heel and strode out.

Jack caught up with him in the corridor a dozen yards beyond Tregarron's door.

"I'm sorry," he said in little more than a whisper. "But he does know what he's talking about, and the evidence is pretty thin."

"Of course it is," Pitt said between his teeth. "People don't leave a trail that leads back to them. If they did, we wouldn't need police, let alone Special Branch." He did not slacken his pace, and Jack had to lengthen his own stride to keep up with him.

"Come on, Thomas," he said reasonably. "You can't expect a man in Tregarron's position to accept a story as basically unlikely as this one, unless you have real evidence. He knows Austria, and he gets regular reports from all the people we have there, and a few others as well. He's damned good at his job."

Pitt stopped abruptly and swung around to face Jack. "Would you have said that, in those words, if it had been Narraway who'd come to you with suspicions? Or might you have given him the courtesy of assuming that he also was good at his job?"

The color flushed up Jack's face. "I'm sorry. That was incredibly clumsy of me. I —"

Pitt smiled bleakly. "No, it was regrettably honest. And that is not a quality you can afford to exercise if you hope to rise in the diplomatic corps. One day you may also be damned good at your job, but it isn't today." He started to walk again.

"Thomas!" Jack grabbed him by the arm, hard, forcing him to stop. "Listen. I think you are jumping at shadows, and after the business in St. Malo, and then Ireland and what happened to Narraway, I don't entirely blame you. But you can't force Tregarron to go against his own knowledge of the people and the country. If you really believe something is threatened, then I'll arrange for you to see Evan Blantyre at short notice. I'll tell him it's a matter of urgency, even that there could be very unpleasant consequences if we make a bad judgment." He looked at Pitt expectantly, his eyes wide, his stare direct.

Pitt felt churlish. It hurt that he had to be offered, as if he had never met Blantyre, a meeting that would have been instantly granted to Narraway. Was it his lack of experience, and the fact that Narraway was indisputably a gentleman, while he was not? Or was it that Narraway had amassed a wealth of knowledge about so many people that no one dared defy him? Whatever the case, none of this was Jack's fault, and Pitt knew he would be a fool to squander the few advantages he had: the strength of family and the bonds of friendship, which Narraway had never possessed.

He forced the resentment out of his mind.

"Thank you," he accepted. "That's an excellent suggestion."

Jack went back to Tregarron's office with sharply conflicting emotions. He was certain he had done the right thing in promising to arrange for Pitt to speak in depth with Evan Blantyre right away, yet at the same time, he believed that Tregarron would not approve it. He was not even sure why. To some extent Pitt was overreacting, but that was better than reacting too little, or too late. Belittling him and making him doubt his own judgment helped no one.

He reached Tregarron's door again and tapped lightly. On the command to enter, he went back in.

Tregarron was at his desk. Papers on a different subject were spread out in front of him. He looked up at Jack, his expression still slightly angry.

"I'd like you to look through these and give me your opinion, Radley," he said, pulling the papers together more neatly. "I think Wishart is right, but I'm predisposed to that view anyway. Do you know Lord Wishart? Good chap. Very sound."

"No, sir, I don't," Jack replied, holding out his hand and taking the papers.

"Must introduce you some time." Tregarron's smile lit his face, giving it a unique charm. "You'll like him."

"Thank you, sir." Jack was flattered. Many people wanted very much to meet Lord Wishart, and few did. Emily would be delighted. He could picture her face when he told her. Then he had a sudden, uncomfortable feeling that it was a sop, for having been so abrasive toward Pitt. Tregarron was quite aware that Pitt was Jack's brother-in-law. He wanted to say something further, but he had no clear idea what it would be.

He looked down at the papers Tregarron had given him. They were to do with a proposed British diplomatic mission to Trieste, one of the Italian cities still under Austrian rule. This matter was largely cultural, with some mention of Slovenia. It was complicated, as was every issue that dealt with the Austrian Empire.

He saw an opinion written in Tregarron's flowing hand and read the first two sentences. Then he went back and reread it, thinking he had made a mistake. It was in direct contradiction to information Tregarron had received only yesterday.

"By this afternoon, Radley," Tregarron prompted.

Jack looked up. Should he question what he had just read, or would it be seen as exceeding his duty, perhaps even criticizing Tregarron himself? He decided to say nothing. There would be an explanation for it, some additional fact of which he was not yet aware. If he read the whole report, it would explain the apparent anomaly.

"Yes, sir," he replied, forcing himself to meet Tregarron's eyes and smile briefly. "Thank you."

Tregarron nodded and bent his attention to the papers on the desk again.

■ ■ ■ ■

Word from Blantyre came more rapidly than
Pitt had expected. He had thought their
meeting would be arranged the following
day, at the earliest, but Blantyre asked for
him that same afternoon.

Pitt grasped his coat and, forgetting his
hat, went out to catch the next passing
hansom. He ran up the steps two at a time,
arriving a little breathlessly at Blantyre's office door. Uncharacteristically for him, he
straightened his tie, eased his shoulders to
help his jacket lie a little more gracefully,
and then raised his hand to knock.

The knock was answered almost immediately. A secretary ushered him in and,
without any waiting at all, he found himself
in Blantyre's office. They shook hands, and
then Blantyre motioned for him to be
seated.

"Sorry for the haste," Blantyre apologized.
"I have another appointment I couldn't
shelve, and tomorrow I have one meeting
after another. Tell me as briefly as you can,
and still make any sense of it, what you
know and what you've deduced."

Pitt had already prepared what he meant
to say during the hansom ride. He began

without a preamble.

"We followed all the leads you gave us, and we are almost certain of the identities of the men asking questions about the timetables, signals, and points. There are various pieces of further information, observations of new and unlikely alliances formed by people we know as troublemakers and sympathizers with anarchy or violent change. Such evidence as we have indicates that the intended target is Duke Alois Habsburg, as you said."

Blantyre nodded. "What is the weight of the evidence now, in your judgment?"

"Too serious to ignore," Pitt said without hesitation. "It may be an extraordinary collection of coincidences, but surely that happens once in a hundred times, or less."

"From my own experience of Austro-Hungarian affairs, which is considerable, I still think it's extremely unlikely. But 'unlikely' isn't good enough; we must be sure it's impossible. I need more details, and I haven't time to get them now, or to give this appropriate thought." Blantyre frowned and stood up. "Can you come to dinner at my home this evening? You and your wife would be most welcome. We can allow the ladies to retire to the withdrawing room, and we can talk at length, and you

225

can tell me all the details you are free to discuss, bearing in mind that I also serve the government, and Her Majesty. I know how to keep a secret. Between us we should be able to judge the gravity of the threat, so you may react appropriately."

Pitt rose to his feet feeling as if a great weight had been taken from him. He had found an ally: perhaps the one man in England able to help him assess the value of his information.

"Thank you, sir," he said with profound feeling. "We would be delighted."

Blantyre held out his hand. "No need to be particularly formal, but we'll make a pleasure of it all the same. Eight o'clock is a trifle early, but we will need the time. This matter may, after all, be very grave."

Pitt took his leave and walked down the corridor rapidly, smiling. It had been more than a professional success. A man of substance and high office had treated him with the same dignity as he would have treated Narraway. There had been no condescension in his manner. For the first time in a while, Pitt was happy as he went down the stairs and out into the bitter wind knifing along the street.

While Pitt was speaking with Evan Blantyre, Charlotte had decided that she should telephone Emily, no matter how awkward she felt. Though the quarrel had been primarily Emily's fault, one of them had to make the first move toward reconciliation, before the rift became too deep. Since Emily apparently was not going to do it, then she must. She was the elder anyway; perhaps it was her responsibility.

When she picked up the receiver to put the call through, she half hoped Emily would be out making calls. Then she could satisfy herself with the virtue of having made the attempt, without actually having to negotiate some kind of peace.

But the footman at the other end brought Emily to the telephone within moments of Charlotte being connected.

"How are you?" Emily asked guardedly.

"Very well, thank you," Charlotte replied. They could have been strangers speaking to each other. The planned conversation disappeared from her head. "And you?" she asked, to fill the silence.

"Excellent," Emily answered. "We are going to the theater this evening. It is a new play, supposed to be very interesting."

"I hope you enjoy it. Have you heard from Mama and Joshua lately?" Joshua Fielding, their mother's second husband, was an actor. It seemed a reasonable thing to ask. At least it stopped the silence from returning.

"Not for a couple of weeks," Emily replied. "They are in Stratford. Had you forgotten?"

Charlotte had, but she did not wish to admit it. There was a touch of condescension in Emily's tone. "No," she lied. "I imagine they have telephones, even there."

"Not in theatrical boardinghouses," Emily replied. "I thought you would know that."

"You have the advantage of me," Charlotte said instantly. "I have never had occasion to inquire about one."

"Since your mother frequents them, and you seem to be concerned for her welfare, perhaps you should have," Emily returned.

"For heaven's sake, Emily! It was a simple question — something to say."

"I've never known you to be at a loss for something to say." Emily's tone was still critical.

"There is a great deal you have never known," Charlotte snapped. "I was hoping for an agreeable conversation. Clearly that isn't going to happen."

"You were hoping I was going to say something to Jack about helping Thomas in his present predicament," Emily corrected her.

Charlotte heard the defensiveness in Emily's voice, and hesitated for a moment. Then temper and loyalty to Pitt got the better of her.

"You overestimate my opinion of Jack's abilities," she said coldly. "Thomas will get himself out of any difficulties there may be. I am sorry I disturbed you. This is obviously a conversation better held at another time, perhaps some distance in the future when you are less defensive."

She heard Emily's voice calling her name sharply, but she had already moved the receiver away from her ear. This was only going to hurt more the longer she continued talking. She replaced the instrument in its cradle and walked away with a tightness in her throat. It would be better to find something useful to do.

Charlotte was delighted when Pitt came home and told her of the invitation to dine with Blantyre and his wife. It was a social occasion that promised to be most enjoyable. However, of much more importance to her was the relief she saw in Pitt over the fact that someone had finally listened to his concerns.

For years he had shared with her much of what he had done. She had been of help to him in many cases, especially those concerning people of the class into which she had been born, and he had not. To begin with, he had considered it meddling, and had been afraid for her safety. Gradually he had come to value her judgment, especially her observation of people, and her strength of character, even if he still feared for her safety in some of her wilder interventions.

Emily too had involved herself, demonstrating both courage and intelligence. But that was in a past that now seemed distant; they were much further apart than they used to be. She did not blame Emily for feeling a greater loyalty to Jack than to her sister. She herself gave her first passionate and instinctive allegiance to her husband. But the knowledge still carried a sense of loss, a longing for the laughter and the trust, the ability to talk openly about all kinds of things, trivial or important, which had always been part of her life and her relationship with Emily. There was no one else she would trust in the same way.

But she forced it from her mind and smiled at Pitt. "That will be excellent. It will be lovely, and a decent excuse to wear a new gown I have bought for myself, rather than one borrowed from Emily or Aunt Vespasia. I have a very fashionable one, in a curious shade of blue. It will be more than equal to the occasion."

She saw Pitt's amusement.

"Adriana Blantyre is very beautiful, Thomas. I shall have to do my best to not be constantly overshadowed!"

"Is she brave and clever as well?" he asked with sudden gentleness. "Or funny and kind?" He did not add the rest of what he implied. She knew it, and felt the blush of self-consciousness creep up her cheeks, but she did not lower her eyes from his.

"I don't know. I liked her. I look forward to knowing her a little better." Then suddenly she was serious again. "Thomas, does Blantyre matter to you? Is he going to help you?"

"I hope so," he replied. "Jack arranged it."

A hurt inside her slipped away. "Good. Good. I'm glad."

She wished he were free to tell her what troubled him, apart from the burden of taking on Narraway's job. She wanted to assure him that he was equal to it, but such assurances would be meaningless, because she had very little idea what it was that bothered him in the first place. She did not know whether his skills matched Narraway's, or even if they ever could. They were very different from each other. Until their experience in Ireland, she had thought of

Narraway as intellectual, and happy to be alone. Whether that was natural to him or he had learned it, it had become his habit. Only when he lost his position in Special Branch had she seen any vulnerability in him, any need at all for the emotional warmth of others. How blind she had been. It was something she thought of now with a dull ache of guilt. She preferred to put it from her mind. That would be easier for Narraway too. He would not wish to think she remembered every emotion in his face, perhaps regretted now. Some things should remain guessed at, but unspoken.

Regardless of such moments, there was a professional ruthlessness in Narraway that she believed would never be natural to Pitt. Indeed, she hoped it would not.

That was part of the difficulty. Two of the things she loved most in Pitt were his empathy and his love of justice, which would make leadership and its terrible decisions more difficult for him.

She had not yet found any way in which she could help him. Blind support was all she could offer, and it had a very limited value. It was, in some ways, like the love of a child; in the dangerous and painful decisions, he was essentially alone.

She looked at him now, standing in the

middle of the kitchen as Daniel came in with his homework, and she saw the deliberate change of expression as he turned to his son. She knew the effort it cost him to put aside his worry, saw his hands clenched in frustration even as he smiled at Daniel and they spoke of history homework, and how best to answer a complicated question.

"But how is that the Holy Roman Empire?" Daniel asked reasonably, pointing to the map in his schoolbook. "Rome is way down there!" He put his finger on the middle of Italy. "It isn't even in the same country. That's Austria. It says so. And why is it holier than anywhere else?"

Pitt took a deep breath. "It isn't," he said patiently. "Have you got a map of where the old Roman Empire used to be? I'll show you where it became the Eastern and the Western Empires."

"I know that, Papa! And it wasn't up there!" He put his finger on Austria again. "Why is all that bit part of the Holy Empire?"

Charlotte smiled and left Pitt to do his best with conquest and Imperial politics. No one else had ever been able to give a morally satisfying answer, and she knew Daniel well enough to expect a long argument.

■ ■ ■ ■

Charlotte dressed for the dinner as she had done in her early twenties, before her marriage, when her mother had been trying desperately, and unsuccessfully, to find her a suitable husband.

She had chosen a color and style that flattered the warmth of her skin and the hints of auburn in her hair. The cut of her dress showed the soft curves of her figure to their best advantage. It was fashionable enough to feel up to date, but not so much that in a few months it would be outmoded. She had Minnie Maude help her coil and pin her hair so it had no chance of slipping undone. To have one's hair falling out of its coiffure would be deemed just as disastrous as having one's clothing fall off! And rather more difficult to put right again.

In the lamplight, she was not sure if she observed one or two gray hairs, or if it was only a nervous imagination. Her mother, many years her senior, had only a few. And of course there was a remedy for it. Apparently iron nails steeped in strong tea for fifteen days make an excellent dye for darker hair! Rinsing the hair in tea was, she considered, good for it every so often anyway.

She wore very little jewelry. This was not only as a matter of style, but also because she owned very little, a fact she did not wish to make obvious. Earrings were sufficient. There was natural color in her face, but she added a little rouge, very, very discreetly, and put a tiny dab of powder on her nose to take away the shine. Once she was satisfied that it was the best she could do, she would forget it entirely and focus on whoever she was speaking to, listen with attention, and answer with warmth, and if possible, a little wit.

They had hired a carriage for the evening. To keep one all the time was an expense they could not afford, nor was it needed. If that day were to come in the future, perhaps it would be after they had moved to a house with stables. It would be exciting to make such an upward climb in society, but it would also force her to leave behind a place in which they had known much joy. Charlotte was perfectly happy not to have such a burden at the moment. She sat back in her seat, smiling in the dark as they were driven through Russell Square, its bare trees thrashing in the heavy wind. They turned left up Woburn Place, past Tavistock Square, open and windy again, then along the shelter of Upper Woburn Place and into the flickering lamplight of Endsleigh Gardens.

The carriage stopped and they alighted at the Blantyres' house, where they were welcomed in by a liveried footman. He showed them immediately to a large withdrawing room where a blazing fire shed red and yellow light on leather-upholstered chairs and sofas, and a carpet rich in shades of amber, gold, and peach. The gaslamps were turned low, so it was difficult to see the details of the many paintings that decorated the walls. In a quick glance all Charlotte noticed was their ornamental gold frames, and the fact that they seemed to be mostly land- and seascapes.

Adriana Blantyre came forward to welcome them, a step ahead of her husband. She was dressed in burgundy velvet. Its glowing color emphasized the fairness of her face and the amazing depth of her eyes. She looked both fragile and intensely alive.

Blantyre himself greeted Charlotte with a smile, but his glance returned to his wife before he offered his hand.

"I'm so pleased you could come. How are you, Mrs. Pitt?"

"Very well, thank you, Mr. Blantyre," she replied. "Good evening, Mrs. Blantyre. It is such a pleasure to see you again." That was not merely good manners. On the brief occasions she had met Adriana, she had found her to be quite different from most of the society women she knew. She possessed a sparkling energy and a dry sense of humor that lay more in what she did not say than in any quick ripostes.

They sat and talked casually: light comments on the weather, the latest gossip, rumors that were of no serious consequence. Charlotte had time to look at the paintings on the walls, and the very beautiful ornaments that graced the mantel and two or three small tables. One was a porcelain figurine of a woman dancing. It had such grace that it seemed as if, at any moment, it would actually move. One of the largest ornaments was a huge statue of a wild boar. It stood with its head lowered, menacing, yet there was a beauty in it that commanded admiration.

"He's rather fine, isn't he?" Blantyre remarked, seeing her gaze. "We don't have boar here anymore but they still do in Austria."

"When did we have them here?" Charlotte asked, not really because she wanted to know, but because she was interested in drawing him into conversation.

His eyes opened wide. "An excellent question. I must find out. Have we progressed because we no longer have them, or regressed? We could ask that question of a lot of things." He smiled, as if the possibilities amused him.

"Have you hunted boar?" Charlotte asked.

"Oh, long in the past. I lived for several years in Vienna. The forests around there abound with them."

Charlotte gave an involuntary little shiver.

"I imagine you would greatly prefer the music and the dancing," he said with certainty. "It is a marvelous city, one where almost anything you care to dream of seems possible." He looked for a moment at Adriana, and there was an intense tenderness in his face. "We first met in Vienna."

Adriana rolled her dark eyes and a flash of amusement lit her expression. "We first *danced* in Vienna," she corrected him. "We met in Trieste."

"I remember the moonlight on the Danube!" he protested.

"My dear," she said, "it was the Adriatic. We didn't speak, but we saw each other. I knew you were watching me."

"Did you? I thought I was being so discreet."

She laughed, then turned away.

For an instant Charlotte thought it was out of modesty, because the look on Blantyre's face was openly emotional. Then she caught something in the angle of Adriana's head, the light catching a tear in her eye, and felt that there was something she had missed entirely, far deeper than the words conveyed.

A few minutes later they were called to the dining room, and its lush, old-fashioned beauty took all Charlotte's attention. It was not the least bit English; there was a simplicity to the proportions, which lent an extraordinary grace, and a lush warmth to the coloring.

"Do you like it?" Adriana asked, standing close behind her. Then she apologized. "I'm sorry. If I ask, how could you possibly say you did not?" She gave a rueful smile. "I love England, but this room carried the memory of my home; I want people here to like what I used to know and love as well." Without waiting for an answer, she moved away to take her place at the foot of the table, while Blantyre sat down at the head.

The meal was served by footmen and a parlormaid, silently, and with a discretion born of long practice. First there was a clear soup, followed by a light fish, and then the main course of lamb in red wine sauce. The conversation moved easily from one subject to another. Blantyre was a highly entertain-

239

ing host, full of anecdotes about his travels, especially his time in the capitals of Europe. Watching his face, Charlotte saw an undisguised enthusiasm for the individuality and culture of each place, but a love for Austria that superseded all the others.

He spoke of the gaiety and sophistication of Paris, of the theater and art and philosophy, but his voice took on a new intensity when he described the Viennese operetta, the vitality of it, the music lyrical enough to make everyone wish to dance.

"They have to nail the chairs and tables to the floor," he said, almost seriously. He was smiling, his eyes staring into the distance. "Vienna's always in my dreams. One minute you cry there, the next you laugh. There is a unique richness in the blend of so many cultures."

Adriana moved very slightly, and the change in the light on her face made Charlotte look toward her. For a moment, she saw pain in Adriana's eyes, and in the shadows around her mouth, which was still too young for lines or hollows. Then it was gone. But for a second, Adriana had seemed utterly lost. Her hand was on her fork, and then she set it down with a clink, as if she could not eat any more.

Blantyre had seen it — Charlotte was

quite certain of that — yet he went on with his tale of music and color, as if to avoid drawing attention to it.

The next course was served. Blantyre changed the subject and became more serious. Now his attention was directed toward Pitt.

"It has changed lately, of course," he said with a little grimace. "Since the death of Crown Prince Rudolf."

Adriana's eyes widened in surprise, probably that he should mention such a subject at the dinner table, and with people they hardly knew.

Instantly, Charlotte wondered if Pitt's real reason for being here could possibly be connected to the tragedy at Mayerling. But what concern could that be to British Special Branch? She looked at Pitt and saw a slight frown on his face.

"The emperor is a martinet," Blantyre went on. "Sleeps in an old army bed and rises at half-past four in the morning to begin his work on the papers of state. He dresses in the uniform of a junior officer, and I wouldn't be surprised if he eats only bread and drinks only water."

Charlotte looked at him closely to see if he was joking. His stories had been full of wit and lighthearted mockery but always gentle. Now she saw no lightness in his face at all. His nostrils were slightly flared, and his mouth was pulled a little tight.

"Evan . . ." Adriana began anxiously.

"Mr. Pitt is head of Special Branch, my dear," Blantyre said, very slightly criticizing her. "He has few illusions. We should not add to them."

Adriana went very pale, but did not argue.

Charlotte wondered where the conversation was heading. How much of it was information that Pitt was seeking, and why had they come to learn it this way? She turned to Blantyre.

"He sounds rather grim," she observed. "Was he always like that, or is it the effect of grief over the death of his son?"

Blantyre replied, "I'm afraid he was pretty much always a bore. Poor Sisi escapes whenever she can. She's a trifle eccentric, but who could blame the poor woman?"

Charlotte looked from Blantyre to Pitt; she saw the mystified expression on his face before he could hide it.

"The empress Elisabeth," Blantyre explained, eyebrows arched a little. "God knows why they call her Sisi, but they all do. A bohemian at heart. Always taking off for somewhere or the other, mostly Paris, sometimes Rome."

Charlotte plunged in, hoping she was judging correctly that in some fashion this had to do with Pitt's current case.

"Which came first?" she asked innocently.

Blantyre turned to her with a bright stare. Was that a ghost of amusement in his eyes? "First?" he inquired.

She looked straight at him. "Her desire to escape his being a bore, or his retreating into solitude because she was always off on some adventure?"

He nodded almost imperceptibly. "Neither, so far as I know. But Crown Prince Rudolf was caught up in a considerable conflict between his father's rigid military dictatorship and his mother's erratic flights of fancy, both metaphorical and literal. He was really rather clever, you know, when given half a chance to escape the straitjacket of duty." He turned to Pitt. "He wrote excellent articles for radical newspapers, under a pseudonym, of course."

Pitt straightened, his fork halfway to his mouth.

Blantyre smiled. "You didn't know? It doesn't surprise me. Not many people do. He was of the opinion that an Austrian invasion of Croatia would be a cause for war with Russia, which Austria would start against a completely anti-Austrian Balkan peninsula, from the Black Sea to the Adriatic. He said not only the present would be at stake, but also the whole future, for which Austria was responsible to the coming generation."

Pitt stared at him. There was complete silence at the table.

"Almost a direct quote," Blantyre said. "As closely as I can match the English to the German."

"Evan, the poor man is dead," Adriana said softly. "We will never know what good he might have done had he lived." There was intense sadness in her voice, and her eyes were downcast.

Charlotte's mind raced. She could think of no way in which a suicide pact between a man and his mistress, however tragic, could concern British Special Branch. And yet it appeared that Blantyre had introduced the subject very deliberately, even though it was hardly polite dinner conversation among people who barely knew one another.

Now Blantyre was looking at Adriana. "My dear, you mustn't grieve for him so much." He reached out a hand toward hers, but the table was too long for them to touch. Still his fingers remained in the open gesture, resting lightly on the white cloth. "It was his own choice, and I think perhaps all that was left to him. He was tired and ill, and desperately unhappy."

"Ill?" she said quickly, meeting his gaze for the first time since Rudolf's death had been mentioned. "How can you know?"

"Because now Princess Stéphanie is also infected," he replied.

The expression in Adriana's face was unreadable: surprise, pity, but — more complex than that — it seemed to Charlotte to include a kind of hope, as if a long-standing problem had at last been resolved.

"So it would have been the Archduke Franz Ferdinand anyway?" Adriana said after a couple of seconds.

"Yes," Blantyre agreed. "Did you think poor Rudolf's death could have had something to do with the succession? It wasn't political, at least in that sense. If Rudolf had become emperor, he had planned to make the empire a republic and be president of it, with far greater freedom for the individual nations within."

"Would that have worked?" Adriana asked dubiously.

He smiled. "Probably not. He was an idealist, very much a dreamer. But maybe."

Pitt looked from one to the other of them. "Is there any doubt that it was suicide?"

Blantyre shook his head. "None at all. I

245

know there are all kinds of rumors flying around, but the truth is far beyond that which is known to the public. But I believe that some griefs should remain the property of those who are the victims. That is about the only decency we can offer them. I am quite certain that his death and that of Marie Vetsera were by their own hands, and there were no others involved. Who has blame for the patterns of their lives is not an issue for us."

Pitt seemed about to say something, then changed his mind, and instead made some remark about one of the many beautiful paintings on the wall.

Adriana's face lit with pleasure immediately. "The Croatian coast," she said eagerly. "That's where I was born." She went on to describe it, her words full of nostalgia.

Charlotte noted Blantyre's face. There was a lingering sadness in his eyes as he listened to his wife remembering her childhood, the changing seasons, the sounds and the touch of the past.

Adriana said nothing more of Vienna, as if it were part of another world.

After dinner Charlotte and Adriana returned to the withdrawing room for tea and delicate, prettily decorated sweets.

"Your country sounds very beautiful," Charlotte said with interest.

"It's unique," she said, smiling. "At least it was. I haven't been back for several years now."

"Surely you can go back, at least to visit?" Charlotte asked.

Suddenly Adriana was very still. The delicate color of her skin became even lighter, almost as if it were translucent.

"I don't think I would like to. Evan is very protective of my feelings. He keeps telling me that it would bring back old pain that is best left to heal, and perhaps he is right."

Charlotte waited, believing an explanation would come. Even if it did not, it would be clumsy to ask.

"I'm sorry, I am making no sense. My father died a long time ago, and my mother some time before that. His death is something I still find hard to think about. Others loved him and grieved also, but not as I did." For some minutes she had difficulty keeping her emotions under control. She looked at Charlotte with startling trust, as if there was clearly a friendship between them, but she did not say anything more.

Charlotte thought of her own elder sister's death: the grief, the fear, the disillusionment that had followed it. It was during that series of murders that she had first met Pitt. She had grown up during that time, had learned to look more honestly at the people she loved. She had tried to accept failure, her own and theirs, and learn not to blame them because they fell short of her idealistic and rather immature perceptions of them.

She had no idea how Adriana's father had died, but clearly it had been part of some complicated situation that had caused her much pain, if, even now, she would not speak of it.

Charlotte looked around the withdrawing room and chose a lovely, very ornate piece of carving in wood to admire and ask about.

The tension was broken, and Adriana responded with a flush of gratitude, giving an account of its history.

In the dining room, the butler brought in port and cigars; at Blantyre's request he left them alone. Then the serious conversation began. Blantyre offered no preamble.

"I have looked more closely at the situation, Pitt. I have been obliged to change my mind. I admit, I thought you were being a little hasty and had jumped to conclusions. I was mistaken. I now believe that you are right to consider the danger serious, possibly even as catastrophic as it looks."

Pitt was stunned.

Blantyre leaned forward. "Of course, the indications are slight: an inquiry about timetables, which seems natural enough; a desire to know how the signals work, in more detail than the average person knows, or wishes to; a technical description of how the points work. They do not indicate to the Foreign Office that there is anything amiss." He gave a rueful, self-deprecating smile. "To me, knowing the names of the men concerned, it indicates that they plan something large and complicated enough to require the use of men who have killed before, and are willing to cause any number of civilian casualties in order to succeed."

"Why Duke Alois?" Pitt asked him. "Does he actually have far more political significance than we realize?"

Blantyre's face was very grave.

"I am unaware that he has any significance at all, but there may be a number of things that have changed since my last accurate bulletin. But even if he does not, this is a far bigger issue than the death of any one man, whoever he is." He spread his hands on the white cloth. They were lean and strong.

"The Austro-Hungarian Empire is pivotal to the future of Europe. I don't believe the government of Britain fully realizes that. Perhaps no other government does either. Look at the map, Pitt. The empire is enormous. It lies in the heart of Europe between the rising industrial strengths of the Protestant countries in the west, especially Germany, newly united and growing in power every year, and the old, fractured east, which includes all the quarrelsome Balkan states, and Greece, Macedonia, and of course, Turkey — 'the sick man of Europe.' ”

Pitt did not interrupt. The brandy sat forgotten, the cigars unlit.

“And to the south is Italy,” Blantyre went on. “Like Germany, it is newly united, but still with that open wound in the north, an Austrian-occupied territory containing some of its most valuable cities. And then there are Serbia, Croatia, Montenegro, and the other Adriatic countries, where the real powder keg lies. Small as they are, if they explode, they could eventually take the whole of Europe with them.”

His hands tightened a little. “And to the north lies the vast, restless bear of Russia: Slavic in its loyalties, Orthodox in its faith. It's ruled by a tsar in Moscow who hasn't the faintest idea what really lies in his own people's hearts, never mind anywhere else.”

Pitt felt cold. He began to understand where Blantyre was going with this train of thought.

"And Austria lies in the heart of it." Blantyre moved his hand very slightly, as if it lay on a map, not the white linen tablecloth. "The empire has twelve different languages, and a multitude of faiths — Catholic, Orthodox, Muslim, and Jewish. Although admittedly the anti-Semitism is ugly, and rising, still the general tolerance is there. The culture is old and deeply sophisticated, and the government is long practiced at holding the reins of power strongly enough to govern, but lightly enough to give individual countries their breathing space."

He looked at Pitt, judging his reaction.

"Teutonic Germany is impatient, chomping at the bit of its own power. Bismarck said, 'chaining the trim, seaworthy frigate of Prussia to the ancient, worm-eaten galleon of Austria.' We have not taken enough notice of that. The Germans are dangerous and growing increasingly restless. Their young lions are waiting to take down the old. But even that is only peripheral to the real danger. Austria is the heart where all the different interests meet, safely. Remove it, and there is no neutral core. Teutons and Slavs are face-to-face. Protestant, Catholic,

Muslim, and Jew have no forum in which to speak familiarly. There is no longer a single culture where all take part."

Pitt could see the indisputable logic in what Blantyre was saying.

"But why kill a minor member of the Austrian royal family, and here in England? What purpose does that serve?" he asked.

Blantyre smiled, his face tight, eyes bleak. "It doesn't matter who it is; the victim is incidental. Assassinate him at home and the authorities might be able to cover it up, make it seem like some horrible accident. Do it in England, where they have no control, in the territory of one of the best secret services in Europe, and it cannot be hidden. And no doubt when you catch whoever is responsible, they will unmistakably prove to be Croatian. Austria will have no choice whatsoever except to try him and execute him, then to find all his allies and do the same — do you see?"

Pitt began to see, and the vision was appalling.

Blantyre nodded slowly. "It is in your face. Of course you see. Austria would then be at war with Croatia. Croatia is Slavic. It will appeal to its mighty Russian cousins, who will weigh in on its side, even if not invited to. Then Germany will come in on the side of German-speaking, German-cultural Austria, and before you can stop the landslide, you will have war, the likes of which we have never seen before."

"No sane man would . . ." Pitt began, and trailed off.

"No sane man," Blantyre repeated softly. "How many sane nationalist revolutionaries do you know? How many dynamiters and assassins who see only a few days ahead of them, instead of looking to the future, to six months, a year, or a decade?"

"None," Pitt said almost under his breath. "God, what a mess."

"We must prevent it," Blantyre answered. "Special Branch may never have had a more important job to do. Any help I can give, any service I can provide, I offer it to you, day or night."

Pitt stared down at the table, shoulders hunched, all the muscles of his face and neck aching.

"Thank you."

CHAPTER 6

The early afternoon was sunny, but very cold, when Vespasia set out to visit Serafina again. She was not looking forward to it this time; to see Serafina in such confusion was distressing, and the very obvious fear she felt was even more difficult, as it made Vespasia feel helpless and a poor friend, unable to alleviate it.

The carriage passed through the long-familiar streets. Vespasia noticed a woman almost knocked off balance when a gust of wind caught her skirts; a hundred yards farther a man in gray held his hands up to keep his hat from being blown off. The clip of horses' hooves rang loudly on the iron-hard stones.

Then suddenly Vespasia realized that the sound had vanished. They were slowing down, but still moving. With a chill of horror she recognized the familiar hush of sawdust in the road, and knew its meaning:

They were passing the home of someone very recently dead. Except that they were not passing; they had stopped and the coachman was at the carriage door.

"My lady . . ." He sounded uncomfortable.

"Yes," Vespasia knew the words he was reluctant to say. "I see what has happened. I will still go in. Please wait for me here. I do not imagine I shall be long."

"Yes, my lady." He held out his hand and helped her alight.

She walked over the sawdust to the footpath. The curtains were drawn. The dark blue dress she was wearing was no longer appropriate. It should have been black, but she had not known. She knocked on the door, and was about to knock again, when it was answered by Nerissa. Her face, normally stressed and a little colorless, looked completely bleached from shock, her eyes red-rimmed, the lids puffy. She drew in a breath to speak, and let it out again in a gasp. She looked on the verge of collapse.

Vespasia mastered her own feelings and took Nerissa by the arm, gently propelling her inside. She closed the door before turning to speak to her.

"I can see what has happened," she said quietly. "I'm very sorry. It is always a shock, no matter how well one imagines one is prepared. I admit, I had not thought it would be so soon, or I would not have come so ill-prepared, and perhaps intrusively early."

"No . . ." Nerissa gulped. "No, you are not intrusive in the slightest. You were so kind . . . to come . . ." She gulped again.

Vespasia felt a rush of pity for her. She was an unattractive young woman, not so much plain of feature as lacking in charm. Now she had lost perhaps the only relative she had, and even if she had inherited the house, it would do little to give her entrée to desirable social circles. Certainly it would bring her no friends of true value. In her sudden new loneliness she would be even more vulnerable than before. Vespasia hoped the lover she believed Nerissa had was indeed real, and in no way in pursuit of her inheritance from Serafina.

"Perhaps a cup of tea?" Vespasia suggested. "I am sure you would benefit from a chance to sit down for a few moments. It must be a heavy burden for you. Is there anyone who will assist you in whatever needs to be done? If not, I'm sure I can recommend a suitable person, and instruct them as to your wishes, and of course Serafina's."

"Thank you . . . thank you." Nerissa seemed to compose herself a little more. "I have barely had time to think of it. But certainly tea. Tea would be excellent. I'm so sorry I did not offer it. My good manners seem to have evaporated . . ."

"Not at all," Vespasia assured her. "I daresay the kitchen is in a bit of a state. Servants need a firm hand at such times, and something to do, or they tend to go to pieces. It is all very distressing. They will be worrying about their own positions, no doubt. The sooner you can reassure them, the better able they will be to assist you."

"Yes . . . I hadn't even thought . . ." Nerissa very deliberately steadied herself and turned to lead the way into the morning room. It was bitterly cold, as the fire was not lit. She stopped in dismay.

"Perhaps the housekeeper's sitting room?" Vespasia suggested. "That is very often comfortable even when all else is in disarray."

Nerissa seemed grateful for the suggestion. Ten minutes later they were in the small but very cozy room in the servants' quarters from which Mrs. Whiteside governed the domestic arrangements. She was a short, stout woman with a surprisingly handsome face. At the moment she was clearly very distressed, but grateful to have something useful to do. Nerissa disappeared to address the servants and Mrs. Whiteside brought Vespasia a pot of tea while she waited.

There was a brief knock on the door. Vespasia answered, expecting Mrs. Whiteside back again, but it was Tucker who came in, closing the door behind her. She looked suddenly older, as if ten years had stricken her in one night, but she stood straight, head high. She was wearing a black dress without a white apron, and was completely without adornment of any kind. Her white hair was neatly dressed as always, but her skin was so colorless it looked like wrinkled paper.

Vespasia rose to her feet and went toward her. She took Tucker's hands in hers, something she would normally never have imagined doing to a servant of any sort.

"My dear Tucker, I am so sorry. For all the warning one has of such an event, one can never anticipate the sense of loss."

Tucker stood rigid, overcome by her emotions. She had lost a lifetime's companionship. She wanted to speak, but she was painfully aware that she could not do so without losing her composure. She might have come intending to say something, but now was not the time.

"Would you care for tea?" Vespasia asked, gesturing toward the tray that had been prepared for her. There was still plenty left in the pot. All it required was another cup.

Tucker swallowed. "No, thank you, my lady. I just came . . ." She was unable to complete the sentence.

"Then please return to your duties," Vespasia said gently. "No doubt we shall have other opportunities to speak."

Tucker nodded, gulped, and retreated to the door.

It was another five minutes before Nerissa came back.

"Thank you," she said with intense feeling. "It was kind of you to come." She sat with her hands knotted in her lap, her knuckles white. "It . . . it seems much easier when there is something to do."

"Indeed," Vespasia agreed. "I gather from what Mrs. Whiteside said that Serafina died some time during the night, and it was you who found her this morning. It must have been extremely distressing for you."

"Yes. Yes, we were not expecting it . . . for weeks . . . even months," Nerissa agreed.

"We? You mean you and her doctor?"

"Yes. He . . . I . . . we sent for him, of course. Mrs. Whiteside and I. He came almost straightaway. Of course there was nothing he could do. It seemed she . . . died . . . quite early in the night." She was gasping for breath, her speech disjointed.

Vespasia looked at the young woman sitting opposite her, tense, desperately unhappy, perhaps even feeling guilty because she had not been there when her aunt had died. That was natural, but not reasonable; there was nothing at all she could have done except make it so that Serafina had not died alone. But it was also true that Serafina may have gone in her sleep, and would not have known the difference.

Nerissa was waiting for Vespasia to speak, perhaps to offer some words of comfort. The silence between them had grown heavy.

Vespasia gave a bleak smile. "The fact of death is always painful. You are not alone, nor should you feel so. I am sure the doctor assured you that there was nothing you could have done to alter things, or even to help."

"Yes . . . yes, he did say that," Nerissa agreed. "But one feels so helpless, and as if one should have known."

"It would not have comforted Serafina to have you sitting up with her day and night on the assumption that at any moment she might die," Vespasia said drily.

Nerissa managed a small smile. "Would you care to go up to her room and say a last good-bye?"

Vespasia did not believe it was "good-bye," only a last *au revoir.* But she was certainly curious to see if there had been any struggle, any fighting for the last breath, the final sleep. It would be more of a relief than she had imagined if there had not.

"Thank you." She rose to her feet and Nerissa stood too. Vespasia followed her out of the housekeeper's room back into the main hall, then up the stairs to the room where only a few days earlier she had visited Serafina.

Vespasia went in and stood alone. She looked at the body of the woman with whom she had never truly been friends, yet with whom she had had so much in common. The passion of their beliefs had separated them from others they knew day by day, even from their own families — perhaps especially from them.

Now all the fear was ironed out of Serafina's features. The worst she could imagine had either happened, or the danger of it had passed, and she had moved beyond all earthly success or failure. Vespasia looked at her, and saw nothing but the shell. The spirit was gone.

What had she imagined she could learn? Whatever Serafina had been afraid of must be discovered in some other way. She turned and went back outside to thank Nerissa, and to offer her condolences once again. Then with increasing urgency, she gathered her cape and went outside. She was determined to visit Thomas Pitt.

She was kept waiting at his office at Lisson Grove no more than twenty minutes. The young man named Stoker knew who she was and insisted that Pitt would wish to see her right away.

"Aunt Vespasia?" Pitt said with some alarm, when Stoker led her into the office. He rose from his chair and came over to her as she closed the door behind her. She did little more than glance at the pictures on the wall and the books, but she noticed the difference from when Victor Narraway had occupied the room.

"Good afternoon, Thomas. Thank you for seeing me immediately. I have just called at the home of Serafina Montserrat, and found that she died unexpectedly, some time last night."

"I'm sorry," he said gently. "I know that you knew her."

"Thank you. She was a remarkable

woman. But it is not the loss of a friend that concerns me. We were not especially close. Last time I visited her, a few days ago, she was profoundly afraid — indeed, I would say terrified — that her mind was affected to the point where she was lost in memory, and might have forgotten where and when she was, and to whom she was speaking. That in itself is not a unique circumstance in old age." She gave a small, sad smile. "But in her case it was dangerous, or so she believed. She knew many secrets from her time as something of a revolutionary in the Austrian Empire many years ago. She was afraid there were people to whom she was still a danger."

She saw the sudden, sharp attention in his face.

"I thought that at best she was romanticizing," she continued. "But I took the precaution of asking Victor Narraway if perhaps it might be the truth. He inquired into it. At first it seemed that she was deluding herself, but he did not give up easily, and it transpired that she might have been understating her importance, if anything."

"How far in the past?" he interrupted.

"A generation ago, at least. But she felt that some of her knowledge concerned people still alive, or those whom they might have loved and wished to protect. I can give you no names because I don't know any. But she was very, very frightened, Thomas."

He looked puzzled. "Of betraying someone accidentally, even now? Who? Did she tell you?"

"No. To me, she was very discreet. I suppose part of what made me think she was romanticizing was the fact that she gave no names. But Victor said that she was even more involved in events at the time than she claimed. And Thomas, I am not absolutely certain that she was mistaken in her fear. One moment she was as lucid as you or I, when we were alone, then when someone else came in she seemed to lurch into near insanity, as if she had no idea where she was."

She took a deep, rather shaky breath, and let it out with a sigh. "I'm afraid that someone may have frightened her to the point where she took her own life, rather than continue with the risk of betraying a friend, an ally in the cause." Pity overwhelmed her, and a sense of guilt because she had done nothing to prevent this. She had known about it, and Serafina had begged for her help. Now she was safe in Pitt's office talking about it, too late, and Serafina was dead. "I feel like I should've done something more to help her."

"What could you have done?" Pitt's voice, gentle and urgent, intruded on her thoughts.

She looked at him. "I don't know. Which is not a good enough excuse, is it?"

"Unless you were willing and able to move in and sleep in the room beside her, or perhaps be certain that she saw no visitors without your being present, there is nothing you could've done."

"I tried to have Nerissa Freemarsh do that. I even asked her to engage a nurse," Vespasia said bleakly. "I did not try hard enough."

Thomas waited a beat. "What else is bothering you?" he prompted.

She stared at him, for long, level seconds. "As I said, there is the possibility that she was not afraid unnecessarily. And if there was someone she could still have betrayed, knowingly or not . . ." She saw the tension increase in Pitt, from the rigidity of his body. He knew what she was going to say. "They could have killed her," she finished in a whisper.

Pitt nodded slowly. "Her address?"

"Fifteen Dorchester Terrace," she replied. "Just off Blandford Square. It is only a few streets away. You may need to hurry, in case things are moved . . . or hidden . . ."

Pitt rose to his feet. "I know."

Pitt took Stoker with him, explaining as they went. It was, as Vespasia had said, no more than a quarter of a mile away, and they walked at a rapid pace. He barely had sufficient time to acquaint Stoker with a little of Serafina's history, and the reasons her fears were realistic enough that Special Branch must make certain they had not come to pass. Stoker did not question his reasoning; the mention of Austria was sufficient.

The door was opened by a parlormaid who was grim-faced and clearly in mourning. She was drawing in breath to deny them entrance when Nerissa came across the hall behind her.

"Good afternoon, Miss Freemarsh," Pitt said to Nerissa. "I am Thomas Pitt, Commander of Special Branch. This is Sergeant Stoker. We are here regarding the very recent death of Mrs. Montserrat. May we come in, please?" He said it in a manner that did not allow her to refuse, and he took the first step across the threshold before she replied.

Beneath the red blotches from weeping, her face was ashen white.

"Why? What . . . what has happened?" She

was shaking so badly that Pitt was worried she might faint.

"Please let us come in, Miss Freemarsh, where you can sit down. Perhaps your maid might bring us tea, or some other restorative. It is possible that this is unnecessary, but your aunt was a woman of great importance to her country, and there are aspects of her death that we need to assure ourselves are in order."

"What do you mean?" Nerissa gulped. "She was old and ill. Her mind was wandering, and she imagined things." She put her hands to her mouth. "This is Lady Vespasia's doing, isn't it!" she said accusingly. "She's . . . meddling . . ."

"Miss Freemarsh, is there something about your aunt's death that you wish to conceal from us?"

"No! Of course not! I want only decency and respect for her, not — not policemen tramping through the house and . . . and making a spectacle out of our family tragedy."

"It is not a tragedy that the old should die, Miss Freemarsh," he said more gently, "unless there is something about their death that is not as it should be. And I am not a policeman, I am the head of Special Branch. Unless you tell them so, no one needs to

267

think me anything other than a government official come to pay my respects to a much-admired and -valued woman."

Stoker stepped in behind Pitt and closed the front door.

Nerissa backed a little farther into the center of the beautiful hallway with its sweeping staircase and newel lamp.

"There is nothing for you to do!" she protested. "Aunt Serafina died in her sleep some time last night. The doctor says it was probably early, because . . . because when I touched her this morning, she was cold." She shivered. "Why are you doing this? It's brutal!"

Stoker fidgeted behind Pitt, shifting his weight from one foot to the other. Pitt did not know if his impatience was with Pitt or Nerissa Freemarsh, and he could not afford to care.

"If I was in your place, Miss Freemarsh, I believe I would prefer to have my mind set at ease," he said quietly. "But whether that is what you wish or not, I am afraid I must be certain; I would like to see Mrs. Montserrat, and then have the name and address of her doctor so I can see him, and perhaps the name of her lawyer as well. Special Branch will take care of the funeral arrangements, according to whatever her wishes were."

Nerissa was aghast. "Can you do that?"

"I can do whatever is necessary to safeguard the peace and welfare of the nation," Pitt replied. "But it can all be dignified and discreet, if you do not oppose it."

Nerissa waved her hand reluctantly toward the stairs. "The doctor is upstairs with her now."

Pitt swiveled around and went up the stairs two at a time. He threw open the door of the first bedroom facing the front of the house, and saw a young, fair-haired man in black bending forward over the bed. There was a gladstone bag on the floor beside him. He straightened up and turned as Pitt came through the door.

"Who the devil are you, sir, barging into a lady's bedroom like this?" he demanded. His face was fair, but his features were stronger than might have been suggested by the slenderness of his build.

Pitt closed the door behind him. "Thomas Pitt, head of Special Branch. You, I presume, are Mrs. Montserrat's physician?"

"I am. Geoffrey Thurgood. The reason for my presence here is obvious. What is the reason for yours?"

"I think our reasons are the same," Pitt

replied, coming further into the room. The ashes were cold in the grate but the colors in the room still gave it a suggestion of warmth. "To be certain as to the cause of Mrs. Montserrat's death, although I may need to know more about the exact circumstances surrounding it than you do."

"She was of advanced years, and her health was rapidly deteriorating," Thurgood said with barely concealed impatience. "Her mind was wandering more with each day. Even with the most optimistic assessment, her death could not have been very far away."

"Days?" Pitt asked.

Thurgood hesitated. "No. I would have expected her to have lived another several months, actually."

"A year?"

"Possibly."

"What was the cause of her death, exactly?"

"Heart failure."

"Of course her heart failed," Pitt retorted impatiently. "Everybody's heart fails when they die. What *caused* it to fail?"

"Probably her age. She was an invalid." Thurgood too was losing what was left of his patience. "The woman was almost eighty!"

"Being eighty is not a cause of death. I have a grandmother-in-law who is well over eighty. Regrettably, she is as strong as a horse."

Thurgood smiled in spite of himself. "Then your mother-in-law may well have another thirty years."

"There is nothing wrong with my mother-in-law, except her own mother-in-law." Pitt pulled his face into an expression of pity and resignation, thinking of Charlotte's grandmama. "Mrs. Montserrat was not a fantasist, Dr. Thurgood. She had done some remarkable things in her earlier years, and knew a great many secrets that might still be dangerous. It was not ghosts she was afraid of, but very real people."

Thurgood looked startled, stared at Pitt for a moment, then went pale. "You're serious?"

"Yes."

"May I see proof that you are who you claim to be?"

"Of course." Pitt fished in his untidy pockets and pulled out the proof of his identity and office, along with a ball of string, a knob of sealing wax, and a handkerchief. He gave the identification to Thurgood.

Thurgood read it carefully and handed it

back. "I see. What do you want of me?"

"Complete professional discretion, then the exact cause, time, and any other details you can give me about Mrs. Montserrat's death, and whether it is what you expected, or whether there are any aspects of it that surprise you or that are hard to explain."

"I can't tell you that without a postmortem . . ."

"Of course not," Pitt agreed.

"I doubt the family will agree."

"The family consists only of Miss Freemarsh," Pitt pointed out. "But I'm afraid it is not within her rights to prevent it if there is the possibility of a crime."

"You'll have to have the necessary legal —" Thurgood began.

"No, I won't," Pitt interrupted him. "I'm Special Branch, not police. I will have no trouble ensuring that the law does not stand in our way. This may turn out to be unnecessary, but it is too important to ignore it."

Thurgood's lips tightened. "I shall begin the arrangements immediately. I leave it to you to inform the family solicitor, who is bound to object; Miss Freemarsh is sure to see that he does."

Pitt nodded. He was beginning to like Thurgood. "Thank you."

■ ■ ■ ■

As Thurgood had foretold, the lawyer, Mr. Morton, was less than obliging when Pitt went to see him at his office. He sputtered and protested, and talked about desecration of the body, but in the end he was forced to yield, albeit somewhat ungraciously.

"This is monstrous! You overstep yourself, sir. I have always been of the opinion that the police force is a highly dubious blessing, and the body that calls itself Special Branch even more so." His chin quivered, and his blue eyes sparked with outrage. "I demand the name of your superior!"

"Lord Salisbury," Pitt said with a smile. "You will find him at Number Ten Downing Street. But before you leave to appeal to him, I would like a very approximate figure as to Mrs. Montserrat's estate, and information as to whom it is bequeathed to."

"Certainly not! You trespass too far." The old man folded his arms across his ample chest and glared at Pitt defiantly.

"If I have to find out by asking questions outside the family, it will be a great deal less discreet," Pitt pointed out. "I am trying to deal with this as delicately as possible, and to protect Mrs. Montserrat's heirs from unpleasantness, and possibly danger."

"Danger? What danger? Mrs. Montserrat died in her sleep!"

"I hope so."

"What do you mean, you 'hope so'?"

"She was a woman of great distinction. She deserves the best attention we can give her. If there is something untoward in her death, or in the property and papers she leaves, I wish to keep it private. Indeed, I intend to. Allow me to do it gently."

The lawyer grunted. "I suppose you have the power to force me if I refuse. And from the look on your face, and your taste for authority, you will do so."

Pitt forbore from speaking.

"She left a nice bequest for her maid, Tucker," the lawyer said reluctantly, "for whom she had considerable affection. It will take care of her for the rest of her life. Apart from that, the house in Dorchester Terrace and the balance of her estate go to her niece, Nerissa Freemarsh. It is several thousand pounds. If she is careful it will provide an income sufficient for her to live quite comfortably."

"Thank you. Are there any papers other than the ordinary household and financial ones you would expect? Any diaries?"

The lawyer looked at Pitt with gleaming

satisfaction. "No, there are not!"

Pitt had expected that answer, but it would have been remiss not to ask.

"Thank you, Mr. Morton. I am obliged to you. Good day."

Morton did not reply.

The following day Thurgood sent a message to Pitt telling him that he had completed his examination and was prepared to offer his report. He was ready to give, at least, the exact cause of death, but the circumstances he would leave to Pitt to discern.

Pitt had been to morgues before. It had been a grim part of his duty for most of his adult life, although rather less often since joining Special Branch. The moment he stepped from the bright, windy street into the building with its uncanny silence, he could smell the odors of death and chemical preservation and feel a dampness in the air. It was as if the constant washing away of blood prevented the building from ever being fully dry, or warm. To him the smells of carbolic, vinegar, and formaldehyde were worse than any other scent.

"Well?" he asked when he was alone with Thurgood in the doctor's office and the door was closed.

"Simply, it was laudanum," Thurgood

replied unhappily. "She took it regularly. She found that sleep eluded her, and often she would be awake all night, hearing every creak in the timbers of the house, imagining footsteps."

"Are you saying she finally took too much?" Pitt asked with disbelief. "Could that be accidental? Wasn't she given it by someone who knew what they were doing? Miss Freemarsh? Or the lady's maid? Tucker had been with Mrs. Montserrat most of her life. She would never have made such a mistake." It occurred to him then that Tucker could have done it on purpose, as an act of mercy to a woman living in such terrible fear. She would only have been hastening something that was inevitable. Then he remembered how, when he had interviewed Tucker briefly, before leaving for Mr. Morton's office the previous afternoon, he had seen only grief in her face. The idea melted away.

"No. This was too large a dose to have been an accident," Thurgood replied, his face betraying his unhappiness. "It was at least five times as much as she would have taken for sleep. Laudanum is not easy to overdose on because the solution is weak. One would have to take a second, or, in time, even a third dose within a short time to have it be fatal. I deliberately prepared it that way, precisely to avoid such accidents. And I made sure that both Tucker and Miss Freemarsh kept the supply out of the main bedroom or bathroom, in a cupboard with a lock."

Pitt was growing even colder. "And the key?"

"On a ring in a cupboard, whose handle was higher than Mrs. Montserrat could have reached." Thurgood looked as if he was chilled too. He stood stiffly, his hands clenched together, the bloodless skin stretched over his knuckles. "If Mrs. Montserrat had taken the same dose she was normally given at night before settling down to sleep, even if she was awake, she would have been too drowsy to have gotten up, gone from her room across the landing to the chambermaid's room, and climbed on a chair to open the key cupboard, and then a second chair to reach the medicine cabinet. No, the laudanum was administered to her by someone else. What I cannot say is whether it was an accident, but I find it hard to believe anyone could give so much accidentally." He met Pitt's eyes. "I'm relieved to say that it is not my responsibility to find out."

"I see. Thank you." Pitt was bitterly disappointed, although in all honesty he had to admit that he had not wanted to think Serafina was so far departed from reality as to have taken her own life in a haze of fear and confusion — or even deliberately, as an alternative to the mental disintegration that had already begun. It would've been a humiliating end for a brave woman.

But this looked like murder.

Was it a simple domestic tragedy fueled by greed and impatience? Nerissa unwilling to play companion and dreamer-in-waiting another year or two, or even three? Perhaps her lover was losing the will to wait for her, or she was afraid he might soon? Perhaps it was just another wretched story of family misery turning into hatred, for an imprisonment in loveless tedium. How old would Nerissa be? Mid-thirties, perhaps. How many more childbearing years did she have? Desperation was a strong force, all but overwhelming.

Perhaps it had nothing to do with Serafina's past, or Special Branch. But he must be sure.

"Thank you," he said.

Thurgood smiled without pleasure. "I'll send you a written report: amounts, and so on. But there is no doubt as to what it is, and I can't tell you anything more."

"No marks on the body?" Pitt asked. "Scratches, bruises? Anything to indicate her being held? Wrists? A cut inside the mouth? Anything at all?"

"Several," Thurgood said thinly. "She was an old woman and she bruised easily. But if she had been forced to take it against her will I would have expected to find bruises all around her wrists. It takes some strength to hold a person fighting for her life, even an old woman."

"Would you know if you were drinking laudanum?" Pitt persisted. "What does it taste like?"

"You'd know," Thurgood assured him. "If she took that much, believe me, either she took it intentionally, or under some kind of duress. The only other alternative, and I've been thinking about this, is that she took the normal dose. Then, when she was in a half-asleep state, the rest was given to her. If there were some spilled, it could be mopped up, perhaps with a little water, and there'd be no discernible trace." He shrugged with an air of hopelessness. "Even if there was, it would prove nothing. She might often spill things. She was old and shaky, sitting up in bed."

"I see. Thank you."

■ ■ ■ ■

Pitt arrived back at Dorchester Terrace later that afternoon. Already the light was fading from the sky. The footman admitted him and had him wait in the cold morning room until Nerissa sent for him to come to the withdrawing room. The curtains were drawn closed, as they had been the previous day, but she was rather more composed this time, even if just as tense.

"What is it now, Mr. Pitt? Have you not caused us sufficient distress?" she said coldly. "The doctor tells me that you have obliged him to perform an autopsy on my aunt. I don't know what purpose you believe that will possibly serve. It is a horrible thing to do, a desecration of her body that I cannot protest against strongly enough — for all the good it will do now."

"It was necessary to know how she died, Miss Freemarsh," he replied, watching her face, her anger, the clenched hands by her side. "And I regret to say that it was from an overdose of laudanum." He stopped, afraid she was going to faint. She swayed and grasped the back of the settee to steady herself.

"An . . . overdose?" she repeated hoarsely.

"I thought . . . I thought laudanum was safe. How could that happen? It was not even kept in the same room with her. We were so careful. It was in an upstairs cupboard and Tucker has the key. Even if my aunt felt that she was not sleeping well enough, she could not have gotten up to dose herself. That makes no sense!"

"What *would* make sense, Miss Freemarsh?" Pitt asked more gently.

"I beg your pardon?"

"What do you think happened?"

"I . . . I don't know. How could I? She must have . . ." She sat still, unable to finish.

"What?" He did not allow her to wait. "You have just told me that she could not have gotten up to find the laudanum herself."

"Then . . . then someone must have . . ." Her hand went to her throat. "Someone must have . . . broken in . . . or . . ."

"Is that possible?"

"I would not have thought so." She was beginning to regain a little of her composure. "But I do not know the facts. If you are quite certain that she died of too much laudanum, then I don't see what other explanation there can be. I did not give it to her, and I cannot believe that Tucker did.

She has been loyal to Aunt Serafina for years." She was staring at Pitt defiantly now. She lowered her voice just a little. "Aunt Serafina used to speak rather a lot about her past. I always believed she was making up most of it, but perhaps she wasn't. She was afraid someone would try to hurt her, to keep her from revealing secrets. If the doctor is right — and I have no idea if he is — then that may be the answer."

Pitt waited, still watching her.

"I don't know what else you expect me to say." She shook her head very slightly. "Lady Vespasia came to see her several times. Perhaps she may know who would wish my aunt harm. Aunt Serafina trusted her. She may have confided in her. I really cannot help, and I will not have you distressing the servants. None of us knows anything. I will ask them if they heard noises of any sort in the night. And of course you may ask them if anything was found, but I will not have you frightening them with the idea that we have had a murderer in the house. Do you understand me?" She shook herself a little and glared at him. "I will hold you responsible if you have them walk out in terror and leave me alone here."

It was not graceful, but it was a reasonable statement. If it was even remotely possible that someone had indeed broken in, then she had a right to be afraid.

"I will check the windows and doors myself, Miss Freemarsh," he promised. "There is no need for any of your servants to be aware that Mrs. Montserrat's death was anything but natural, unless you choose to tell them."

"Thank you." She gulped. "How am I supposed to explain your presence here?"

"Mrs. Montserrat was a woman of great distinction, to whom the country owes a debt," he replied. "We are taking care of the arrangements for her funeral, and you will not argue with us over this. It will explain my continued presence perfectly."

She let out her breath with a sigh. "Yes. Yes, that will do. I am obliged. Now what is it you wish to look at? Will it wait until tomorrow?"

"No, it will not. I'm sure your housekeeping staff is excellent. They may unintentionally remove all trace of anyone having broken in, if indeed such a thing happened."

"I . . . see. Then I suppose you had better look. Although it is more than possible that they have removed such a thing already."

Pitt gave a very tiny smile. "Of course." But if he waited until the following day, it would allow her time to *create* such evidence, and he had no intention of permitting that. "Now, if you would be good enough to show me all the windows and doors, I will examine them myself."

She obeyed without speaking again. They went to every door and window one by one, any place where anyone could possibly have gained entry. As he had expected, he found nothing that proved, or disproved, that someone might have broken in. He examined the key to the cupboard where the laudanum was kept, then the cupboard itself. It was all exactly as he had been told.

He thanked Nerissa and left.

Outside in the lamplit street, wind-whipped and cold, he hailed the first hansom he could find, and gave the driver Narraway's address. He climbed in and sat sunk in thought as they bowled along, almost oblivious of where he was.

In spite of Vespasia's fears, he had not expected the doctor's findings. Suddenly the world that Serafina had apparently hinted at had become real, and he was not prepared for it. When Vespasia had told him everything, it had sounded very much like the ramblings of an old woman who was losing her grip on life and longed to be thought important and interesting for just a little longer. He had to admit he had assumed that Vespasia was seeing in Serafina a ghost of what might happen to herself one day, and was exercising kindness rather than critical judgment.

Now he needed Narraway's opinion, something to balance the thoughts that teemed in his own mind. Narraway, of all people, would not be swayed by fancy.

It did not occur to him until he was almost at Narraway's door that at this time in the early evening he might very well not be at home. He felt a sense of desperation rise inside himself and leaned forward, as if traveling faster would somehow solve the problem. He realized the stupidity of it and leaned back again with a sigh.

The hansom pulled up and he asked the driver to wait. There was no purpose in staying here if Narraway was out. He could be gone all evening. He was free to do as he wished — even take a vacation, if he cared to.

But the manservant told him Narraway was at home. As soon as he had paid the hansom, Pitt went in and was shown to the sparse, elegant sitting room with its book-lined walls. The fire sent warmth into every corner, and the heavy velvet curtains were drawn against the night.

Pitt did not bother with niceties. They

285

knew each other too well, and had long ago dispensed with trivia. Now the balance was more even between them. Though Narraway was the elder, the command was Pitt's.

"Serafina Montserrat is dead," Pitt said quietly. "She died some time during the night before last."

"I know," Narraway replied gravely. "Vespasia told me. What is there about it that concerns you? Is it not better that she went before her mind lost all its grasp, and fear and confusion had taken over? She was once a great woman. The cruelties of old age are . . . very harsh." He waited, dark eyes steady on Pitt's, knowing that there had to be something else. Pitt would not have come simply to share grief. "Did she say anything dangerous before she died?"

"I don't know," Pitt answered. "It seems possible, even more so than I thought. She died of an overdose of laudanum." He saw Narraway flinch but he did not interrupt. "According to the postmortem, it was many times the medically correct amount," Pitt continued. "Miss Freemarsh said that the bottle was kept locked in a cupboard in the maid's pantry, and was higher than Mrs. Montserrat could have reached, even had she had the key. I checked and she is right. I questioned the lady's maid, Tucker, and

she agrees. I searched the house, and while it is not impossible that someone broke in, there is nothing that indicates it."

Narraway bit his lip, his face troubled. "I assume there is no possibility she could have accidentally been given a large dose? Or that she deliberately took it?"

"No, the doctor has assured me that it couldn't have been done unknowingly. And she didn't handle the bottle herself, which rules out deliberately too, unless Tucker helped her."

"A killing performed out of mercy to hasten what was inevitable, but before Serafina betrayed all that she had valued?" Narraway asked. "Not a pleasant thought, but imaginable, in extreme circumstances?" His lips tightened into a bitter line. "I think I would be grateful if someone were to do that for me."

Pitt considered it. He tried to picture the frail, elderly maid, after a lifetime of service, doing her desperate mistress the last kindness she could, the final act of loyalty to the past. It made perfect sense, and yet, thinking of Tucker's face, he could not believe it.

"No. After having spoken to Tucker, I don't believe that she would do such a thing."

"Not even to save Serafina from having

the same thing done to her by somebody else, perhaps more brutally? Not a quiet going to sleep from which she didn't waken, but perhaps strangling, or suffocating with a quick, hard pillow over the face?" Narraway asked. "This would have been gentle. If not Tucker, perhaps the niece, Miss Freemarsh? She could have done it as easily."

"I thought of that," Pitt replied. "But I don't think the niece has any understanding of what Serafina accomplished in the past, or any profound loyalty to her. The possibility that someone else coerced Tucker into it is more likely, but I don't believe that either."

"Reason? Instinct?"

"Instinct," Pitt replied. "But they could have gotten to the niece. That's possible. And I think she's lying about the circumstances of Mrs. Montserrat's death, at least to some degree. There are two reasons I can see as to why she might lie. One, a certain amount of fairly natural resentment could blossom out of spending one's youth as a dependent, a companion and housekeeper, while childbearing years slip away."

Narraway winced. "You make it sound pretty grim."

"It is pretty grim. But it's better than not having a roof over your head," Pitt pointed out. "Which may well have been her only alternative. I'll have it looked into, just in case it matters."

"And the other reason?"

"I think she has a lover."

Narraway smiled. "So her life is not as grim as you painted it, after all?"

"Depends on who he is, and what he's after," Pitt responded drily. The thought flickered through his head that Narraway seemed to know comparatively little about women. It was a surprise to perceive how having a wife, and also children, was such a large advantage in that sense.

Narraway was watching him, his face grave, an intense sadness in his eyes.

"Poor Serafina," he said softly. "Murdered after all." He rubbed the heel of his hand across his face. "Damn! If someone killed her, it means she knew things that still matter. She had all sorts of connections in the whole Balkan area: Austria, Hungary, Serbia, Croatia, Macedonia, and of course most of all in northern Italy. She was part of all the nationalist uprisings from '48 onward. If there's something brewing now, she might have known who was involved: connections, old debts."

Pitt did not have to weigh whether he should tell Narraway about the current assassination threat. It was never a possibility in his mind that Narraway would betray anything.

"We have word that there might be an assassination attempt on Duke Alois Habsburg when he visits here in a couple of weeks," he said very quietly. He did not yet want to tell Narraway what a bloody and violent plan it was.

"Alois Habsburg?" Narraway was stunned. "For God's sake, why?" He took a deep breath. "Is he far more important than we ever supposed? What does the Foreign Office say?"

"That I have a severe case of inflated imagination," Pitt replied. "Due, in all likelihood, to having been promoted beyond my ability."

Narraway swore, with a vocabulary Pitt had not known he possessed.

"But Evan Blantyre is taking it very seriously, and has already given me a great deal of help," Pitt added.

"Blantyre? Good. He knows as much about the Austrian Empire as anyone, probably more than the Foreign Secretary. If he thinks it's serious, then it is. God, what a mess! But I don't understand: Why Duke Alois?" He bit his lip. "Have you considered the possibility that Special Branch is actually the target, and Duke Alois is incidental?"

"Yes," Pitt said softly. "He may be simply a convenient pawn, the man in the right place at the right time. Perhaps it doesn't matter who's killed, as long as it's done here."

"But could he be a troublemaker, like Crown Prince Rudolf?" Narraway asked doubtfully. "Socialist sympathies? Does he write articles for left-leaning papers, with dangerous philosophical ideas, or subversive elements of any sort?"

"No," Pitt replied. "As far as we can find out, he's a totally harmless dabbler in science and philosophy. If he hadn't been distantly royal, and with money, he probably would have been a university professor."

Narraway frowned. "There's a hell of a lot we don't know about this, Pitt, and you need to find out damn quickly. How much help is Blantyre being? And why?"

Pitt smiled bitterly. "I thought of that too, but the answer's fairly simple. He sees the pivotal position of Austria in Europe, and the increasingly fragile threads that hold the empire together. One really good hole ripped in it, such as would be caused by a major scandal — something that, say, forced the Austrians to react violently against one of the smaller member nations like Croatia — and the whole fabric could unravel."

Narraway looked skeptical. "Croatia has caused trouble for years," he pointed out. "And Blantyre, of all people, knows that."

"There is something new in it," Pitt argued. "Blantyre pointed it out to me. We now have a unified Germany, with the strong, energetic power of Prussia at the head. If Slavic Croatia seems to be the victim of German-speaking Austria's aggression, Slavic Russia will very naturally come to its aid. Newly unified German-speaking Teutonic Prussia will come to Vienna's aid, and we will have a European war in the making that we might not be able to stop."

"God Almighty!" Narraway said in horror as the enormity of it dawned on him. "Then guard Alois with your life, if necessary. Use Blantyre, use everybody. I'll do all I can, starting with finding out what happened to poor Serafina Montserrat, particularly whether she knew anything about this." His face was ashen but there was a tension in his body, as if every nerve in him had come alive. His breathing was faster. There was a tiny muscle jumping in his temple, and his slender hands were locked rigidly together as he leaned forward. "We have to succeed."

"I know," Pitt agreed quietly.

"And Serafina's death?" Narraway asked. Then, when Pitt did not answer immediately, he continued. "I have nothing to do, at least nothing that matters. Let me look into that. It may be important, but even if it has nothing to do with politics and is merely some miserable domestic tragedy, she deserves better than having it be ignored."

Pitt stared at him for several seconds.

"I assure you, I have solved the occasional crime before now," Narraway said, his eyes bright with amusement. "You will be challenging me no more to step into your shoes than I have you stepping into mine."

Pitt drew breath to apologize, then changed his mind and simply smiled.

"Of course. She does deserve better."

Charlotte reasoned that just because Pitt could not tell her about his current case, that did not mean that she could not use her own intelligence and considerable deductive powers to work out what she could do to be of use to him anyway.

It was perfectly obvious that Evan Blantyre was important to Pitt. At dinner at the Blantyres' house, the men had spent the rest of the evening in the dining room with the door closed, and had given instructions to the butler not to interrupt them unless sent for. When they had finally emerged, they had seemed in close agreement about something. Pitt had expressed a gratitude that was far deeper than the thanks one owes for a good dinner and a pleasant evening.

On the way home he had said nothing, but Charlotte had seen that the tension in him had eased somewhat; certainly that night he had slept better than for over a week.

Therefore she judged it a good idea to cultivate a friendship with Adriana Blantyre. This was not in the least difficult, since she had liked her instinctively, and found her unusually interesting. Having grown up in Croatia and then northern Italy, Adriana had a different perspective on many things. And she was certainly a very agreeable person, in spite of the anxiety that was often in her face, and the sense Charlotte had that there were secrets within her that she shared with no one. Perhaps that was because those secrets were rooted in experiences an Englishwoman could not even imagine.

So Charlotte had invited Adriana to visit an exhibition of watercolors with her that afternoon. Adriana had accepted without hesitation.

They met at two o'clock on the steps of the gallery and went inside together. They laughed a little as they clutched at their hats, the wind picking up even the heavy cloth of winter skirts, whose edges were dampened by rain.

Adriana was dressed in a warm wine color, which lent a glow to her pale skin. It was a beautifully cut costume with a slightly sporty air, which made one think of a hunting dress. Her hat was narrow-brimmed, tipped well forward, and had a towering crown. It looked vaguely Austrian. Charlotte saw at least a dozen other women glance at Adriana and then look away, their faces filled with disapproval and envy. Everyone else looked dull in comparison, and they knew it.

Adriana saw, and seemed a little abashed.

"Too much?" she asked almost under her breath.

"Not at all," Charlotte said with amusement. "You may guarantee that at least three of them will go straight to their milliners tomorrow morning and demand something like it. On some it will look wonderful, and on others absurd. Hats are the hardest things to get right, don't you think?"

Adriana hesitated a moment to make sure that Charlotte was serious, then her face relaxed into a wide smile. "Yes, I do. But with hair like yours it seems a shame to wear a hat at all. But I suppose you must, at least out in the street — oh, and in church, of course." She laughed lightly. "I wonder if God had the faintest idea how many hours we would spend in front of the glass rather than on our knees, fussing over what to wear to worship Him."

"In what to be seen while worshipping Him," Charlotte corrected her. "But if He is a man, as everyone says, then He probably did not think of it." She smiled, and walked side by side with Adriana across the wide entrance hall and into the first display room. "But if He is a woman, or had a wife, then He would certainly know," she continued softly, so as not to be overheard. "Presumably He invented our hair. He must have at least some idea how long it takes to pin it up!"

"Every picture I have seen of Eve, she has hair long enough to sit on!" Adriana exclaimed. "To cover her . . . womanly attributes. I don't think mine would ever grow so long."

"Of course, a number of gentlemen have very little hair at all, especially in their advancing years," Charlotte replied. "You should feel free to have as wide a skirt and as large a hat as you please."

They went around the paintings slowly, looking at each one with care.

"Oh, look!" Adriana said in sudden excitement. "That is just like a bridge I used to know near where I was born." She stood transfixed in front of a small, delicate pastoral scene. It was simple: a small river meandering over its bed and disappearing beneath a stone bridge, the light shining in the water beyond. Cows grazed nearby, so perfectly depicted that it seemed as if at any moment they would amble out of the painting.

Charlotte looked at Adriana and saw a range of emotions in her face. She seemed very close to both laughter and tears.

"It's beautiful," Charlotte said sincerely. "You must find it very different here. I sometimes wish I had grown up in the country, but if I had, I think I would miss it so terribly that I might never reconcile myself to paved streets and houses close to each other — not to mention noise, and smoke in the winter."

"Oh, there's mud in the country," Adriana assured her. "And cold. And in the winter it can be unbearably tedious, believe me. And so much darkness everywhere! It closes in on you in every direction, almost without relief. You would miss the theater, and parties, and gossip about famous people, rather than just the talk of your neighbors: Mrs. This about her grandchildren; Mr. That about his gout; Miss So-and-so about her aunt, and how bad the cook is."

Charlotte looked at her closely, trying to see how much she meant what she was saying, and how much she was very lightly mocking. After several seconds, she was still uncertain. That was invigorating. It was a bore to always be able to read people.

"Perhaps one should have a city home for the winter to go to the theater and operas and parties," she said with an answering half-seriousness, "and a country home for the summer, to go for rides and walks, to dine in the garden, and . . . whatever else one chooses to do."

"But you are English." Adriana was close to laughter now. "So you spend the summer in town and go to your country estate for the winter, where you gallop around the fields behind a pack of dogs, and apparently enjoy yourself enormously."

Charlotte laughed with her, and they moved to the next painting. Charlotte only barely noticed Adriana glance back once at the gentle bridge in the sun, with the cows grazing nearby. She must have loved Blantyre very much to have left behind the country she clearly adored and come to England.

"Have you traveled to many places in Europe?" she asked aloud. "I have never been to Italy, for instance, but from the pictures I have seen, it is very beautiful indeed."

"It is," Adriana agreed. "But I have found that it isn't really places that matter; it all comes down to people, in the end." She turned to look at Charlotte. "Don't you agree?" There was complete honesty in her eyes, and almost a challenge.

"Yes. I suppose I like London because the best things that have happened to me have happened here," Charlotte agreed. "Yes, of course it is all to do with people; in the end, it comes down to being with those you love. Beauty is exciting, and thrilling; you never entirely forget it, but you still need to share it with someone."

Adriana blinked and turned away. "I don't think I really want to go back to Croatia. It wouldn't ever be the same. My family is gone . . ." She stopped abruptly, as if she regretted having begun. She straightened her back and shoulders, and moved to another painting, depicting a girl of about sixteen sitting on the grass in the shade of a tree. She was wearing a pale muslin dress, and the dappled light made her seem extraordinarily fragile, as if not altogether real. She had dark hair, like Adriana. In fact, the resemblance was remarkable.

Adriana stared at her. "It was another world, wasn't it? Sixteen?" she said at last.

"Yes," Charlotte agreed, thinking back to being with Sarah and Emily in the garden at Cater Street every summer when they were young.

Adriana moved a little closer to her. "She looks so delicate," she said, facing the painting. "She probably isn't. I was ill a lot as a child, but I have been well for years now. Evan doesn't always believe it. He treats me as if I need watching all the time: extra blankets, another scarf, gloves on, don't step in the puddles or you'll get your feet wet. You'll catch a cold." She pulled her lips into a strange, rueful half-smile. "Actually I hardly ever get colds. It must be your bracing climate here. I have become English, and tough."

This time it was Charlotte who laughed. "We get colds," she admitted. "Some people seem to always be coughing and sniffling. But I'm very glad to hear that you have outgrown your ill health. If you are strong now, that's all that counts."

Adriana turned away quickly, tears slipping down her cheeks.

"I'm sorry!" Charlotte said instantly, wondering what she had said. Had Adriana lost someone to a simple illness? Perhaps a child? How tragic and painful, if that was the case.

Adriana shook her head. "Please don't be. One cannot go backward. There are always losses. I don't think there is anyone in the world I ever loved as I cared for my father. I wish he could know that I am well and strong here, and that I . . ." She waved her hand impatiently. "I apologize. I shouldn't even allow the memories to come to my mind. We all lose people." She looked back at Charlotte. "You are very patient, and gentle."

"I had two sisters. I lost one of them," Charlotte said quietly. "Sometimes I think of her and wonder what it would be like if she were still alive. If we would be better friends than we were then." She forced her memory back to those dreadful days when the family, the whole neighborhood, looked at each other with fear, when she had realized how little she knew of what the people closest to her really believed in, loved, or dreamed of.

She blushed now, when she wondered if

Sarah had known that Charlotte had been in love with Dominic, Sarah's husband. That was something she preferred not to recall. Everyone had embarrassing moments in their past, pieces they would like to live over again, to create a better outcome.

She linked her arm in Adriana's. "Come on, let's go and get a hot cup of tea, and maybe some cake, or crumpets. You mentioned where you first met Mr. Blantyre the other evening. It sounded far more romantic than London. I first met Mr. Pitt when he was investigating a fearful crime near where I lived, and we were all suspect, at least of having seen something and lying about it, in order to protect those we loved. It was all grim and awful. You have to have a better tale to tell than that."

Adriana looked at her with interest, and then, as their eyes met for longer, with understanding. "Certainly," she said cheerfully. "Tea and crumpets, then I'll tell you how Mr. Blantyre and I met, and more about some of the really wonderful places I've been. The blue and green lakes in the mountains in Croatia. You've never even imagined such colors! They lie like a necklace dropped carelessly by some great goddess of the sky. And I wish I could really describe for you the forests of Illyria," she

went on. "They are all deciduous trees, and in the spring, when the young leaves are just out, it is as if the whole world were newly made."

Charlotte tried to imagine it. Perhaps it was something like a beech forest in England, but she did not want to put words to it, or try to compare.

"And we have the Dinaric Alps," Adriana went on. "And caves, dozens of them, seven or eight hundred feet deep."

"Really?" Charlotte was amazed, but mostly she was moved by the depth of emotion in Adriana's voice, the passion behind her words. "Have you been in some of them?"

Adriana shivered. "Only once. My father took me, and held my hand. There is nothing on earth darker than a cave. It makes the night sky, even with clouds, seem full of light. But you should see Istria, and the islands. There are over a thousand of them strung all along the coast. Those in the farthest south are almost tropical, you know."

"You must miss such beauty, here."

"I do." Adriana gave her a sudden smile of great warmth; then she changed the subject abruptly, as if the memories of her own country were too overwhelming to continue discussing. "Vienna is marvelous," she said cheerfully. "You have never really danced till you have heard a Viennese orchestra play for Mr. Strauss. And the clothes! Every woman should have a dress to waltz in, once in her life. Come!"

Charlotte obeyed, falling into step with her.

The following day Charlotte was in the parlor giving serious consideration to the matter of whether to buy new curtains, possibly in a different color, when she heard Daniel shouting angrily. He must have turned at the bottom of the stairs to go along the passage to the kitchen, because his feet were loud on the linoleum.

The next moment Jemima came after him.

"I told you you'd break it!" she shouted. "Now look what you've done!"

"I wouldn't have if you hadn't left it there, stupid!" Daniel shouted back.

"How was I to know you'd go banging around like a carthorse?" Jemima was at the bottom of the stairs now.

Charlotte came out of the parlor. "Jemima!"

Jemima stopped in the passage and swung around, her face flushed with anger. "He broke it!" she said, holding up the remnants

of a delicate ornamental box. She was close to tears from fury and disappointment.

Charlotte looked at it and knew it was beyond mending. She met Jemima's eyes, so much like her own.

"I'm sorry. I don't think there's anything we can do with that. I don't suppose he meant to."

"He didn't care!" Jemima retorted. "I told him to be careful."

Charlotte looked at her, and imagined how tactful Jemima's warning had likely been. "Yes," she said calmly. "You'd better put it in the wastebasket, under the lid so you don't keep looking at it. I'll go and speak to him."

Jemima did not move.

"Go on," Charlotte repeated. "Do you want to make it better, or worse? If I talk to him about it in front of you, it will definitely make it worse, that I can promise you."

Reluctantly Jemima turned around and climbed slowly back up the stairs.

Charlotte watched her until she had disappeared up the next flight as well, to her own bedroom, then she went along to the kitchen.

Minnie Maude was peeling potatoes at the sink. Daniel was sitting on one of the chairs at the kitchen table, swinging his feet and looking miserable and angry. He glared at Charlotte as she came in, ready to defend himself from Jemima if she was immediately behind.

"Did you break it?" Charlotte asked.

"It was her fault," he responded. "She left it in the way!"

"Did you mean to?"

"Of course I didn't!"

"Daniel, are you sure?"

"Yes! That's not fair! I didn't see it."

"That's what I thought. So what are you going to do about it?"

He looked at her resentfully. "I can't put it together again," he protested.

"No, I don't think anybody can," she agreed. "I think you'll have to find her another one."

His eyes widened. "I can't! Where would I get it?"

"You won't get one just like it, but if you save up your pocket money, you might find one nearly as nice."

"She shouldn't have left it there!" He drew in a deep breath. "It'll be all my money for weeks! Maybe months!"

"What if she puts in half?" Charlotte suggested. "Her half for leaving the box in the way, your half for not looking where you were going and breaking it?"

Reluctantly he agreed, watching to see if she was pleased.

"Good." She smiled at him. "Now Minnie Maude will get you a piece of cake, then you will go upstairs and tell Jemima you are sorry, and offer to share pocket money with her to find another box."

"What if she says no?" he asked.

"If you ask nicely, and she refuses, then you are excused."

He was happy. He turned to Minnie Maude and waited for the promised cake.

"I'm going out for a little while," Charlotte told them both. "I may be an hour or two, or even longer. Minnie Maude, please tell Mr. Pitt, if he comes home before I do, that I've gone to visit my sister."

"Yes, ma'am," Minnie Maude agreed, reaching for the cake.

Charlotte did not bother to change. She took her coat, hat, and gloves and left immediately, before she could lose the conviction within herself that she must go to Emily and make peace with her.

She walked briskly along Keppel Street to Russell Square, where she caught a hansom. During the ride, she composed in her mind, over and over, what she would say, how she would vary her answers according to Emily's responses, and how best to keep both of their tempers in check.

The weather was getting milder. She passed several carriages bowling along briskly with ladies out visiting, or simply taking the air. Another month and it would be a pleasure to go to the botanical gardens. Trees and shrubs would begin to show green leaves, even flower buds. There would be daffodils in bloom.

She arrived at Emily's spacious, handsome house and alighted. She paid the driver, then walked up to the front door and pulled the bell.

She waited only a few moments before the door was opened and a footman greeted her with apologies.

"I'm sorry, Mrs. Pitt, but neither Mr. nor Mrs. Radley is at home. You are welcome to come in and take a little refreshment, if you would care to?" He held the door wide and stepped back to allow her to pass.

Charlotte felt ridiculously disappointed. It had never occurred to her that Emily would be out at this hour, but of course that was perfectly reasonable. All her screwing up of courage, her swallowing of pride, was to no avail.

"Thank you," she accepted, going into the warmth of the hallway. It was windy outside. Already the light was fading from the sky, and dusk was in the air. "That would be very pleasant. Perhaps I may leave a message for Mrs. Radley?"

"Certainly, ma'am. I shall bring you a pen and paper, unless you would prefer to use Mrs. Radley's desk in the morning room?"

"That would be a very good idea. Thank you."

"I'll have your tea served here when you return. Would you care for hot crumpets and butter as well?"

She smiled at him, liking his thoughtfulness. "Yes, please."

She found the paper in Emily's desk and wrote:

Dear Emily,

I came by on the spur of the moment, because I quite suddenly realized how little I wish to quarrel with you. There is nothing of such importance that I should allow it to make me unreasonable or illtempered.

She hesitated. Maybe she was taking rather too much of the blame for what had been, at the very least, quite as much Emily's fault? No, better to continue in this vein. She could always be a trifle sharper if Emily took advantage. And it was true: none of the differences mattered, in the end.

All that is good outweighs everything else, and small differences must not be allowed to matter.

Affectionately,
Charlotte

She folded the note and put it in her reticule, then put the top back on the ink and laid the pen down.

She returned to the morning room, and hot tea and crumpets were served to her a few moments later. She gave her note to the footman, thanked him, and sat down to enjoy her treat, before going back outside into the cold to look for a hansom to take her home again.

CHAPTER 7

Breakfast on Keppel Street on March the fifth was as busy as usual. Daniel and Jemima had to get off to school, homework packed in satchels, boots on, coats buttoned, and with scarves and gloves that matched each other. No matter how much care was taken the evening before, there always seemed to be something to hunt for. It was a sharp, icy morning with a knife-edge to the wind. Scarves were tied tightly. A button was found hanging loose. Charlotte hastily fetched a needle, thread, thimble, and scissors to attach it more securely before she bundled them both out the front door. At least there was now a tentative peace between them and they went down the pavement side by side.

Pitt had been debating with himself whether to seek Charlotte's opinion about the next step he planned to take in the case of Duke Alois, or not to trouble her with it.

If he was mistaken, either way, he would jeopardize his position, and therefore the future of them all. Even Minnie Maude, standing at the sink washing dishes, would be without a job, or a home.

Did he want to tell Charlotte because she might actually help, or simply because it would be less lonely for him?

Charlotte took a small piece of cheese out of the cupboard near the door. "Have we got any more of this in the back pantry?" she asked Minnie Maude.

Minnie Maude took her hands out of the water. "I'll go an' look, ma'am," she said quickly.

"No, it's all right. You're busy. I'll see myself," Charlotte replied, turning to do so.

"No!" Minnie Maude dripped water on the floor in her haste, then wiped her hands on her apron. "I'll go. I'm not sure where I put it." She went almost at a run, her heels clattering on the floor. Archie and Angus, the two cats curled up together in the wood basket by the stove, opened their eyes. Archie spat with irritation.

Charlotte shook her head, glancing at Pitt. "I don't know what it is with that girl," she said with a sigh and a smile. "I'd think she was keeping a lover in that pantry, if I didn't know better."

Pitt was startled. He put his empty cup down and stared at her in alarm.

"Oh, don't be ridiculous!" she said with a laugh. "There's nobody there, Thomas! It's just her own little bit of space. I think she goes out there just to sit and think sometimes. Coming here is a big change for her. She's very aware of trying to fill Gracie's shoes, you know." As she passed him, moving to the cupboard over the sink, she touched him gently, just brushing her hand over his hair. "You should understand that."

So she had seen his apprehension about trying to fill Narraway's place, perhaps more keenly than he had wanted her to. But why should he have doubted it? She had known him longer and better than anyone else in his life. Hers was not a blind love, nor one that chose to believe only what was comfortable. It was open-eyed, which perhaps was the only type of love that was safe in the end, and therefore infinitely precious.

"She's good, though, isn't she?" he asked.

"Yes, she's excellent," Charlotte answered. "But she's not Gracie, and I have to keep remembering that. By the way, Gracie came by the other day. She looks so happy I couldn't but be happy for her too."

"You didn't mention it!" he said quickly.

"You were rather occupied with Jack and

Lord Tregarron."

"Oh. Well, I intend to see the prime minister today, so that will probably make it even worse. I'm sorry."

She bit her lip. "Don't be. Emily'll get over it. She's desperate for Jack to succeed. I hope he doesn't know how much. I hope he has no idea how afraid she is that he might not. I can't imagine living with that."

"I don't think she needs to worry —" he began.

"Thomas! I'm not talking about her!" she protested. "I mean him! He would know she doubted him."

He drew in a deep breath. "Aren't you afraid for me . . . at least sometimes?" He instantly wished he had not asked, but it was too late.

"You've already succeeded at enough things that I can live with a failure or two," she said perfectly steadily. "Nobody wins all the time, unless what they're aiming at is pretty easy."

For a moment emotion robbed him of any words at all. His chest was so tight that he gulped in a breath. He grasped her hand and pulled her toward him and held her until he heard Minnie Maude's footsteps in the corridor.

She came in holding a large wedge of

cheese and Charlotte took it from her with a wide smile.

Pitt said good-bye, and went into the hall for his coat.

Pitt sent his request through the right channels, but he refused to explain himself to footmen or secretaries.

"I am Commander of Special Branch, and I need to advise the prime minister of an incident that, if we do not prevent it, could be disastrous to Great Britain." He gave no more detail than that, except that the matter was urgent.

It was a little after midday when he was received at Downing Street, residence of the prime minister, the Marquess of Salisbury.

"Good afternoon, Commander," Salisbury said grimly. He held out his hand, since it was the first time they had met in this present capacity. "I trust this is as grave as you imply?" There was warning in his tone that, if he had been misled, the consequences for Pitt would be unpleasant.

"If it takes place, yes, sir," Pitt replied, sitting in the chair Salisbury indicated. "I am hoping we can prevent it."

"Then you had better tell me what it is, and quickly. I have a meeting with the chancellor of the Exchequer in forty minutes." Salisbury sat opposite him, but was clearly not at ease.

Pitt had already decided, while walking here through the rising wind, trying to keep his hat on, that he would say nothing about the likelihood of the threat to European stability, unless he was asked. His answer should be clear: no prevaricating or defending himself in advance.

"The assassination of Duke Alois Habsburg, grandnephew of Emperor Franz Josef of Austria, sir. He is due to visit one of our own queen's great-nephews, here in London, in eleven days' time. It appears as if the murder itself may be committed by causing a major rail crash between Dover and London." He forced himself to add no more. Salisbury's expression of dismay told him that the Foreign Secretary had not relayed the earlier warning Pitt had given him.

"A rail crash? Good God!" Salisbury's long, pale face went a shade paler. "I suppose you are perfectly sure of what you're saying?" He squinted at Pitt, as if it was his eyesight he disbelieved rather than his hearing.

Pitt chose his words carefully. The prime minister's reaction today, and his future confidence in Pitt's judgment, depended on them.

"I am sure that such an attempt is being planned, sir. However, I do not know by whom, nor where it will take place. So far I am certain only that the duke's route from Vienna all the way to London is being checked by people we know as anarchists, men with backgrounds of violence. We cannot afford to take the threat lightly."

"Lightly? What sane man would?" Salisbury was irritated; he had been caught on the wrong foot because no one had prepared him.

Pitt tried to think what Narraway would do. Pitt could not treat the Marquess of Salisbury as an equal, as Narraway might have, but he needed to remain in control of the situation.

"Only someone who disbelieved it, sir," he said quietly. "And on the face of it, there seems to be no reason to harm Duke Alois, so the attempt makes little sense."

Salisbury nodded.

Pitt continued, "I need to find out if in fact someone else is the intended target, or alternatively, if Duke Alois is far more important than he seems. All I can learn so far is that he is a quiet, rather academically inclined young man who spends his time studying philosophy and science, but at no one else's expense. He is quite well liked, has plenty of money of his own, is unmarried so far, and has no political affiliations that we can trace. In other words, he is perfectly harmless."

Salisbury's face was grim. "Whose wife or daughter is he sleeping with?" he asked.

Pitt grimaced. "That I don't know. But if that were the case, it seems an extreme way of dealing with it — plotting such a violent assassination, and in a foreign country."

"You are right," Salisbury agreed. "Quite likely he has political convictions we don't know about — and that's not impossible; Crown Prince Rudolf certainly had. He was a walking disaster waiting to occur, according to my information, after the fact, of course."

Pitt made no comment. That was a diplomatic issue, not Special Branch's.

"It could be that either Duke Alois is very much cleverer than he pretends to be," Salisbury went on, "or the target is someone in his retinue. Alternatively, the whole thing has another purpose, such as to embarrass Britain and put us at a serious disadvantage in some future negotiation. You must prevent it. Whatever help you need, get it. What is it you want from me?" He frowned. "Why aren't you in the Foreign Secretary's Office?"

"Lord Tregarron does not believe the threat is real, sir," Pitt replied. "But Mr. Evan Blantyre does."

Salisbury sat without moving for several moments. "I see," he said finally. "Well, we'll go with your judgment, Pitt. Take whatever steps you need to make absolutely certain that when Duke Alois comes to England, he has a safe and happy visit, and leaves in peace. If he is killed, let it be in France, or Austria, not here. And, please God, not by an Englishman." He bit his lip and stared at Pitt, his voice suddenly husky. "You don't suppose that this rail crash is a diversion, and it is actually the queen these lunatics are after, do you?"

That was a thought that had not even crossed Pitt's mind. "No, sir, I don't," he said, hoping to God he was right, but far from sure. "Although it might be advisable for Her Majesty not to visit this young man in Kensington Palace. We have more than enough guards present to take care of her in Buckingham Palace." He allowed himself the barest smile. "I am sufficiently acquainted with Her Majesty to know that advice for her safety will be received well."

Salisbury grunted. "True. And I have not

forgotten your accomplishments at Osborne. That is principally why you are in the position you are, and why I listen to you."

Pitt felt the heat burn up his face. He had not referred to that incident in order to remind the prime minister of his own success, and now he felt extraordinarily clumsy to have mentioned it at all.

Salisbury smiled. "You are not in an enviable position, Commander. But it is my belief that you are the best man for the job. I would be deeply obliged if you would prove me right."

Pitt stood up, his legs a little stiff. "Yes, sir. Thank you."

When Pitt returned to Lisson Grove he found a message from Blantyre waiting for him, asking Pitt to contact him as soon as possible. Pitt telephoned, and they met at Blantyre's club for a late luncheon.

Pitt had never been in such a place before, except as a policeman investigating a case and thus coming to speak to one of the members. Now, he was conducted by a uniformed steward who treated him with the respect he'd show any other guest. They walked through the oak-paneled corridors, hung with hunting scenes and Stubbs's paintings of horses. The men's feet were soundless on the carpet. Blantyre was waiting for Pitt at the entrance to the dining room, and together they went to the table and took their seats, watched by life-sized portraits of the Duke of Wellington, the Duke of Marlborough, and a rather fanciful portrait of Henry V at Agincourt.

"All a bit military, isn't it?" Blantyre said with an apologetic smile. "But the food's excellent, and they'll leave us alone as long as we wish, which is rather what I need at the moment. I recommend the roast beef — it's really very good — with a decent Burgundy. A trifle heavy, I know, but well worth it."

"Thank you," Pitt accepted. His mind was too occupied with why Blantyre had called this meeting to be concerned with what he might eat.

The steward came and Blantyre ordered for both of them, including the wine. As soon as they were alone, he started to speak.

"This young man, Duke Alois," he said, looking at Pitt, his dark brows puckered. "Did you find out anything more about him?"

"I can find nothing that would make him worth anybody's time or energy to assassinate," Pitt replied. "If he is indeed the target, then I have to assume that there is a completely different reason for killing him."

"My thoughts precisely," Blantyre agreed. "I have called on friends in Austria, and in Germany too. All I can find is that he is a harmless young aristocrat who intends nothing more adventurous than to while away his life studying the subjects that interest him."

"Are you certain?" Pitt pressed.

Blantyre indicated the food just served them. "Please eat. You will enjoy it. And yes, I am certain. My informants tell me he was offered a very agreeable post in diplomacy, and declined it. At least he was honest enough to say that he had no disposition to be restricted in such a way."

Pitt was beginning to feel impatient with Duke Alois, but he did not show it.

"On the other hand," Blantyre went on, beginning to eat his meal, "he also appears to listen with great attention to the music of Gustav Mahler, and even Schoenberg, this new young composer who creates such odd, dissonant sounds. Is he interested and looking for meaning, or merely for a new experience? I think the latter more likely." There was a sadness in his voice and in his dark eyes. "A typical Austrian: one eye laughing, the other weeping. But I think it is better to do a small thing well than nothing at all. However, I am not a royal duke, thank God. Nothing is expected of me."

Pitt looked at him with a new appreciation of his sympathy and imagination. He had raised, as if perfectly natural to him, issues that Pitt had not considered.

"It is peculiarly repugnant to kill someone so innocent of any harm, or use," Blantyre said wryly. There was no malice in his tone, only a slight sadness. "Is it a good thing or a bad thing not to be worth anyone's effort to kill you?" He said it with a gentle, droll humor, looking at Pitt very directly.

Pitt answered with hesitation. "At times, most comfortable, and unquestionably safer, but I think in the end I should regret it. It seems like an opportunity wasted, let slip through your fingers like dry sand."

Blantyre sighed. "I suppose you sleep better, for whatever that is worth? But I'd rather not spend my entire life emotionally asleep, however intellectually absorbing my pursuits."

Pitt watched silently as the steward poured more of the dark Burgundy into their cut-crystal glasses; the light burned red through them.

"But this is not why I asked you to come," Blantyre said, his face emptying of all pleasure. "Events seem to have taken a new turn. A man named Erich Staum has been seen in Dover, apparently working as a road sweeper." He stopped, watching Pitt closely. "He is known to certain political authorities in Vienna as an assassin of unusual skill and imagination."

To give himself time to think, Pitt sipped more wine. It was extremely good, a quality he was totally unused to. Perhaps it would have been familiar to Narraway.

"I suppose you are sure about this?" he asked with a smile, looking at the wine in his glass.

"There is doubt," Blantyre admitted. "But very slight. He has a face that is not easy to forget, especially his eyes. The man in question was dressed in ill-fitting and dirty clothes, with a broom in his hands; but if one imagines him upright and shorn of the submissiveness, he is too like Staum to ignore the probability. He has used the guise of a railway porter before, and also a hansom cab driver, and a postman."

"I see," Pitt said quietly. Dustmen pushed carts with their equipment, and collected rubbish. No one gave them a second glance. It was the perfect disguise to carry explosives. People take no notice of a road sweeper, not to mention his cart. "Why

Duke Alois?" he asked, looking up at Blantyre again. "We still have not answered that."

"Staum is for hire." Blantyre shook his head very slightly, barely a movement at all. "Anarchists don't always select victims for any reason. But you know that better than I do."

His hands clenched on his knife and fork. "Things are getting worse, Pitt, more dangerous every year. Violent socialism is rising, national borders are moving around like the tide. There seems to be unrest everywhere and wild ideas and philosophies multiplying like rabbits. I admit, I am afraid for the future." There was no melodrama in his voice, just a foreboding and the darkness of real fear. It shadowed his face, making his features pinched, more ascetic.

Because Pitt respected him, he felt the weight of his responsibility settle even more heavily on him.

"We'll protect Duke Alois, regardless of whoever's after him, and whatever the reason," he said grimly.

Blantyre let out a sigh. "I know. I know." He reached out and poured the rest of the Burgundy into their glasses. He did not offer a toast.

Pitt had no difficulty reaching the Foreign

Secretary. Clearly Salisbury had been as good as his word. However, as far as canceling Duke Alois's visit, nothing had changed.

"I'm sorry," the Foreign Secretary said grimly. "It would be quite impossible to cancel the visit now. Such a thing would signal to all Europe that Britain cannot guarantee the safety of a member of a foreign royal family visiting our own monarch." His voice became even sharper. "It would be a flag of surrender to every predator in the world. Surely you see that it cannot even be considered?"

Reluctantly, Pitt had to agree. He could imagine with horrible clarity the results that would follow.

"Yes, sir, I do see," he said quietly. "I would very much like to know who is behind this. I will not let it go until I do."

It was late and Pitt was tired, but he felt that he must speak with Narraway; however, he was torn, because to do so was a kind of yielding, an admission that he needed advice. He hesitated even as he walked along the cold street, his breath making wispy trails in the air.

But not to speak with him was to set his own vanity above the lives of the men and women who would be killed if there really was a train crash. Not to mention the all-but-crippling damage to the service to which he was sworn.

He reached Narraway's door with no indecision left, and when the manservant let him in, he accepted the offer of supper and hot tea. Blantyre's wine at luncheon had been more than he was used to.

"Any progress on Serafina Montserrat's death?" he asked Narraway as they sat by the fire, Pitt leaning toward it, warming his hands after the cold walk.

"Not yet," Narraway answered. "But you didn't come just to ask me that."

Pitt sighed and sat back in the chair. "No," he conceded. "No, it is something rather bigger than that."

"Pitt, stop beating around the bush," Narraway ordered.

Briefly Pitt told him what he feared about a possible rail crash and what Blantyre had said at lunchtime about Duke Alois's visit.

"If it's Staum," Narraway said quietly, "then there's a lot of money involved. He has no loyalty to anyone, and he is expensive. If he has ever failed, we don't know about it." He thought for a few more moments in silence, staring at the fire.

Pitt waited.

"Staum has no loyalties, no interests,"

Narraway said at last. "A rail crash, with all the civilian casualties, is very extreme. Even anarchists are not usually so indiscriminate; this could kill scores of people."

"I know."

"Either the target is someone so well guarded they cannot reach him any other way — but that profile doesn't fit Duke Alois at all — or else it is a decoy."

"I've thought of that!" Pitt said more sharply than he had intended. It was not anger speaking but fear.

"Any rumor of something else that might be happening, however slight?" Narraway asked. "What else is vulnerable?"

Pitt gave him a thorough update on every issue, even the most trivial and seemingly irrelevant. They were all issues going back to Narraway's own time as head of the Branch, so there could be no question of confidences broken.

"Who else is traveling with the duke?" Narraway asked when he had considered them all and come up with nothing.

"No one who seems important," Pitt replied, feeling the sense of helplessness twist even more tightly inside him. "And time is short. We have little more than a week before he comes."

Narraway sighed. "Then my best guess is

that the rail crash is a diversion, because the assassination will happen before they ever reach the train. Staum will get Duke Alois somewhere in the streets of Dover. He won't know that we have anyone who can recognize him."

"That's true. In fact, how did Blantyre recognize him, do you think?" Pitt asked.

"Austrian connection, I presume," Narraway replied. "Staum has committed a few assassinations in Europe, but never here before, so far as we know."

"Blantyre could be wrong," Pitt said.

"Of course he could. Are you willing to take that risk?"

"No. We don't have enough men to guard all the streets in Dover, especially if it means drawing them back from the points and the signals."

"Which they are counting on," Narraway agreed.

"If they blow up the main street of Dover, they'll kill scores of people, and they might still miss Duke Alois —"

"They won't," Narraway cut across him. "They'll cause a diversion at the last moment, an overflowing drain, an overturned cart, anything to force him to go down a side street, or else stand around as a stationary target while they clear the way. In those situations you must keep moving. Have several alternative routes. Never allow yourself to be cut off and have to stop." Narraway's face was deeply lined, almost haggard in the firelight. "You haven't much time, Pitt."

"Find out who killed Serafina, and why," Pitt urged.

"You really think that what she was afraid of telling someone had to do with this? She was rambling . . ."

"Do you know of a better reason someone is willing to go to this length to kill Duke Alois?" Pitt asked. "Or someone else in his retinue?"

"I think he could be incidental, just the excuse," Narraway reminded him, his voice gravelly with weariness and the tension of knowledge and fear. "Special Branch is important, Pitt. It's our defense against all kinds of violence from slow treason to anarchy that kills in minutes. If I wanted to cripple England, I would try to get rid of Special Branch first. And if I can think of that, so can others."

"I know." Pitt stood up slowly, surprised how his muscles ached from clenching them. "I'll start again tomorrow morning."

Early the next day at Lisson Grove, Pitt and

Stoker went over every detail of Alois's visit from the time he stepped aboard the steamer at Calais until he boarded it again at Dover to leave.

The office was warm, the fire beginning to burn well in the clear air after the sluggishness of rain, but there was no ease in the room.

"He'll be bringing just four men with him," Stoker said, pointing to Calais on the map spread across Pitt's desk.

"What do we know about them?" Pitt asked.

"All part of his family's regular household retainers," Stoker replied. "As far as we can tell. Nothing we can find that would make them vulnerable to betrayal. None of them gambles or has debts out of the ordinary, no love affairs with anyone of suspicious background or politics. No one drinks more than average, which is pretty high." He pulled his face into an expression of distaste. Pitt had no idea whether it was for what he imagined these men in particular to be like, or for foreigners in general.

"They're just what you'd expect of hangers-on of a minor royal duke," Stoker went on. "Decent enough, in their own way, I expect." He looked up from the map to meet Pitt's eyes, but his own were unreadable.

"Competent to guard him from an attack?" Pitt asked.

Stoker shrugged. "Can't say, because they've never had to. Honestly, sir, he's not somebody anyone would bother to attack. Are we going to put someone in with them?"

"Yes. It'll need to be someone who speaks German, if possible."

"He speaks good English," Stoker replied.

"Good. But we need to understand what they say to each other as well," Pitt pointed out.

"We've got Beck, sir, and Holbein. They're both pretty good."

"We'll use them," Pitt agreed.

Stoker raised his eyebrows. "Both?"

"Yes, both. We can't afford to fail, you know that."

Stoker stiffened. "Yes, sir. Whatever happens to the Duke, it bloody well won't happen while he's in England!" He bent to the map again, intense concentration in his face. "The ferry leaves Calais at nine in the morning, weather permitting. It should arrive in Dover at noon. He'll be the first to disembark. He has a special carriage set apart for his use." He looked up at Pitt. "What about this man Staum, sir? Are we sure it's him? How do we know it isn't someone who just looks a bit like him? His face can't be that memorable, or he'd have been caught by now."

"No, we're not certain it's him," Pitt conceded. "But using such a man makes more sense than creating a train crash that kills scores of people."

"Depends what this person, or people, hope to gain," Stoker said bitterly. "Anarchists don't usually make that much sense. That's why they're so damn difficult to predict."

"I know. And people who don't care whether they are caught always have a kind of advantage over those who do. But I don't envy them. Who the hell wants to have nothing worth living for?"

"I can't imagine what that's like." Stoker shook his head, his expression puzzled and sad. "I suppose that's why we find them so hard to catch. We just don't understand them. What about this duke, sir? Do you think he's going to do pretty much what we tell him? Or will he want to show everyone how brave he is, and behave like a fool?"

"I don't know," Pitt admitted. "I'm still trying to find out more about him, and the rest of his men."

Stoker swore gently and colorfully, under

his breath.

"Couldn't have put it better myself," Pitt agreed, surprised at the width of Stoker's imagination.

Stoker colored. "Sorry, sir."

"Don't be." Pitt smiled briefly. "I am thinking much the same, but I can't put it as concisely as you do! Your vocabulary makes me think you spent some time in the navy, but I didn't see it on your record, at least not the one they showed me."

"No, sir." Stoker was clearly uncomfortable. "It was . . . not quite official . . ." He stopped, lost for an explanation.

"Learn anything?" Pitt asked.

"Yes, sir, quite a lot." He stood still, waiting for the rest of the interrogation.

"Then it wasn't time wasted," Pitt answered. He was determined to ask Narraway one day what Stoker's story was. It would be wise to know, but it did not matter now.

"Sir —" Stoker began.

"Doesn't matter," Pitt cut him off.

"Sir . . . I was going to say that if you want me to go to Dover and travel on the train with Duke Alois, I'll do that."

"You don't have to," Pitt replied. "It'll be dangerous."

"Aren't you going?" Stoker challenged.

"Yes, I am."

"Then I'm coming too, sir. Anyway, I could use the bit of extra pay." He smiled slightly.

"Really?" Pitt spoke lightly. "Saving for something, are you?"

"Yes, sir." Stoker straightened his shoulders a little. "I want to buy a cello, sir."

Pitt could think of no possible answer to that, but he felt inordinately pleased.

CHAPTER 8

Narraway sat by the fire in his study, the gaslight turned low, and thought about Serafina Montserrat. Pitt said he had asked the doctor to keep his own counsel regarding the conclusion that her death could not have been accidental. He said he had given the doctor his word that the death would not be investigated by the police, but by Special Branch, because of its possible connection with a current case.

The possible plot against Duke Alois needed to occupy all of Pitt's attention; he could not afford to be distracted by anything else. But Narraway was not certain if his promise to investigate Serafina's death was wise. Detection was not a skill he had refined to anything like Pitt's degree. However, he still believed it possible that there was a direct link between Serafina's fears and the proposed assassination of Duke Alois. If there was, it was imperative that he find it before it was too late.

If Serafina's death was a political act by someone afraid she might reveal a long-dead scandal or personal indiscretion, surely it must have ceased to be embarrassing to anyone but the attacker himself?

He did not think, from what Vespasia had said of her, that Nerissa Freemarsh had the nature to contemplate killing her aunt as an act of compassion to free her from the mental suffering of knowing that her own mind was betraying her.

Tucker, the lady's maid? That was more likely. She was devoted to Serafina. Vespasia had told him that, and he trusted her judgment without question. She had certainly had enough maids to know, and seen dozens of others.

But then Tucker would also lose her position at Serafina's death. And she must know that she would be suspected before anyone else if an overdose was discovered. After the years of looking after Serafina, no one would believe her capable of doing such a thing accidentally.

That left only the far uglier thought that Nerissa Freemarsh had killed her aunt for personal reasons: possibly the inheritance of the house and whatever money Serafina possessed, before it was too late for her to enjoy it — or perhaps before the money had been spent on Serafina's care.

He would have to interview the household staff. There was no one else who could answer the difficult, probing questions he needed to ask. He stared up at the firelight patterns on the ceiling and tried to think of facts, physical evidence, anything at all that could prove who had given Serafina the extra laudanum. Nothing came to mind. Whoever had done it would have cleaned up after themselves. The house would be dusted and polished every day, the dishes washed, everything put back into the cupboard or onto the shelf where it was normally stored. All household staff would have access to all parts of the house, though it was likely that only Tucker and Nerissa would spend time in Serafina's bedroom, and perhaps one of the housemaids.

Had anyone else been there? Would they have been noticed? And what reason would they have to harm Serafina . . . unless they had been paid by someone? But no, that thought was absurd.

By midnight the fire had burned down. Narraway stood up, turned off the lights, and went upstairs to bed. He had not thought of any solution to his quandary, except to investigate personal motives. He had little more than a week before Duke Alois arrived in Dover.

In the morning he decided to ask Vespasia's opinion. He dressed smartly, as was suitable for a visit to a lady for whom he had not only a deep affection, but also a certain awe.

"Victor! How pleasant to see you," Vespasia said with some surprise when he was shown into the withdrawing room a little after ten o'clock. She wore a highly fashionable dress of a pale blue-green shade with white lace at the throat, large sleeves, and her customary pearls. She was smiling. She knew, of course, that he had come for a specific reason.

"Well?" she inquired, when she had sent the maid for tea.

He told her briefly the thoughts he had entertained the previous evening. She listened to him in silence until he had finished, merely moving her head fractionally every now and then in agreement.

"There is one thing you have apparently not considered," she observed. "Nerissa is not a particularly charming young woman, and, judging from her present position as companion to her aunt, she has no great means of her own."

"I know that," he said. "Maybe she decided not to risk Serafina spending all of what would be her inheritance."

Vespasia smiled. "My dear Victor, there is another consideration far more urgent in a woman's mind than mere money." She noted his expression with amusement. "Nerissa is not plain in appearance, but she is quite unaware of how to flatter or charm, to amuse, to make a man feel high-spirited or at ease. She is also rapidly coming toward the end of her childbearing years. At the moment her prospects are good; but if Serafina were to have lived even another five years, which she might have, then it would have been a different matter. Her present lover may not be willing to wait so long for Nerissa to come into her inheritance."

Narraway froze. "Her present lover! Are you certain?"

"Yes. But I am not certain if it is an affair that has any realistic hope of ending in marriage. If it does not, then privacy may be all that she desired."

"But surely Serafina Montserrat would be the last woman on earth to interfere in an affair, let alone disapprove of one?" he said reasonably.

"Perhaps. But Nerissa may not have realized that. I am not sure whether she is fully aware of Serafina's earlier life. These are things it might be profitable for you to discover."

"Yes," he agreed, ceasing the conversation while the maid brought in the tea and Vespasia poured it.

Vespasia smiled at him. "Tucker will know," she remarked, taking one of the tiny crisp cookies off the plate. "Treat her with respect, and you will learn all kinds of things."

He thought for a moment. "If this lover of Nerissa's is serious, might he have killed Serafina, to preserve the money Nerissa could inherit? With the house, it would make him very comfortable."

"Possibly." Vespasia's face expressed her pity for such a thought, and her contempt. "Which is why it is important that you discover who he is." Her eyes softened with a deeper kind of sadness. "It is also possible that his reason was nothing to do with money, or with Nerissa at all, except insofar as she gave him access to Serafina, and her disintegrating memory."

"I know," he agreed. "I will investigate that too."

After leaving Vespasia's home, Narraway rode in the hansom to visit Serafina's doctor, consumed in thought. He was starting

341

to realize how much more difficult detection was than he had originally appreciated. He was guilty of having taken Pitt's skill very much for granted in the previous years. He did not even notice the brilliant blue sky darken over, or the people on footpaths hastening their steps. He did not see the first heavy spots of rain. He was unaware of the swift change in the weather until one man lost grip of his umbrella and it whisked into the street, startling horses and causing a near-accident.

Dr. Thurgood was unable to give any further assistance. There was nothing medical to add to the bare fact that Serafina had died of an overdose of laudanum so huge that it was impossible that she had given it to herself accidentally.

He caught a hansom to go to Dorchester Terrace. On the journey he turned over in his mind the practical facts, which severely limited the number of people able to administer such a dose.

The most obvious person was Nerissa Freemarsh; not that he seriously thought it *was* Nerissa, unless her lover had built up the nerve, or the desperation, to force her into it. What could have caused that? A sudden, urgent financial need? The longing to marry before it was too late for children?

Then why now? Why not sooner? Was it really coincidental that Serafina's death had happened just before Duke Alois's visit? It was not easy to believe.

He arrived at Dorchester Terrace, alighted, and paid the cabbie, then walked up the pathway to the door. He was admitted by the footman and gave him his card.

"Good morning," he said quickly, before the man could protest that the house was in mourning and would receive no callers. "I need to speak with Miss Freemarsh. I hope she is still at home?" He was certain she would be. She was very traditional in her manner and dress, and, so newly bereaved, he was certain she would not leave the house for some time.

The man hesitated.

"Will you inform her that Lord Narraway is here, on business to do with the recent death of her aunt, Mrs. Montserrat." He did not pitch his voice to make it a request. "I shall also need to speak with the house-keeper, the maids, the cook, yourself, and Miss Tucker."

The man paled. "Yes . . . yes, sir. If you . . ." He gulped and cleared his throat. "If you would like to wait in the morning room, my lord?"

"Thank you, but I would prefer to use the

housekeeper's sitting room. It will make people more at ease."

The man did not argue. Five minutes later Narraway was seated on a comfortable chair by the fire, facing the plump, pink-faced housekeeper, Mrs. Whiteside. She looked angry and bristling.

"I don't know what you are thinking, I can tell you that much," she began, refusing to sit, even though he had asked her to.

"You are in charge of the house, Mrs. Whiteside. You can tell me about each of the servants employed here."

"You can't imagine that any of them killed poor Mrs. Montserrat!" she accused him. "I'm not standing here while you say wicked things like that about innocent people, lordship or not, whoever you are."

He smiled with amusement at her indignation, and with quite genuine pleasure at her loyalty. She looked like an angry hen ready to take on an intruder in the farmyard.

"Nothing would give me more pleasure than to prove that true, Mrs. Whiteside," he said gently. "Perhaps with some detail, you can assist me in that. Then we widen the circle to include others who might have observed something of meaning, even if they did not realize it at the time. The one thing that seems impossible to deny is that someone did give Mrs. Montserrat a very large dose of laudanum. If you have any idea who that might be, or even why, then I would be obliged to you if you would tell me."

It was the last sort of response she had expected. For several seconds she could not find words to answer him.

He indicated the chair opposite him again. "Please sit down, Mrs. Whiteside. Tell me about the members of your staff, so that I can imagine what they do when they are off duty, what they like and dislike, and so on."

She was thoroughly confused, but she did her best. A quarter of an hour into her description, she began to speak naturally, even with affection. For the first time in his life, Narraway was offered a vivid picture of a group of people utterly unlike himself, all away from the homes and families in which they grew up, slowly forming a new kind of family, with friendships, jealousies, loyalty, and understanding that gave comfort to their lives, and a certain kind of framework that was of intense importance. Mrs. Whiteside was the matriarch, the cook almost as important. The footman was the only man, Serafina not requiring a butler, and therefore he had a place of unique privilege. But he was young, and not above bickering with the maids over trivia.

Tucker, as the lady's maid, was not really either upstairs or downstairs. Her position was senior to the others, and as Narraway listened to Mrs. Whiteside's descriptions, he came to the conclusion that Tucker's position was an oddly lonely one.

"I don't know what else you want," she finished abruptly, looking confused again.

Narraway was quite certain that none of the staff had had anything to do with Serafina's death. Their own lives had been sadly disrupted by it; now, even their home was no longer assured. Sooner or later Nerissa might choose to sell the house, or might have to, and they would be separated from one another and without employment. Then again, if she suspected them of disloyalty, or of speaking out of turn to Narraway, she might dismiss them without even a reference, and that would be worse. He became suddenly sensitive to the fact that he must phrase his questions with care.

"I would like to speak to them one at a time," he responded. "And see if anyone has noticed anything out of the ordinary in the house. Something not in its usual place, moved, or accidentally destroyed perhaps."

She understood immediately. "You think somebody broke in and killed poor Mrs. Montserrat?" Her face was horrified.

"The more you describe the people here, the less likely I think it is that one of them could have gone upstairs, found the laudanum, and given Mrs. Montserrat a fatal dose."

"I must stay right in this room while you talk to the maids," she warned him.

"Of course," he agreed. "I wish you to, but please do not interrupt."

His questioning proved fruitless, as he had expected, except to confirm in his own mind that Serafina's staff was ordinary, an artless group of domestic servants, capable of occasional idleness, gossip, and petty squabbling, but not of sustained malice or evil. For one thing, they seemed far too unsophisticated for the degree of deception required to poison someone and hide all traces. For another, they confided in one another too freely to keep such a secret. Mrs. Whiteside's estimate of them was reasonably accurate. He made a mental note that if he was ever involved in detective work again, he would pay more attention to the observations of housekeepers.

Tucker was a different matter. She had been with Serafina for decades. She looked pathetically frail now, and somewhat lost; she would be cared for now, but never needed in the way Serafina had needed her.

She sat in the chair opposite Narraway and prepared to answer his questions.

He began gently, and was amused to find her observations of the other servants very similar to Mrs. Whiteside's, if a trifle sharper. But then she did not have to work with them anymore. She no longer had a position to guard.

She was not without humor, and he regretted having to move his line of inquiry to more sensitive areas.

"Miss Tucker, I have heard from Lady Vespasia Cumming-Gould that Mrs. Montserrat was losing her ability to remember exactly where she was, and to whom she was speaking. Did you know that she was afraid of letting secrets slip that might affect other people very adversely?"

She sighed and looked at him carefully. "Of course I was aware. If you had asked me five years ago, I'd never have believed such a thing could happen to a lady like Mrs. Montserrat." She had difficulty controlling her grief, and her eyes blazed at him through tears.

"Someone killed her, Miss Tucker. I am thinking it less and less likely that it was someone already in this house."

She blinked and said nothing.

"Who has visited Mrs. Montserrat in the

last three or four months?"

She looked down. "Not many. People like to feel comfortable, to be entertained or amused. If you are of a certain age yourself, seeing a living example of what can happen, or what may yet happen to you, is unpleasant."

Narraway winced internally. He had many years before he reached Serafina's age, but it would come soon enough. Would he bear it with grace?

Then he realized with a chill like ice that perhaps he too would be terrified of what he might say, and might even be murdered to ensure his silence. Suddenly Serafina became of intense importance to him, almost an image of himself in a future to come.

"Miss Tucker, someone killed her," he said with a catch in his voice. "I intend to find out who it was, and to see to it that they answer to the law. The fact that Mrs. Montserrat was old and had very little family is irrelevant. Whoever she was, she had the right to be cared for, to be treated with dignity, and to be allowed to live out the whole of her life."

Miss Tucker now let the tears roll down her thin cheeks, which were almost colorless in the late winter light.

"No one here would hurt her, my lord," she said in barely more than a whisper. "But there were others who came into the house, some to visit her, some to visit Miss Freemarsh."

He nodded again. "Of course. Who were they?"

She pursed her lips slightly in concentration. "Well, there was Lady Burwood, who came twice, as I recall, but that was some time ago."

"To visit whom?"

"Oh, Mrs. Montserrat, although of course she was very civil to Miss Freemarsh."

Narraway could imagine it: Lady Burwood, whoever she was, being polite and indefinably condescending; and Nerissa hungering for recognition, and receiving none, except secondhand through her relationship to Serafina.

"Who is Lady Burwood?" he asked.

Miss Tucker smiled. "Middle-aged, married rather beneath her, but happily enough, I think. She has a sister with a title and more money, but fewer children. She found Mrs. Montserrat more interesting than most of her other friends did."

Narraway nodded. "You are very observant as to the details that matter, Miss Tucker," he said sincerely. "Why did she stop coming?" It was a cruel question, and he knew it, but the answer might be important.

Tucker's face flushed with amusement. "Not what you assume, my lord. She fell and broke her leg."

"I stand corrected," he said wryly. "Who else?"

She mentioned two or three others, and a fourth and fifth who had come solely to visit Nerissa. None of them seemed to have the remotest connection with Austria, or past intrigues anywhere at all.

"No gentlemen?" he inquired.

She looked at him very steadily. She had kept decades of secrets, and many of them were probably of a romantic or purely lustful nature. A good lady's maid was a mixture of servant, artist, and priest, and Tucker had been superb at her job. A maid to Serafina Montserrat would have had to be.

"Please?" he said gravely. "Someone murdered her, Miss Tucker. I shall repeat nothing that is not relevant to the case. I am good at keeping secrets; until a few months ago, I was head of Special Branch." It was still painful to say that.

Perhaps she saw it in his face. "I see." She nodded very slightly. "You are too young to retire." She did not ask the question that lay between them.

"One of my own secrets came back and caught me," he told her.

"Oh, dear." There was sympathy and the very faintest possible humor in her eyes.

"Who visited the house, Miss Tucker?" he asked.

"Lord Tregarron came to see Mrs. Montserrat, twice I think. He did not stay very long," she replied. "Mrs. Montserrat was not very well on either occasion. I did not hear their conversation, but I believe it was not . . . not amicable."

"How do you know that, Miss Tucker? Did Mrs. Montserrat tell you?"

"Mrs. Montserrat knew the first Lord Tregarron, in Vienna, a long time ago."

"Tregarron's father?"

"Yes."

"Do you know the circumstances of their acquaintance?"

"I surmise them, but I do not know for sure. Nor will I imagine them for you."

"Did Tregarron speak with Miss Freemarsh?"

"Yes, at some length, but it was downstairs in the withdrawing room, and I have no idea what was said. I know it was some time only because Sissy the housemaid told me."

"I see. Anyone else?"

"Mr. and Mrs. Blantyre both came, separately. Several times."

"To see Mrs. Montserrat?"

"And Miss Freemarsh. I imagine to discuss Mrs. Montserrat's health, and what might be done to make her happier and more comfortable. I think Mrs. Blantyre was very fond of her. She seemed to be."

"Mr. Blantyre also?"

"He is very fond of his wife, and very concerned for her health. Apparently she is delicate, or at least he is of that opinion."

"And you are not?" he asked quickly.

She smiled. "I think she is far stronger than he appreciates. He likes to think she is delicate. Some men are pleased to believe themselves protectors of the weak, caring for some beautiful woman like a tropical flower that needs to be defended from every chill draft."

Narraway had never thought of such a thing, but it seemed obvious after hearing Tucker say it.

"So you believe Blantyre came in order to ensure that Adriana was not distressed by her visits to Mrs. Montserrat?"

"I think that is how he wished it to appear," she said carefully.

He noted the difference. "I see. And Miss

Freemarsh?" he asked. "Would she say the same?"

"Most certainly." A tiny flicker of amusement touched her mouth.

"Miss Tucker, I think there is something of importance that you are deliberately not telling me."

"Observations," she said quickly. "Not facts, my lord. I think you do not know women very well."

He was now realizing this for himself.

"I am learning," he said ruefully. "A difficult question, Miss Tucker, and I ask you not from personal curiosity, but because I need to know. Does Miss Freemarsh have an admirer?"

Tucker's face remained completely impassive. "You mean a lover, my lord?"

Narraway watched her intently, and still could not read the emotion behind the words.

"Yes, I suppose that's what I mean."

"Yes, she does. But I know that because I have been a lady's maid all my life, and I know when a woman is in love: how she walks, how she smiles, the tiny alterations she will make to her appearance, even when she is forced to keep the matter secret."

He nodded slowly. It made perfect sense. Tucker would know everything; those who had grown up with servants in the house came to look at them as furniture: familiar, useful, to be looked after with care, and treated as if they had neither eyes nor ears.

"Who is it, Miss Tucker?"

She hesitated.

"Miss Tucker, whoever it is may, knowingly or not, be behind the death of Mrs. Montserrat."

Tucker winced.

"Please?"

"It is either Lord Tregarron or Mr. Blantyre," she said, in little above a whisper.

Narraway was stunned. His disbelief must have shown on his face, because Tucker looked at him with a disappointment that verged on a kind of hurt. She started to speak again, then changed her mind.

"You surprise me," he admitted. "I considered both men to be very happily married, and I gather Miss Freemarsh is . . . not . . ."

"Attractive to men," Tucker finished for him.

"Quite," he agreed.

Tucker smiled patiently. "I have known of perfectly respectable middle-aged men who have been uncontrollably attracted to the strangest women," she answered. "Sometimes very rough women, laborers with their hands not even clean, and most certainly ignorant. I have no idea what it is that appeals, but it is true. With Mrs. Montserrat, men loved her courage, her passion, and her hunger for adventure. And she could make them laugh."

Narraway believed it. Briefly, for a swift, perfect moment, he thought of Charlotte, and knew why he found her in his own thoughts far too often. She had courage and passion too, and she made him laugh, but he also loved her so much because of her fierce loyalty, and the fact that she would never betray Pitt, would never even wish to.

Then he thought of Vespasia and what made her so appealing. Curiously enough, it was not her beauty. Even in her youth it had not been her beauty, dazzling though she was. It was the fire in her, the intelligence and the spirit; and, more recently, a vulnerability he would never have perceived in her, even a year ago.

"Thank you, Miss Tucker. You have been extraordinarily helpful," he said. "I promise you I will do everything I can to see that the truth of Mrs. Montserrat's death is discovered, and that whoever is responsible is dealt with justly." He did not say "according to the law." In this case, he was not certain that the two were one and the same.

■ ■ ■ ■

When Narraway finally saw Nerissa, he had already been at Dorchester Terrace for three hours. He had eaten a luncheon of cold game pie and pickles, with a dessert of suet pudding and hot treacle sauce, the same as had been eaten in the servants' dining room.

Nerissa came in and closed the door behind her. She was wearing black, with a brooch of jet. Her face was bleached of even the faintest color, and she looked tired. The skin around her eyes was shadowed. Narraway felt a moment of pity for her. He tried to imagine what her daily life had been like, and the picture he conjured up was monotonous, without light or laughter, without thoughts to provoke the mind or a sense of purpose. Had she been desperate to escape that prison? Wouldn't anyone, but especially a woman in love?

"Please sit down, Miss Freemarsh. I am sorry to have to disturb you, but there is no alternative."

She obeyed, but remained stiff-backed in the chair, her hands folded in her lap.

"I assume you would not do so if you did not have to, my lord," she said with a sigh. "I find it very difficult to believe that any of the staff here would have contributed to my aunt's death, even negligently. And I . . . I cannot think of anyone else who might have done so. But since you seem convinced that it was neither an accident, nor suicide, then there must be some other explanation. It is . . . distressing."

"I have to ask you about visitors, Miss Freemarsh," he began. "Since the laudanum was given directly to your aunt and had an almost immediate effect, it must have been given by someone who came to the house that evening." He looked down and saw that Nerissa's hands were gripping each other so tightly that the knuckles were white. "Who could that have been, Miss Freemarsh?"

Nerissa opened her mouth, gulped air, and said nothing. He could see that her mind was frantically racing as she searched for the right words; if she denied that anyone came, then the only conclusion to be drawn was that it was someone already in the house: either herself, or one of the servants. He knew from the servants themselves that after dinner had been eaten and cleared away, they had taken their own meal and retired for the day. Unless at least two of them were in collusion with each other, their time was accounted for.

Nerissa had been alone. He imagined the

long, solitary evenings, one after the other, every week, every month, stretching ahead into every year, waiting for a lover who could come only rarely. If he had called, then Nerissa herself would have let him in, possibly at a prearranged time. It might well have been their intent that the servants would be gone, so as not to know of it.

"Mrs. Blantyre came," Nerissa said softly. "Aunt Serafina was fond of her, and she enjoyed her visits. But I can't . . ." She left the rest unsaid.

"And she was alone with Mrs. Montserrat?"

"Yes. I had some domestic business to deal with . . . a slight problem with the menu for the following day. I'm . . . so sorry."

Narraway could scarcely believe it. If Tucker was not mistaken, and either Blantyre or Tregarron was Nerissa's lover, was it even conceivable that Adriana Blantyre knew this?

How could any man prefer Nerissa Freemarsh — plain, humorless, desperate Nerissa — over the beautiful, elegant Adriana? Perhaps Blantyre was weary of Adriana's delicate health, which might deny him the marital privileges he wished, and felt that that was a good enough reason to stray.

But why on earth with a plain, respectable woman like Nerissa? Perhaps because she loved him, and love was what he craved? And perhaps because no one would imagine it? What could be safer?

How had Adriana learned of it? Had it been through some careless word from Serafina? Could Adriana really be jealous to the degree that she would murder an old woman in her bed? Why? So Blantyre would have no more excuse to come to Dorchester Terrace? That was absurd.

But Adriana was Croatian; and Serafina had lived and worked in Vienna, northern Italy, and the Balkans, including Croatia. He must look more closely into their pasts before he leaped to any conclusions.

"Thank you, Miss Freemarsh," he said quietly. "I am grateful for your candor. I don't suppose you could offer any reason Mrs. Blantyre should wish your aunt any harm?"

Nerissa lowered her eyes. "I know very little, except what Aunt Serafina said, and she was rambling a lot of the time. I am really not sure what was real and what was just her confused imagination. She was very . . . muddled."

"What did she say, Miss Freemarsh? If you can remember any of it, it may help explain what has happened, especially if she also mentioned it in someone else's hearing."

Nerissa's eyes opened wide. "Mrs. Blantyre's, you mean? Do you think so?"

"Well, we don't know who else she may have spoken to." He was trying to suggest a further person, someone Nerissa could blame more easily. He did not know what he was looking for, but he could not assume it was Adriana, whatever the reason, until he had exhausted all other possibilities, and learned who Serafina herself had feared.

Nerissa sat silent for so long that Narraway was beginning to think she was not going to speak. When she finally did, it was steadily and reluctantly.

"She mentioned many names, especially from thirty or forty years ago. Most of them were Austrian, I think, or Croatian. Some Italian. I'm afraid I don't recall them all. It is difficult when they are not in your own language. She said Tregarron, but it made no sense, because Lord Tregarron could not have been more than a child at the time she seemed to believe it was. It was all very muddled."

"I understand. Who else?" he prompted.

Again she considered for several moments,

digging into memories that were clearly painful.

Narraway felt guilty, but he had to see if there were any connections, however oblique, to the proposed assassination of Alois. And even if Adriana had left Croatia as a young woman, family ties might still exist that could be relevant.

"Miss Freemarsh?"

She looked up at him. "She . . . she spoke of Mrs. Blantyre's family, the name Dragovic. I don't know what she said; it was difficult to catch it all. But Mrs. Blantyre was . . . distressed to hear it. Perhaps it awoke old tragedies for her. I can't say. Naturally I did not speak of it to her. I asked Aunt Serafina later, but she appeared to have forgotten it. I'm sorry, but that's all I can tell you about it."

"I see. Thank you very much." He rose to his feet and allowed her to lead the way back to the hall. He left her standing on the exquisite floor of the house that was now hers, looking dwarfed, crushed by the beauty of it.

"See what you think of that, Radley," Lord Tregarron said, handing Jack a sheaf of papers. They were in Tregarron's office and had been working on a delicate matter concerning a British business initiative in Germany.

"Yes, sir." Jack accepted the papers with a sense of acute satisfaction. He knew that Tregarron meant him to read them immediately. Such documents were never allowed to be taken from the building. He left the room and went to his own, smaller office. Sitting in the armchair in front of the fire, he began to read.

It was interesting. He was continually learning more about Europe in general, and the delicate balance between one nation and another, most particularly the old, ramshackle, and crumbling power of the Austrian Empire and the new, rising Germany with its extraordinary energy. Germany's culture was as old as the land itself; it had produced some of the world's great thinkers, and brilliant composers of music to enrich the human spirit. But as a political entity, it was in its infancy. All the strengths and weaknesses of youth were very evident in its behavior.

The same could be said in many ways of Italy, on Austria's southern border. The country had been unified only in language and heritage, but politically it remained the patchwork of warring city-states that it had been since the fall of the Roman Empire.

The more he read of all of it, the more fascinated he became. He was more than halfway through the pages when he came to a passage he did not fully understand. He read the passage again, made a note, and then continued until he came to the end. He went back and reread the page that had troubled him. Then he picked up the whole and took it back to Tregarron's office. He knocked on the door.

It was answered immediately and he went in.

"Ah, what do you think?" Tregarron asked. He was smiling, leaning back a little in his chair, his powerful face relaxed, eyes expectant. Then he saw Jack's expression and he frowned. "A problem?" he asked without any anxiety, but rather with a look of very slight amusement.

"Yes, sir." Jack felt foolish, but the matter troubled him too much not to raise it. "On page fourteen the phrasing of the second paragraph suggests that the Austrians are not aware of the Germans' agreement with Hauser, and we know that they are. The Austrians would profit from this quite unfairly."

Tregarron frowned and held out his hand.

Jack passed him the papers.

Tregarron read the entire page, then read

it again. Finally he looked up at Jack, his heavy brows drawn together. "You are quite right. We need to rephrase that. In fact, I think it would be better if we omitted that paragraph altogether."

"That would still mislead Berlin, sir," Jack said unhappily. "I don't know how Vienna knows about the agreement, but it's quite clear from the dispatch we had yesterday that they do. Shouldn't that be stated here?"

"Whatever Austrian intelligence has learned, it is not our concern to inform Berlin of it," Tregarron replied. His eyes hardened. "But you are perfectly correct to bring that to my attention. The reference must be taken out. Good work, Radley." He smiled, showing strong, white teeth. "You have saved us from what could have been a very considerable embarrassment. Thank you."

Later that evening, as Jack escorted Emily to a dinner party she very much wished to attend, he found his thoughts returning to Tregarron's explanation of the discrepancy in the document. It seemed an uncharacteristic error to have made; Tregarron was not a careless man. Far from it: He was meticulous in detail. How had he not seen the anomaly himself?

Emily was across the table from him dressed in pink, an unusual color for her. She had always said it was too obvious, better suited to someone darker. But this gown, with its huge sleeves emphasizing her slender shoulders and neck, and the white lace inserts in the low bodice, was extraordinarily flattering. She was enjoying herself this evening, but he could tell by the carefully controlled pitch of her voice, and the slight stiffness in the way she held her head, that she was still troubled by her quarrel with Charlotte, though she was determined not to give in until she received a more specific form of apology. His attempts to persuade her to answer Charlotte's letter had only made matters worse. She had called him an appeaser in a tone of total contempt. Her anger was with Charlotte, not him, but he knew very well not to interfere again, at least not yet.

The chatter swirled around him. He joined in politely. His charm had always been effortless, and he could give only half his attention and still seem as though he was thoroughly engaged.

Tregarron was not at this particular function, but someone mentioned his name. Jack saw the respect on Emily's face, and she spoke warmly of Lady Tregarron. Jack's mind returned again to the papers. How had Vienna known about Germany's agreement? If it was through their own intelligence service, as Tregarron had said, that meant they must have an agent operating within the British Foreign Office. And if that was true, it should have caused far greater alarm than it had in Tregarron.

Surely that must mean there was some other explanation, then? He did not know what it was, though, so he put it to the back of his mind and turned to the woman next to him, devoting his attention to her.

They did not call their carriage to take them home until well after midnight.

Emily stifled a yawn with elegance. "I enjoyed that so much," she said with a tired smile, leaning her head against his shoulder.

He put an arm around her. "I'm glad."

She turned toward him, although in the dimness of the carriage, with the shadow and light from streetlamps moving across their faces through the windows, she could not see him clearly.

"What were you worrying about? And don't tell me you weren't worrying; I know when you are giving someone your whole mind and when you are not."

He had never lied to her, but discretion was an entirely different thing.

"Political papers I saw today," he said, perfectly truthfully.

"You can manage the problem, whatever it is," she responded without hesitation. "Tomorrow it will be clear enough. I've long thought nothing much is ever well solved when you are tired."

"You are quite right," he agreed, and leaned his head back. But he did not forget it. He had already made up his mind that tomorrow he would call upon Vespasia.

"Good morning, Jack," she said without concealing her surprise when he was standing in her morning room just after breakfast. "There must be some matter of concern, to bring you so early." She studied him more closely. He had always been an unusually handsome man; now he looked restless, hiding unease with less than his usual skill.

"May I speak to you in complete confidence, Lady Vespasia?" he asked.

"Oh, dear." She sat down and gestured for him to do the same. "This sounds very grave. Of course you may. What is it that concerns you?"

In as few words as possible, he told her about the agreement with Berlin, omitting the substance of it except for the one matter that concerned Vienna. Then he explained the sentence that troubled him, and watched for her reply, never taking his eyes from hers.

"I am afraid," she said at length, "that if you are correct, then someone in the Foreign Office is giving sensitive information to Vienna that should be kept from it. I suppose you have read this particular document very carefully and you cannot be mistaken?"

"I asked Lord Tregarron if there had been an error," he replied. "He said that he would attend to it, and thanked me for my diligence."

"But that does not satisfy you, or you would not be here telling me," she pointed out.

He looked profoundly unhappy. "No," he said almost under his breath.

"Have you mentioned this to Emily?"

He looked startled. "No, of course not!"

"Or Thomas?"

"No . . . I . . ."

"Then please do not. If you speak to Thomas, he is now in a position where he will have no choice but to act. I shall deal with it."

"How? I don't expect you to do anything except advise me. I suppose I was hoping you would say that I am starting at shadows, and to forget the matter."

She smiled. "My dear Jack, you know perfectly well that you are not starting at shadows. At the very least, there has been a mistake of the utmost carelessness."

"And at worst?" he asked softly.

She sighed. "At worst, there is treason. Keep your own counsel. Behave as if you consider the matter closed."

"And what will you do?"

"I shall speak to Victor Narraway."

"Thank you."

Narraway listened to Vespasia with increasing concern. When she had finished she had no doubt that he regarded the matter with even more gravity than she had.

"I see," he said when she fell silent. "Please don't speak of it to anyone at this point, especially Pitt. We must not take his attention from Duke Alois at the moment. We have only a little more than a week before he lands in Dover."

"Is he really only a trivial person, Victor?" she asked.

"If he's more, I haven't been able to find out. At the moment it seems likely he is a victim of convenience. It is the crime that matters."

"I see. And Serafina's death?"

"Another matter that is not yet concluded."

"Then I had better leave you to pursue whichever issue you consider most urgent. I apologize for bringing you further concerns." There was the faintest gleam of humor in her eyes. He understood it perfectly, just as he knew she understood him.

"Not at all," he murmured, rising to bid her farewell. In other circumstances he would have asked her to stay, but he was already turning over in his mind how he would pursue this new investigation: which favor he would call in, which debts he might collect, upon whom to apply a certain type of pressure.

At the door she hesitated.

"Yes," he said to her unasked question. "I shall tell you."

"Thank you, Victor. Good evening."

Narraway lay awake a great deal of the night, turning over and over in his mind what Vespasia had told him, and how it might fit in with Serafina's death. He reviewed all the people he had known, in any context, who might be of help. Who could he even ask regarding such a subject as the betraying of confidential information regarding German interests? Was it a deliberate sabotaging of an Anglo-German agreement?

Why? Was it an intended deviousness, something the Foreign Office, specifically Tregarron, had not thought that Jack Radley should know? He was new to his position, perhaps a trifle idealistic, so perhaps not yet to be trusted with less-than-honest dealings?

If that was Tregarron's judgment, then it was correct. Jack had been troubled, and he had not been able to turn a blind eye.

Narraway decided that the first thing he should do was find out more about Tregarron. The Foreign Office was certainly not above deceit, as long as it was certain it could claim innocence afterward, if it became known.

Where should he begin so that his inquiries would never be learned of by Tregarron himself? The answer came to him with extraordinary clarity. Tregarron had gone to Dorchester Terrace, probably to see Serafina, perhaps to see Nerissa Freemarsh. Had Serafina still been alive, and fully possessed of her wits and her memory, she would have been the ideal person to ask. But surely a great deal of anything she knew, the excellent and loyal Tucker might also know.

He debated whether to take her some gift

as an appreciation of her time, and decided that doing so would be clumsy. Perhaps afterward he would. To begin with, simple respect would be the subtlest and most important compliment.

When he arrived at Dorchester Terrace at midmorning the following day, fortune played into his hands. Nerissa was out; Special Branch, thanks to Pitt, was paying for the funeral, but it had left it to Nerissa to deal with the actual arrangements, which had been somewhat delayed because of the necessity for an autopsy.

"I came to see Miss Tucker," Narraway informed the footman. "It is extremely urgent, or I would not disturb you at such a time."

The footman let him in and fifteen minutes later Narraway was again sitting before the fire in Mrs. Whiteside's room. Tucker was perched on the chair opposite him, a tray of tea and thinly sliced bread and butter between them.

"I am sorry to intrude on you again, Miss Tucker, but the matter cannot wait," he said gravely.

She had poured the tea but it was too hot to drink yet. It sat gently wafting a fragrant steam into the air.

"How can I help you, Lord Narraway? I

have told you all I know."

"This is a completely different matter. At least I believe it is. I would have asked Mrs. Montserrat, were she here to answer me. But as I was turning the matter over and over in my mind, I realized that a great deal of what she knew, you might also know."

She looked startled, then very distinctly pleased.

He smiled, only faintly. He did not wish her to think him self-satisfied.

"What is it you think I might know?" she inquired, picking up her cup and testing to see if it was cool enough to sip. It was not, and she took instead a slice of bread and butter.

He took one also, then began. "This is of the utmost confidence. I must ask you to speak of it to no one at all, absolutely no one."

"I shall not," she promised.

"I shall ask you as I would have asked Mrs. Montserrat. What can you tell me of Lord Tregarron? It is imperative to Britain's good name, to our honesty in dealing with other countries, most particularly Germany and Austria, that I know the truth."

She sat very upright in her chair. A tired, proud old woman, at the end of a lifetime of service, was now being asked by a man

374

— a lord — to help her country.

"The present Lord Tregarron, my lord, or his father?" she inquired.

Narraway stiffened, drew in his breath, and then let it out slowly. "Both, I think. But please begin with his father. You were acquainted with him?"

She smiled very slightly, as if at his innocence. "Mrs. Montserrat knew him intimately, my lord, at least for a while. He was married, you understand. Lady Tregarron was a nice woman, very respectable, at times a trifle . . ." She searched for the right word. ". . . Tedious."

"Oh, dear." Without realizing it, he had exactly mimicked Vespasia's tone of voice. "I see." He did see. A vision of endless polite, even affectionate, boredom sketched before him. "Was it love?"

She made a slight move with her lips. "Oh, no, just a romance, a straying to pick flowers that belonged to someone else. Vienna has a certain magic. One is away from home. People forget that it is just as real, just as good, or bad!"

"And did Mrs. Montserrat and Lord Tregarron part with ill feeling, or not?" he asked.

"Enmity, not at all. But ill feeling?" She sipped her tea. "I think Lord Tregarron was very afraid that Lady Tregarron might find out, and that would have troubled him greatly. He loved her. She was his safety, not just the mother of his children — they had one son and several daughters — but also she was socially very well connected. She was a good woman, just unimaginative, and — heaven help her — rather humorless."

"Who else knew of the affair?"

"I don't know. People are sometimes more observant than one would wish."

"I see. And the present Lord Tregarron?"

"I know less of him. He thought well of his father, but even better of his mother. He is devoted to her."

"But he wasn't devoted to his father?" he asked.

"There was some estrangement between them," she answered.

"Did Mrs. Montserrat know why?"

Tucker hesitated.

"Please, Miss Tucker. It may be of some importance," he pleaded.

"I believe he learned of his father's affair with Mrs. Montserrat, even though by that time it had been over for many years," she said reluctantly.

"Thank you, I am very grateful to you." He picked up his tea. It was at last cool enough to sip.

She frowned. "Is it of use?"

"I'm not sure. I'm not sure at all." But an idea, vague and ill-defined as yet, was beginning to form in his mind.

CHAPTER 9

Pitt felt uncomfortable sitting in the big carved chair behind the desk that used to be Narraway's and looking at Narraway himself sitting opposite, as a visitor. It was only months since their positions had been reversed.

Narraway was smartly dressed, as always: slim and elegant, his dark suit perfectly cut, his thick hair immaculate. But he was worried. The lines in his face were deeply etched, his expression without even the shadow of a smile.

It was just a few days until Duke Alois would arrive at Dover.

"I've just come from Dorchester Terrace," Narraway said without hesitation. "It's not impossible that Serafina's murder was domestic, but it's extremely unlikely."

"Who was it?" Pitt was saddened by the events at Dorchester Terrace, but not yet concerned. The infinitely deeper question of Duke Alois's possible assassination engaged all his attention.

"It seems most likely that it was Adriana Blantyre," Narraway replied. His voice was low, his face pinched with regret.

"Adriana Blantyre?" Pitt repeated, as if saying it aloud would make Narraway correct him, explain that she was not really who he had meant.

"I'm sorry," Narraway said gravely. "I know that you have had great help from her husband, and that you like Adriana herself, but I can see no reasonable alternative."

"There has to be," Pitt protested. "Why in God's name would Adriana Blantyre murder Mrs. Montserrat? How well did they even know each other? It makes no sense!"

Narraway sighed. "Pitt, you're thinking with your emotions. Use your brain. There are a dozen ways in which it might make sense. The most obvious connection is Blantyre himself. He is an expert on the Austrian Empire, against whose dominion in Italy Serafina spent most of her life fighting. They would have had a hundred acquaintances in common, friends and enemies. There could have been a score of causes on which they were on opposite sides."

"Causes that still matter now?" Pitt asked with an edge of disbelief. Adriana was at least a generation younger than Serafina. True, she was loyal to the country of her birth. He had seen her face light up at the mere mention of it. But she had been in England now for more than ten years, and Pitt had never seen her show more than a passing interest in politics, nothing to suggest that she had ever been actively involved in them before or was now.

"Did Nerissa suggest it? Perhaps she is trying to move suspicion away from herself to the only other person she could think of," he said.

"Possibly," Narraway conceded. "But Adriana was there at Dorchester Terrace the night Serafina died, and she was alone with her. Tucker confirmed that. We will probably never know what Serafina said that was the catalyst, but she was rambling, raking up all sorts of old memories, in bits and pieces that made little sense. We need to know a great deal more about Adriana Blantyre's past, and what Serafina might have inadvertently given away about it. I'm sorry.

"I can't do it," Narraway went on, a slight edge to his voice, a self-lacerating humor. "You'll need to look at Special Branch records, such as we have, of old Austrian and Croatian plots, things Serafina might have been involved in, or known about.

There isn't very much, and I can tell you where it's filed."

Pitt was pleased not to see regret in Narraway's eyes, or anything to suggest a sense of feeling excluded or isolated.

"I'll look," he said quietly. "Are we sure no one else could have been in the house?"

"Not according to Tucker. But Blantyre himself and Tregarron were both there that week."

Pitt stiffened. "Tregarron? Whatever for?"

"To see Serafina. They would hardly have gone to see Nerissa, except as courtesy demanded. At least on the surface."

"The surface?" Pitt raised his eyebrows.

"There is still the question of Nerissa's lover," Narraway said drily.

"So Tregarron knew Serafina?" Pitt picked up the original thread. "Or else he went because of the questions I asked him about Duke Alois."

"Presumably."

"Thank you."

Narraway smiled and rose to his feet. "Don't sidestep any part of this matter, Pitt," he warned. "You need to have the truth, whatever you decide to do about it."

Pitt read all the files about the Austrian oppression and revolts of the last forty years.

They were exactly where Narraway had said they would be. He learned very little of use, except where to find a certain elderly gentleman named Peter Ffitch, who had once served in Special Branch, and had an encyclopedic memory. He had retired twenty years earlier and was a widower now, living quietly in a small village in Oxfordshire.

Pitt caught the next train and was in Banbury just after lunchtime. He then took a small branch line further into the country, and after a stiff walk through the rain, arrived at Ffitch's steeply thatched house on a cobbled road off the main street.

The door was answered by a dark-haired woman of uncertain years, a white apron tied over a plain brown skirt and blouse. She looked at him with suspicion.

Pitt introduced himself, with proof of his identity, and told her that it was extremely important that he speak with Mr. Ffitch. After some persuasion she admitted him.

Ffitch must have been in his eighties, with the mild features of a child and quite a lot of white hair. Only when Pitt looked more closely into his eyes did he see the startling intelligence there, and a spark of humor, even pleasure, at the prospect of being questioned.

At Ffitch's request the woman, mollified

by his assurances, brought them tea and a generous portion of cake, and then left them alone.

"Well," Ffitch said with satisfaction. "It must be important to bring the new head of Special Branch all the way out here. Murder or high treason, at the least. How can I help?" He rubbed his hands together. They were surprisingly strong hands, not touched by age or rheumatism. He reached forward and put several more pieces of coal on the fire, as if settling in for the full afternoon. "What can I tell you?"

Pitt allowed himself to enjoy the cake and tea. The cake was rich and full of fruit, and the tea was hot. He realized momentarily how long the train journey had seemed, and how chilly the carriage had been. He decided to tell Ffitch the truth, at least as far as Serafina was concerned.

"Oh, dear," Ffitch said when Pitt was finished. His seemingly bland face was filled with grief, altering it completely. "What a sad way for such a marvelous woman to end. But perhaps whoever killed her did not do her such a great disservice."

"Perhaps not," Pitt agreed. "But I still need to know who it was, and why."

"For justice?" Ffitch said curiously.

"Because I need to know the players in

this particular drama, and what their ultimate goal is," Pitt corrected him. "There is very much on the table currently, to win or lose."

"Well, well." Ffitch smiled, his body relaxing. "I am often reminded that not even the past is safe. Strange business we are in. More than most people, our old ghosts keep haunting us." He frowned. "But you speak of present danger. Have some more tea, and tell me what I can do."

"Thank you," Pitt accepted. He glanced around the room. Ffitch may have lived in many countries, but the room was English to the bone. There were Hogarth cartoon prints on the walls, and leather-bound books on the five shelves on the far wall. From what Pitt could see they were mostly history and some of the great works of literature and commentary. He saw the light flicker on the gold lettering of Gibbon's *Decline and Fall of the Roman Empire,* and Milton's *Paradise Lost.*

Ffitch poured the tea and passed Pitt back his cup.

"Serafina," Ffitch said thoughtfully. "I knew a lot about her, but I only ever met her a few times." He smiled. "The first was at a ball in Berlin. I remember it very well. She was dressed in gold, very soft, like an evening sky. Still, she looked like a tigress, only temporarily made friendly by warmth and good food."

The smile of memory left his face. "The second was in a forest. She came on horseback, slim as a whip, and lithe. She dismounted easily and walked with such grace, wearing trousers, of course, and carrying a pistol. What is it you need to know? If you are looking for whoever murdered her, it could have been any of a hundred people, for any of a hundred reasons."

"Now, in 1896?" Pitt said skeptically.

Ffitch bit his lip. "Point taken, sir. No, not now. But some of those old victories and losses still matter, at least to those who were involved. It sounds as if you're looking for something that came to light only recently, but from some old story?"

"Looks like it," Pitt replied.

Ffitch pursed his lips. "So something she remembered, and let slip in her confusion of mind, affects someone alive today so deeply that the betrayal of it still matters." He nodded slowly. "Interesting. There were some bad things. Some treason against England in Vienna, but I never knew who was involved. I tried very hard to find out because it was important. Quite a lot of information went from the British Embassy to the Austrians, and it embarrassed us severely. Not being able to stop it was one of my worst failures." He could not hide the distress in his face.

Pitt hated embarrassing him, but he pressed the matter further. "Was it ever widely known within Special Branch?"

Ffitch looked at him bleakly. "No, not when I retired. If they had learned, I like to think someone would have told me. Perhaps I delude myself as to either my own importance or the regard they had for me."

"I doubt that," Pitt replied, hoping it was true. "I think at least Victor Narraway would have spoken of it, because if he had known, he would not have agreed that it was good for me to come out here and trouble you now."

"Ah . . . yes, Victor Narraway. Always thought he would do well. Clever man. Ruthless, in his own way. Wondered why he left. Would have thought he had many good years in him yet. But I don't imagine you'll tell me." His eyes narrowed. He looked at Pitt closely, quite openly assessing his ability, and almost certainly also his nerve.

Pitt waited, taking another piece of cake.

Ffitch sighed at last. "Serafina might have known," he said thoughtfully. "Perhaps that was what she was afraid of." He shook his head, the firelight flushing his cheeks. "In her prime she could keep a secret better than the grave. What a damn shame."

"Adriana Blantyre," Pitt said softly.

Ffitch blinked. "Blantyre? Evan Blantyre was young then, but clever, very clever. Always at the edge of things, never in the middle — at least that's how it looked from the outside."

"What things?" Pitt asked.

Ffitch looked surprised. "Plots to gain greater freedom from the Austrian yoke, what else? Italian plots, Croatian plots, even the odd Hungarian plot, although most Hungarians were willing enough to pay lip service to Vienna, and carry on with whatever they wanted to do in Budapest."

"Not Serafina?"

"Certainly not. You want to know about the ones that went badly wrong? Of course you do. They all went wrong somehow. Most simply failed, fizzled out, or succeeded for a few months. One or two ended really badly, men shot before they could succeed, tricked or trapped one way or another. Probably the best organized, the bravest of the fighters, was Lazar Dragovic. Fine man. Handsome, funny, a dreamer with intelligence and courage."

"But he failed . . ." The conclusion was

obvious.

Ffitch's eyes were sad.

"He was betrayed. Never knew by whom. But yes, he failed. The rest of the people involved escaped, but Dragovic was summarily executed. They beat him right there on the spot, trying to get the names of the others, but he died without telling them anything. They put the gun to his head and shot him, kneeling on the ground." Even so long after, the misery of it pinched Ffitch's face.

"Might Serafina have known who betrayed him?" Pitt asked quietly.

"Yes. I suppose so. But I've no idea why she wouldn't have done something about it — shot whoever it was herself. I would have. She cared for Dragovic, perhaps more than for any of her other lovers. If she knew and did nothing, she must have had a devil of a good reason."

"What sort of reason?" Pitt asked.

Ffitch considered for a few moments. "Hard to think of one. Perhaps it would've affected the lives of others, possibly several others? A better revenge? But Serafina wasn't one to wait; she would've taken whatever chance she could get at the time." He turned and looked into the flames of the fire. "I did hear a story — I don't know if it's true — that Dragovic's eight-year-old daughter was there and saw her father executed. They say Serafina had to choose between going after the man who was behind Dragovic's betrayal, or saving the child. She did what she knew Dragovic would have wanted, which was of course saving the child." He turned from the flames and looked at Pitt, eyes filled with sudden understanding. "The child's name was Adriana — Adriana Dragovic."

The room was so quiet Pitt heard the coals settle in the grate.

"What did she look like?" he asked.

"No idea, but she had delicate health. I don't even know if she lived."

Pitt was already certain in his mind as to the answer. "She did," he said quietly.

Ffitch stared at him. "Adriana Blantyre?"

"I believe so, but I will find out."

Ffitch nodded, and reached to pour them both a third cup of tea.

Pitt looked through all the old records he could find dating back thirty years to the story of Lazar Dragovic, his attempted uprising, his betrayal, and his death. There was very little, but it removed any doubt that Adriana Dragovic was his daughter, and that she had later married Evan Blantyre.

There was also little room for doubt that it was Serafina Montserrat who had taken the child Adriana from the scene of the execution, and looked after her until she could be left with her grandparents.

What was conspicuously missing was any statement indicating who had betrayed Dragovic to the Austrians, resulting in the failure of the uprising and Dragovic's own torture and murder.

Had Adriana found out who it was, after all these years? Or had she listened to Serafina's ramblings and imagined that she had learned the truth?

What damage had been done to her when she had seen her father killed? What trust had been warped forever? Pitt had spent his professional life tearing the surface from secrets so well hidden that no one else had imagined them. He had found scorching pain concealed by facades of a dozen sorts: duty, obedience, faith, sacrifice. He had seen rage so silent that it had been completely overlooked, until the dam burst and every-one in its path was destroyed.

All sorts of emotions can mask themselves as something else, until they grow too unbearable. That could be as true of Adriana Blantyre as of anyone.

■ ■ ■ ■

Pitt was too late getting home that evening to visit Blantyre, but he did so the following morning. He could not afford to allow any more time to slip through his fingers.

He arrived at Blantyre's house early, in case Evan had intended to go anywhere other than to his office.

"Another development?" Blantyre said with surprise when Pitt was shown into his study. He was busy answering correspondence; notepaper and envelopes were stacked on the corner of the desk, the cap was off the inkwell, an elegant thing in the shape of a sleeping lion, and there was a pen in his hand.

"I apologize for disturbing you," Pitt began.

"I assume it must be necessary." Blantyre put his pen down and recapped the ink. "Something has happened? More word of Duke Alois? Please sit, and tell me."

He indicated a comfortable, leather-padded captain's chair.

Pitt obeyed.

"It is the death of Serafina Montserrat that concerns me today," he answered. "I don't know whether it's connected to Duke

391

Alois or not, but I can't afford to assume that it isn't." He hated having to tell Blantyre this, but there was no escape. "I'm afraid there is no question that she was murdered. There is no other possible conclusion from the evidence." He saw the surprise and dismay in Blantyre's face and dreaded the possibility that Narraway was right. Was that why Blantyre had seemed so protective of Adriana? Because he knew she was so emotionally fragile that she could be capable of such a thing? How does any man protect the woman he loves from the demons within herself?

Blantyre was waiting, his dark eyes searching Pitt's face.

"The amount of laudanum in her body was far more than an accidental second dose could explain," Pitt went on, knowing it was irrelevant. "I have to consider the possibility that she knew something that has bearing on the reasons for the attempt on Duke Alois. And what she knew might tell us who is behind it."

Blantyre nodded slowly. "Of course. Poor Serafina. What a sad ending for such a brave and colorful woman." He lifted his shoulders very slightly. "What can I tell you that would be useful? If I had the faintest idea who was behind the attempt to assassinate

Duke Alois, I would have already told you. I am still learning whatever I can, but there are dozens of dissident groups of one sort or another within the Austrian Empire. All of them are capable of violence. I still don't know if Alois is any more than he seems to be on the surface, or if he is merely a pawn to be sacrificed in some cause we haven't yet identified — at least not specifically. All I know is, if it happens here, no one will be able to cover it up, or pass it off as an accident." His expressive face reflected a sharp, sad humor. "Or a suicide," he added.

"Are you suggesting that what happened at Mayerling was a concealed murder?" Pitt asked with surprise.

"No." Blantyre did not hesitate. "I think they did what they could to keep it private, perhaps mistakenly. Rudolf was always high-strung, veering between elation and melancholy, and his childhood was enough to turn anyone into a lunatic. God knows, his mother is eccentric, to put it as gently as possible. He grew up with literally dozens of tutors, and no friends, no parental support . . ."

Pitt did not interrupt. Blantyre spoke softly, looking not at Pitt, but somewhere beyond him.

"Austrian politics are infinitely more

complicated than ours. The Hungarians are afraid of both Germany overtaking Austria itself, to their west, and all the Slavic parts of the empire, backed of course by Russia, to the east. The Ottoman Empire is falling apart, and Russia will surely pounce there, wherever it can. Serbia and Croatia could be the gateway to a slow erosion that will eventually eat into the heart of Austria itself."

He smiled bleakly, looking at Pitt now. "And of course Vienna is a hotbed of ideas about the socialism that is raging all over Europe, the ideas and philosophies that Rudolf admired. There was nothing of the autocrat in him. He was a dreamer, a man in love with the idealism of the future as he wanted it to be."

The ashes settled in the fire with a very slight sound, but Blantyre did not move to restoke it.

"He was friendly with our own Prince of Wales," he went on. "They were distantly related, as most European royalty is, but far more than that, they were in extraordinarily similar positions. Like Edward, everything was expected of him, but he seemed to be waiting for it indefinitely. Unlike Edward, he had a wife he couldn't abide: cold, critical, boring, but eminently suitable for a

Habsburg emperor."

"And then he fell in love with Marie Vetsera," Pitt concluded.

"No. I think he just came to the end of the road," Blantyre said sadly. "There was nothing left for him to hope for. He had syphilis, among other things. Not a pleasant disease, and of course incurable."

"I have learned a great deal more about Serafina Montserrat's past," Pitt said quietly, wanting to turn the conversation back to the matter. "Including her presence at the beating and execution of one Lazar Dragovic, and her rescue of his eight-year-old daughter, Adriana." He saw Blantyre's face lose its color. If any proof had been needed of Adriana's identity, the expression on Blantyre's face would have been sufficient. "Apparently, it is still not known who betrayed Dragovic to the Austrians," he added. "Unless, of course, Serafina knew."

Blantyre breathed in and out, and swallowed. His eyes met Pitt's without wavering, but he did not speak.

"In her rambling, it is possible that Serafina told Adriana, either directly," Pitt continued, "or enough in bits and pieces that Adriana was able to piece it together and deduce the truth."

Blantyre swallowed again, with difficulty.

"Are you saying that Adriana believed it was Serafina who betrayed her father?" he asked. "Why, for God's sake? Serafina was an insurgent herself. Are you suggesting that she was secretly on the side of the Austrians?" There was intense disbelief in his voice.

"I don't know why," Pitt admitted. "It makes no political sense, from what we know, but there may be other elements that we know nothing about."

Blantyre thought for several seconds. "Personal?" he said at last.

"Perhaps." Pitt waited for him to say that Dragovic and Serafina had been lovers. Did Blantyre know that? If he had been involved in the uprisings himself, on either side, then he might. Or he might have deduced it from what others had said.

Blantyre's face twisted into a gesture of misery and contempt. "Are you suggesting that they were once lovers, and she took his rejection so bitterly that she was prepared to betray him, and the cause, to have her revenge? I find that impossible to believe. Serafina had many lovers. I never knew of her taking revenge for anything. Life was too short and sweet for that."

"And Dragovic was loyal to the cause?"

Pitt explored another line of thought.

Blantyre's eyes widened. "As far as I know. But if he wasn't, what has that to do with Serafina's death now? Are you saying that she admitted to betraying him because he was a traitor himself? That's nonsense. No one would believe her. Dragovic was a hero. Everyone knew that; he was willing to die rather than tell the Austrians who else was involved. There is no doubt about that, because no one else was ever arrested. I know that myself."

"Could he have been betrayed by one of Serafina's other lovers, out of jealousy over her?" Pitt asked. He hoped that was true. It would remove suspicion from Adriana, and he wanted that very much, for her sake, for Charlotte's, and above all for Blantyre himself.

"Yes . . ." Blantyre said slowly. "Yes . . . that makes more sense. Though God knows who!"

"Someone who cares about their reputation enough to kill Serafina in order to preserve it, and is not only still alive, but is here in London, aware that Serafina was rambling and could betray the truth accidentally," Pitt replied. "And of course, the person would have to have had access to the house in Dorchester Terrace in order to poison Serafina with laudanum. That must restrict the possibilities to a very few indeed."

Blantyre rubbed a hand across his face in a gesture of intense weariness. He sighed. "Nerissa Freemarsh?"

"Do you think so?" Pitt asked with surprise.

"She has a lover," Blantyre said. "Though I doubt very much that you will get his name from her. She is a . . . a very desperate woman, no family except Serafina, no husband, no child. Such women can be very . . . unpredictable." He frowned.

Pitt thought of Lord Tregarron, and what Tucker had told Narraway about Tregarron's visits to Dorchester Terrace. He needed to know a great deal more about that, absurd as it seemed. What on earth could Nerissa Freemarsh offer a man in Tregarron's position? A hunger, a need for his attention that perhaps his wife no longer had, unquestioning praise, a willingness to do anything he wished, which again, perhaps his wife would not? Maybe it was no more than simply a safe escape from pressure, duty, and fulfilling other people's expectations. The more he thought about it, the more reasons there seemed to be.

Had Serafina somehow discovered that,

and raised a fierce objection? Considering her own past, it would surely not be on moral grounds; possibly a concern for Nerissa's reputation and the damage such an affair would do to it, if discovered?

Nerissa might misinterpret whatever Serafina said as a moral judgment, even a condemnation. If she loved Tregarron she would see it as her aunt ruining her last chance for love.

"Apparently Lord Tregarron called to see Mrs. Montserrat."

Blantyre stiffened. "Tregarron? Are you sure?"

"Yes." There was no avoiding it any longer. "And Mrs. Blantyre visited her often. But you know that."

"They have been in touch, on and off, since that time," Blantyre said quietly, "and the death of Adriana's father is never spoken of. I don't know how much Adriana remembers. I hope very little: just confusion and pain, and then of course the loss. Her mother was also dead. Serafina had no time for a child, especially one with extremely delicate health. Adriana lived with her grandparents until I met her. She was nineteen then, and the most beautiful girl I had ever seen.

"The shadow of tragedy gave her a haunting quality, a depth other women did not have," Blantyre continued. "I would be grateful to you if you did not mention that time to her, unless it is absolutely necessary for the safety of the country. I can promise you that if she knew anything about Duke Alois, or about Tregarron, for that matter, she would have already told me, and I would have told you."

"Of course I won't mention it," Pitt promised, "unless my hand is forced — and I can see no reason that should be. But I may have to ask her about her visit to Dorchester Terrace on the night Mrs. Montserrat died, in case she saw or heard anything that can shed light on her death."

"Then you will do so when I am present." It was said gently, but it was not a request. The power in Blantyre's voice, the force of his emotion, filled the room.

"As long as you will not cause delays I cannot afford," Pitt agreed. "Of course."

Blantyre smiled very slightly, but there was a warmth in it. "Thank you. I am obliged."

Charlotte had had a delightful day with Adriana. Their friendship had become much easier and more fluid, and they laughed together often, over the amusing and the absurd.

Today they had been to an afternoon soi-rée. The singing had been very pleasant, but agonizingly serious. They had looked at each other in the middle of the performance, and had been forced to stifle giggles and pretend a sudden fit of sneezing had attacked them. An elderly lady of a very sentimental nature had been concerned for Adriana, and she had then been obliged to pretend she had suffered an unfortunate reaction to some lilies.

Charlotte had come to her rescue with a long and totally fictitious story about lilies at a funeral affecting her the same way. She had added to the verisimilitude of it by weeping, and everyone had praised her good nature and gentleness of heart — qualities she was perfectly sure she did not possess, as she admitted to Adriana later.

She had accepted the elderly lady's admiration with a straight face, and she and Adriana had excused themselves hastily before they burst into giggles.

Charlotte had arrived home still smiling. She found Minnie Maude in the kitchen clearing away tea after Daniel and Jemima. There was a pile of crusts on the plate. She whisked them away very quickly when she heard Charlotte's footsteps, swinging around to hide them with her body. Her eyes widened.

"You do look lovely, ma'am," she said sincerely. "You should get another dress that same color of goldy-brown. There's not many as can wear that."

"Thank you," Charlotte said, but in her head she was wondering why Minnie Maude was not making the children eat their crusts. She would let it go today. It would seem churlish to make an issue of a small thing after such a nice compliment. But next time she would have to say something.

"I shall be down for dinner, but I must change out of this gown. It is rather too much for the parlor, I think!" She laughed, and turned to leave.

"Can I 'elp yer, ma'am?" Minnie Maude offered. "Them back buttons, any rate."

"Thank you. That would be a good idea." Charlotte turned and allowed Minnie Maude to undo the top half dozen or so at the back of her neck. Then she started for the door again. She had reached the bottom of the stairs when she recalled that she had not asked Minnie Maude to set the table in the dining room. As she turned back, she saw Minnie whisk into the cellar with what looked like the dish of crusts in her hand.

She went up the stairs slowly. Was she not giving Minnie Maude enough to eat? The girl should not have to pick at crusts. There was plenty of food in the house, and she was more than welcome to have as much as she wished. She had settled in so well, Charlotte thought, in the way she performed her duties and with her extremely agreeable nature. She should make time to look into the matter more carefully.

But when Pitt came home he was clearly worried, and for the first time since the present case began, he wished to talk to her about it. After supper, when they retired to the parlor, she had barely begun to tell him about the soirée when he interrupted her.

"You know Adriana quite well now. You must talk to each other about many things. Does she ever mention Serafina Montserrat?" he asked.

She saw the earnestness in his face. This was not a question of polite interest.

"Only briefly," she replied, trying to read his expression. "She was very saddened by her decline."

"And her death?"

"Of course. Why are you asking, Thomas?"

"I need to know."

"That means it has something to do with Special Branch." The deduction was obvious. "So Serafina knew something of great importance, after all."

She was so used to asking questions that the old habit asserted itself before she could think. She realized it too late. "I'm sorry . . . I didn't mean to pry."

He smiled. "Not at all, Charlotte. I asked you in the first place. I need to understand Adriana a great deal more than I do. Who better to ask than you? And I cannot expect you to give me the answers I need if I don't tell you what the questions are."

His eyes were gentle, and there was an oblique humor in his face. But she heard the emotion in his voice; Adriana was somehow tied into the case, and he could not tell her about the issue that kept him at work late into the evenings and stopped him from sleeping through the night.

"What do you need to know about her?" she asked. "She talks quite freely now. I hate breaking confidences, but you wouldn't ask if it was not necessary."

"Do you know when she first met Serafina Montserrat?"

Charlotte thought back to their conversations. "No. She speaks as if she has known her as long as she can remember."

"As a child?"

"Yes. I think their encounter was brief, and at a time very painful to Adriana. They met again after Adriana was married, but I don't think she ever knew her as well as she did in the last few months. Why?"

He ignored the question. "What does she say of her father?"

Charlotte felt increasingly uneasy. "Quite a lot. Not so much directly, but she mentions him in passing; she adored him, and she had already lost her mother when he died. He seems to have been brave, funny, kind, and very clever, and to have been devoted to her. He died when she was eight. She still misses him terribly. I suppose when you lose someone when you're that young, you tend to idealize them a little, but if even half of what she recalls is true, he was a fine man. Certainly they were very close."

Pitt's face was bleak, his lips pressed close together for a moment. The sorrow his face showed worried her.

"He was," he answered. "His name was Lazar Dragovic. He was a fighter for Croatian freedom from Austrian rule. He was the leader of a spectacular plot, which failed because he was betrayed by one of the conspirators. All of the others escaped but he didn't. He was beaten and then shot because he would not give away the names of the others involved."

Charlotte was stunned, even though she had known from the way Adriana had spoken of it that her father's death had been tragic.

"I'm sorry. That's terrible. But it was thirty years ago, and in Austria. Why does it matter to Special Branch now?"

"Serafina was there. She rescued Adriana from the scene," he said simply.

"Adriana saw it?" Charlotte's stomach lurched and knotted inside her. She thought of Jemima at eight, her face soft and innocent, her eyes unafraid. She ached to reach back in time and protect the child Adriana had been.

Pitt nodded. "It was Serafina who took her away. She left Adriana with grandparents."

Charlotte had known Pitt long enough to make the leap of deduction. "Did Serafina know who betrayed Adriana's father? Is that what you are afraid of? She knew, and she told Adriana, whether she meant to or not?"

"What I'm afraid of is that Adriana thought that Serafina herself did," he admitted.

Charlotte sat frozen in her seat. She could see now why Pitt had looked so wretched. "You think Adriana killed her out of revenge?" she asked softly. "The poor old woman was dying anyway! She wouldn't do such a thing! That's horrible!"

"Her father's death was horrible, Charlotte," he pointed out. "He was betrayed by his own and — worse than that — from what my informant told me, Serafina and Dragovic were lovers. That's the worst kind of betrayal. He was beaten and killed, in front of his child. I think that warrants final revenge."

She thought of her own father, Edward Ellison; she knew him only as a rather stern man, affectionate but without the passion she believed was required in a revolutionary: a man prepared to suffer appallingly in order to change an injustice.

But then, how well had she known her father as a human being? She had taken him for granted. He was always there, calm, at the head of the table in the evenings, walking to church on Sundays, sitting by the fire with his legs crossed and a newspaper spread open. He represented safety: the comfortable, unchanging part of life; the things you miss only when, suddenly, they are not there anymore.

Adriana had lost that part of her life when she was only a child, and in a horrible way; soaked in blood and pain, right in front of her.

"Yes," she said softly. "I suppose I can imagine it easily enough."

"But did Adriana think it was Serafina who betrayed her father?" Pitt persisted. "She can't have known until very recently. Revenge like that is not content to wait thirty years. Think back; was there a time when you could see a change in her? Did she speak of Serafina at all? Even a chance remark in passing, a change in attitude, a shock of any sort. She can hardly have learned something like that without it affecting her profoundly."

They sat still for several moments. Pitt glanced at the fire and put more coal on it. There was no sound from the rest of the house.

Charlotte went over every meeting in her mind, and recalled nothing. "I'm sorry . . ." She meant it. She was torn in her affection for Adriana, but she wanted to help Pitt find the truth. "She didn't speak of Serafina often, and she didn't show any intense reaction to her at all, except pity. Honestly, Thomas, I don't think she remembers Serafina as part of her father's death."

Pitt did not immediately reply.

"Are you certain she would remember any details about it, after this length of time, even if she knew them then?" she asked softly. "And if so, wouldn't she have seen the fear in Serafina, the fact that she was helpless and slowly losing her mind, as a far better revenge than a quick way out, falling asleep painlessly in her own bed and never waking up?"

"Possibly," Pitt admitted. "But I'm not Adriana."

Charlotte thought for several moments, recalling every time she had seen Adriana: from the first meeting at the musical performance through the afternoons they had spent together, talking, laughing, each sharing with the other memories of things that had mattered to them. She did not believe Adriana could have murdered an old woman, whatever she might have been guilty of in the past.

She looked up at Pitt. "I don't know. I'm sorry. I don't believe it, but that's because I like her, and I don't want to believe it. But I know people who plan murder don't wear it in their faces, before or after. If they did, we wouldn't need detectives; we would all be able to solve crimes very easily."

"I seem to remember that you were rather good at solving crimes," he observed.

"Out of practice," she replied ruefully. "I don't want to spy on Adriana, but I'll try."

"Thank you." He reached forward and held out his hand, palm open.

She placed her hand in his, and he closed

it gently.

Charlotte was in the kitchen a couple of hours later when the telephone rang in the hall. She went to answer it. Emily was put through.

"Charlotte?" Her voice was a little tentative. "How are you?"

It was unquestionably time to accept peace, even if she had no idea what had prompted it. Had Jack said something to her? She would not ask; it did not matter at all.

"I'm very well, if a little tired of the cold," Charlotte replied. "How are you?"

"Oh . . . well. I went to the theater yesterday evening and saw a new play. It was very entertaining. I thought perhaps we could go see it together . . . I think you might enjoy it . . . that is, if you and Thomas have time?" There was a note of uncertainty in her voice that was out of character for her.

"I'm sure we can make time," Charlotte answered. "It is very good to take one's mind from anxieties for a while. I imagine it will run for another few weeks, at the very least."

"Oh . . ." The disappointment was sharp in Emily's voice now. Clearly she had hoped they would meet sooner, and now she feared this was a rebuff. "Yes, I'm sure it will."

The silence was heavy. How much could Charlotte say without breaking Thomas's trust in her discretion?

"But even if Thomas cannot come at the moment, I would like to," she said quickly. "It seems to be one of those plays worth seeing more than once. I can always take him to see it later."

She heard Emily breathe in quickly. "Yes . . . yes, it is just that type of play."

The bridge had been created. "Good," she went on aloud. "Because Thomas is so busy at the moment, he is often away from home late into the evening. Thank goodness Minnie Maude is working out so well."

"Don't you miss Gracie?" Emily asked.

"Yes, of course. But I'm also happy for her."

They talked for a few moments about trivial things: the latest word from Gracie in her new home, china she had bought and been proud to show Charlotte. None of the conversation mattered in the slightest, but as they spoke, Charlotte became more and more certain that Emily was afraid of something. Charlotte wanted to ask her outright, but their newfound peace was still far too delicate for that, so she ended the conversation cheerfully, with a silly story about a mutual acquaintance. She had Emily laughing before she replaced the receiver on its hook.

After dinner, when Daniel and Jemima had gone to bed, Charlotte told Pitt about the call.

"It was Emily who telephoned me earlier, while you were in your study," she began. "She was very agreeable. We didn't discuss our differences at all.

"She didn't mention Jack," she went on. "Not that she does always . . . but . . . Don't look at me with that patient expression! I think she's worried, even frightened. Thomas, does this thing you are investigating really have anything to do with Jack? Is he making some kind of mistake?"

"I don't know," he said quietly. "And I'm not being oblique. I just really don't."

"Would you tell me if you did?" she asked, uncertain what answer she wanted to hear.

He smiled. He knew her so very well. "No. Then you would feel guilty because you wouldn't be able to warn Emily. Better she blame me."

"Thomas . . . ?"

"Charlotte, I don't know," he repeated. "I really don't. Perhaps I am the one who is mistaken, and I'm not even sure what about. You can tell Emily we don't know anything, and do it with a clear conscience."

She made herself smile, and saw the relief in his eyes. They laughed together, but it was a little shaky. They were too much aware of what could not be said.

CHAPTER 10

Stoker was pacing back and forth in Pitt's office, his hands pushed hard into his pockets, his outdoor scarf still wound around his neck. The windowsill behind him was white with a dusting of snow, and flakes were drifting past, almost invisible against a flat, leaden sky.

"The street sweeper is Staum all right," he said, stopping and facing Pitt. "I've seen a photograph of him now."

"What happened to the previous sweeper?" Pitt asked.

"Took a vacation," Stoker replied. "Came in and told the office he'd come into a little money from some relative who'd died, and he was going away for a while. Staum was the first person to apply for the job, and no one else showed up within a day or two, so they gave it to him. Don't know what money changed hands." He pulled his face into an expression of disgust. "Might not have taken much." He winced. "On the other hand, I suppose, from what I know of Staum, he wouldn't shrink from killing the man, if it was necessary."

Pitt felt the heaviness settle inside him. "Then we can expect an attack in Dover itself. But I don't dare take men away from the signals and points, just in case." He slumped against his chair. "The dust cart was a brilliant idea. He can wheel the thing anywhere, and no one'll be surprised, or suspicious. Wear dirty clothes, a cap, keep his face down, and he's practically invisible."

"Are we going to tell the local police?" Stoker asked.

"Not yet. Once they know, it'll be public in hours. They won't be able to hide it. Everyone's behavior will be different. And a man of Staum's skill will be watching for that. He'll change plans."

Stoker's face tightened. A small muscle in his jaw flickered.

"I know," Pitt said quietly. "And I still can't find out anything more useful about Duke Alois. They say he has a nice, very dry sense of humor, and he's very fond of music, especially the heavier sort of German stuff, Beethoven's last works."

"Doesn't make any sense." Stoker was

unhappy. "We've missed something."

"Perhaps that's the point," Pitt replied thoughtfully. "You can't guard against what you can't understand or foresee."

"I want to arrest Staum, any reason at all, but I know we need to have him where we can see him in case he leads us to other conspirators," Stoker said miserably, his voice edged with anger.

"Yes, we do," Pitt agreed sharply, sitting up straight suddenly. "Watch him. He's probably too clever to give anything away, but if he doesn't know we're onto him he may slip up, contact someone."

"And then on the other hand, he may know very well that we're watching him, and keep our attention from what's really happening." Stoker hunched his shoulders. "I want to get this man."

Pitt smiled bleakly. "So do I, but it's second place to getting Alois in and out of Britain safely."

"Yes, sir."

This time Pitt was granted fifteen minutes with the prime minister without any difficulty. He did not waste any of it.

"Anything further?" Salisbury asked, standing with his back to the fire, his long face grave, his fluff of white hair standing on end.

"Yes, my lord," Pitt replied. "We know who is in place in Dover, and along the railway line, but we don't know where they intend to strike. Some of the men are definitely decoys."

Salisbury sighed. "What a bloody mess. Anything good in it at all? Such as who is behind it, and why? Why Duke Alois, and why here in England?"

"The more I learn about Duke Alois the more I believe he is of no tactical value himself."

Salisbury's eyebrows rose but he smiled. "Really . . ." His expression gave nothing away, but the amusement in his eyes conveyed his opinion of minor royal dukes. Europe was teeming with distant relatives to Queen Victoria, and at one time or another he had had dealings with most of them. "So he would be an incidental victim," he said.

"Yes, sir. Most anarchists' victims are. One person's blood is as good as another's to protest with."

"As long as it isn't your own," Salisbury added a little acidly.

"For some," Pitt agreed. "For others that's all part of it. Dying for the cause."

"God Almighty! How do we fight madmen?"

"Carefully." Pitt shrugged. "With knowledge, observation, and keeping in mind that they are mad, so don't look for sanity in their intentions."

"What do they actually want? Do you know?"

"I'm not sure that even they know what they want," Pitt answered. "Except change. They all want change."

"So they can be the ones with power, money, and privilege." It was a conclusion rather than a question.

"Probably, yes. But they are not thinking things through. If they were, they'd know that sporadic assassinations have never achieved social change. If they kill Duke Alois they'll make him out to be a martyr."

"And they'll make us out to be incompetent fools!" Salisbury said bitterly. "Which is probably what they are really after. Duke Alois is just the means to an end, poor devil."

"Yes, sir. As they see it, to the greater good."

"Stop them, Pitt. If they win, not just Britain but all civilized mankind is the loser. We can't be held ransom to fear like this."

Pitt decided to try one last time, though

418

he was fairly certain what Salisbury would say.

"Are you sure there is no point in letting him know how serious the threat is, and asking him to come at another time?"

"Yes, I'm quite sure," Salisbury replied.

Pitt drew in his breath to argue, but decided against it.

Salisbury looked at him wearily. "I'm sure because I have already tried. He insists he will be perfectly safe in your hands."

"Yes, sir," Pitt replied, his mind using many different and far less civil words.

Salisbury smiled. "Quite," he said grimly.

Charlotte was in the hall about to pick up the ringing telephone when she saw Minnie Maude come out of the cellar door and catch sight of her. Minnie Maude colored unhappily, brushed something off her arms, gave a brief smile, and turned away.

Charlotte ignored the telephone. Something was troubling the girl and it was time Charlotte learned what it was. She followed Minnie Maude into the kitchen. She was standing at the sink with a string of onions on the counter and a knife in her hand. She had cut into the first onion and the pungent scent already filled the air.

The table was completely cleared away,

the dishes washed and dried and back on the dresser. An uneaten slice of toast had disappeared. Was that why Minnie Maude had been in the cellar, to eat it herself? Had she grown up in such poverty that food was still so treasured that she felt compelled to take scraps in secret?

"Minnie Maude," Charlotte spoke gently.

Minnie Maude turned around. Her eyes were red, perhaps from the onion, but she looked afraid.

Charlotte felt a tug of pity, and of guilt. The girl was only four or five years older than Jemima, and would possibly spend the rest of her life as a servant in someone else's home, with only one room she could call her own. And in their house she was the only resident servant, so there was not even anyone else to befriend. She knew she was replacing Gracie, who had been so beloved. The loneliness, the constant effort to be good enough, must be a heavy burden at times, and yet she had nowhere to go to escape it, except the cellar.

"Minnie Maude," Charlotte said again, this time smiling, "I think it would be a good idea if you toasted some teacakes. I know we have some. Let's have them hot-buttered, with a cup of tea. Perhaps in half an hour? You work hard. A break would be nice for both of us."

Minnie Maude's shoulders relaxed. "Yes, ma'am. I'll toast 'em then." Clearly she had been expecting Charlotte to say something else.

"Are you getting enough to eat, Minnie Maude?" Charlotte asked. "You may have as much as you wish, you know. If necessary, please cook more and help yourself. We have no need to restrain ourselves. Just don't waste it." She smiled. "We have had our difficult times in the past, and it is good not to forget them, but now there is more than enough for you to eat as you like."

"I'm . . . I'm fine, ma'am." Minnie Maude's face colored pink with embarrassment, but she said nothing more. Very slowly, uncertain whether she had permission, she turned back to continue cutting the onions.

Charlotte knew she had not arrived at the truth. Perhaps the trips to the cellar had nothing to do with food; maybe Minnie Maude just wanted to be alone? That made no sense. The cellar was cold. Minnie Maude had a perfectly good bedroom upstairs, which was properly furnished and warm. The problem was something else. Temporarily defeated, she went back to the hall.

She was almost beside the telephone when it rang. She picked it off its hook and answered, and Adriana Blantyre was put through. Her voice was a little altered by the machine, but still perfectly recognizable with its huskiness, and very slight accent.

"How are you?" Adriana asked. "I am sorry to call you so hastily. This is all most improper, but there is an exhibition in a private gallery that I am very eager to see, and I thought you might enjoy it too. Have you ever heard of Heinrich Schliemann?"

"Of course!" Charlotte said quickly. "He discovered the ruins of Troy, through his love of Homer. He died a few years ago. Is something of his work on display?" It was not difficult to sound enthusiastic. It was the perfect opening for her to see Adriana again, and perhaps learn something of the evidence Pitt needed. She hoped fervently that she could help prove Adriana innocent.

"Yes," Adriana replied instantly, excitement lifting her voice. "I only just heard of it. I've canceled my other engagements and I'm going. But it would be so much more fun if you were to come with me. Please don't feel obliged . . . but if you can . . ."

"I can. We shall make a journey through time, and for a few hours today will disappear. Where shall we meet?"

"I shall come for you in my carriage in an hour. Is that too early?"

"No, not at all. I assure you, I have nothing more pressing to do, and anything else that arises can wait."

"Then I shall see you in an hour. Goodbye."

Charlotte replaced the receiver. She would tell Minnie Maude where she was going, and then change into the smartest morning dress she had and prepare to be charming, friendly, and intelligent, and — if she found out a difficult truth — betray her friend to Pitt.

She sat in front of her bedroom mirror but found it difficult to face her reflection. She despised what she was about to do, and yet she could see no alternative, except refusing to help Pitt, which wasn't an alternative at all. Someone had murdered Serafina, lying frightened and alone in her bed, terrified of the darkness that was closing in on her mind, robbing her of everything she had been, betraying her in a way against which there was no defense.

All she could hope was that her discoveries would prove Adriana innocent, not guilty.

As soon as they entered the doors of the

exhibition, the past seemed to close in around them and whisk them away. The whole display was as much about Schliemann himself as the objects he had discovered. He had died in Naples, the day after Christmas in 1890, but his energy and the power of his dreams filled the gallery. A large portrait of him hung at the entrance: a balding man with spectacles, wearing a neat formal suit with a high-buttoned waistcoat. He looked to be in his late fifties or early sixties.

"That's not how I imagined him," Adriana said with a little shrug. "He should be fierce and magnificent, a man who would not have been out of place at the time when Troy still lived."

Charlotte smiled. "Just don't let us find out that Helen of Troy was really quite plain. I couldn't bear it."

Adriana laughed. "They burned the topless towers of Ilium for her, so the poets tell us." Her eye caught another portrait on the wall a few yards away. It showed a dark-haired woman, quite young, wearing a gorgeous headdress with long, trailing pieces at the ears, and also a heavy necklace comprised of fifteen or more strands of gold.

Charlotte walked over to it, Adriana immediately behind her.

"She's rather beautiful," Charlotte said, regarding her closely. She read the inscription below: "Sophie Schliemann, wearing the treasures discovered at Hisarlik, said to be the jewels of Helen of Troy." She turned to Adriana. "I wonder what Helen was really like. I can't imagine anyone being so beautiful that a whole city and all its people were ruined because of it. Not to mention the eleven-year war, and all the death and despair it brought. Is any love worth that?"

"No," Adriana said without hesitation. "But I have often wondered about the connection between love and beauty. To marry a woman because of the way she looks, when you do not care about who she is inside that shell, is no more than acquiring a work of art for the pleasure it gives you to look at it, or to exhibit it to others. If she is not a companion to you, one with whom you share your dreams, your laughter and pain, is that not like buying food you cannot eat?"

Adriana's face was quite calm, the skin unblemished across its perfect bones, her eyes fathomless.

Charlotte was left speechless; such a life would be terribly empty. Was that how Blantyre felt about Adriana: that she was a fragile, exquisite possession? What would he feel when the first lines appeared, when the bloom faded from her cheeks, when her hair thinned and turned gray, when she no longer moved with such grace?

Charlotte had always secretly wanted to be beautiful: not merely handsome, as she was, but possessed of the kind of beauty that dazzles, the kind Aunt Vespasia had had. Now she was almost dizzy with gratitude that she looked as she did; Pitt was not only her husband, he was also the dearest, most intimate friend she had ever had, closer than Emily, or anyone else.

Collecting herself, she replied, "Poor Helen. Do you suppose that is all it was: a squabble over possessions that a whole nation paid for?"

"No," Adriana shook her head. "The classical Greek idea of beauty was as much about the mind as the face. She must have been wise and honest and brave as well."

"And gentle?" Charlotte continued. "Do you think that she had a wild and vivid sense of humor as well? And that she was quick to forgive, and generous of spirit?"

Adriana laughed. "Yes! And no wonder they burned Troy for her! I'm surprised it wasn't the whole of Asia Minor! Let's look at the rest of this." She touched Charlotte's arm and they moved forward together, marveling at the ornaments, the golden masks, the photographs of the ruins, the walls that must once have kept out the armies of Agamemnon and the heroes of legend.

"How much of it do you think is true?" Charlotte said after several minutes of silence. She must not waste this opportunity to try to learn some information that could help Thomas. "Do you think they felt all the same things we do: envy, fear, the hunger for revenge for wrongs we can't forget?"

Adriana turned from the photographs she was looking at and faced her. "Of course. Don't you?" A flicker of fear crossed her face. "Those things never change."

Charlotte racked her brain for something relevant that could continue the conversation. "Agamemnon killed his daughter, didn't he? A sacrifice to the gods to make the winds turn in his favor and carry his armies to Troy. And when he came home again eleven years later, his wife killed him for it."

"Yes," Adriana agreed. "I can understand that. Mind, she had married his brother in the meantime, so there were a lot of different emotions there. And then her son killed her, and on and on. It was a pretty nasty mess."

"Revenge often is," Charlotte said with a sudden change of tone, as if they were speaking of something present.

Adriana looked at her curiously. "You say that as if they were people you knew."

"Aren't all good stories really about people we know?"

Adriana thought for a moment. "I suppose they are." She gave a sudden, brilliant smile. "I knew coming here with you would be more fun than with anyone else! Can you spare time to have luncheon as well? There is a most excellent place near here where the chef is Croatian. I would like you to taste a little of the food from my country. It is not so very different. You will not find it too strong, or too heavy."

"I would be delighted," Charlotte said sincerely. "I know so very little about Croatia. I wish you would tell me more . . ."

"That is a dangerous request," Adriana said happily. "You may wish you had never asked. Stop me when it gets dark and you have to go home."

Charlotte felt the guilt well up inside her, but it was too late to turn back. "I will," she promised. "Now let us see the end of what

Mr. Schliemann found in Troy and Mycenae."

"Did you know he spoke thirteen different languages?" Adriana asked. "He wrote in his diary in the language of whatever country he was in. English, French, Dutch, Spanish, Portuguese, Swedish, Italian, Greek, Latin, Russian, Arabic, and Turkish. And German, of course. He was German." Her face was animated with excitement and admiration.

"He actually wrote a paper on Troy in Ancient Greek," she went on. "He was an extraordinary man. He made and spent at least two fortunes. He named his children Andromache and Agamemnon. He allowed them to be baptized, but placed a copy of *The Iliad* on their heads at the time, and recited a hundred hexameters of it. Wouldn't life be so much emptier without the world's eccentrics?" She was laughing as she said it, but there was a ring of passion in her voice and a vividness in her face that lent her the sort of beauty that made others in the room turn to look at her, as if she might, for an instant, have been Helen herself.

Charlotte thought back to the intensity of the emotion she had seen in Blantyre's face when he looked at Adriana: the protection, the pride, something that could have been lingering amazement that she should have chosen him, when she had had perhaps a dozen suitors, a score. How much did her beauty matter to him? Would he still have loved her had she been ordinary to look at? How much was her vulnerability, and his need to protect her, a part of his feelings for her?

Charlotte knew she had to learn more about Croatia, about the past there, about Adriana's father's death, and above all about Serafina Montserrat.

They finished the tour of the exhibit and Adriana's carriage took them to luncheon at the restaurant she had spoken of. She was eager to share everything about her country and the culture with which she had grown up.

"You'll enjoy this," she said as each new dish was brought. "I used to like this when I was a child. My grandmother showed me how it was made. And this was always one of my favorites. It is mostly rice with tiny little shellfish, and very delicate herbs. The art is in cooking it to just the right tenderness, and being careful with the seasoning. Too strong and it is horrible."

"Do the Croatians eat a lot of fish?" Charlotte asked.

"Yes. I don't know why, except that it's

easy to cook, and not very expensive."

"And like us, you have a long coastline," Charlotte added.

Adriana gazed at some vision inside her own mind. "Ah." She let out a sigh. "Beautiful as England is, you've never seen a shore like ours. The air is warm, and the sky seems so high, with tiny drifting clouds in wonderful shapes, delicate, like feathers, and bright. The sand is pale, no shingle, and the water is colors you wouldn't believe."

Charlotte tried to see it in her mind. She pictured blue water bright in the sun, warmth that seeped through the skin to the bones. She found that she was smiling.

"Croatia is very old," Adriana went on. "Not older than England, of course. We became part of the Roman Empire in AD 9, and we had Greek colonies before that. In AD 305 the Roman emperor Diocletian built a palace in Split. The very last emperor, Julius Nepos, ruled from there, until he was killed in AD 408. You see, we too have great Roman ruins." She said it with pride.

"Our first king, Tomislav, was crowned in AD 925." She stopped and pulled her face into an expression of resignation. "In 1102 we entered a union with Hungary; that would be after you were conquered by William of Normandy. Then in 1526 we chose a Habsburg king, and I suppose that was the beginning of the end. At least that is what my father used to say." Pain laced through her voice, and was apparent in her eyes. She looked down quickly. "That was about the time of your Queen Elizabeth, wasn't it?"

"Yes, yes, it was," Charlotte said quickly, struggling to remember. Elizabeth had died around 1600, so it must be close. She felt brutal, but she had no better chance than this. She might betray Adriana's guilt, but on the other hand, she might prove her innocence. That would be infinitely worth all her efforts and discomfort.

The second course was a white fish baked in vine leaves with vegetables Charlotte was unfamiliar with. She tried them, tentatively at first, then, aware that Adriana was watching her, with more relish. Their time was slipping away. She must introduce the subject of Serafina; how could she do it without being appallingly clumsy?

"I wish I could travel," she said, not knowing where that subject might lead. "You must miss your home. I mean the one where you grew up."

Adriana smiled with an edge of sadness. "Sometimes," she admitted.

"Do you know other people who have

lived there, beside Mr. Blantyre, of course?"

"Not many, I'm afraid. Perhaps I should seek a little harder, but it seems so . . . forced."

Charlotte took a deep breath. "Did you know Mrs. Montserrat, who died recently? She lived in Croatia once, I believe."

Adriana looked surprised. "Did you know her? You never mentioned it before." Her voice dropped. "Poor Serafina. That was a terrible way to die."

Charlotte struggled to keep from contradicting herself and letting too much of the truth into her questions.

"Was it?" She affected ignorance. "I know very little. I'm sorry if I gave the impression that I knew her myself. She was a great friend of my aunt Vespasia — Lady Vespasia Cumming-Gould."

"Lady Vespasia is your aunt?" Adriana asked with delight.

"Actually she is my sister's great-aunt, by marriage to her first husband. But we hold her in higher regard and affection than any other relative we have."

"So would I," Adriana agreed. "She is quite marvelous."

Charlotte could not afford to let the conversation slide away from Serafina. "I'm so sorry about Mrs. Montserrat. Aunt Vespasia said she died quite peacefully. At least I thought that was what she said. Was I not listening properly? Or was she . . . ? No, Aunt Vespasia would never circle around the truth to make it meaningless."

Adriana looked down at the table. "No. She wouldn't. She was a fighter for freedom too, I believe."

"Like Mrs. Montserrat," Charlotte agreed. "They knew each other long ago. Aunt Vespasia said Mrs. Montserrat was very brave — and outspoken in her beliefs."

Adriana smiled. "Yes, she was. I remember her laughter. And her singing. She had a lovely voice." She struggled for a moment, trying to catch her breath and steady her voice before going on. "My father used to say she was the bravest of them all. Sometimes she succeeded just because no one expected a woman to ride all night through the forest, and then be able to think clearly by daylight, and even hold a gun steady and shoot. He said . . ." Tears filled her eyes and ran down her cheeks. Blindly she fumbled in her bag for a handkerchief, finally finding it and blowing her nose gently.

"There is no need to apologize," Charlotte assured her. "The loss of your father must have been terrible, and I know that you still miss him very much. Did you say that Serafina was there, when he died?"

Adriana was surprised. "Yes. I . . . I must have. I don't talk about it because it always makes me lose my composure. I apologize. This is ridiculous. Everyone must be looking at me."

"Lots of people were looking at you anyway," Charlotte responded with a smile. "Men look at beautiful women with pleasure, women with envy, and if they are stylish as well, to see what they might copy. Or to see if they can find a flaw, if they are particularly catty."

"Then I will have satisfied them," Adriana said wryly.

"Nonsense. There is nothing wrong with a tender heart," Charlotte assured her. She was losing her grip on the conversation. "Did Mrs. Montserrat talk to you about your father? That must have been sweet as well as painful for you, to have someone to remember with, who could tell you stories of his courage, or just the little things he liked and disliked."

Adriana's eyes softened. "Yes. She told me about his love of history, and how he could tell all the old tales of the medieval heroes: Porga who went to the Byzantine emperor Heraclius, and had the Pope send Christian missionaries to the Croatian

Provinces in AD 640. And Duke Branimir, and on and on. Serafina knew all their names, and what they did, even though she was Italian. She enabled me to recall the stories he told me, when I had only bits of them in my mind."

Charlotte tried to imagine Adriana sitting beside Serafina's bed, waiting patiently as the old woman salvaged fragments from her wandering mind and pieced them together, bringing back for a brief moment the presence of her beloved father.

Did she remember that she had seen him beaten, covered in his own blood, and then forced to his knees and shot in the back of the head? The sight of faces distorted with rage, the gleam of light on gun barrels, the cries of terror and pain, then the stillness and the smell of gun smoke; and then Serafina coming, grasping her, holding her, hurrying her away, perhaps on horseback, on the saddle in front of her as she rode like a wild thing to escape, to protect the child Adriana.

Looking at her now, so exquisitely dressed, her skin paper white, Charlotte could see that the demons were still in her eyes. If Serafina had let something slip, been careless in even a couple of words, had she led Adriana to believe that it was she who had betrayed Lazar Dragovic?

Or had she given the name of someone else who had?

"I'm so sorry she's gone," she said to Adriana. "But Aunt Vespasia told me it was peaceful. As if she had taken much laudanum, and simply gone to sleep." Was that enough? It was a lie, of course. It was Pitt who had told her, but it was unimportant.

Adriana stared at her. "Would a double dose of laudanum kill you?"

Charlotte hesitated. What should she say? Should she evade the truth, or tell it, and see how Adriana reacted? She had to know. Pitt's case might rest on it.

"No," she answered levelly. "I believe it takes far more than that, several times a single dose."

Everyone else in the restaurant seemed as if they were moving in slow motion as Adriana stared at Charlotte. She started to speak but her mouth was so dry her voice faltered. She tried again. "Several times?"

Charlotte nodded. "Apparently."

"Then . . ." Adriana did not finish the sentence, but it was not necessary. They both knew what the end was.

"I'm sorry," Charlotte said softly. "Perhaps I should not have told you. Would a lie, or at least an evasion, have been better?"

"No." Adriana sat motionless for a few more moments. "I'm sorry, I can't eat any more. I think I need to go home. Do you know who gave it to her? Was it Nerissa Freemarsh, do you think? Serafina was so distressed by her failing memory . . . her mind . . ." She did not complete the train of thought.

"I don't know," Charlotte said honestly. "It might be considered an act of mercy by some, but the law would regard it as murder, all the same."

"Perhaps she took it herself?" Adriana said desperately.

Charlotte knew that was not possible. Care had been taken to prevent that, but perhaps this was not the time to say so.

"Perhaps," she agreed. "She was terribly afraid of being indiscreet and letting slip old secrets that might cause harm to someone who is still alive and vulnerable. I have no idea who that could be, or indeed if there even is such a person. Do you know?"

"No . . . she said nothing about anyone to me. I can't think of a person . . ." Adriana spoke hesitantly, as if she was raking her memory for anything Serafina might have said.

"No one at all?" Charlotte pressed. Was

she being deliberately and pointlessly cruel?

"Well, Serafina knew Lord Tregarron," Adriana said tentatively. "Quite well, it seemed, from the way she spoke of it."

Charlotte was puzzled. There had been the faintest flicker of amusement in Adriana's eyes, gone again the next instant. Tregarron was at least twenty-five years younger than Serafina, if not more. Thirty-five years ago that might have mattered less, but then he would have been very young, no more than a boy, and she in her late thirties. That was ridiculous. Adriana must be mistaken.

"Could it have been someone else, whose name sounded like his?" she suggested. "Someone Austrian, or Hungarian, for example?"

"No, it was Tregarron," Adriana insisted. "He visited her at Dorchester Terrace."

"Then she could not have known him far in the past."

"No. I must have misunderstood that." Adriana looked at Charlotte's plate and the unfinished dessert.

"Oh, I've had sufficient," Charlotte said quickly. "Let us go. It was a delicious meal. I shall have to eat Croatian food again. I had no idea it was so very good. Thank you for all you've shown me, and for the pleasure of your company."

Adriana smiled, her composure almost returned. "Didn't your Lord Byron say that happiness was born a twin? Pleasures tasted alone lose half their savor. Let us go and find the carriage."

Charlotte arrived home in the middle of the afternoon, a trifle earlier than she had expected. She had much more information to give Pitt but no conclusions, other than the growing certainty in her own mind that Serafina had known who had betrayed Lazar Dragovic, but for some reason had never spoken of it to anyone. Was that the secret she had been so afraid of letting slip? It made sense. At least to Adriana Dragovic, it still mattered passionately, and Serafina had always tried to protect Adriana, whether out of love for Lazar, or simply human decency. She would have known what that knowledge would do to Adriana.

Charlotte walked down the hall to the kitchen. It was too early for Daniel and Jemima to be home from school, but she was surprised to find the kitchen empty. Minnie Maude was not in the scullery either, nor was she in the dining room or the parlor. Could she be out shopping? Most of the household goods they required were delivered, and those that needed to be bought in person were bought in the morning.

Charlotte went up the stairs and looked for Minnie Maude without finding her. Now she was worried. She even looked in the back garden to see if she could have tripped and been hurt. She knew even as she did it that the thought was absurd. Unless Minnie was unconscious, she would have made her way back into the house, even if she had been injured.

She must be in the cellar; it was the only place left. But Charlotte had been home a quarter of an hour! Why on earth would Minnie Maude be in the cellar for that length of time? There was nothing down there that could take so long to collect, and it would be perishing cold.

She opened the door. The light was on — she could see its dim glow from the top step. Had Minnie Maude slipped and fallen here? She went down quickly now, holding on to the handrail. Minnie Maude was sitting on a cushion in the corner, a blanket wrapped around her, and in her arms was a small, dirty, and extremely scruffy little dog, with a red ribbon around its neck.

Minnie Maude and the puppy both looked up at her with wide, frightened eyes.

Charlotte took a deep breath.

"For goodness' sake, bring it upstairs into the kitchen," she said, trying to keep the overwhelming emotion inside her under some kind of control. Relief, pity, a drowning comprehension of Minnie Maude's loneliness, and all the conflicting feelings for Adriana, and for Serafina, everything to do with need and loss churned in her mind. "And wash it!" she went on. "It's filthy! I suppose one can't expect it not to be, living in the coal cellar."

Minnie Maude climbed to her feet slowly, still holding the dog.

"You'd better give it some dinner," Charlotte added. "Something warm. It's very young, by the look of it."

"Are you going to put it out?" Minnie Maude's face was white with fear, and she held the animal so tightly it started squirming around.

"I daresay the cats won't like it," Charlotte replied obliquely. "But they'll just have to get used to it. We'll find it a basket. Wash it in the scullery sink, or you'll have coal dust all over the place."

Minnie Maude took a long, shuddering breath, and her face filled with hope.

Charlotte turned away to go up the stairs. She did not want Minnie Maude to think she could get away with absolutely anything.

"Does it have a name?" she asked huskily.

"Uffie," Minnie Maude said. "But you can change it if you want to."

"Uffie seems perfectly good to me," Charlotte replied. "Bring her, or is it him, upstairs, and don't put her down until you get to the scullery, or you'll spend the rest of the day getting coal dust out of the carpets, and we'll all have no dinner."

"I'll carry 'er ter the kitchen," Minnie Maude promised fervently. "An' I'll see she don't make a mess anywhere, I promise. She's ever so good."

She won't be, Charlotte thought, not when she's warm enough and properly fed, and realizes she can stay. But maybe that is better. "She's your responsibility," she warned as she held the cellar door open. Minnie Maude walked through into the hall, still holding the dog close to her, her face shining with happiness.

When Pitt returned home, late and tired, Charlotte told him very briefly about the dog, not as a question, but simply so he would not be surprised when he found the little animal in the scullery. Daniel and Jemima had both fallen instantly in love with it, so no further decision could really be made.

443

In the evening, alone with the parlor fire dying down and the embers settling in the hearth, Charlotte told Pitt what she had learned from Adriana.

"Are you sure she said Tregarron?" he asked, sitting a little forward in his chair.

"Yes. But of course I'm not sure that is what *Serafina* said, or if it was, that it was who she actually meant. But I believe that Serafina knew who betrayed Lazar Dragovic, and that, whether she meant to tell her or not, somehow Adriana realized who it was too."

"Well, it couldn't have been Tregarron," Pitt said reasonably. "He was too young to have been involved at all, and was here in England at boarding school anyway. He would have been about fourteen at the time. And why would Adriana have killed Serafina, even if Serafina did tell her? Who would she be protecting? That doesn't make any sense."

"Yes, it does." Charlotte spoke so quickly her voice was almost lost in the crackle from the fire as another log fell apart in a shower of sparks. "It makes sense if it was Serafina herself who betrayed Dragovic."

"Serafina?" He was startled. "But she was on the same side as him. And she rescued Adriana. My sources say she and Dragovic were lovers, at least for a while."

"Thomas, don't be so naive," Charlotte said. "The most passionate lovers also make the bitterest enemies, at times. And who knows now, or even then, if they were really lovers? Perhaps either one of them was only using the other?"

He started to argue. "But they were both fighting for the same . . ." He trailed off.

"Balkan politics are not so simple," she said. "At least that is what I hear, from those who know. And love affairs hardly ever are."

He smiled with a flicker of ironic humor. "At least that is what you hear from those who know?"

She blushed very slightly. "Yes."

"Do you think Adriana believed that Serafina betrayed her father?" he asked, all humor vanished.

"I think it's more likely than Nerissa Freemarsh murdering her aunt out of frustration, because she didn't die quickly enough," she said quietly.

"And Tregarron?" he asked. "What was he doing at Dorchester Terrace?"

"I don't know," she admitted. "Perhaps trying to make sure that Serafina didn't tell any more secrets in her confused state. Ones we don't even know about. They would be old, but perhaps still embarrassing. He's responsible for a lot of the British relations with the Austrian Empire, and the countries around its borders. Maybe Poland, Ukraine, or the Ottoman Empire? Even if the people concerned are dead, or out of office, the matters might still be better left alone."

"But who could she tell?" he asked thoughtfully. "Not many people came to see her."

"Would he leave that to chance? Would you?"

"No." He sighed and leaned back again. "Tomorrow I had better go and speak to Nerissa Freemarsh, and to Tucker again. I don't think it can have anything to do with . . . present cases . . . but I need to be certain. Thank you."

"For what?" She was puzzled by his gratitude.

"For questioning Adriana," he explained. "I know you didn't wish to."

"Oh. No. Thomas, you don't mind about Uffie, do you?"

"Who?"

"The dog."

He laughed quietly. "No, of course I don't."

In the morning Pitt went to see Narraway and told him about Charlotte's conversation with Adriana Blantyre, and the conclusions he was forced to draw from it.

"I was hoping the answer would be different," Narraway said quietly. "I was sure it had to do with this wretched Duke Alois threat, but it seems the timing is coincidental after all. I'm sorry. What are you going to do?"

"Go back to Dorchester Terrace and check on the exact amount of laudanum that was in the house," Pitt replied. "And whether anyone from the outside ever had access to it."

"You think Adriana learned the truth from Serafina, went away and thought about it, then came back with laudanum? That's cold-blooded."

"If Serafina betrayed her father to his death, perhaps. I hope to be wrong."

Narraway spread his hands in a small, rueful gesture. He said nothing, for which Pitt was grateful.

At Dorchester Terrace he spoke first with Tucker and then with Nerissa Freemarsh. He checked on the laudanum, as he had told Narraway he would. The conclusion was inescapable: Whoever had given her the extra dosage had brought it with them. Killing her had been carefully planned.

447

Tucker had nothing new to add; yes, Mrs. Blantyre had called several times, bringing flowers and once a box of candied fruit. She was always kind. Yes, she had seemed distressed the last time she had called, on the evening of Mrs. Montserrat's death. Pale-faced, Tucker noted that Adriana had spent some time alone with Mrs. Montserrat in the bedroom. It had seemed to be what Mrs. Montserrat had wanted.

With Nerissa, it was a different matter. She was tense as she came into the house-keeper's sitting room, and closed the door behind her with a sharp snap. She was still in black, but today she had several rows of very fine jet beads around her neck, and excellent-quality jet earrings, which added a fashionable touch to her appearance.

"I don't know what else I can tell you, Mr. Pitt," she said with a certain briskness. Being mistress of the house at last gave her a new air of confidence. The slightly nervous demeanor was gone. She stood straighter and somehow she looked taller. Perhaps she had new boots with a higher heel. Under the swirl of her black bombazine skirt it was not possible to tell. But there was unquestionably a touch of color on her skin.

Pitt had decided to be totally open.

"Did Lord Tregarron visit here often?" he asked.

"Lord Tregarron?" she repeated.

She was playing for time. It was a question she had not expected, and she needed to think what to say.

"Is that something you find difficult to answer, Miss Freemarsh?" He met her eyes challengingly. "Why would that be? Surely he did not ask anyone to keep that fact hidden?"

Now there was an angry flush on her cheeks. "Of course not! That is absurd. I was trying to recollect how often he did come."

"And have you succeeded?"

"He came to visit my aunt because he had heard she was ill, and he knew how much she had done for England in her youth, particularly with regard to the Austrian Empire, and our relationship with Vienna."

"How very generous of him," Pitt said with only the slightest asperity in his voice. "Since, as far as I can learn, Mrs. Montserrat was passionately on the side of the rebels, against the Habsburg throne. Was that not so? Or was she a spy for Austria perhaps, planted there to betray the freedom fighters?"

Now Nerissa was really angry. "That is a

dreadful thing to say! And completely ir-responsible. But —" Suddenly she stopped as if a new and terrible thought had filled her mind. "I . . . I had not even . . ." She blinked. "I don't know, Mr. Pitt. She always said . . ." Again she stopped. "Now I don't know. Perhaps that was what it was all about. It would explain Mrs. Blantyre . . ." Her hand had flown to her mouth as if to stop herself from crying out. Now it fell to her side again. "I think perhaps I had better say no more. I would not wish to be unjust to anyone."

He felt cold, as if the fire had suddenly died, though it was burning so hot and red in the hearth that the whole chimney breast was warm.

"Mrs. Blantyre visited your aunt quite often, including the evening she died." His voice sounded hollow.

"Yes . . . but . . . yes, she did."

"Alone?"

"Yes. Mr. Blantyre remained downstairs. He thought it would be less strain on Mrs. Montserrat. She did not find it easy to speak to several people at a time. And sometimes she and Adriana would converse in Italian, which he does not speak — at least not flu-ently."

"I see. Does he speak Croatian?"

"I have no idea." Her face was very pale. She sat rigidly, as if her bodice was suddenly constrictingly tight. "Perhaps. He speaks German, I know. He spent quite a lot of time in Vienna."

"I see. Thank you." He was left with no choice. He must go and question Adriana Blantyre. There was nothing to be gained by delaying it, not that he wished to. If he went now, Blantyre himself might still be at home. That would make it more difficult, more embarrassing and emotionally wrenching, but it was the right way to do it.

He thanked Nerissa again and left Dorchester Terrace to walk the short distance to Blantyre's house.

He was admitted by the butler, and Blantyre himself met him in the hall.

"Has something happened?" he asked, searching Pitt's face. "Some word about Duke Alois?"

"No. It concerns Serafina Montserrat's death."

"Oh?" Blantyre looked tired, and his face was deeply lined. He waved the butler away and the man disappeared obediently, leaving them standing alone in the middle of the beautiful hall. "Have you learned something further?"

"I am not certain, but it begins to look

like it," Pitt replied. It was the worst part of his position as head of Special Branch, and he could pass the responsibility to no one else; Blantyre had been more than a friend; he had gone out of his way, even taken professional risks, to help Pitt learn the reality of the threat to Duke Alois and to persuade the prime minister to take the issue seriously. It made this investigation acutely painful, but it did not relieve him of the necessity of pursuing it.

Blantyre frowned. When he spoke his voice was level and perfectly under control. "There's something I can do? I know nothing about her death at all. Until you told me otherwise, I assumed it was natural. Then when you mentioned the laudanum, I thought perhaps she had dreaded the loss of her mind to the point where suicide had seemed preferable. Is that not the case?"

"Is it possible that Serafina was working for the Austrian monarchy all the time, and that it was she who betrayed Lazar Dragovic to his death?" Pitt asked.

"Dear God!" Blantyre gasped and swayed a little on his feet. Then he turned and strode across the floor to the foot of the stairs. He grasped the banister, hesitated a moment, then started up.

Pitt followed after him, seized by a shadow

of fear, but with no idea why he was afraid.

Blantyre increased his speed, taking the steps two at a time. He reached the landing and went to the second door. He knocked, then stood with his hand still raised. He turned to Pitt a couple of yards behind him. There was a terrible silence.

Blantyre lowered his hand and turned the knob. He pushed the door open and walked into the room.

The curtains were still closed but there was sufficient daylight filtering through them to find their way across to the big bed, and to see Adriana's black hair fanned across the pillow.

"Adriana!" Blantyre choked on the word.

Pitt waited, his heart pounding.

"Adriana!" Blantyre cried out loudly. He lurched forward and grasped her arm where it lay on the coverlet. She did not move.

Pitt looked and saw the empty glass on the bedside table, and the small piece of folded paper, such as holds a medicinal powder. He would not need to taste it to know what it was.

He walked silently over to Blantyre and put his hand on his shoulder.

Blantyre buckled at the knees and collapsed onto the floor, his body racked with pain, his sobs hollow, making barely a sound.

CHAPTER 11

Pitt was in his office, looking yet again through the plans for Duke Alois's visit, when Stoker knocked on the door.

Pitt looked up as he came in.

Stoker's expression was anxious, and he was clearly uncomfortable.

"Mr. Blantyre's here, sir. He looks pretty bad, like he hasn't eaten or slept for a while, but he wants to see you. Sorry, but I couldn't put him off. I think it's about Staum."

"Ask him in," Pitt replied. There was no way to avoid it. Assassins do not stop for private grief; it might solve at least part of the problem if Staum was connected to Adriana, but there was nothing to suggest it. Adriana had killed Serafina in revenge for her father, and then apparently in remorse or despair, taken her own life. There was no reason to think she had even heard of Duke Alois, who would have been a child, even younger than herself, at the time of the uprising and the betrayal.

"Fetch brandy and a couple of glasses," he added, then, seeing the look on Stoker's face, "I know it's early, but he may well have been awake all night. It's civil to make the offer. Poor man."

"I don't know how he can bear it," Stoker said grimly. "Wife killing an old lady who was dying anyway, then taking her own life. Mind, he looks as if he'd be better off dead himself, right now."

"Ask him in, and don't be long with the brandy," Pitt told him.

"Yes, sir."

Blantyre came in a moment later. He looked like a man stumbling blindly through a nightmare.

Pitt stood to greet him. It was impossible to know what to say. Pitt remembered Charlotte's grief when he had told her about Adriana; she had been stunned, as if his words had made no sense to her. Then as understanding filled her, followed by horror at the torment she imagined Adriana must've been feeling, she had wept in Pitt's arms for what seemed like a long time. Even when they had finally gone to bed, she had cried in the dark. When he touched her, her face had been wet with tears.

She and Adriana had been friends for only a few weeks. What Blantyre must be feeling was a devastation imaginable only to those who had experienced it.

Blantyre eased himself into the chair like an old man with brittle bones. Stoker came in almost on his heels with the brandy, and Blantyre accepted it. He held the glass in both hands as if to warm the bowl and send the aroma up, but his fingers were bloodless and shaking.

"Stoker said you had some news," Pitt prompted him after a few moments of silence.

Blantyre looked up. "Staum is no longer alone in Dover," he said quietly. "There is another man called Reibnitz there. Elegant, ineffectual-looking fellow, very tidy, humorless. He looks like an accountant, and you half expect his fingers to be stained with ink. Until he speaks; then he sounds like a gentleman, and you take him for some third son from a decent family, the sort in England who would go into the Church, for the lack of something better to do."

"Reibnitz," Pitt repeated.

Blantyre's face tightened. "Johann Reibnitz, so ordinary as to be almost invisible. Average height, slender build, light brown hair, gray eyes, pale complexion. Could be any one of a million men in Austria or any of the rest of Europe. Speaks English without an accent."

"Nothing to distinguish him?" Pitt asked with growing alarm.

"Nothing at all. No moles, no scars, no limp or twitch or stutter. As I said, an invisible man." There was no expression in Blantyre's eyes; he spoke mechanically.

"So Staum might be a decoy, as we feared?" Pitt said.

"I think so. He would be, if I were planning it."

"How do you know this?"

The ghost of a smile crossed Blantyre's face but vanished so completely Pitt wasn't sure he had actually seen it. "I still have contacts in Vienna. Reibnitz has killed several times before. They know, but they cannot prove it."

It was Pitt's turn to smile. "And you expect me to believe that a lack of proof prevents them from removing him? Is Vienna so . . . squeamish?"

Blantyre sighed. "Of course not. You are quite right. They use him also, as it suits them. He was one of their own originally. They believe that he has gone rogue." He looked at Pitt with sudden intensity, as if something alive had stirred within him again. "Would you order one of your own shot, simply because you believed he had become unreliable? Would you not want him tried, given a chance to defend himself? How could you be sure the evidence was good? Should he not face his accuser? And would you detail one of your men to do it? Or would you feel that as head of the service, it was your burden to bear?"

Pitt was startled. It was a question he had avoided asking himself since the O'Neil affair. It was one thing to defend yourself in the heat of the moment; it was very different to order an execution, a judicial murder, in cold blood.

Blantyre sipped his brandy. "You are a detective, a brilliant one." There was sincerity in his voice, even admiration. "You uncover truths most men would never find. You make certain. You weigh evidence, you refine your understanding until you have as much of the whole picture as anyone ever will. You have intense emotions. You empathize with pain; injustice outrages you. But you hardly ever lose your self-control." He made a slight gesture with his strong, graceful hands. "You think before you act. These are the qualities that make you a great leader in the service of your country. Perhaps one day you will even be better than

Victor Narraway, because you know people better."

Pitt stared at him, embarrassed. He understood that there was a "but" coming and he did not want to hear it.

Blantyre twisted his mouth in a grimace. "But could you execute one of your men, without trial?"

"I don't know," Pitt admitted. It was difficult to say. The expression on Blantyre's face gave him no indication as to whether he respected Pitt's answer, or despised it.

"I know you don't." Blantyre relaxed at last. "Perhaps your counterpart in Vienna hasn't decided yet either. Or perhaps Reibnitz is a double agent, working for the head of the Austrian Secret Service, and betraying his other masters to them, as the occasion arises."

"Well, if he attempts to murder Duke Alois, perhaps we can relieve them of the decision," Pitt said grimly. "Is there anything more you can tell me about Reibnitz? Where he has been seen? Habits, dress, any way we can recognize him? Anything known of his likes and dislikes? Any associates?"

"Of course. I have written down everything known." Blantyre pulled a folded piece of paper from his inside pocket and handed it to Pitt. "The name of my informant is there separately. I would be obliged if you would note it somewhere absolutely safe, and show it to no one else, except possibly Stoker. I know you trust him."

Pitt took it. "Thank you," he said sincerely. "Duke Alois will owe you his life, and we will all owe you for saving us from a national embarrassment, which could have cost us very dearly indeed."

Blantyre finished his brandy. "Thank you." He put the glass down on the desk and stood up. He hesitated a moment as if to say something more, then changed his mind and walked unsteadily to the door.

As soon as he was gone, Pitt sent for Stoker and told him all that Blantyre had said, including the name of the informant regarding Reibnitz. It took them the rest of that day to follow it up, but every fact that Blantyre had offered was verifiable, and proved to be true.

Leaving Stoker and the others under his command to check and double check all the arrangements from the moment the ferry landed in Dover, Pitt went to see Narraway.

It was the middle of the afternoon with rain sweeping in from the west. Pitt was soaked, and put his hat, gloves, and scarf on the leather-padded brass railing in front of the fire.

Narraway put more coal and wood on the embers and settled in his chair, gazing at Pitt.

"You are certain about Reibnitz?" he asked gravely.

"I'm certain that what Blantyre told me is true," Pitt replied. "I've checked on the few Austrian political murders we know about. It's difficult to pin them down. Too many are anarchists striking at anyone at all, just as they are here, or else the cases are unsolved. Reibnitz fits the description for a murder in Berlin, and one in Paris. As Blantyre said, there's no proof."

"But he's here in Dover?" Narraway pressed.

Pitt nodded. "There is an ordinary-seeming man answering his description, calling himself John Rainer, just returned from Bordeaux after apparently having been away on business for several months. He has no friends or family who can confirm it, only a passport with that name."

Narraway pursed his lips. "He doesn't sound like an anarchist; more like a deliberate and very careful assassin."

"He could still be paid by anarchists," Pitt reasoned. The rain beating on the windows sounded threatening, as if it were trying to come in.

Narraway looked at him steadily, the shadows from the firelight playing across his face.

"In case it's all a misdirection, I have put only four men on the Duke Alois case, until he actually gets here. Everyone else is on their usual rounds, watching for any movement, any change that stands out. We've got a socialist rally in Kilburn, but the regular police can deal with anything there. An exhibition of rather explicit paintings in one of the galleries in Piccadilly; some protests expected there. Nothing else that I know of."

"Then you'd better prepare for the worst." Narraway's eyes were bleak, his mouth pulled into a thin line. "You need all the allies you can find. It might be time to exert a little pressure, even call in a few favors. This information from Blantyre needs further checking. It doesn't smell like casual anarchist violence."

It was what Pitt had thought, and feared.

"I don't have any favors to call in," he said grimly. "Blantyre is crippled by his wife's death. I still have no idea if any of it had to do with Duke Alois or not, but I can't see any connection. The duke is Austrian, and

463

has no visible ties with Italy or Croatia. He has no interest we can find in any of the other smaller parts of the Austrian Empire."

"Prussia? Poland?" Narraway asked.

"Nothing."

Narraway frowned. "I don't like coincidences, but I can't think of any way in which Serafina's rambling mind, or the secrets she might have known forty years ago, have anything to do with anarchists today, or Duke Alois at any time. Tragically, the connection with Adriana and Lazar Dragovic is all too obvious. Although it surprises me. I would never have thought of Serafina Montserrat as one to betray anyone. But then I knew her only through other people's eyes."

"Vespasia's?" Pitt asked.

"I suppose so. You have no doubt that it was Adriana who killed her?"

"I wish I did, but I can't see any. She was there that night." A deep, painful heaviness settled inside him. "We know that Serafina was one of Dragovic's allies, and that she was there when he was executed. She took Adriana away and looked after her. It was an appalling piece of duplicity, whatever reason she did it for, whoever's power or freedom was bought that way. No wonder she was afraid when she knew that Adriana, as a grown woman, was coming to see her. That explains the terror that Vespasia saw."

"And when she realized you knew, Adriana killed herself," Narraway added. He watched Pitt steadily, his eyes probing to see how harshly Pitt felt the guilt.

Pitt gave a bleak smile in return. "There is one other person to consider in all this," he said, not as an evasion, but to move the conversation forward.

Narraway nodded, lips drawn tight. "Be careful, Pitt. Don't create enemies you can't afford. If you're going to use people, be damned careful how you do it. People understand favors and repayment, but no one likes to be used."

He leaned forward and picked up the poker from the hearth. He pushed it into the coals, and the flames gushed up.

"There are a few people you can set at each other's throats, if you need to shake things up a little. See what falls out," he added.

Pitt watched him closely, waiting for the next words, dreading them.

"Tregarron," Narraway went on, replacing the poker gently. "He is devoted to his mother, but had a certain ill feeling toward his father."

"Wasn't his father a diplomat in Vienna?"

"Yes. You might see if he knew anything about Dragovic, or Serafina, for that matter. There are one or two others, people I could . . ." He looked for the right word. "Persuade to be more forthcoming. But they're heavy debts, ones I can call in only once." He looked up at Pitt, whose face was tense, uncertain in the flickering light. "You tell me what you would like me to do."

Pitt could not answer. He wanted to ask someone's advice — perhaps Vespasia's — but he knew that it was his decision. He was head of Special Branch.

"I want to know if the betrayal of Dragovic was the only secret Serafina was afraid of revealing," he said aloud. "And who Nerissa Freemarsh's lover is, if he exists at all."

"Freemarsh's lover?" Narraway's head jerked up. "Yes, find that out. Find out if it was Tregarron. Find out what he really went to that house for."

"I intend to."

Pitt went to one of the sources that Narraway had mentioned. He took the train on the Great Eastern Line to just beyond Hackney Wick. From there he walked three-quarters of a mile through sporadic sunshine to Plover Road. It overlooked Hackney Marsh, which was flat as a table, and crossed

466

by narrow, winding waterways.

There he found the man whose name Narraway had given him, an Italian who had fought with the Croatian nationalists when Dragovic was one of their leaders. He was well into his eighties now, but still sharp-witted, in spite of failing physical health. When Pitt had identified himself and proved to the man's satisfaction that he knew Victor Narraway, they sat down together in a small room with a window overlooking the marsh.

Beyond the glass, flights of birds raced across the wide sky, chasing sunlight and shadows, and wind combed the grasses in ever-changing patterns.

"Yes, of course I remember Serafina Montserrat," the old man said with a smile. He had lost most of his hair, but he still had beautiful teeth. "What man could forget her?"

"What about Lazar Dragovic?" Pitt asked.

The old man's face filled with sadness. "Killed," he said briefly. "The Austrians shot him."

"Executed," Pitt put in.

"Murdered," the old man corrected him.

"Wasn't he planning to assassinate someone?"

The old man's seamed face twisted with contempt. "A butcher of the people, put there to rule. He had no damned business being set on the throne there. Foreigner. Barely even spoke their language. And he was brutal. Killing *him* — now that would have been an execution."

"Was Dragovic betrayed by one of his own?" Pitt asked.

"Yes." The old man's eyes burned with the memory. "Of course he was. Never would have been caught otherwise."

"Do you know who?"

"What does it matter now?" There was weariness and a sudden overwhelming defeat in his voice. He stared out the window. "They're all dead."

"Are they?" Pitt asked. "Are you sure?"

"Must be. It was a long time ago. People like that are passionate, vivid. They live with courage and hope, but they burn out."

"Serafina died only a few weeks ago," Pitt told him.

He smiled. "Ah . . . Serafina. God rest her."

"She was murdered," Pitt said, feeling brutal to deliver such news.

"Is that why you came?" That was an accusation. "English policeman, with a murder to solve?"

"There have been three deaths counting Lazar Dragovic. And, more urgently, there is the threat of more death to come," Pitt corrected him. "Who betrayed Lazar Dragovic?"

"Who else is dead? You said three deaths, but Serafina and Lazar makes two."

"Adriana Dragovic."

Tears filled the old man's eyes and slipped down his withered cheeks. "She was a lovely child," he whispered.

Pitt thought of Adriana, picturing her vividly in his mind: beautiful, delicate, and yet perhaps far stronger than Blantyre had imagined. Or was she? Had she killed Serafina, after all these years? Or not? Why did he still question it? He had all the evidence.

The old man blinked. "When did it happen? When?"

"A few days ago."

"How? Was she ill? She was fragile as a child. Lung diseases, I think. But . . ." He sighed. "I thought she was better. It's so easy to wish. But you said only a few days ago? Was it her lungs still?"

"No. She killed herself. But I don't know why, not for certain."

The old man blinked again. "What can I tell you all this time later that can help? It was all long ago. Dragovic is dead; so are those who fought with him. And now you say Serafina and Adriana are dead too. What could I know that matters anymore?"

"Who betrayed Dragovic," Pitt answered.

"Do you think if I knew, that person would still be alive? I would've killed him long ago!" The old man's voice shook with anger. His face was crumpled, his eyes wet.

"Did Serafina know?" Pitt persisted.

Seconds ticked by and the silence in the room remained unbroken. More cloud shadows chased one another over the marsh. There would be rain before sunset.

Pitt waited.

"I'm not sure," the old man said at last. "I didn't think so, at first. Later I began to wonder."

"Weren't she and Dragovic lovers?"

"Yes. That's why I was sure at first that she didn't know. She'd have taken her revenge if she had, I thought. She grieved for him, inside. Few people saw it, but it was there. I'm not sure it ever really healed."

"You are certain of that?"

"Of course I am. I knew Serafina." Now there was anger in the old man's voice, a challenge.

Pitt wondered how well he had known her. Had he been her lover too? Might Dragovic's betrayal have been nothing political at all, but an old-fashioned triangle of love and jealousy?

"Did you know her well?" he asked.

The old man smiled, showing the beautiful teeth again. "Yes, very well. And before you ask, yes, we were lovers, before Dragovic. But you dishonor me if you think I would betray the cause out of personal jealousy. The cause came first, always."

"For everyone?"

"Yes! For everyone!" Anger flared in his eyes, against Pitt, because he was young and knew nothing about their passion and their loss.

"Then, logically, whoever betrayed Dragovic was secretly on the side of a different cause." Pitt stated the only conclusion.

The old man nodded slowly. "Yes, that must be so."

"But if Serafina knew, why wouldn't she expose that person?"

"She would have. She cannot have known. I was wrong."

"When did you think she might have learned?"

"Oh . . . ten, maybe fifteen years later."

"How would she have found out, so long after?"

"I've thought about that too, and I don't know."

"Are you certain it was not Serafina

herself?" Pitt loathed asking, but it was un-avoidable.

"Serafina?" The old man was shocked, and angry again, sitting more upright in his chair. "Never!"

"Then perhaps it was someone she loved." It was the most obvious conclusion.

"No. Men came and went. There was no one she would have forgiven for betraying Dragovic." His voice was filled with cutting contempt. Pitt could imagine the young man he must have been, slightly built but wiry, handsome, filled with passion.

"Are you certain?" he probed.

"Yes. The only person she loved that much was Dragovic's child, Adriana."

Adriana had been only eight when her father was killed. Could she have let something slip by accident, something that ended up killing her father? Was that terrible realization what Blantyre had been trying to protect her from? If Serafina had told her in one of her ramblings, little wonder that Adriana had gone home and killed herself.

Except the timing made no sense. If she had found out such a thing, surely she would've been wild with distress on the day Serafina told her, driven to take her life then, not several days and social engage-ments later. And why would she kill Serafina for that?

The old man was studying his face. "What is it?" he asked anxiously. "Do you know something?"

"No, I don't," Pitt replied. "What I was thinking makes no sense. But Serafina knew. That's why she was killed, to prevent her from telling anyone else."

"That doesn't explain why Adriana killed herself," the old man said. "Unless she killed Serafina to silence her, and then couldn't take the guilt of it. But what reason could she have had to do that?"

"To protect her husband." Pitt had spoken the words before he realized the full impact of what he was saying.

"Her husband?" The old man was aghast. "Evan Blantyre?"

Pitt looked at him, studying the fragile skin, the deep lines, the strength in the bones. In its own way, it was a beautiful face. "Yes — Evan Blantyre."

The old man crossed himself. "Yes . . . God forgive us all, that would make sense. That would be why Serafina never told. She didn't know it until later, when Blantyre returned and courted Adriana. He must have let something slip, and Serafina put it together."

"And she let Adriana marry him?" Pitt

asked incredulously.

"How was she going to stop it? They were in love, passionately and completely. Adriana was beautiful, but she had nothing: no money, no status. She was the orphan daughter of a traitor to the empire, an executed criminal. And Serafina probably had no proof, only her own inner certainty." He shrugged his thin shoulders. "Not that proof would have made a difference. Blantyre would have been regarded as a hero by the Viennese emperor. No, she would have kept her silence and let Adriana be happy. She was delicate, needing someone to look after her, to help her regain her health. In poverty, she would have been left to die young and alone. Serafina never had a child of her own. Adriana was the only thing left of the man she loved."

Pitt tried to imagine it: Serafina watching the marriage of Adriana to the man who had betrayed them both. And perhaps that was it: the depth of real love, more powerful than the need for revenge, and deeper, infinitely more selfless than any kind of hate or hunger for justice. He felt a pain in his chest and a tightness in his throat; tears glistened in the old man's eyes.

The first drops of rain spattered against the windows.

If Blantyre had betrayed Lazar Dragovic, and Serafina knew it, then she might well have let something slip to Adriana. And if Adriana had confronted Blantyre with it, what would he have done?

Serafina was terrified that she would say something that sooner or later would lead to the truth. That made perfect sense. But Blantyre must have also feared that it would happen, so he killed her to prevent it. Then when Adriana knew Serafina had been murdered — and realized she was about to be blamed for it by Pitt — she had killed herself in despair!

Or Blantyre thought that Adriana would put together all the different things Serafina had said and deduce the truth, so with terrible, agonizing regret, he had killed her, to protect himself.

Everything suddenly crystalized in Pitt's mind: the detail with which Blantyre had explained to Pitt and Charlotte the crucial place of the Austrian Empire in European politics, the passion he had shown while discussing the subject.

Was he right? Was the empire's survival necessary to the continued peace of Europe?

Perhaps it was.

It did not excuse the murder of Serafina Montserrat. Even less did it excuse the murder of Adriana.

Pitt rose to his feet. "Thank you, sir," he said gravely. "You have saved the good name of two women who were murdered and defamed. I will do all I can to see that that injustice is corrected, but I may not be able to do it quickly. Believe me, I will not forget or abandon it."

The old man nodded slowly. "Good," he said with conviction. "Good."

On the train home, Pitt stared out the window, even though it was streaked with rain and there was little he could see. He ignored the other two men sitting in the carriage reading newspapers.

If Blantyre had been with Serafina long enough to hear that she knew the truth, then he must've spent quite a lot of time with her. How often had he visited her? Why had neither Adriana nor Nerissa mentioned it?

The answer to the first was simple: Adriana might not have known.

The answer to the second was more complicated. Nerissa could not escape knowing, unless Blantyre had visited when she was out of the house, possibly in the afternoons. The more probable answer was that she did know, and had chosen not to tell Pitt. Had that been to protect herself, because she had allowed him to see Serafina without anyone else in the room? Or — more likely — to protect him from suspicion, perhaps because he had asked her to? Or — most likely of all — because he was her lover?

Except what, in heaven's name, would the brilliant, charming Evan Blantyre see in a woman like Nerissa Freemarsh? But then, who knew what anyone saw in another person? The outer appearance was trivial, if one understood the mind or the heart. Perhaps she was generous, easy to please, uncritical. Maybe she listened to him with genuine interest, laughed at his jokes, never contradicted him or compared him with others. It could be as simple as that she loved him unconditionally, and asked nothing in return, except a little time, a little kindness, or the semblance of it. Perhaps it was in defiance of the beautiful, and maybe demanding, Adriana?

The rain beat harder on the carriage window now, and it was growing dark outside. The rattle of the train was rhythmic, soothing.

The most likely explanation of all was that Blantyre had visited Dorchester Terrace once with Adriana, realized how dangerously Serafina was rambling, and secured for himself an ostensible reason for returning again and again so he could figure out just how great the danger might be.

Then a new thought occurred to Pitt: Blantyre could've learned from Serafina's disintegrating mind any other secret she might know about anyone or anything else. He might now have stored in his own mind all the secrets Serafina was so afraid she would let slip: names of men and women who had participated in indiscretions of all sorts, over half of Europe, for the last forty years.

Most of them were probably trivial: affairs, illegitimate children, romantic betrayals as opposed to political ones; possibly thefts or embezzlements, purchases of office, blackmails or coercions. The list was almost endless.

What would Blantyre do with them? That was a troubling thought, but it might have to wait until after Duke Alois had safely completed his visit.

But then, had Blantyre gained his knowledge about the assassination plot from Serafina? It did not seem possible. Serafina had been ill and confined to her bed for half a year. It was far longer than that since she had been involved in any affairs of state in England or Austria.

Was it even conceivable that Duke Alois was connected with someone else from that time? That seemed fanciful in the extreme. Pitt was skeptical of coincidences. Ordinary police work had taught him that, even before Special Branch. But on the other hand, it was equally foolish to imagine that everything was connected, or to see cause and effect where there was none.

He sat back and let the rhythm and movement of the train lull him into near sleep. It was still at least half an hour before he would reach the station in London, and then as long again before he was home.

Pitt found Charlotte waiting for him, with the kettle on the burner and the fire still burning in the parlor. He stood by the scrubbed table as she made tea and cut him a sandwich of cold beef and pickles. He glanced at the basket beside the stove and saw the little dog, Uffie, half asleep, her nose twitching as she smelled the meat.

He smiled, took a tiny piece from where Charlotte had sliced it, and offered it to the dog. She snapped it up immediately.

"Thomas, I've already fed her!" Charlotte smiled.

He picked up the tray and carried it through to the parlor. He had not realized how hungry he was, or how cold. He set it down and watched while she poured tea for both of them. The room was warm and silent except for the slight crackling of the flames in the hearth, and, now and then, the sound of wind and rain on the window-panes beyond the closed curtains. He glanced at the familiar pictures on the walls: the Dutch water scene he was so used to, with its soft colors, blues and grays, calm as a still morning. On the other wall was a drawing of cows grazing. There was some-thing very beautiful about cows, a kind of certainty that always pleased him. Perhaps that was based on some memory from child-hood.

Charlotte was watching him, waiting.

How much could he tell her? He could fail to see something important, something she might catch. Especially if it was based on something Adriana had told her that she had not previously understood the relevance of.

On the other hand, there were the prom-ises of secrecy he had made regarding his office in Special Branch. If he could not be trusted to keep them, he was no use to anyone, and no protection to Charlotte herself. He must choose his words carefully.

"You don't believe that Adriana killed Serafina, do you." He made it more of a statement than a question.

"No," she said instantly. "I know you think Serafina was responsible for Lazar Dragovic's death, but even if she was — and I don't know that you're right — Adriana wouldn't have murdered her. It would be stupid, apart from anything else. Serafina was dying anyway, and in some distress. If you hate someone deeply, you want them to suffer, not to be let off lightly."

"Revenge is usually stupid," he said quietly. "For an instant it feels wonderful, then the fury dies away and you're left empty, and wondering why it didn't make you feel any better, what it was you were expecting that didn't happen."

She stared at him. "When did you ever take revenge on anyone?"

"I've wanted to," he replied, with a sense of shame. "Some people I've arrested, some people for whom I didn't have enough proof that they were guilty, or simply couldn't catch them at the crime. Even recently, people I just had to arrest calmly, but whom I would like to have beaten with my fists. The only thing stopping me was the fact that I wasn't alone with them; I don't know whether I would have, if I'd been certain of getting away with it."

She looked at him with amazement, and a degree of curiosity. "You've never told me that before."

"I'm not proud of it."

"Do you tell me only the things you're proud of?" she challenged.

"No, of course not." He smiled ruefully, softening the moment. "I would probably have told you if I'd actually done it."

"Because I'd find out?"

"No, because it was a weakness I hadn't overcome."

She gave a little laugh, but there was no edge to it, no criticism. "What about Adriana? If she didn't kill Serafina, who did? And why did she then kill herself?" Her voice dropped. "Or didn't she?"

Pitt avoided her question. "You spent quite a lot of time with her. Do you think you learned to know her at all? I want your true opinion of her. A great deal may depend on it, even people's lives."

"Whose?" she came back instantly. "Blantyre's?"

"Among others. But I wasn't principally referring to him. It has to do with other people, most of whom you don't even know." He made a slight, rueful gesture. "And my job as well."

The last vestige of amusement vanished

from Charlotte's face. Her eyes were steady and serious. "I don't think she was fragile at all. She had been hurt terribly, seeing her father beaten and then executed. But many people see very bad things. It's painful. One never forgets them, but they don't make you deranged. Nightmares, maybe? I've had a few. Sometimes if I sleep really badly, or I'm worried or frightened, I remember the dead people I've seen."

She did not move her gaze from his, but he saw the sudden return of memory in her eyes. "One of the worst was the skeleton of the woman on the swing, with the tiny bones of the baby inside her. I still see that sometimes, and it makes me want to weep and weep until I have no strength left. But I don't."

Pitt started to reach across to touch her, then changed his mind. This was not the moment. "Adriana?" he said again.

"She wasn't hysterical," she said with conviction. "And I don't believe she would ever have killed herself. Who killed her, Thomas? Why? Wouldn't it have been the same person who betrayed her father? Did Serafina know who that was? She would have. That was why she was killed too. That's the only thing that makes sense."

"I imagine so." Should he tell her? Did

she have to know, for her own safety? Or would knowing endanger her? And even if he did not tell her, Blantyre might assume he had.

"It was him, wasn't it?" Her voice interrupted his thoughts.

"Him?"

"Blantyre!" she said sharply. "He was the only one who could have betrayed Dragovic, killed Serafina, and killed Adriana." She made it sound so simple. "Thomas, I don't care what secrets he knows, or what kind of office he holds, you can't let him get away with that! It's . . . monstrous!"

"You want revenge?" he asked.

"Maybe! Yes. I want revenge for Adriana. And for Serafina. She deserved better than to die like that! But call it justice, if you like. It is — and you'll feel better."

"Justice can mean many different things to different people," Pitt pointed out.

"Then call it an act of necessity. You can't have someone like that in a high office in the government. Such a man could do anything!"

"Oh, indeed. And probably will. Some of it we will praise him for, and some we will be glad enough not to know about."

Charlotte said nothing. He looked across at her and could not read what she was thinking.

First thing in the morning, Pitt went to see Vespasia. It was far too early to call, but he disregarded courtesy and told the maid that it was urgent. Vespasia's maid had become used to him, his polished boots and crooked ties, and above all, the fact that Vespasia was always willing to receive him.

He found her in the yellow breakfast room, sitting at the cherrywood table with tea, toast, and marmalade. The maid set another place for Pitt and went to fetch fresh tea and more toast.

"Good morning, Thomas," Vespasia said gravely. "Please sit down. You give me a crick in my neck staring up at you."

He smiled bleakly and accepted the invitation. He loved this room. It always seemed as if the sun were shining inside it.

"Serafina Montserrat knew who betrayed Lazar Dragovic," he said without preamble.

Vespasia inclined her head very slightly. "I thought she might. She was seldom fooled, and she loved him enough to not rest easily until she knew. Her fear makes perfect sense now; if she had not told Adriana already, then it was because she did not wish her to know. She was probably worried that she would ultimately let it slip."

"You are right," he agreed.

The maid returned with fresh tea, a second cup, and more toast. She left without speaking and closed the door behind her.

"Which must mean it was Evan Blantyre," Vespasia concluded. "If it was anyone else, Serafina would not have gone to such lengths to bury the truth."

"Did she care about him?" he asked.

Vespasia raised her eyebrows in exasperation. "Don't be absurd, Thomas! She must have found out after Adriana was committed to marrying him. That would have made it impossible for her to do anything! She would have stifled her own feelings and kept silent for Adriana's sake."

"In the end it served neither of them," Pitt said unhappily. "Poor Serafina. She paid a very high price for nothing."

"Not for nothing," she corrected him simply. "Adriana had many happy years. She grew to be a strong, beautiful woman, and I think she always knew that Serafina loved her like a mother."

"And Blantyre?" he asked bitterly.

"Perhaps, in his own way, he also loved her. But not as he cared for his ideals and his beliefs in Austria."

"I'll prove it, one way or another," he said grimly, as if he were making an oath.

"I daresay you will." She poured a cup of tea for him and passed it over.

"Thank you." He took it and then a piece of toast, buttering it absentmindedly.

"That is hardly your most urgent concern," she observed.

He looked up at her.

"My dear, if Evan Blantyre spent long enough at Dorchester Terrace to realize that Serafina knew he was the one who betrayed Lazar Dragovic, then he must have listened to a great deal that she said. What else was there, do you suppose? Most of it may be irrelevant now, but what about that which is not? Who does it concern?"

"I don't know," he admitted. "That same thought occurred to me. I could find out all the places where Blantyre has served, but it wouldn't tell me much, except the extent of the possibilities, and I can already guess that."

She spread more butter on her piece of toast.

"All kinds of people have served in the embassies of Europe at some time or another, especially that of Vienna," Vespasia said.

She passed him the marmalade. "And apart from government positions, most of the aristocracy travels for pleasure, to hunt, to drink beer, to exchange ideas — philosophy, sciences. To climb mountains in the Tyrol, or to sail on the lakes. To visit Venice and the Adriatic, especially the coast of Croatia with its islands. And always we go to the glory and the ruin of Rome, and imagine ourselves heirs to the days of its empire. Some of us go to Naples to gaze at Vesuvius and imagine the eruption that burned Pompeii. We see the sunlight on the water and dream for a little while that it always shines."

"What does that have to do with Austria's survival as an empire?" he asked.

"Very little," she replied. "But a great deal to do with indiscretions, with secrets that people might still wish to keep, even forty years later."

The crisp toast and sharp marmalade lost their taste. Pitt could have been eating cardboard.

"You mean Serafina was in those places and would have known all sorts of things?"

"She was very observant. It was part of her skill."

"So there were likely many Austrians she could've blackmailed," he concluded.

"Certainly. Britishers as well. She was neither spiteful nor irresponsible," Vespasia said gently, "but she understood the weaknesses of people. And now Blantyre may know a great many things from Serafina's confused mind, and he may well have no moral boundaries in his crusade to preserve the power of the Austro-Hungarian Empire, and all that he believes depends upon it."

Pitt leaned forward slowly, his hands pressed hard against his face.

"It is time for some very difficult decisions, my dear," Vespasia said after a moment or two. "When you have made sure that Duke Alois is safe, you are going to have to deal with Evan Blantyre. You have the heart of a policeman, but you must have the brain of the head of Special Branch. Don't forget that, Thomas. Too many people are relying on you."

CHAPTER 12

Pitt sat in the housekeeper's room at Dorchester Terrace waiting for Nerissa Freemarsh to come. He had expected her to deliberately keep him waiting, and he was not disappointed. It gave him time to think very carefully about what he intended to say, how much of the truth to tell her, and how much pressure to exert. He had felt a certain compassion toward her when they had first met. At one time or another during his career in the police he had seen many single young women who were dependent upon a relative who made full use of them as unpaid servants. Occasionally, a parent had intentionally kept one daughter home for precisely that purpose.

It was wretched for anyone being such a dependent, an onlooker at life but never a participant. Nerissa had been one of those with very little choice. She did not have the charm or the daring to have set out on her own. She could not create adventure for herself, as Serafina had done; perhaps Serafina had secretly despised her for that. If so, Nerissa would've realized it, even if she could not have put a name to it or explained why.

Was Nerissa flattered that another woman's husband had made advances to her, professed a kind of love? Or had she genuinely cared for him, probably far more than he had for her? Was Pitt insulting her in assuming that Blantyre's interest was solely in Serafina, and that Nerissa was merely the excuse to visit? He felt a certain anger for a man who could use a woman's obvious vulnerability in such a way.

The door opened, without a knock, and Nerissa came in, closing it behind her. She stood facing him as he rose to his feet. Today she had a jet-and-crystal brooch at her throat and matching earrings giving light to her face. They were beautiful. Pitt wondered briefly if they had been Serafina's.

"Good morning, Miss Freemarsh," he said quietly. "I'm sorry to disturb you again, but several new facts have come to light, and I need to ask you some further questions."

She seemed calmer today. There was no

sign of anxiety in her face as she heard this news.

"Indeed? I am aware of Mrs. Blantyre's suicide," she answered coolly, facing him with her hands folded in front of her. "A tragedy, and yet it appears to have been inevitable. I gather that she held my aunt responsible for her father's death, or at least for his being caught by the Austrians and executed for insurrection. I was aware that she was . . ." She looked for the right word, cutting but not overtly cruel. ". . . fragile. I was not aware that it was so very serious. I'm sorry. I know that suicide is a sin, but in the circumstances, perhaps it is better that she should have taken her own life, rather than face arrest and trial, and the shame of all that." Her face tightened. "And they might have locked her away in an asylum, or even hanged her, I suppose. Yes, I . . . I have to respect her for her choice. Poor creature."

Pitt looked at her, a well of pity, disgust, and revulsion building up inside him. Did she know that it was Blantyre who had betrayed Lazar Dragovic, killed Serafina, and then Adriana too? Was she a party to it, or ignorant of everything, guilty of nothing but falling in love with another woman's husband? He did not know.

"Please sit down, Miss Freemarsh. I'm afraid the situation is not as simple as that."

She sat obediently, hands folded in her lap, and he returned to the housekeeper's chair.

"You're not going to make the case public, are you?" she asked in dismay. "Surely that is not in the government's interest? It is simply the tragedy of a woman who suffered as a child, and did not recover from it." She scowled. "You would drag her husband through a mire of shame and embarrassment he does not deserve, and to what purpose? Please do not say that it is justice. That is complete nonsense, and would be the utmost hypocrisy on your part. My aunt caused the death of Mrs. Blantyre's father, politically justified or not. Mrs. Blantyre's mind was unhinged as a child because of it. I believe she was actually there and witnessed the whole appalling thing. She never knew who betrayed him, until Aunt Serafina's own mind began to wander, and somehow in her ramblings she gave herself away. In a hysteria of revenge, Mrs. Blantyre killed her, and then, realizing what she had done, took her own life. Justice has already been more than served."

He looked at her and wondered how much of that she truly believed, and how much

493

she had convinced herself of.

"Are you sure?" he asked, as if he was seeking proof himself.

"Quite sure," she replied. "And if you consider it, you will see that it makes perfect sense." There was no doubt visible in her, no unease. He could see no sign of real pity either. She could not, or did not, wish to imagine herself in Adriana's place.

"When did your aunt tell you about Lazar Dragovic's death?" he asked, affecting only mild interest. "And when did you realize that Dragovic was Adriana's father?"

Nerissa looked startled. "I beg your pardon?"

She was playing for time, trying to understand what he was looking for, and how to answer him.

"You know about Dragovic, and that Adriana witnessed his death herself, as an eight-year-old child," he explained. "Someone told you. It is not recorded in any written history, obviously, or Adriana would have known it all the time. Only those present knew the truth."

Nerissa swallowed. He could see her throat convulse.

"Oh. Yes, I see." Her hands were knotted in her lap now, her knuckles white.

"So when did your aunt tell you this?" he

persisted. "And why? She cannot have wished you to tell anyone, least of all Adriana Blantyre."

"I . . . I can't recall." She took a deep breath. "I must have pieced it together from her ramblings. She was very incoherent at times. Lady Vespasia would tell you that. Bits and pieces, jumbled, not knowing who was with her."

"And you realized from all those 'bits and pieces' that Adriana Blantyre was actually Lazar Dragovic's daughter, that Serafina had betrayed him to the Austrians, that she and Adriana had witnessed his execution, and that it had turned Adriana's mind, although she did not know who was behind the betrayal." He kept the disbelief from his tone, but barely. "And then Adriana later pieced together the truth, also from Mrs. Montserrat's ramblings, and lost her mind so completely that she murdered her, using the laudanum whose whereabouts she happened to know. But you did not think to mention this to anyone when Mrs. Montserrat was killed. You are a brilliant, complex, and quite extraordinary woman, Miss Freemarsh." Now he did not even attempt to keep the sarcasm out of his voice.

What little color was in her face was draining away, leaving her almost gray.

"I don't . . . I don't know what you mean," she stammered.

"Yes, you do, Miss Freemarsh. You know a great deal about Mrs. Blantyre and her past, which you did not learn from her, because she did not know it herself. Her whole motive for killing Mrs. Montserrat would've been that she had just discovered this apparent betrayal. And Mrs. Montserrat was quite unaware that she had revealed it, or she would have taken precautions to protect herself, would've at least told Miss Tucker. Mrs. Blantyre also could not have told anyone, because that would've immediately made her suspect in Mrs. Montserrat's death. So again, how did you know all of this?"

"I . . ." She gulped again, as if starving for air. "I told you. I . . . learned it from Aunt Serafina's rambling, the same way Mrs. Blantyre learned. Why is it difficult for you to understand that?"

"Because you would have me believe that she acted on it, and yet you did not mention any of this to me, even after we discovered that Mrs. Montserrat was murdered."

Nerissa was rigid now, her muscles locked so tight her shoulders strained against the fabric of her dress. She started to speak, and then stopped, staring at him defiantly.

496

"So. If I am to understand it, you assume that Mrs. Blantyre learned the truth from your aunt's disjointed ramblings, and was certain enough of what she pieced together to kill Mrs. Montserrat, without making any attempt to check the truth of it with anyone?" he asked patiently.

Nerissa's eyebrows rose. "Check the truth of it? With whom?" she demanded. "Where would she find anyone who could do that? Are you saying she should have taken a trip to Croatia and started searching for survivors of the rebels and insurgents of thirty years ago? That's absurd!" She gave a little snarl of laughter. "And even if she succeeded, Aunt Serafina could have been dead by the time she returned," she added.

"Exactly," he agreed. "No satisfaction in killing someone who is dying anyway. In fact, there's really very little purpose in that, don't you think?"

Her eyes were like pinpoints. "Then why are we having this ridiculous conversation?"

"Croatia was your suggestion, Miss Freemarsh. I was not thinking of her going there, or anywhere else. I was thinking of her simply going home."

Now she was sarcastic. "I beg your pardon?"

"I was supposing she would have asked

her husband," he explained. "After all, he was involved with the insurgents at that time. He was one of them. Or pretending to be. I think, actually, he was always loyal to Austrian unity and dominance in all the regions of its empire."

She said nothing.

"If it had been me, I would simply have gone home and asked him. Isn't that what you would've done?" he pressed.

She stared at him in angry silence, as if his question did not merit an answer.

"Unless, of course, Serafina did let something slip." He went on relentlessly now. "But it was not that *she* was the betrayer. And why would she be? She was always an insurgent, a fighter for freedom — if not for Croatia, then for that part of northern Italy that was under Austrian rule."

"What are you saying?" Nerissa's voice was hoarse.

"That the betrayer was not Serafina. It was Evan Blantyre himself. That is what Adriana discovered."

She was struggling now, to find a way to deny the truth. "That makes no sense!" she said sharply. "How dare you say such a thing? If Aunt Serafina knew that, or even believed it, why didn't she say so long ago? Why did she ever let Adriana Dragovic marry him?"

"I wondered that myself," Pitt admitted. "Then I realized that Adriana was beautiful, but poor, the orphan daughter of a man who had been executed by the Austrians. She was in ill health. She might very likely not bear children. What were her opportunities? She had met Evan Blantyre; he was in love with her and could offer her a very good life. Serafina probably had no proof against him. He had acted according to his own loyalties to Austria, because he believed passionately that the empire acted for the good of Europe — a conviction he still holds. Serafina loved Adriana enough to let her be safe, and happy. Accidentally revealing the truth and giving her a burden she could not live with was the thing she was most afraid of, when she knew that her control was slipping away and that she might forget where she was, or to whom she was speaking."

Nerissa breathed out slowly. "Then it seems she was right to fear it, since that was exactly what happened."

"Really?" he said with a disbelief she could not miss. "And when it did, Adriana killed her, then waited several days before going home and killing herself? Why, for God's sake?"

Nerissa started to shake her head.

Pitt leaned forward a little, his voice urgent now. "It was her husband who betrayed her father, not Serafina. So surely if Adriana was going to kill anyone, it would have been him? Except she didn't know, Miss Freemarsh. Serafina kept her secrets and died with them, before she could tell anyone else — except perhaps *Mr.* Blantyre. He spent time with her, didn't he? He came here telling you it was to see you, as your lover, but he sat with her, so it would look respectable. Only it was really the other way around; he came to see Serafina, not you, to find out how far her mind had disintegrated, and what of the past she might betray to Adriana."

"No!" she cried out. "No! That's horrible!" She made a swift movement with her hand, as if to sweep the suggestion away.

"Yes, it is," he agreed. "But we are speaking of a man who believes in the value of the Austrian Empire above all else. He betrayed his friend Lazar Dragovic, to his torture and death. He married Dragovic's daughter, perhaps from guilt, perhaps because she was beautiful and vulnerable. Maybe he felt safer, knowing where she was. And it would give him standing in the community of those who still seek to throw off

500

the Austrian yoke. Heaven knows, the whole Balkan Peninsula is teeming with them."

"That's . . ." she began, but could not finish the sentence.

"Logical," he said. "Yes, it is. And you are just one more of his victims, both emotionally and morally."

She stiffened but the tears were sliding down her face. "I have done nothing . . ." She stopped again.

"I am prepared to accept that you did not know beforehand that Blantyre would kill Serafina, and perhaps not immediately after," he said more gently. "You may have willfully refused to think about Adriana's death, or to work out for yourself what the truth had to be. At the moment I can see no purpose in charging you as an accessory. But if you do not cooperate now, that will change."

"Co . . . cooperate? How?" She started to deny her complicity, even her knowledge, but the words died on her tongue. She had known — or at least guessed — but refused to allow the thoughts to complete themselves in her mind. She knew that Pitt could see as much in her eyes.

"Tell me who was in the house the day Serafina Montserrat was killed, and the day before as well."

"The . . . day before?" Her hands twisted around each other in her lap.

"Yes. And please don't make any mistakes or omissions. If you do, and we discover them afterward, it will point very powerfully to guilt on your part — and probably to whoever you are attempting to protect."

She was trembling now.

"You have no choice, Miss Freemarsh, if you wish to save yourself. And I will, naturally, be speaking to at least some of the staff again."

It was several seconds before she spoke.

He waited for her in silence.

"Mr. Blantyre was here the day Aunt Serafina died," she said at last. "He came often. I don't remember all the days. Two or three times a week. He spent some time with me . . . and some with her."

"And he was definitely here the day she died?" he persisted.

"Yes."

"Did he see her alone, before Mrs. Blantyre was here?"

"Yes." Her voice was barely audible.

"What reason did he give?" he pressed her.

"What you said. For the . . . sake of appearance."

"Anyone else?" He was not even certain why he asked, except that he sensed a reluctance in her. "I would prefer to have it from you rather than from the staff. Allow yourself that dignity, Miss Freemarsh. You have little enough left. And by the way, I would not let your staff go, if I were you. Employed here, they have an interest in maintaining some discretion. If they leave, it will make a great many people wonder why, and they will most certainly talk, no matter what threats you make. You are not in a good position to do anything other than maintain silence yourself. If you are not prosecuted for anything, you will be in a comfortable financial situation, and free to conduct yourself as you please."

Her eyes widened a little.

"Who else was here?" he pressed.

"Lord Tregarron." It was little more than a whisper.

"Why?"

"I beg your pardon?"

"Why was Lord Tregarron here? To see you, or to see Mrs. Montserrat? I assume it was both, or you would not have been so reluctant to say so."

She cleared her throat. "Yes."

"Why did he wish to see Mrs. Montserrat? Were they friends?"

She hesitated.

He did not ask again.

503

"No," she said at last, speaking in gasps as if it caused her an almost physical pain. "His calling on her was . . . an excuse. I'm not certain if he was interested in me — he pretended to be — or in Aunt Serafina and her recollections."

"He spent time talking to her?"

"Not . . . much. I . . ." She breathed in and out several times, struggling to control her emotions. "I had the feeling that he did not like her, but that he wished to hide it. But not merely from good manners, or to spare my feelings because she was my aunt."

"Thank you," he said sincerely. "Did he express any interest in Mr. or Mrs. Blantyre?"

"Not . . . more than I would expect . . ." She trailed off again.

"I understand. Thank you, Miss Freemarsh. I think that is all, at least for the time being. I would like to speak to Miss Tucker now."

Tucker confirmed all that Nerissa had said, including several visits from Tregarron, over the period of the last four or five weeks.

Pitt thanked her and left. He walked back to Lisson Grove with his mind in turmoil. The heart of this case was no longer anything to do with Serafina's death, or Adriana, but two other matters.

The first and most urgent was the question of Evan Blantyre's loyalties. Had he given Pitt the information regarding Duke Alois out of loyalty to the Austrian Empire, which it seemed he had never lost, in spite of working for the British government? If that was so, and his betrayal of Lazar Dragovic, and the later murders of Serafina and Adriana, were to preserve the unity at the heart of Europe, then his information would be safe for Pitt to rely on. He could deal with Blantyre's prosecution and conviction after Duke Alois had come and gone.

If, on the other hand, Blantyre had some other purpose, his information about Duke Alois was very far from reliable.

And then the other obvious question arose: After Duke Alois left, what was Pitt going to do about Blantyre? What could he do? What evidence was there? He had no doubt now that Blantyre had killed Serafina and Adriana, but he doubted that there was sufficient proof to convict a man of such prominence and high reputation.

But that would have to wait. It was two days until the duke crossed the Channel and landed in England. Murder, however tragic, would pale beside the effects of a political assassination in London.

■ ■ ■ ■

Pitt checked in with Stoker at Lisson Grove. Then, after one or two items of urgent business, he left again and took a hansom to Blantyre's office. In spite of his bereavement, Blantyre had chosen to continue working. Duke Alois's visit could not be put off; there were arrangements to make and details to be attended to, and Blantyre, with his intimate and affectionate knowledge of Austria, was the best man for the job.

"Anything further?" Blantyre asked as he sat down in his large chair close to the fire. He poured whisky for both of them without bothering to ask. In spite of it being the middle of March, it was a bitter day outside, and they were both tired and cold.

"Yes," Pitt answered, accepting the exquisite glass, but putting it down on the small table to his right without drinking from it. "I now know who killed Serafina, and why. But then so do you." He watched Blantyre's sensitive, haggard face and saw not a flicker in it, not even a change in his eyes.

"And who killed Mrs. Blantyre," Pitt continued. "But again, so do you."

This time there was a twitch of pain, which Pitt believed was perfectly real. Blantyre must have hated killing her, but had known that if he himself were to survive, then he had no alternative. Adriana would never forgive him for her father's death, and maybe not for Serafina's either. Even if she told no one, he would never be able to sleep again if she was in the house; perhaps not eat or drink. He would always be aware of her watching him. His mind would run riot imagining what she felt for him now and when she would lose control and erupt into action.

Pitt went on levelly. "I also know who betrayed Lazar Dragovic to the Austrians, which of course was the beginning of all this."

"It was necessary," Blantyre said almost conversationally. They could have been discussing the dismissal of an old but ineffectual servant.

"Perhaps you don't understand that," he went on. "You are a man of reason and deduction who comes to conclusions, and leaves it for others to do something about those conclusions. My father was like that. Clever. And he cared. But never enough to do anything that risked his own moral comfort." Bitterness filled his face and all but choked his voice. "Whoever lived or died, he must always be able to sleep at night!"

Pitt did not answer.

Blantyre leaned forward in his chair, still holding the whisky glass in his hand. He looked steadily at Pitt. "The Austrian Empire lies at the heart of Europe. We have discussed this before. I tried to explain to you how complex it is, but it seems you are a 'little Englander' at heart. I like you, but God help you, you have no vision. You are a provincial man. Britain's empire covers most of the globe, in patches here and there: Britain itself, Gibraltar, Malta, Egypt, Sudan, most of Africa all the way to the Cape, territories in the Middle East, India, Burma, Hong Kong, Shanghai, Borneo, the whole subcontinent of Australia, New Zealand, Canada, and islands in every ocean on Earth. The sun never sets on it."

Pitt stirred.

Temper flared in Blantyre's eyes. "Austria is completely different! Apart from the Austrian Netherlands, it stretches in one continuous landmass from parts of Germany in the northwest to Ukraine in the east, south to most of Romania, north again as far down the Adriatic coast as Ragusa, then west through Croatia and northern Italy into Switzerland. There are twelve main languages there, the richest, most original culture, scientific discoveries in every field of human endeavor . . . but it is fragile!"

His hands jerked up, and apart, as if he were encompassing some kind of explosion with his strong fingers.

"Its genius means that it is also liable to be torn apart by the very nature of the ideas it creates, the individuality of its people. The new nations of Italy and Germany, born in turmoil and still testing their strength, are tearing at the fabric of order. Italy is chaotic; it always has been."

Pitt smiled in spite of himself.

"Germany is altogether a different matter," Blantyre went on with intense seriousness. "It is sleek and dangerous. Its government is not chaotic; anything but. It is highly organized and militarily brilliant. It will not be contained against its will for long."

"Germany is not part of the Austrian Empire," Pitt pointed out. "It has a language in common, and a certain culture, but not an identity. Austria will never swallow it; it will not allow that."

"For God's sake, Pitt, wake up!" Blantyre was nearly shouting now. "If Austria fractures or loses control of its possessions, or if there is an uprising in the east that is successful enough to be dangerous, Vienna will have to make reprisals, or lose everything. If there is trouble in northern Italy it hardly matters, but if it is in one of the Slavic possessions, like Croatia or Serbia, then it will turn to Russia for help. They are blood brothers, and Russia will not need more than an excuse to come to their aid. And then teutonic Germany will have found the justification it needs to take German Austria."

His voice was growing harsher, as if the nightmare was already happening. "Hungary will secede, and before you know how to stop any of it, you will have a war that will spread like fire until it embroils most of the world. Don't imagine that England will escape. It won't. There will be war from Ireland to the Middle East, and from Moscow to North Africa, maybe further. Perhaps all of Africa, because it is British, and then Australia will follow, and New Zealand. Even Canada. Perhaps eventually the United States as well."

Pitt was stunned by the enormity of it, the horror and the absurdity of the view.

"No one would let that sort of thing happen," he said soberly. "You are suggesting that one act of violence in the Balkans

510

would end in a conflagration that would consume the world. That's ridiculous."

Blantyre took a deep breath and let it out slowly.

"Pitt, Austria is the linchpin, the glue that holds together the political body of Europe." He was staring intently. "It wouldn't be overnight, but you'd be appalled how quickly it would happen, if Vienna loses control and the constituent parts of the empire turn on one another. Picture a street riot. You must have had to deal with them, in your days on the beat. How many men does it take before the crowd joins in, and every idiot with a grudge, or too much to drink, starts swinging his fists? All the old enmities under the surface smolder and then break out."

Pitt remembered a time that was very similar to what Blantyre had just described: rage, hysteria, violence spreading outward until it took hold for no reason at all. Too late to regret it afterward, when houses were in ruins and broken glass was everywhere among fire-blackened walls and blood.

Blantyre was watching him. He knew Pitt understood what he was saying.

"There will be a vacuum at the heart," Blantyre went on. "And however much you like to imagine that Britain is the center of

Europe, it isn't. England's power lies in pieces, all over the globe. We have no army and no presence at the core of Europe. There will be chaos. The Austrian and German part of Europe will be at the throats of the Slavic northern and eastern parts. There will be a pan-European war, economic ruin, and in the end possibly a new and dominant Germany. Is the peaceful death, in her sleep, of one old woman so important to you in the face of that?"

"That is not the point," Pitt said quietly, facing Blantyre across the two untouched glasses of whisky. "I have no intention of pursuing Serafina's death right now. What concerns me is the validity of the information you have given Special Branch regarding Duke Alois, and the apparent threat of his assassination."

Blantyre raised his eyebrows. "Why should you doubt it? Surely you can see that I, of all people, do not want an Austrian duke assassinated. Why the hell do you think I turned Dragovic over to the Austrians? He was planning the assassination of a particularly brutal local governor. He was a pig of a man, but the vengeance for his death would have been terrible." He leaned forward, his face twisted with passion. "Think, damn it! Use whatever brain you have. Of course I don't want Alois assassinated."

Pitt smiled. "Unless, of course, he is another dissident. Then it would be very convenient if he was killed while he was here in London. Not the Austrians' fault — it's all down to the incompetent British, with their Special Branch led by a new man, who'll swallow any story at all."

Blantyre sighed wearily. "Is this all about your promotion, and the fact that you don't think you are fit for the job?"

Pitt clenched his jaw to keep his temper. "It's about the fact that most of the information we have on the assassination planned here came from you, and that you are a murderer and a liar, whose principal loyalty is to the Habsburg crown, and not the British," he replied, carefully keeping his voice level. "If Duke Alois was your enemy rather than your friend, you would be perfectly capable of having him murdered wherever it was most convenient to you."

Blantyre winced, but he did not speak.

"Or alternatively, there is no plot at all," Pitt continued. "You wanted to keep Special Branch busy, and the police away from investigating the murder of Serafina Montserrat, and then, most regrettably, of your wife. You had to kill Serafina, once you knew she was losing her grip on her mind, and might betray you to Adriana. And you need to survive now, or else how can you be of service in helping Austria keep control of its rapidly crumbling empire, after the suicide of its crown prince, and his replacement by Franz Ferdinand, who the old emperor despises?"

Blantyre's jaw was tight, his eyes hard.

"A fair estimate," he said between his teeth. "But you will not know if I am telling the truth or not, will you? You have checked all the information I gave you, or you should have. If you haven't, then you are a greater fool than I took you to be. Dare you trust it?" He smiled thinly. "You damned well don't dare ignore it!"

Pitt felt as if the ground were sinking beneath him. Yet the fire still burned gently in the hearth, the flames warming the whisky glasses, which shone a luminous amber.

"Be careful, Pitt," Blantyre warned. "Consider deeply what you do, after Alois has been here and gone. Assuming you manage to keep him alive, don't entertain any ideas of arresting me, or bringing me to any kind of trial." He smiled very slightly. "I visited Serafina quite often, and I listened to her. A good deal of that time she had no idea who I was. But then you know that already. You will have heard it from Lady Vespasia, if nothing else."

"Of course I know that," Pitt said tartly. "If you were not afraid of her talking candidly again, to others, you would not have taken the risk of killing her."

"Quite. I regretted doing it." Blantyre gave a slight shrug. "She was a magnificent woman, in her time. She knew more secrets about both personal and political indiscretions than anyone else."

Pitt was aware of a change in the atmosphere: a warmth in Blantyre, a chill in himself.

Blantyre nodded his head fractionally. "She rambled on about all manner of things and people. Some I had already guessed, but much of it was new to me. I had no idea that her circle was so wide: Austrian, Hungarian, Croatian, and Italian were all what I might have imagined. But the others: the French, for example; the German; and of course the British. There were some considerable surprises." He looked very steadily at Pitt, as if to make certain that Pitt grasped the weight of what he was saying.

Pitt thought of Tregarron, also using Nerissa Freemarsh to disguise his visits to Serafina. What did he fear that could be so much worse than being thought to have an affair with a plain, single woman of no significance, and almost on his own doorstep? It was a despicable use of a vulnerable person whose reputation it would permanently ruin.

"The British Special Branch, and various other diplomatic and intelligence sources, have a record of some very dubious actions," Blantyre continued. His voice dropped a little. "Some have made them vulnerable to blackmail, with all its shabby consequences. And of course there are also the idealists who set certain values above the narrow love of country. Serafina was another little Englander like you. She kept silent." He left the suggestion hanging in the air. It was not necessary to spell it out.

Pitt stared at him. He had no doubt whatsoever that Blantyre meant everything he was saying. There was a confidence in him, an arrogance that filled the room.

Blantyre was smiling broadly. "Victor Narraway would have killed me," he said with almost a kind of relish. "You won't. You don't have the courage. You may think of it, but the guilt would cripple you.

"I like you, Pitt," he said with intense sincerity, his voice thick with emotion. "You are an intelligent, imaginative, and compassionate man. You have quite a nice sense of humor. But in the end, you haven't the steel in your soul to act outside what is predictable, and comfortable. You are essentially bourgeois, just like my father."

He took a deep breath. "Now you had better go and make sure you save Duke Alois. You can't afford to have him shot in England."

Pitt rose to his feet and left without speaking. There was no answer that had any meaning.

Outside he walked along the windy street. He was chilled and shivering in spite of the sun, which sat low in the sky, giving off a clean-edged, late winter light. Was Blantyre right? Would Narraway have shot Blantyre? Would he find himself unable to do the same, standing with a pistol in his hand, unable to kill in cold blood a man he knew, and had liked?

He did not know the answer. He was not even certain what he wanted the truth to be. If he could do such a thing, what would he gain? And what would he lose? His children might never know anything about it, but it would still be a barrier between them and him.

And what ruthlessness would Charlotte see in him, which she had not seen before, and had not wanted to? Or Vespasia? Or anyone? Above all these, what would he learn about himself? How would it change him from who he was now? Was Blantyre right that his inner comfort was what he cared about most, in the end?

He was walking rapidly, not certain where he was going. He was less than half a mile from the part of the Foreign Office where Jack worked. There were no secrets left about Blantyre. Pitt knew the worst. But the resolution as to what to do was lost in the turmoil of his own mind.

Vespasia knew from the moment Victor Narraway came into her sitting room that he had serious news. His face was pinched with anxiety, and he looked cold, even though it was a comparatively mild evening.

Without realizing she was doing so, she rose to greet him.

"What is it, Victor? What has happened?"

His hands were chill when he took hers, briefly, but she did not pull away.

"I have learned something further about Serafina, which I am afraid may be more serious than I had supposed. Tregarron visited Dorchester Terrace several times. I thought at first it was primarily to see Nerissa . . ."

"Nerissa?" For an instant she wanted to

laugh at the idea, then the impulse died. "Really? It seems an eccentric idea. Are you sure?"

"No, I'm not sure. Men do sometimes have the oddest tastes in affairs. But now I believe that Nerissa was the excuse and Serafina the reason."

"She was at least a generation older than he, and there is no proof, in fact, not even a suggestion, that they knew each other," she pointed out.

"But his father knew Serafina," Narraway said grimly, watching her face. "Very well."

"Oh. Oh, dear. Yes, I see. And you are assuming that perhaps Serafina was indiscreet about that too. Or perhaps others were able to deduce that the present Lord Tregarron was visiting for fear of her saying something unfortunate. Who is he protecting, though? His father's reputation? Is his mother still alive?"

"Yes. She is very old, but apparently quite clear in her mind." His expression was sad and gentle. "What a devil of a burden it is to know so many secrets. How much safer it would be to understand nothing, to see all manner of things before you, and never add it up so you perceive the meaning."

It was not necessary for either of them to say more. Each carried his or her own burden of knowledge, differently gained but perhaps equally heavy.

They sat by the fire for a few more moments, then he rose and wished her good night.

But when he left, going out into the mild, blustery wind, Vespasia remained sitting beside the last of the fire, thinking about what he had said. Of course Tregarron would rather his mother never heard of her husband's affair with Serafina, on the assumption that she did not already know. But it did not seem a sufficient motive for Tregarron to make quite so many visits to see Serafina; surely there was something else, possibly something about that affair uglier and more dangerous than just unfaithfulness?

She must make her own inquiries. The day after tomorrow Duke Alois Habsburg would land in Dover. There was no time to spare for subtlety. It was not a thought she wished to face, but she knew who she must ask for this possibly dangerous piece of knowledge. She had reached the point where the price of evasion would be greater than that of asking.

Vespasia alighted in Cavendish Square the next morning at a quarter to ten. It had been a long time — over two decades — since she had last seen Bishop Magnus Collier. He was a little older than she, and had retired several years earlier.

The footman who answered the door had no idea who she was. She offered her card, telling him that she was an old acquaintance and the matter was of extreme urgency.

He looked doubtful.

"His lordship would not be amused should you leave me standing on the step in the street," she said coldly.

He invited her in and, in a manner no more than civil, showed her to a morning room where the fire was not yet lit. It was fifteen very cool minutes before he returned, pink-faced, and conducted her into the bishop's study. There, the fire was burning well, and the warmth in the air wrapped around her comfortingly.

She accepted the offer of tea, and occupied herself looking at the rows of bookshelves. Many of the titles she was familiar with from long ago, though they were works she had never read herself. She found the writings of most of the very early Church fathers more than a trifle pompous.

She heard the door open and close and turned to find Bishop Collier standing just inside, a curious smile on his lean face. He was very thin, and far grayer than when they had last met, but the warmth in his eyes had not changed.

"All my life it has been a pleasure to see you," he said quietly. "But I am concerned that you say it is a matter of such urgency. It must be, to bring you here, after our last parting. What can I do to help?"

"I'm sorry," she said softly, and she meant it. The impossible feelings they had once had for each other were no longer there, but it had still been wise for them to decide not to meet again. They had to consider the perceptions of the outside world.

He gestured toward the chairs near the fire and they both sat. She arranged her skirts with a practiced hand, in a single, graceful movement.

"Perhaps you read that Serafina Montserrat died recently?" she began.

"Time is catching up with us rather more rapidly than I expected," he said ruefully. "But perhaps that is its nature, and ours is to be taken by surprise by what was utterly predictable. But I'm sure you did not come to discuss the nature of time and its peculiar elastic qualities. I hope her passing was easy. She was a remarkable woman. She would have faced death with courage. I would be surprised if it had the temerity to inconvenience her overmuch."

Vespasia smiled in spite of herself. She was reminded sharply of what it was in him that she had liked so much, and why they had decided to stay apart.

"I think it was simply a matter of going to sleep and not waking again," she replied. "The part of it that brings me here is that the sleep was the result of having been given a massive overdose of laudanum."

All the light vanished from his face. He leaned forward a little. "Are you saying that it was given to her without her knowledge, or that she took it herself, intending to die? I find the latter very difficult to believe."

"No, that isn't what I am saying. She rambled in her mind, sometimes forgot what year it was, or to whom she was speaking, which caused her profound anxiety. She was worried she would accidentally let slip a confidence that could do much damage." She recalled the terror on Serafina's face with acute pain. "She did make such slips, and she was murdered because of it."

He shook his head. "Are you certain beyond doubt?"

"Yes. But that is not why I have come. My concern is with one of the secrets she let slip, and the damage it could cause now."

"What can I do to help?" He looked

puzzled.

"The secret concerns an affair she had very many years ago, with the late Lord Tregarron." She stopped, seeing the change in his face, the sudden darkness. It would be impossible now for him to deny that he was bitterly aware of what it was she was going to ask.

"I cannot repeat to you things that were told to me in confidence," he said. "Surely you know better than to ask?"

"There is a very slight deviousness in you, Magnus," she said with a curve of her lips that was almost a smile. "Anything Tregarron might have told you may be confidential, although the man has been dead for years. What Serafina told you, though, I doubt was in the nature of confession. Is keeping confidence about an old affair really so very important that we can allow it to cost a man his life now? And, if the worst comes to pass, it may be more than one life at stake."

"Surely you are exaggerating?" he demurred, but there was no conviction in his eyes.

This time she did smile. "You are not built for deceit, Magnus."

"What is it that you imagine I am hiding, Vespasia?" he asked.

"A truth that is a great deal uglier than a mere indiscretion," she replied.

"He was married," he pointed out reasonably. "It was a betrayal of his vows to his wife."

"Would you excommunicate him for it?" She raised her silver eyebrows curiously.

"Of course not! And I daresay he repented. I do not have the right to assume that he did not."

"Of course you don't," she agreed. "So we may dispense with the fiction that it had anything to do with that."

"But it did, I assure you," he said immediately.

"A sophistry, Magnus. I gather it sprang from that. By having an affair with Serafina he laid himself open to blackmail. He may have wished profoundly at the time to keep the matter secret. He was in a senior diplomatic position in Vienna. It would have made his discretion severely suspect."

His gaze wavered for an instant. "I cannot tell you, Vespasia."

"You do not need to, my dear. I can deduce it for myself. Now that I know where to look, I can inform the appropriate people."

"I believe Victor Narraway is no longer in office," he observed, this time meeting her gaze squarely.

"That is true. His place has been taken by Thomas Pitt, who is married to my grand-niece. I have known Thomas for years. His brother-in-law is Jack Radley, who is assistant to the present Lord Tregarron."

"Vespasia! Please . . ." he began, then stopped.

"I assume it was treason of which his father was guilty?" she said so quietly it was almost a whisper.

"I cannot say," he answered, but his face showed that she was right.

She stood up slowly. "I'm sorry. You deserved better from me than this. Were it not now a matter of treason, and more murder yet to come, I would not have asked."

He rose also. "You always had the better of me, in the end."

"It was not a battle, Magnus. I understood you more than you did me, because your beliefs were never hidden. It is a good way to be. I am glad you have not changed. That is your victory; don't regard it as anything else."

He smiled, but his eyes were still grave. "Be careful, Vespasia. Although I suppose that is a foolish thing to say. You haven't changed either."

■ ■ ■ ■

Vespasia had no doubt now what she must do. She would have liked to have seen Jack at his rooms in the Foreign Office, but she could not go there without Tregarron being aware of it. Instead she would have to speak to Emily, and hope to impress on her the desperate urgency of what she had to say.

As it transpired, Emily was not at home. Vespasia had to either wait for her or leave and return again in the late afternoon. She went home and used her telephone — an instrument of which she was becoming increasingly fond. However, on this most urgent occasion it did not help her. She failed to contact Victor Narraway, or Charlotte, and she did not dare spark curiosity or alarm by trying to reach Jack.

So, in the end, she returned to Emily's home at five o'clock. She had only half an hour to wait before Emily herself arrived.

"Aunt Vespasia!" She was instantly concerned. "The butler tells me you called this morning as well. Is everything all right? What has happened? It . . . it isn't Jack, is it?" Now she was afraid.

"No, not at all. As far as I know Jack is perfectly well, at least so far," Vespasia replied. "But there is a situation of which he is unaware, which may endanger him very badly, unless he acts now. It will not be easy, but I am afraid circumstances may not allow him the luxury of waiting."

"What?" Emily demanded. "What is it?"

"When do you expect him home?"

Emily glanced at the ormolu clock on the mantel. "In half an hour, maybe a little more. Can you not tell me what it is?"

"Not yet. Perhaps you would care for a cup of tea while we wait?" Vespasia suggested.

Emily apologized for her oversight in hospitality and rang the bell for the maid. When she had requested the tea, she paced the floor, unable to relax. Vespasia thought of asking her to desist, and then changed her mind.

When Jack got home, the butler informed him of the situation. He stopped only to hand his overcoat to the footman before he went to the withdrawing room.

He saw Emily at the window. She swung around to face him as soon as she heard the door. Vespasia was sitting on the sofa before the fire. The remnants of cookies and tea were on the tray, Emily's undrunk.

"Is it something serious?" Jack said, as soon as he had greeted them both.

"I am afraid it is," Vespasia replied. "If Emily is to remain, then she will have to give her word that she will repeat no part of this to anyone at all, not even Charlotte or Thomas. And in my opinion it would be better if she left."

"I'm staying," Emily said firmly.

"You are not," Jack responded. "If I think it is wise, I shall tell you afterward. Thank you for keeping Aunt Vespasia company until I arrived."

Emily drew in her breath to argue. Then she looked again at his face, and obediently left the room. On the way out, she instructed the footman to see that no one intruded into the withdrawing room for any reason.

Briefly, and with as few explanations as she could manage, Vespasia told Jack what she had learned.

He stood by the fire, his mind racing, his whole body feeling battered. He wanted to cry out that it was impossible: only a collection of circumstances that did not fit together and, in the end, meant nothing at all.

But even as the words formed in his mouth, he knew that it was not so. There were other things that Vespasia did not know, but that fit into place like the last pieces of a jigsaw: the way Tregarron had dismissed Pitt, the contradictions in the reports that Jack had tried not to see. The small items of information that had turned up with people who should not have known them.

"I'm sorry," Vespasia said quietly. "I know you believed that Tregarron was a good man, and that it was a considerable promotion for you to assist him as closely as you do. But he will be brought down, Jack, sooner or later. You must see to it that you do not go down with him. Treason is not a forgivable offense."

But Jack's mind was already elsewhere. Tomorrow Alois Habsburg was due to arrive in Dover. Pitt would go there tonight to be on the train with him when he came up to London. Tregarron had left the office at midday. There was no decision to be made. Of course Tregarron had denied that there was going to be an attempt on Alois's life — he was the one who was going to make it!

"I'm going to warn Thomas," he said, his voice shaking. "I must go immediately. We'll leave for Dover tonight. Please tell Emily." He turned and strode toward the door.

"Jack!" Vespasia called after him.

"I have no time to stay. I'm sorry!"

"I know you don't," she replied. "My carriage is at the door. Take it."

"Thank you," he said over his shoulder. He ran out onto the footpath and looked for the carriage. It was only a few yards away. He called out to the coachman and gave Pitt's home address. Then he stopped. Should he go to Lisson Grove?

"Sir?" The coachman waited for his confirmation.

"No — right! Keppel Street." Jack scrambled into the carriage and it pulled away from the curb. He sat white-knuckled while they raced through the streets. It was not far, but it seemed as if they must've crossed half of London.

They skated to a stop. He flung the door open and strode over the pavement. He knocked on the door, which was opened by Minnie Maude.

"Yes, sir?"

"Is Commander Pitt at home?"

"No, sir. I'm afraid yer just missed 'im."

"Has he gone to Lisson Grove?"

"No, sir. 'E's gone ter the railway station."

"How long ago? Quickly!"

"Quarter of an hour, sir. Mrs. Pitt's at 'ome, if you'd like to see her."

"No . . . thank you." He swung around and went back to the carriage. He was too late. There was nothing he could do now but go home and get money, and perhaps a swordstick from the library, and go down to Dover himself.

CHAPTER 13

Pitt woke up in the morning with a jolt, taking a moment to adjust to his strange surroundings and remember where he was. It should not have been difficult. He had spent enough of the night lying awake staring at the unfamiliar streetlamp patterns on the ceiling of his hotel room in Dover.

This was the day Alois Habsburg was to land and take the London train. From the moment he set foot on English soil he was Pitt's responsibility.

He had gone over the plans in his mind, trying to think of anything more he could do to foresee the attack, exactly where it would come, and how, if it would even come at all. But doubt nagged him: Had they been carefully misdirected here, to Dover and Duke Alois, when in reality the crime waiting to be committed was something entirely different? In the small hours of the night he thought of the Bank of England, the Tower of London, and the crown jewels, even the Houses of Parliament.

Pitt had fallen asleep without any answers.

Now he rose quickly, washed, shaved, and dressed. There was time for a quick breakfast, and it would be stupid not to eat. The best decisions were seldom made on an empty stomach.

He found Stoker in the dining room but they sat separately, to draw less attention to themselves. They left a few moments apart too. It was probably completely unnecessary, but better than being careless.

They were close to the docks anyway. It took them only ten minutes to be at the pier, where the cross-Channel ferry was already approaching. Pitt stood with his hands in his pockets watching the outlines of the boat as it came closer across the choppy gray water. He hunched his shoulders and turned his collar up against the chill of the wind. He liked the smell of salt, even the tar and oil and fish odors, but somehow sea wind was colder. It crept through every crevice in clothing, no matter how carefully one dressed.

He knew where Stoker was, and the other three men he had brought, but never once did he look at them. He had not asked assistance from the Dover police. They were there as a courtesy, knowing from the Austrian Embassy of Duke Alois's visit, but he had weighed the issues and decided it was better not to let them think there was any particular danger.

He was standing in the wind, part of the crowd, when he felt a nudge next to him and half-turned. Jack was standing beside him, pale-faced, cold, his coat collar turned up.

"You were right," Jack said before Pitt could speak. "It's Tregarron. I'm sorry. Serafina seduced his father into an affair, then because of it, he was blackmailed into committing treason. It was all a long time ago, and obviously he's dead now, but the present Lord Tregarron was desperate to conceal it, for his own protection, and his mother's too, I imagine. It . . . it explains a few other things he was doing. I should have seen it earlier. I didn't want to."

Pitt looked at him with surprise and a sudden warmth of affection. "You came down here to tell me?"

"Of course."

"Thank you."

"Be careful . . ." Jack warned urgently.

Pitt smiled. "I will. You should get back home, before you're missed."

"Can't I help?"

"You just did. We may need you back home yet, if Tregarron's at the party this evening."

Jack smiled and moved off into the crowd.

The ferry was nosing in gently; in a few minutes the gangway would be lowered. The Port Authority had told Pitt that Duke Alois would be disembarking first. It would have been better had he come amid the other passengers, less conspicuous, but it would have been contrary to protocol, and thereby would have signaled that Special Branch felt unable to protect him under normal circumstances. It was a debate Pitt had had with himself, and he was still not sure if he had come to the right answer.

He watched as the docking procedure took place. It seemed infinitely slow, and yet when the slender, elegant figure appeared at the top of the gangway, dark hair blowing in the wind, Pitt felt a leap of alarm. His mind raced to think of anything he might have missed, failed to do, or not thought of, and what Reibnitz, if he was really here, would have prepared for.

Alois came down the steps, slowly, giving a slight salute and smiling at the dignitaries waiting at the bottom to welcome him. He was followed by four casually dressed, very fashionable men around his own age. None of them was in uniform. Pitt was seized with a sudden conviction that they didn't have the faintest idea that there would be any danger. They were on a foreign vacation to a country where they had no enemies, no rivals, and no one who could be anything but delighted to see them.

The mayor of Dover stepped forward and the welcome began. It was a long, highly formal affair.

Pitt watched the small crowd of people gathered to observe the event, or who were simply here to meet their own friends and family. He tried to appear as if he was looking for some family member himself. He saw Stoker and his other men come a little closer as Duke Alois moved away with the mayor and his officials.

"Looks as if he has no idea of danger," Stoker said quietly as they walked side by side from the dock along the street toward the railway station. "I suppose somebody did tell him?"

Pitt did not reply; Salisbury had said he had informed the duke — so perhaps the duke's nonchalance was an act? He wasn't sure.

Stoker grunted, and increased his pace.

Pitt was tense as Duke Alois and his men stepped up into a carriage and the horses moved off at a walk. The general traffic had been held back to allow them passage. Pitt looked down and across the street, but he saw no dust carts, no sweepers. Where was Staum?

He and Stoker followed after the carriage on foot, watching every movement, occasionally glancing up at higher windows above shops and offices. The wind was gusty, with a light spatter of rain, and as far as he could see, none of the stores were open. Still, he was nervous.

He glanced at Stoker, and saw the same anxiety in his face, in the stiff, tight-muscled way he walked.

If there was no attack in Dover, did that mean it was going to be on the train after all? A diversion? A crash?

The station was in sight. Two hundred yards to go.

A dust cart trundled by, wheels bouncing on uneven stones. Pitt and Stoker stared at the man wheeling it, but he was very old and wizened, and was steering the cart in the opposite direction.

Fifty yards, and then they were there. Duke Alois and his men alighted. The mayor of Dover conducted them inside. Pitt and Stoker gave a last look around, saw nothing suspicious, and followed them in.

The railway station was large and busy. A porter pushed a trolley weighed down with trunks and cases, its wheels rumbling over the platform. A few yards away a family was arguing excitedly, children jumping up and down. A small boy wailed with frustration. A man waved his arms and shouted a greeting. Half a dozen carriage doors slammed in the nearest train, and ahead of them the engine blew out great clouds of steam and smut. Pitt brushed it off his face, unintentionally smearing the dirt across his cheek, to Stoker's amusement. For an instant the tension was broken.

Pitt wiped away the smut and they pushed their way past other passengers. They reached the train, where the mayor was bidding Duke Alois good-bye. His escort seemed far more attentive now, standing on the platform looking first one direction, then the other, eyes searching.

As Pitt drew closer, he saw that one of them had a hand out of sight under his coat. Pitt knew it rested on the grip of his revolver. Pitt stopped and looked straight at the man's face.

"Commander Pitt, Special Branch," he introduced himself. "If you will allow me, I shall show you my identification."

Before the man could reply, Alois turned

from the mayor and stepped toward Pitt, smiling. He had a pleasant face: ascetic and filled with a kind of lopsided amusement.

He held out a hand. "How good of you to come," he said cheerfully. "Quite unnecessary, I'm sure, but a damned decent gesture." He spoke English with no trace of an accent.

Pitt offered a hand and met a firm, surprisingly strong grasp.

"How do you do, sir?" he replied. "It probably is unnecessary, but it might still be a good idea to get into the carriage anyway, if you don't mind."

"Certainly. Cold out here. Always damned cold, railway platforms, don't you think?" With alacrity, Duke Alois gave the mayor a small salute, and disappeared into the very handsomely decorated first-class carriage, Pitt a step behind him.

Duke Alois looked around approvingly. "Oh, very comfortable," he said with satisfaction. "Plenty of room." He looked at his own escort, standing to attention, waiting for his orders. "You chaps can busy yourselves doing whatever you do, looking out of carriage windows, or watching doors, or whatever. The commander here will have a cup of tea." He looked at Pitt. "Won't you?" It was a question, but the look in his light blue eyes was level and unflinching. In its own discreet way it was an order.

"I'd prefer to make sure of the rest of the carriage, sir, if you don't mind," Pitt answered.

Duke Alois laughed. "For heaven's sake, man, have your fellow here do it." He gestured toward Stoker. "I'm sure he's excellent. If you brought only him, you can't really imagine that there's anything to worry about."

"There are others," Pitt told him.

"Very good. Then we shall have a cup of tea, and leave them to it. Come." He opened the compartment door, and Pitt was obliged to accept.

The duke closed the door, sat down in one of the very comfortable seats, and crossed his legs, indicating the seat opposite for Pitt. Pitt sat down awkwardly; Narraway might have been versed in the art of conversation to entertain an Austrian duke, but Pitt was very definitely not. They could not have had less in common.

Pitt had no interest whatsoever in philosophy, or the more abstract sciences he had been told Duke Alois devoted his time to.

"Very good," Duke Alois repeated with a smile, stretching out his long legs. "Now we can talk."

Pitt swallowed. This was the one nightmare he had not foreseen, and he had no idea how to deal with it. What possible excuse could he make to escape?

"I was hoping you would come," Alois continued. "Rather overplayed the bit about Staum," he went on. "Nasty little swine, but actually he's one of ours. Reibnitz too. Have to use them, now and then. I expect you have such men yourself."

"I beg your p-pardon, sir?" Pitt stammered.

Duke Alois looked amused. His face radiated a pleasure that made him look more relaxed, less studious, and far more like a man on vacation. Was it possible he was even in some way enjoying this? Had he no conception of danger?

Pitt drew in his breath and tried to speak levelly, courteously. For all Duke Alois's divorce from reality — and, heaven knew, the Habsburgs had bred more than their fair share of imbeciles — he was still a royal duke.

"Sir, we cannot afford to take any threats lightly," he began.

"I don't," Alois assured him. "I am quite aware that it is serious, which is why we should have our conversation immediately, just in case we should be disturbed."

"Sir —" Pitt began.

Duke Alois held up a hand. "Please don't interrupt," he requested. "It is the whole purpose of my journey." He saw Pitt's bewilderment. A brief, wry smile lit his face for a moment, then disappeared. "You find that absurd? Good. That means, at least so far, I am succeeding."

Pitt gritted his teeth.

The duke leaned forward. Now his face was totally earnest. "You have a traitor in your government, Commander Pitt. In your Foreign Office, to be precise. I am happy to give you all the details I have, which are considerable."

Pitt swallowed. He was out of his depth, but he did not wish Alois to know it.

"And why would you do this, sir?" he asked with what he hoped was an expression of polite interest.

"Because I wish to establish a good working relationship with British Special Branch," Alois replied. "I believe we may turn this particular gentleman into a double agent, to both our advantages."

A wild idea occurred to Pitt. He looked at Alois's face, at his level, intense stare. It was suddenly very apparent that the man had a depth of political intelligence he chose to mask. Pitt took a deep breath and plunged in. "You are speaking of Lord Tregarron, I presume?" His heart pounded so hard it almost choked him.

Slowly Alois smiled, ruefully, like a child whose game has been spoiled. He let out a sigh. "Damn! I thought I had something worth trading. Have I tipped my hand for nothing?"

More wild ideas chased across Pitt's imagination. "Not necessarily," he replied. "I have only just realized Tregarron's treason. I assume it has to do with his father, and Serafina Montserrat, at least to begin with?"

"Indeed. Rather before my time. Even before my predecessor's," Alois replied.

"Your predecessor?" Pitt questioned.

"As Victor Narraway was yours," Alois answered. "The difference between your position and mine is only that I prefer to allow everyone to presume that my only interests are science and philosophy, intellectual hobbies that are of no practical use. It allows me a much greater freedom. Everyone of importance to your position knows exactly who you are. That also must have its advantages, but then, our systems are different. We, alas, are an empire very much in decline. And our emperor is less checked by any parliament than your queen is — or perhaps I should say empress, since she is empress of India, I believe."

"For what purpose might Tregarron be turned to both our advantages?" Pitt managed to ask, stunned by this revelation.

Alois gave a slight shrug. "I am head of my country's 'Special Branch,' as you are of yours. I do what I think is in our best interest. It is not always exactly what my government would do. But then, I have knowledge that it does not, and perhaps I can see a little further ahead than it can. I am sure you will find yourself in the same position occasionally. It would be to my advantage if Tregarron's information came directly to me."

"Doesn't it anyway?" Pitt asked drily.

"Unfortunately not. It is dictated by Mr. Blantyre, the only one who is aware of Tregarron's late father's treason, and his adultery with Mrs. Montserrat. The present Lord Tregarron is particularly concerned that his mother, who is still very much alive, should not learn of it."

"I think she was probably perfectly aware of it at the time," Pitt observed.

"Of the affair, probably," Alois conceded. "The treason is an entirely different matter. How did you know of it, by the way?"

"I deduced it," Pitt replied, wanting to

keep Jack's name out of the matter.

Duke Alois waited, his clear blue eyes steady, searching Pitt's face.

"It was the only answer that fit with certain other information I had," Pitt told him. Then he smiled to indicate that that was all he was going to say on the subject.

"I see. A pity that I had no opportunity to tell you sooner. It is not something I would like known any more widely. It would destroy its possible usefulness." Alois made a slight gesture of regret, but he did not evade Pitt's gaze, leaving the question open.

Pitt wanted to weigh every possibility and discuss them with Narraway, but knew that was impossible. He tried to think of any comparable arrangement in the past, and could remember none. If it had ever happened, it was not recorded. But then if he accepted Duke Alois's offer now, he would make no written record of it, at least not for general Special Branch availability. He must decide within the next few minutes. Was he giving Alois a weapon to use against him? Making an agreement perhaps useful to both of them? Earning a favor that might be reclaimed at some future time? Were such favors repaid?

Duke Alois was waiting.

"Fine," he said. "Tregarron is a man in an

extremely awkward position, but he is not a fool."

Duke Alois smiled with wry regret, and perhaps a touch of pity. "I know what you mean, and of course you are right. Excellent. We shall both prosper from it, if we are careful."

Pitt was far less certain, but he did not want Alois to know that; it would make him appear indecisive. He tried to keep the doubt from his face. "And how will you know if the information I give to Tregarron is true or false in the first place?" he asked.

"A gentleman's agreement," Duke Alois said drily, meeting Pitt's eyes.

"You are a gentleman," Pitt responded. "I'm not."

"You are a gamekeeper's son," Alois said. "Which means you have a good servant's sense of honor. I am a prince, which means I have very little sense of honor at all, only such as I choose."

Pitt was startled that Alois knew so much about him, then realized that he should have expected it. He also appreciated that Alois's comments were at least half ironic.

"I imagine that after the affair at Buckingham Palace, you are little inclined to trust princes," Alois went on. "Whereas I am much inclined to trust a man raised by a good gamekeeper. Gamekeepers are men who nurture the earth and the creatures on it. Nature forgives no mistakes."

"Nor does Special Branch, yours or mine," Pitt told him.

"Precisely. One might say the same of the tides of history." Alois was very serious now. There was no amusement in his eyes, only intense emotion. Pitt could not look away from him. "Social change is coming in all of Europe, whether the House of Habsburg wants it or not," Alois went on. "If we release our grip voluntarily, it may come without bloodshed. If we try to prevent change using oppression, then the end will be bloody, and the hate will remain."

"Emperor Franz Josef does not agree with you," Pitt said grimly.

"I know." A flash of bitter humor crossed Alois's face. "There is little I can do about that. But what I can do, I will, which is why I would find it very useful to be more aware of Tregarron's information, and perhaps have a few more . . ." He hesitated. ". . . more managed details going in both directions."

Pitt understood very well, even if he was not as certain of Alois's motives as he would like to be.

"Yes," he said, relaxing just slightly. "We

might think of a few ideas that would be profitable to one or the other of us. Perhaps even to both."

Duke Alois held out his hand. Without hesitation Pitt leaned forward and took it. Then he excused himself and went to check with Stoker.

Fifteen minutes later, he was in the hall outside the compartment, standing at the window watching the wooded countryside slip by. Suddenly the train slowed abruptly, as if the driver had jammed on the brakes.

Pitt stiffened, then turned and sprinted back the dozen yards to Duke Alois's compartment. "Stoker!" he shouted above the screech of the wheels on the iron track.

The connecting door to the next carriage flew open and Stoker was there, immediately followed by one of the duke's men.

The compartment door opened and Alois looked out. "What is it?" he asked, his voice steady but his face tight and pale.

"Farm cart on the rails," Stoker answered. "Looks like its load of hay fell off and it got stuck." He looked from Pitt to Duke Alois. "Sir. It's probably nothing, but —"

"Get back in and keep your head down!" Pitt finished for him. He made it sharp, an order.

"Are you sure it was a farm cart?" Duke

Alois questioned.

Stoker took a step toward him. "Maybe just an accident, sir, but maybe not." He stopped close to Alois, as if to push him back inside the compartment.

The duke glanced at Pitt.

The train jerked to a halt.

One of Duke Alois's men, tall, thin, and dark-haired, like the duke himself, came down the corridor.

"What the devil is —" he began.

A shot smashed the glass of the window. The man staggered backward and fell against the compartment wall, then slumped to the floor, a slow red stain spreading across his chest.

Stoker lunged toward Alois and forced him down onto the floor. One of the other men kneeled beside the fallen man, but Pitt knew without bothering to look again that he was beyond help. He turned and ran along the corridor toward the end of the carriage. Throwing open the door on the opposite side, he leaped down onto the track, his hand already on his gun. If he had gone onto the same side as the marksman, he would have been a perfect target, even an expected one. This gave him the cover of the train, but it also meant that he had the length of at least one carriage to run before he could get anywhere near the man.

Would the assassin want to take another shot? Or was he certain he had hit Duke Alois, and so would make his escape immediately? Who was it? Tregarron? Or one of the Austrian factions he had believed it was from the beginning? Tregarron would be alone. But if it was a political assassination attempt simply to draw attention, or any of the minor nations rebelling against Habsburg rule by shooting a member of the ruling family, then there could be half a dozen men. Was Stoker staying to guard Duke Alois? He hoped so. He was still a target.

He reached the end connection, and dropped to his hands and knees. He peered beneath and saw nothing but a narrow strip of woods on the other side. Was the marksman waiting just out of sight, ready to pick off anyone who appeared?

There had been no second shot. He probably knew he had hit someone, but he could not be certain it was Duke Alois. He would surely know that someone, either British, Austrian, or both, would come after him. Would the marksman retreat a little to a point from which he would see the train, but not be easily seen himself? Whoever he was, he had chosen a farm cart to stop the train, and a wooded area from which to attack. Perhaps he was a countryman; he was an excellent shot, possibly a hunter.

Pitt had grown up in the country as well. He had followed Sir Arthur Desmond on pheasant shoots, even deer hunts once or twice. He knew how to stalk, to keep low, to stay downwind, to move silently. He had only a handgun to the other man's rifle, which perhaps even had a telescopic sight on it, judging from the shot that had killed Duke Alois's man. Pitt must take very great care.

He went the length of the next carriage as well, then dropped to his hands and knees again and peered under. No one in sight. He scrambled through the gaps quickly and stayed low, rolling down the embankment into the underbrush and then up onto his feet again as soon as he was within the copse of trees.

Which way would the man go after making the shot? Probably to the high ground, where he would have a chance of still seeing the train, and also of seeing anyone who might come after him. A slight hollow would hide him better. It was instinctive.

But how long would he watch the train to make sure he had killed the right man?

Pitt wished he had told Stoker to make it

appear that they were flustered, and in some way to indicate that it was Alois who was dead. It was too late now. But perhaps he would think of it anyway.

Pitt moved forward through the thickest part of the trees. The ground was damp. He was leaving footprints. That meant the other man would also. If Pitt could find the tracks, he could follow him. But the assassin would realize that.

Pitt moved as quickly as he could toward where he judged the shot to have come from, trying to move silently, looking down to avoid snapping sticks or getting tangled in the long, winding branches of brambles. Every now and then he glanced up, but all he could see was underbrush and tree trunks with glistening wet bark, a lot of them birch, hazel, and black poplar, and here and there a few alder.

He looked backward once. The train was out of sight, except for the engine, which was stopped a few yards short of the huge hay wagon still splayed across the track, its load now largely moved onto the embankment. From the way the whole thing listed, it seemed that one of the wheels had broken, or come off. But if it was off, somebody would have found a way to put it back on again. There were half a dozen men working to clear the track. When they did, surely the train would go, whether Pitt had returned or not? Stoker would see to that? Or the duke?

Pitt stopped and stood still. He strained to hear movement anywhere ahead of him. How long would the marksman wait? Even if he had not seen Pitt through his scope, he would likely assume his presence, or the presence of someone else coming after him. Why had he not shot at Pitt, at least when he was on the embankment? Had he been concentrating on what was going on inside the train?

Pitt could hear nothing except the steady drip of water off the branches onto the wet leaves, which by this point in March almost moldered down into the earth.

Was there any water here? Yes, a stream along the lower ground. That would be the place to hide tracks. What would a clever man do? Go to the stream, leaving footprints easy enough to follow, then walk along the bed of the stream, leaving no trace at all, and then step wherever he would leave the fewest marks. Perhaps he would even create a false trail, and go back into the water again upstream or downstream from his entry.

How did the assassin get here? How would he leave? Not by train, perhaps not by road

— at least for the nearest few miles. Horse-back. It was the obvious way, perhaps the only way in this part of the countryside. Faster and easier than walking.

Then where was his horse? He would have left it tied somewhere; the last thing he needed was to come back and find that it had wandered off. If Pitt could find the horse, then the man would come to him. And where was the main road from London?

He turned and started to make for the high ground himself. Perhaps it would even be a good idea to climb a sturdy tree and look around? The horse would be at some point close to the road. He increased his pace.

At the top of the next rise he selected a strong, well-grown alder. Putting his revolver in his pocket, he began to climb. It was awkward. It must have been at least twenty years since he last climbed a tree.

It took a few moments to reach a satisfactory height, where he could see at least a couple of miles in all directions. As he twisted his body the trunk swayed. Better not to risk going any higher. If it broke, it would not only send him crashing down to possible injury, it would also make a considerable noise and tell the marksman exactly where he was.

Holding the trunk hard with his left arm, he looked around as widely as he could, searching for the road in the distance. It was not hard to see. After a moment or two he could trace it from south to north, swinging away to the west eventually. Surely the marksman would have left his horse near it, for once he reached the road again, he would have escaped pursuit. No one on the train had a horse, or any way of communicating with the outside world to call for help.

Pitt climbed down carefully and set off as rapidly as he could without making noise in the direction of the road. If he was wrong, he would lose his quarry completely, but he had no way of knowing where the marksman was anyhow.

Every now and then he stopped to listen, but he heard nothing more than bird calls and the whir of wings now and then. A dog barked somewhere far in the distance a few times, and then fell silent.

He came out on the road about a mile away from the train, perhaps a little more. He kept to the trees at the side. When he had made certain of his bearings, he went back into the woods again and started moving very carefully, looking for a clearing where someone could leave a horse unseen. He had to be quick. Once the marksman had made certain of his kill, and was back here and mounted, it would be impossible for Pitt to stop him, except by shooting him. Pitt was good with a gun; he had learned from his father. But a handgun is very different from a rifle or a shotgun. He knew his chances of hitting a man astride a fast-moving horse would be pretty poor. There would be no time to even make sure he had the right person. It could be some innocent rider in the wrong place at the wrong time.

And the marksman would know all this too.

Pitt moved as rapidly as he could, sprinting through the few open patches he came to. He was deeper into the woods now. He realized it, and swerved back toward the road. The marksman would have left the horse only far enough in to be hidden from passersby.

When he found it, he almost stumbled into it: a beautiful creature, moving quietly, cropping the grass in as wide a circle as its long tethering rope allowed it. It heard him at the same moment he saw it. It raised its head and looked at him curiously.

Pitt drew breath to speak, then realized the man could be close, so he stepped silently back into the shadow of the trees. The horse lowered its head again.

Pitt did not have long to wait. Less than four minutes later, he heard the faint crack of a twig. A man dressed in brown and green stepped out of the shadows and walked toward the horse, which lifted its head again and blew through its nostrils, taking a step toward him.

The man had a rifle with a telescopic sight fixed to it. It was Lord Tregarron.

Pitt stepped forward, his revolver raised high, pointing at Tregarron.

"If you move any closer to the horse I will shoot you," Pitt said very clearly. "Not to kill, but enough to hurt very much indeed."

Tregarron froze.

Pitt moved farther out of the shadow of the trees. Tregarron had killed a man. He would inevitably learn that he had not hit Duke Alois. Could he be charged with attempted assassination? There would have to be a trial. It would inevitably expose the duke's secret position.

Was the bargain Duke Alois had proposed still useful? It was a risk, but then it always had been.

Pitt came farther forward, angling closer to the horse so Tregarron could not get behind it and spoil his clean shot. The revolver was pointed at Tregarron's chest.

Tregarron smiled. Pitt knew its cruel twist was out of fear.

"Failed, didn't you?" he said with malice edging his voice. "You let Duke Alois be killed. Not likely to remain in your position much longer, especially when the Austrians tell London who he really was. You didn't know, did you?"

"Alois?" Pitt raised his eyebrows. "Is that who you were aiming at?" He saw a moment's doubt in Tregarron's eyes. "I'd like to let you think you succeeded, but you'll know soon enough that you didn't."

Tregarron blinked, not sure if he was being lied to or not.

"But you did kill someone," Pitt went on. "Poor chap was one of Alois's men. Resembled him, certainly."

Tregarron was standing stiffly, the rifle still in his hands.

"Put it down," Pitt told him.

"Or what? You'll shoot me? How would you explain that? I'm out for a ride in the country. Thought I'd shoot a few rabbits. You're a fool!"

"Good idea, shooting rabbits," Pitt lifted the barrel of the revolver an inch higher. "Might shoot a few myself."

"Don't be so damn stupid!" Tregarron

snapped. "You're supposed to be on a train guarding the head of the Austrian Special Branch, not strolling through the woods shooting at small animals!"

"You're right," Pitt agreed. "I wasn't shooting at small animals, I was shooting at the man who killed one of Alois's companions. Didn't see his face. Never realized it was one of our own Foreign Office staff."

A little of the color drained from Tregarron's skin. "You can't try me in court, even if you imagine that you could find proof. You'd create a scandal." But his voice was hollow. "This will look like an accident: tragic, but no one's fault."

"Not even mine, for incompetence?" Pitt asked sarcastically. "Shouldn't I have foreseen that we would have one of our aristocratic ministers wandering around the woods shooting at rabbits — at head height? Roosting in the trees, were they?"

The blood surged up Tregarron's face, and his grip tightened on his rifle till his knuckles were white.

"But as it happens," Pitt went on, "I don't wish to try you. I have a much better idea. You will pass me your rifle, then I will take your horse and ride to the nearest public transport back to London. You will walk to wherever you wish. I will say that I did not find the man who murdered our unfortunate Austrian visitor, and in return for that favor, at whatever time I wish in the future, you will pass on certain information that I will give you to your connections in the Austrian government."

Tregarron stared at him as if he could not believe what he had heard. Then, as he studied Pitt's face, he realized with horror that he really meant it.

"And if I should hear — and I would hear — that you have passed it incorrectly, then you will be exposed as the traitor you are," Pitt continued. "And your father's treason would become equally public, as would his regrettable affair with Serafina Montserrat."

"You filthy bastard!" Tregarron spat.

"I'm a bastard because I would rather use a traitor than shoot him in cold blood and create a scandal I could not control?" Pitt asked, the sarcasm back in his voice. "I suppose that's a matter of opinion. Mine is that you have betrayed your country rather than allow your father's treason to be exposed, or your mother to be embarrassed. You had better make your choice quickly. I am not going to wait."

"And what is to force me to keep my word?" Tregarron asked.

"Fear of exposure," Pitt replied succinctly.

"Pass me the rifle."

Slowly, as if his limbs hurt to move, Tregarron obeyed.

Pitt took the rifle, still keeping his revolver pointed at Tregarron. Then he moved very carefully to untie the horse and walk it beyond Tregarron's line of sight before he mounted it. Slinging the rifle over his shoulder, he urged the horse into a trot along the road.

At home at Keppel Street, Charlotte awaited Pitt with intense nervousness. She kept telling herself that there would be no attack in Dover, that the train journey to London would pass without incident. She busied herself with household tasks, but would stop halfway through, pace around, then forget what she had been doing and start something else.

" 'Ave yer lost summink?" Minnie Maude asked anxiously.

Charlotte swung around. "Oh, no, thank you. I'm just wondering if everything is all right. Which is quite stupid, because I can't help, even if it isn't."

The telephone rang, and she was so startled she flinched and let out her breath in a gasp. Instead of allowing Minnie Maude to pick it up, she dashed into the hall and did it herself.

"Yes? I mean, good afternoon?"

There was a pause while the exchange made the connection. Then: "Charlotte . . ."

It was Pitt's voice, and she was overwhelmed with relief. "Where are you? Are you all right? When will you be home?" she asked.

"I'm still in Kent. I am fine and I shall be home late," he replied. "Please make sure you go to the reception with Aunt Vespasia, or with Jack and Emily, and stay with them the whole time. I shall come when I can."

"Why are you still in Kent?" she demanded. "Are you sure you're all right? Is Duke Alois all right? And Stoker?"

"We are perfectly fine. And you will like the duke when you meet him. And I'll explain later. Please, just go with Aunt Vespasia, or Emily. I am not hurt in the slightest, really."

"Oh . . . thank heaven for that. Yes, I'll go with Emily and Jack." Already she knew what she meant to do. It was the opportunity she needed. "I'll see you there." She replaced the receiver with a smile.

Then immediately she picked it up again and asked to be connected to Emily's number. She had only a few moments to wait before Emily herself was at the other end.

"Emily? It's me. Thomas has been held up and cannot accompany me to the reception at Kensington Palace. May I come with you, please? I . . . I would like to." She said it gently; it mattered very much.

There was a moment's silence, then Emily's voice came back over the wire, filled with relief.

"Of course. That would be excellent. It will be like it was years ago, going together . . ." She stopped, not sure how to finish.

"What are you going to wear?" Charlotte filled in the silence. "I want to wear black and white. It's the only new really grand gown I have."

Emily laughed. "Oh, that's wonderful. I shall wear the palest possible green."

"That is your best color," Charlotte said sincerely.

"Then we shall take them by storm," Emily agreed. "We shall call for you at half-past seven." She laughed; it was a light, happy sound. "Good-bye."

"Good-bye." Charlotte replaced the receiver and went upstairs overwhelmed with relief, smiling all the way. "Minnie Maude! I think perhaps it is time I prepared for the evening," she called from the landing. Jemima's door opened on the next floor; she would want to help too, offer advice, and dream of the day when she would attend such events.

Charlotte arrived at Kensington Palace with Emily and Jack. It was a trifle tight inside their carriage, but both sisters looked superb. Emily's gown was huge in the crown of the sleeve; the Nile-green silk gleamed like sunlight on still water, and the huge skirts, when swept around, revealed a silver lining underneath. It was slender-waisted, and low at the neck. Diamonds shone at her neck and ears, and on a bracelet over her elbow-length white kid gloves.

Charlotte's choice was entirely different. It was a fine, sheer silk black overdress with a gleaming white gown beneath. The effect was all light and shadow, and when she moved it had a most extraordinary grace. The ribbon of black satin around the waist accentuated the natural curves of her body, and she wore pearl-and-jet jewelry with crystals that also caught the light in momentary fire. She knew that as she followed Emily in, she drew more eyes, and she held her head a little higher, feeling the warmth flush her cheeks. She did not normally consider herself beautiful, but perhaps for this occasion, she would make an exception.

The queen herself was not attending. She came to very few functions these days, only those where her absence would have been a serious dereliction of her duty as monarch. The Prince and Princess of Wales were traveling abroad, so — fortunately for Pitt, considering the affair at Buckingham Palace — they were not here either. The atmosphere was relaxed, with plenty of laughter amid the clink of glasses. Somewhere just out of sight, a small orchestra was playing lush, lilting Viennese music so that one could not help but wish to dance.

Vespasia arrived, escorted by Victor Narraway. She was always beautiful, but it seemed on this occasion that she had paid more attention to her appearance than usual. She wore a gown of soft violet; its skirt was not as large as many, and the narrowness of it was very flattering, especially to someone of her height, who walked as if she could have balanced a pile of books on her head without losing a single one. She wore a tiara, a very slender thing, a mere suggestion of amethysts and pearls.

Watching her, Charlotte found herself smiling at what a striking pair Vespasia and Narraway made, and knew that Jack, who was beside her with Emily on his other arm, was wondering why she looked so delighted.

They moved on, talking politely, making conversation about anything and nothing. She missed Pitt. It was odd to be here alone. In spite of the magnificence of the palace, with its great high-ceilinged rooms and its sweeping marble staircases, in spite of the wit, glamour, and ceremony surrounding her, there was an emptiness. Charlotte thought of Adriana Blantyre, and for a moment she felt tears prick her eyes. Would his love of Austria be enough to bring Evan Blantyre here, in spite of all that had happened? She scanned the room to see if she could find his familiar figure. Twice she thought she saw him, but when she looked more closely it was someone else.

She had been in the palace over half an hour when she was introduced to Duke Alois Habsburg. He was tall and a trifle thin, with dark hair and an agreeable, slightly absentminded expression. But the moment his attention focused on her she saw the bright intelligence in his eyes.

"How do you do, Mrs. Pitt?" he asked with a smile.

"How do you do, Your Highness?" she replied with a very slight curtsy. She would not have wished him harm, but she wondered why Pitt had to risk his life to defend a man who played at academic pursuits for pleasure, and served no actively useful purpose.

Someone made a joke and Duke Alois laughed, but he did not move from standing almost in front of her. A young woman in pink was staring at them both, clearly waiting for Alois to notice her; at least that was clear to Charlotte. The duke appeared not to have realized it.

"I imagine your husband will arrive soon," he said to Charlotte.

"Yes, sir," she replied, forcing herself to smile back at him. "He has been held up. I don't know why. I apologize."

"Don't you?" Alois raised his eyebrows. His expression was agreeably interested. "They stopped our train. Put a hay wagon across the track." He said it as if he was commenting on something as trivial as the weather. She barely saw the shadow of grief in his eyes. "Unfortunately, they shot my friend Hans. Your husband went straight after the marksman, without hesitation."

Charlotte was stunned. Suddenly the hubbub of laughter and music drifting from the other room seemed to fade away.

"I'm so sorry. How is your friend?" she asked quietly.

568

"I am afraid he is dead," he replied. Only his voice changed, not the bland look on his face. "I think he may not have suffered. It was a perfect shot, straight through the heart."

She could not think of anything to say. She felt foolish.

"He looked like me," he said. There was a catch in his voice that he could not hide. "Your husband is a good man. I look forward to knowing him better. Perhaps you will come to Vienna one day? You would enjoy it. It is a beautiful city, full of music, ideas, and history."

She took a deep breath. "I look forward to it. Thank you, sir."

He smiled, then turned away to make polite and meaningless conversation with the young woman in pink.

At the farther side of the room, Emily was standing beside Jack. They also finished a courteous discussion and drifted from one group to another.

"Where is Thomas?" Jack said very quietly to Emily. "Why isn't he here?"

"I don't know," Emily replied. "But wherever he is, Charlotte isn't worried about him."

"Are you sure?" he asked anxiously. "She

wouldn't show it if she were."

"Of course I'm sure," Emily said with an elegant shrug of exasperation. "She's my sister. I'd know if she was pretending."

He looked at her with a raised eyebrow. "You haven't read her very well over the last few weeks."

She flushed. "I know, and I'm sorry about it. I thought she was being very self-important." She took a deep breath. "I was." She did not add that she had been afraid that Jack was out of his depth with his promotion to Tregarron's assistant. That was something he might guess, but she would rather that he did not know it for certain. "Charlotte and I understand each other better now," she added. She knew he was still looking at her, so she flashed a quick, confident smile, and saw him relax. Now she wondered how worried he had been, and decided she would prefer not to know either. It would be a good thing for them both to have the chance to deny things, and for each to be able to pretend to believe the other.

She tucked her arm in his. "Let's go and be polite to the duchess of whatever it is. She's a fearful bore. It will take some concentration."

"All you need to do is listen," he replied.

He placed his hand momentarily over hers in a quick, gentle gesture, then removed it again instantly and walked forward with her beside him.

"That's not enough," she whispered, leaning closer. "You have to smile, and nod in all the right places, and try not to fidget, or let your eyes wander to other people . . ."

Almost under the great chandelier Narraway was standing next to Vespasia. For a moment or two they were not engaged in conversation with anyone else.

"Where is Pitt?" he asked quietly. "Charlotte doesn't look worried, but he should be here with Duke Alois. I've seen Stoker, dressed like a footman, but that isn't enough."

She looked at him closely. "You think something could happen here, in the palace?"

"It's unlikely," he replied, almost under his breath. "But it isn't impossible."

She was alarmed. She turned to face him, studying his eyes, his mouth, trying to read whether it was fear or merely caution that moved him. His eyes were shadowed, nearly black, the lines around his mouth scored deep.

"Such a scandal, here?" she whispered.

He put his hand on hers, his fingers warm and strong. "Oh, nothing so melodramatic, my dear. Far more likely to be a quick scuffle in the shadows of a corridor, and then a body behind the curtains to be found in the morning."

She searched his eyes and saw no laughter at all, nothing beyond the wry, gentle irony that softened his words.

"I don't know where Thomas is," she answered his first question. "I think something might have happened that we are not yet aware of. Duke Alois looks as if he is mastering his emotions with some difficulty, and I have not seen Lord Tregarron. Have you?"

"No. Please don't . . . inquire for him . . ." He stopped, uncertain how to continue.

"I won't," she promised. "At least not yet."

This time he did laugh, so quietly it was almost soundless. "Of course you will," he said ruefully. "But please be careful. I have an awful feeling that this threat is not over yet."

"My dear Victor, our concern with threats will never be over. At least, I hope not. And so do you. You would rather go out in a blaze of glory than die of boredom. As would I."

"But I am not ready to do so yet!" He

took a deep breath. "And I am not ready for you to, either."

She felt a distinct warmth of pleasure. "Then I shall endeavor to see that my next blaze of glory is not an exit line."

Pitt arrived at Kensington Palace just under two hours after the reception had begun. He had been home to Keppel Street and washed, shaved, and changed into his evening suit. Leaving Tregarron's rifle locked in the wardrobe, he had then eaten a cold beef sandwich and drunk a cup of tea. Then, with his revolver in his pocket, which felt lumpy and conspicuous, he had caught a hansom cab, paying extra to the driver to take him with the greatest speed possible.

He remembered the jolt of the train stopping, and then the shot, the splintered glass, and the blood as the Duke's man fell. The devil's luck, or a brilliant shot? He thought the latter. Had the victim been chosen to accompany Duke Alois because he looked so much like him? Had he known that, and still been prepared to take that risk?

Had Pitt made the right decision in turning Tregarron, rather than arresting him for Hans's murder? He might never have proved it, and even if he had, what would have been the result? A major scandal, a foreign policy embarrassment of considerable proportions, possibly the loss of his own position, for political clumsiness . . .

Or alternatively, it would never have come to court anyway. That would have left an impossible situation.

Yet it galled Pitt that the man had attempted to murder Duke Alois, had instead murdered the duke's friend, and would now walk away from it with neither injury nor blame.

He entered the glittering reception hall feeling absurdly out of place. And yet, he did not look outwardly different from the scores of men standing around talking, to each other and to the gorgeously gowned women in their brilliant colors, their jewels sparkling like fire in the light of the huge chandeliers pendent from elaborate ceilings.

His eyes searched the crowd for Charlotte. He saw Emily. He recognized her fair hair with its diamond tiara, and the pale, liquid shade of green that suited her so well. She looked happy.

He also saw Vespasia, but then she was usually easy to see in any crowd. She was beside Narraway and they were talking to each other, heads bent a little.

What could Charlotte be wearing? Blue, burgundy, some warmer color that flattered the rich tones of her skin and hair; lots of women were wearing such shades. All the skirts were enormous, the sleeves high and almost winged at the shoulder — it was the fashion.

He saw Duke Alois briefly, laughing at some joke or other and smiling at a duchess. He looked exactly the pleasant, absent-minded sort of academic he affected to be. The serious and idealistic man who was willing to risk his life, to carry a dangerous burden of secret office, the man who had seen his friend shot to death only this afternoon, seemed like something Pitt had dreamed.

It was small wonder Tregarron had tried to kill Duke Alois. What man would not want to rid himself of such mastery by another, such power to manipulate, or destroy? What he had done, he had done to protect his father's name, and his mother's feelings. Not a bad motive. Most people would understand it.

Pitt still could not see Charlotte; he gave up trying from this vantage. He went down the steps slowly and into the crowd. Hardly anyone knew him, so he had no need to stop and acknowledge people.

How had Alois known of Tregarron's vulnerability? That was something that could not have come from Serafina Montserrat. She had been active long before Duke Alois's time, and he had not been to London before.

Yet Pitt could not rid himself of the belief that it was Serafina's crumbling memory that had fired this whole complex series of events. It was Serafina's memory of Lazar Dragovic's death that had driven Blantyre to kill her, and then to kill Adriana.

Blantyre also knew about Tregarron. He had said as much. So had Blantyre told Duke Alois about it?

That made no sense at all. Blantyre might have cooperated with Duke Alois, within limits, but he would never have given him, or anyone else, control of his own means of power, the secret knowledge that enabled him to manipulate Tregarron.

Then, like the sun rising on a hideous landscape, the whole picture became clear in his mind. Blantyre would want Duke Alois dead now. As long as he was alive, he could also control Tregarron. With Duke Alois dead, no one but Pitt knew the secrets, and Blantyre discounted Pitt's courage to act.

Perhaps he also believed that if Duke Alois was murdered while under Pitt's protection in London, Pitt might be disposed of.

Surely it would not be too difficult a task. Pitt was now the head of Special Branch, but he had not proven himself yet. He was still something of an experiment: a man risen from the ranks of the police, rather than a gentleman from the military or diplomatic services. Kill Alois and blame Pitt's incompetence, and Blantyre would be the only man left with the power to manipulate Tregarron into telling Vienna whatever Blantyre wished, and learning whatever he wished in return. He needed both Duke Alois and Pitt out of the way for Tregarron to be of use to him.

It had to have been Blantyre who had sent Tregarron to kill Duke Alois today. It would have worked perfectly. Pitt would like to have seen Blantyre's face when the duke arrived this evening, very clearly alive and well!

Where was Blantyre? Was he here? He started to look more earnestly. He would have to find Charlotte later. He pushed through the gaps in the crowds, excusing himself, brushing past, turning from right to left, searching for Blantyre. He ought to be able to spot him. He was a little taller than average, and he stood and moved with a unique kind of elegance, a trifle stiff. He carried his head in a characteristic way.

Pitt glanced over to where Duke Alois had been talking to a duchess, or whoever she was. She was still there, but now she was speaking with a large, middle-aged man.

Pitt turned around slowly, taking a deep breath and letting it out between his teeth. He could not see the duke. One of his men was standing over near the wall, but there was a slight frown on his face, and he too was looking from side to side.

Pitt started to look for Emily. Her fair hair and the pale green of her gown might stand out. Yes, there she was, and Jack was still beside her.

"Excuse me," Pitt said hastily, brushing his way past a woman in a mulberry-colored silk gown. She glared at him, but he barely noticed. He walked right between two elderly gentlemen, excusing himself again. He must not lose sight of Jack.

"Here! I say!" a young man protested as Pitt bumped him. He in turn trod on a woman's skirt, which was a fraction too long for her.

"I'm sorry," Pitt said over his shoulder, and kept going.

"Jack!" he called just as Jack appeared about to begin a conversation with a young man wearing lush side whiskers. "Jack."

Jack turned, startled. "Thomas! What's

wrong?"

"Excuse me," Pitt said to the young man. "Something of an emergency." He took Jack's arm and pulled him to the side, several steps away from the nearest group. "There was an incident on the train this afternoon. One of Duke Alois's men was shot — killed outright."

Jack looked appalled. The blood drained from his face. His eyes swept down Pitt to reassure himself that he was unhurt, then a flash of relief filled his eyes. "I'm sorry. The duke himself is putting a hell of a good face on it. Or is he too stupid in his studies for physical reality to touch him? He does know, I presume?"

"Yes. And he's anything but out of touch, I promise you."

"Do you know who it was?"

"Yes, but this is not the time to explain. The duke was here a few minutes ago, but I can't see him now. Blantyre was behind the shooting, and I can't see him either. I think he'll try to finish the job . . ."

"Here? For God's sake, Thomas, the place is full of women and —"

"Where better?" Pitt cut across him. "No one will be expecting it. Duke Alois and his men will think he's safe. I nearly did, until I realized exactly why Blantyre has to kill him.

He can't afford to let him get back to Vienna."

Jack gulped. "What do you want me to do?"

"Find the duke, tell him you're my brother-in-law, and keep him in the middle of a crowd, any crowd."

"What about you?"

"I'm going to find Blantyre."

"And do what, for God's sake?"

"Arrest him, but if he forces me to, I'll shoot him." As soon as he said it, Pitt was not certain if he would do it — if he could. He was not even certain if he could prove that Blantyre had murdered Serafina.

Jack stood motionless for an instant, then he gave a very slight nod, and turned on his heel, disappearing into the crowd immediately.

Where would Blantyre have gone? One of two places. He could hide in the crowd, where he would be concealed among hundreds of other men dressed in exactly the same fashion. However, his face was known, so people would stop to speak to him, to express condolences over Adriana's death.

The alternative would be to stay out of sight almost altogether, in the darker, narrower passages, any place where he would not be expected. Change his attitude, his grace of stance or movement, and — from the back at least — he would appear like anyone else, even a servant. The footmen were in livery, but there were always others: a butler, a valet, even a messenger of some sort.

And if he really meant to kill Duke Alois, he would have to do that when he had privacy. He would not intend to be caught.

Pitt went back up the stairs, taking them rapidly. They were too wide and shallow to take two at a time, unless he drew attention to himself by doing it at a run. At the top he stopped, looking for more private rooms, corridors, anterooms, galleries — anything away from the crowd. If he could find Stoker he would ask for his help, but he had no time now to look for him. He too could be anywhere.

There was a door to his left. It was as good a place as any to begin. He had opened it and gone inside when he realized how much better it would be to get some order into his search. Blantyre would not wait forever for the duke; he would stalk him, go where he knew the duke would be, and, sooner or later, get him alone.

Where? The room where the orchestra was playing? A gallery beyond that? A corridor? A lavatory — the one place where a man could spend a few minutes and expect, quite reasonably, to be alone? Blantyre could close a door and be there indefinitely, unseen.

Pitt walked away from the room toward one of the footmen standing at the bottom of the stairs.

"Excuse me," he said calmly. "Can you direct me to the gentlemen's lavatory, please? The most convenient, if there is more than one."

"Just the one available to guests, sir," the footman replied. "If you go along there to your right." He gestured discreetly, so no onlooker would have been aware of where he was pointing. "It is the third door along that passage, sir."

"Thank you," Pitt accepted, and walked quickly in the direction the man had indicated. He came to the door, hesitated a moment, then turned the handle and went inside. It was beautifully appointed, with half a dozen stalls, each with its own door. Only one was occupied. Was Blantyre in there, waiting until Duke Alois came? Surely in the course of the evening it was certain that he would?

Pitt stood silently with his back against the wall, his heart pounding. Seconds ticked by. There was no sound from the occupied cubicle. Perhaps Alois was already there, already dead? Or unconscious and dying while Pitt stood out here like a fool?

There was a noise outside: footsteps, men's voices.

Pitt turned his back to the room and pretended to be drying his hands on a towel.

Behind him two men came in. He glanced around. Neither was Alois. He went to the basin and washed his hands, slowly, as if he had something under a fingernail. After several minutes first one man left, then the other. The door at the far end remained locked. There was no sound from within. Was it someone ill? Someone dead? If it was Blantyre waiting for Alois, why had he not even looked out to see who had come in?

More minutes went by. Another man came in and left.

Was Pitt standing here, incessantly pretending to wash his hands, while outside, Blantyre was stalking Alois, and perhaps catching him? Was the duke already stabbed and bleeding to death behind some curtain?

Pitt went to the outside door and, pulling it open abruptly, slipped out. He closed it, then waited. How had Alois walked? Upright, but not like a soldier. With grace, a sort of lanky elegance, as if nothing troubled him. He tried to picture it exactly. A slight swagger — a very slight limp, as if his left leg was just a little stiff.

He walked away a few steps, turned, and walked back, trying to imitate Alois. He put his hand on the door and opened it, then went in walking casually, dragging his left foot so slightly he was not even certain it was enough. He swallowed, gulping air.

The last door opened and he was looking at Evan Blantyre, a long, curved knife in one hand. For a silent, burning second they stared at each other. Then Pitt's fingers closed around the revolver in his pocket and he lifted it out slowly.

Blantyre smiled. "You don't have the courage," he said slowly.

Pitt did not take his eyes from Blantyre's. "You killed Serafina, Adriana . . ."

"And Lazar Dragovic," Blantyre added. "He was a traitor to Austria. But you can't prove any of it."

"Austria is not my territory," Pitt told him. "London is."

"Austria is the heart of Europe, you provincial fool!" Blantyre said between his teeth. "Get out of my way."

"And London is the heart of England," Pitt replied. "Which is irrelevant, except that it is my responsibility. You blackmailed Tregarron into trying to kill Duke Alois, and only ended up killing his friend instead. But one dead man is as important as another."

"You can't prove that either, without exposing Tregarron, and his father, and the whole sordid mess of treason. And you'll expose Duke Alois as well, of course," Blantyre said. "So there isn't a damn thing you can do. Now get out of my way, and don't oblige me to hurt you."

Pitt stood still, his heart beating so violently he felt certain he must be shaking. His hand ached, gripping the revolver.

Blantyre moved the knife a little so the light caught its blade.

"What are you going to do, stab Alois?" Pitt asked, his voice rough-edged.

Blantyre paled a little.

"Because you can't afford to leave him alive," Pitt added.

There was a flash of understanding in Blantyre's eyes, perhaps of the knowledge that he couldn't afford to leave Pitt alive either. For an instant he moved the knife a fraction, then let it fall again.

"You can't arrest me; you'd only make a fool of yourself. And you don't have the nerve," he said very softly. "I'm walking out of here and I'll find Duke Alois another time. Perhaps I'll follow him back to Vienna.

No reason I shouldn't. You're out of your depth, Pitt. Pity, because I liked you." He gave a slight shrug and took a step forward.

Everything that Blantyre said was true.

Pitt raised the revolver. "God forgive me," he said to himself, and fired.

The sound was deafening.

For an instant Blantyre's eyes were wide with amazement, then he staggered backward against the cubicle door and it crashed open behind him. He fell, his chest soaked in red. He slithered to the floor, and lay still.

Pitt forced himself to walk over to the cubicle and look down. Blantyre's eyes were still open, and sightless. Pitt felt his stomach twist violently with regret. Hours seemed to pass before he heard shouts and footsteps along the corridor. He put the revolver back in his pocket and took out his identification. He had it in his hand when two men in dinner suits flung the door open and stopped abruptly. Narraway was immediately behind them, Jack Radley on his heels.

"God Almighty!" the first man exclaimed, his face ashen, staring first at Pitt, then past him to the open door, and Blantyre covered in blood, lying on the tiled marble floor.

Narraway pushed past him, then stopped.

Pitt started to speak, cleared his throat, and started again.

"I am Thomas Pitt, head of Special Branch. I regret to say that there has been an unpleasant incident, but there is no danger now. You might be civil enough to inform Duke Alois Habsburg that the immediate danger to his life is over."

The first man gaped, then turned very slowly to Narraway.

Narraway looked at him, his eyebrows slightly raised.

"Quite right, Ponsonby," he said. "He is precisely who he says he is, and the facts are as he states. Be a good chap and get everyone out of here while we have someone clear this up, will you?"

When they were gone, too numb with shock to argue, Narraway closed the door.

"Well done, Pitt," he said quietly. "It'll hurt like hell. You'll dream about it as long as you live, but that's the price of leadership, making the gray decisions. Black-and-white ones are easy; any fool can deal with those. You'll have to live with it, but if you hadn't done it, you would have had to live with every grief that followed because of it." He smiled very slightly. "I always knew you'd do it."

"No, you didn't," Pitt replied, his voice hoarse.

Narraway shrugged. "I believed it more

than you did. That's good enough." Then he smiled and held out his hand.

Pitt took it, and held it, hard.

"Thank you." Simple words, but he had never meant them more.

ABOUT THE AUTHOR

Anne Perry is the bestselling author of two acclaimed series set in Victorian England: the Charlotte and Thomas Pitt novels, most recently *Dorchester Terrace* and *Treason at Lisson Grove,* and the William Monk novels, including *Acceptable Loss* and *Execution Dock.* She is also the author of the World War I novels *No Graves As Yet, Shoulder the Sky, Angels in the Gloom, At Some Disputed Barricade,* and *We Shall Not Sleep,* as well as ten Christmas novels, most recently *A Christmas Homecoming.* Her stand-alone novel *The Sheen on the Silk,* set in the Byzantine Empire, was a *New York Times* bestseller. Anne Perry lives in Scotland.
www.anneperry.net

The employees of Thorndike Press hope you have enjoyed this Large Print book. All our Thorndike, Wheeler, and Kennebec Large Print titles are designed for easy reading, and all our books are made to last. Other Thorndike Press Large Print books are available at your library, through selected bookstores, or directly from us.

For information about titles, please call:
  (800) 223-1244

or visit our Web site at:
  http://gale.cengage.com/thorndike

To share your comments, please write:
  Publisher
  Thorndike Press
  10 Water St., Suite 310
  Waterville, ME 04901